Praise for Michael Thomas Ford's
LAST SUMMER

"Sexy, funny and fun."
—*The Washington Blade*

"*Last Summer* is a sprawling tale of a very small cross-section of Provincetown denizens during a particularly momentous summer. . . . Ford delivers the goods again . . . all his creations are refreshing and this novel displays Ford's cutting wit at its keenest. Another Ford trademark prominently on display here is his celebration of the gay Everyman. Unlike the independently wealthy, impossibly handsome protagonists of some gay novels, these characters have an innate reality and credibility that many readers can identify with and will find endearing."
—*Bay Windows*

And more outstanding praise for Michael Thomas Ford

"What Woody Allen did for the world of heterosexual love, sex, and everyday mishaps, Michael Thomas Ford is doing these days for the homosexual."
—*The Letter*

"Michael Thomas Ford is far and away the best gay humorist on the scene today."
—*Seattle Gay Standard*

"He continues to capture the essence of what it means to be gay in America."
—*Booklist*

"Cranky, bemused, and extremely funny, Ford is brilliant."
—*Publishers Weekly*

"His knack for hitting on just the right aspect of humor in everyday events makes him akin to David Sedaris and Ellen DeGeneres."
—*Library Journal*

Books by Michael Thomas Ford

LAST SUMMER

LOOKING FOR IT

MASTERS OF MIDNIGHT
(with William J. Mann, Jeff Mann, and Sean Wolfe)

Published by Kensington Publishing Corporation

MICHAEL THOMAS FORD

LAST SUMMER

KENSINGTON BOOKS
http://www.kensingtonbooks.com

KENSINGTON BOOKS are published by

Kensington Publishing Corp.
850 Third Avenue
New York, NY 10022

ISBN 0-7582-0406-X

First Hardcover Printing: August 2003
First Trade Paperback Printing: July 2004
10 9 8 7 6 5 4

Printed in the United States of America

*it happened one summer
it happened one time
it happened forever
for a short time*

*a place for a moment
an end to a dream
forever I loved you
forever it seemed*

*one summer never ends
one summer never began
it keeps me standing still
it takes all my will
and then suddenly
last summer*

Acknowledgments

Books may have one author, but they come into being only with the help of an enormous number of people. This particular book owes its existence to more individuals than I care to think about or have room to name here. However, there are some who require (or demand) public thanking, among them: Mitchell Waters and John Scognamiglio, who provided pressure and guidance; Katherine Gleason, my best friend and coprocrastinator of many years; my fellow water rats in the Northern California Rainbow Divers and the San Francisco Dive Dogs (particularly Maureen McEvoy, Anna Wan, Kim VandeWalker, Sally Mead, and Julie Coburn), for getting me out of the house and into the ocean; and Abby McAden, Robert Pela, Michael Rowe, Michael Elliott, Amanda Philips, Samuel Ace, Gretchen Breese, Peter McKie, Roger McElhiney, Juliet Swiggum, and Daniel Cullinane for listening to it all on a regular basis.

The writing of this novel coincided with my training for the 2002 National AIDS Marathon. Both the marathon and the book were completed around the same time, and for their generous donations to my marathon fund-raising I owe many, many thanks to Rick Anderson, Rick Andreoli, Bruce and Susan Barnard, Kathleen Billings, C. Paul Bott, Susie Bright, Hillary Carlip and Maxine Lapiduss, Tom Carter and Ellen Walsh, Greg Constante, Barry Creasy, Andrea Curley, June Davies and Joan Gravell, Bronwyn Davis, Emma Dryden and Anne Corvi, Warren Dunford, Charles Flowers, Brenda Garcia, Nancy Garden, Jon Glasgow, Mark Gordon, Paul Grohne, Calvin Gross, Joe Guckin, Dr. June Steffensen Hagen and Rev. Jim Hagen, David Hooban, Andrew Holleran, Ben Jackson, Michael James, Charlie Keating, Robert C. La Mont, Scott A. Lile, Nancy, John, and Ian Muller, Peter Padilla, Regina Sackrider and Yasmine Branden, Kurt Sauer, John Scognamiglio, Barry Shils, Scott Shumaker, Daniel and Dana Sokatch, Andrzej Stankiewicz,

M.D., Deb Stavin, Cecilia Tan, Peggy Thomson, Drew Tosh, Dan Truman, Edo Van Belkom, Lea Wood, and Alan Young.

And finally, for making dinner, doing laundry, walking the dog, reading the manuscript, calming the nerves, enduring the diving, going to Giants games even though he likes the Angels, and generally making every day mean more than just finishing another chapter, my love and thanks to Patrick Crowe.

PART I

May

CHAPTER 1

I could just go back.

Josh stared out at the passing landscape, trying to distract himself from the thought that had been buzzing around his head like a persistent bee for the past hour and a half. He concentrated instead on the scenery around him. The grass on either side of the highway was rich with the promise of the approaching summer, the expanse of green broken here and there with bright flashes of color where some of the hardier flowers had already opened their faces to the light. The sun itself, growing stronger with every passing day, rewarded their enthusiasm by covering everything with the hazy golden blanket of early afternoon.

I could just go back.

Josh sighed. Lovely as it was, the view wasn't going to keep his mind off of where he was going, or why. Ever since leaving he had been playing a game with himself. He'd pretended that he was simply going to the store, perhaps to pick up dinner or a couple of movies. It was, after all, Friday. Those were the things he would normally be doing on a Friday afternoon, gathering up the ingredients for a quiet evening at home: a chicken to roast or steaks to grill, some wine to celebrate the end of the workweek, a copy of a recently released video, or if he was feeling romantic, an old standby like *It Happened One Night* or *Barefoot in the Park*.

But that would be a normal Friday, and this was not a normal Friday. It was anything *but* a normal Friday.

I could just go back.

Simultaneous with the recurrence of the nagging thought was the appearance of the sign announcing the upcoming exit for U.S. 6 East. He had three miles or, at his current speed, about two and a half minutes, to decide what he was going to do. Once he was on Route 6 he knew he wouldn't be going back.

It seemed to Josh as if time stood still while he weighed what lay behind him against what lay ahead of him. If he got on U.S. 6 East, where would it take him? Not in the geographic sense—he knew where the road went—but on a grander scale. What kind of change would he be making in his life if he turned the wheel slightly to the right and took the exit? When he thought about it that way, the off-ramp became much more than just a twist in the asphalt, a sudden diversion from the gray-black ribbon of Massachusetts Highway 3 South.

Fifty miles behind him was Boston. And in Boston was his comfortable apartment, with its familiar furnishings, its view of Fenway Park, and its proximity to the people and places that over the past seven years had become his world. There, too, as comfortable and familiar as the furniture, the view, and the neighborhood, was Doug, his lover of more than eight years. But it was Doug he was driving away from now.

The change in Josh's world had come that morning, shortly after ten o'clock. Returning from his regular morning run, he had found Doug waiting for him on the living room couch, the couch on which Josh had taken so many Saturday afternoon naps, on which the two of them had sat together so often, fingers entwined, watching TV or reading the Sunday *Herald*. They'd bought it together, shortly after moving in to the apartment. It had been their first major purchase as a couple, and even though its covering was faded and starting to wear thin in the places where their bodies most often rested against it, they had never been able to part with the memories it held.

But that morning Doug had looked up at Josh from his seat on the couch they had bought together and said, "There's something I need to tell you."

The "something" had turned out to be a man from their gym. Josh couldn't remember his name now—Stephen or Peter or Roger. It didn't matter. What mattered was that Doug had slept with this man.

"It didn't mean anything," Doug had said afterward.

Josh had laughed, despite being in shock. *Isn't that what they always say?* he'd thought to himself as he'd stared at the face of the man he'd come to think he knew so well, the man he'd believed would never hurt him. It was as if the two of them were suddenly thrust into the worst kind of movie of the week, and for a moment Josh couldn't help but wonder which washed-up former star would play him. Matthew Perry, perhaps, if his movie career was fading. *Or maybe they could get George Clooney,* he'd thought as Doug had waited for him to respond. *George Clooney would be good.*

When he'd finally accepted what Doug had said to him, Josh had replied with the line he'd always wanted the wounded party in such movies to use. "If it didn't mean anything, then why did you have to do it?"

Doug had answered him with the usual repertoire of answers. It had only happened one time. He wasn't really sure why he'd done it. No, they weren't going to see each other again. Josh had listened impatiently, equally as irritated with the predictability of his lover's responses as he was with the revelation of his infidelity. The fact that Doug had engaged in the most common of indiscretions—and that he didn't even know why he'd done it—made everything even worse. At least if he'd had some reason, if it had *meant* something, then Josh would have something to focus on, to blame, to try and understand even while he was reeling from the initial blow. As it was, there was nothing but questions.

"I think I just needed some excitement," Doug had said finally, sounding relieved to have come up with some way of breaking the silence that had settled between them while Josh frantically searched for something that would help him remember that it was *Doug* he was talking to, and not some stranger. "You know, after eight years things do get a little predictable."

That, more than anything else, was what had caused Josh to leave. The predictability of their relationship, the comfortableness of it, was what he loved most about being with Doug. He liked coming home to the same man every day, and sleeping in the same bed with him night after night. He liked knowing that when they went to their favorite Chinese restaurant Doug would always order the General Chow's chicken. He liked knowing that if he heard Tom Petty coming from the stereo it meant Doug was in a good mood or, if it was instead the Cowboy Junkies, that he should give his lover some space. He liked knowing that if Doug asked him to rub his back it meant they would soon be making love.

Wasn't that what being with the same man for eight years was *supposed* to mean? Wasn't that why you stayed with someone that long?

After the initial rush of falling in love, wasn't it the gradual accumulation of shared moments, the daily interactions that revealed the totality of the person you chose to share your life with, that made getting together in the first place worthwhile? Josh had asked Doug these questions, more or less without yelling. However, when all of Doug's replies had begun with "yes, but," Josh had felt himself beginning to lose control.

That's when the clothes had gone into the suitcase. Josh had been surprised at how quickly it was all over. It had really only taken him about twenty minutes to gather up what he needed. Doug had followed him around the entire time, trying to calm him down. But that had only made Josh angrier, and finally he'd stopped speaking altogether, cramming his socks and T-shirts and underwear into his bag without even looking at his lover.

"Where are you going?" Doug had asked him as Josh had snatched up his laptop and carried it, along with his bag, down the two flights of stairs to the street.

"Away," Josh had answered tersely as he'd gotten into his car and pulled away, leaving Doug standing on the street.

The truth was, at the time he really hadn't known where he was going to go. All he knew was that he wanted to be wherever Doug wasn't. So at first he'd just driven around with no particular direction in mind, trying not to think. He'd hoped that if he didn't play the scene over and over in his head, maybe it would turn out not to have happened. Maybe, if he tried hard enough to suppress it, time would somehow be miraculously reversed and Doug's infidelity would never have happened.

After about an hour, though, he'd pulled the car onto a relatively deserted side street and cried. Then he'd used his cell phone to call Ryan at work. His friendship with Ryan went back further even than his relationship with Doug, beginning when both were newly out of college and newly out in Boston. Over the years they'd seen each other through the usual romantic highs and lows, somehow miraculously managing to be on opposite ends of the dating-breakup continuum most of the time, so that whenever one of them was in need of comfort the other was in a position to remind him that true love was still out there somewhere. As Josh dialed Ryan's number he couldn't help but reflect that, true to form, Ryan had recently started dating what appeared to be a great guy after years of suffering through inappropriate and frequently unfaithful boyfriends. It should, he thought bitterly, have been a sign.

When Ryan picked up, the story had spilled out of Josh in a series of tearful bursts interrupted by Ryan having to put him on hold every couple of minutes to take a call from one of the clients whose stock portfolios he tended in hopes of growing their small fortunes into large ones. Each time Josh had been forced to sit and listen to the overly cheerful hold music, he had started crying all over again. It hadn't seemed fair that while his life was falling apart, somewhere in the world Celine Dion was being allowed to record new love songs.

It was Ryan who, after dutifully siding with Josh in declaring Doug the biggest jerk to ever live, had suggested Provincetown. He had, he told Josh, a couple of clients there who owned a guest house. They had frequently extended an invitation for him to come visit them, and he was sure they would let Josh stay for a few days. With Memorial Day more than a week away, the season hadn't yet begun, and the town was still relatively deserted. "Just let me give them a call," he'd told Josh, putting him on hold once again.

The clients, a couple named Ben and Ted, had indeed been more than willing to let Josh stay at their place. Less than ten minutes after hanging up with Josh, Ryan had called back with directions to the house.

"They don't have any guests coming until the holiday weekend," Ryan had told him. "You'll have the place to yourself."

After thanking Ryan and promising to call him later that evening, Josh had hung up and sat in the car, thinking of every reason why he shouldn't go. He didn't know Ted and Ben. He was embarrassed that he was running away. But the truth was that he didn't really have any legitimate reasons for not accepting their offer. His job as a freelance copywriter for various ad agencies meant that he could basically take time off whenever he wanted to. Besides, he told himself, it was only for the weekend. He just needed a few days away from Doug to process what had happened and decide what his next move would be. And if it made Doug feel bad, all the better.

Before he could change his mind he'd started driving. Now, an hour later, he was having second thoughts. Maybe he should have stayed and talked things out with Doug. After all, wasn't he the one who was always stressing the importance of communication in a relationship? He did it so often his lover had taken to calling him Oprah whenever he went into another one of his lectures on the subject, usually to some friend who was having relationship difficulties. Perhaps it was time to take his own advice and find out what exactly had made Doug feel he had to go to someone else for something he clearly wasn't getting from Josh.

But if Doug was so interested in talking things out, why hadn't he even tried once to call? Josh had set the cell phone on the seat next to him, fully expecting it to ring. Surely Doug was wondering where he was, and when he was coming back. Surely he wouldn't let Josh just leave. Despite the way he'd fled the apartment, Josh had truly believed that Doug would try to get him to return after giving him an appropriate amount of time to be furious.

Or would he? Maybe, Josh thought, Doug was glad he was gone. Maybe he wanted the apartment to himself to, like Josh, think things over.

Or maybe he's with Whatshisname, Josh thought grimly.

He wondered what this other guy looked like. Probably a lot like himself, he though miserably. Shortly after he and Doug had started dating, they'd run into Doug's most recent ex at a party. Josh had been a bit taken aback to see that he and the ex resembled each other: tall, medium builds, short dark hair, and green eyes.

He and Doug had laughed about it later, in bed. "What can I say?" Doug had told him. "I have a thing for you dark-haired boys. Especially when you have hairy chests," he'd added, starting to run his tongue down Josh's stomach. He'd kept going, and moments later any jealousy Josh had been feeling about seeing the ex had vanished as the warmth of Doug's mouth had surrounded him.

The memory of that evening eight years earlier almost made him forget about the ugliness of the morning. Then he pictured Doug in bed not with him but with this new man, someone who resembled him visually but wasn't him at all. It would be easier if the guy was his physical opposite: blond, perhaps, and short. Maybe some bulked-up gym queen with bleached teeth and steroid pockmarks on his shoulders. At least if he was physically different from Josh there could be some kind of physical element to blame Doug's behavior on, a momentary yearning for something different, some new taste, touch, or smell that he'd been unable to resist. But if the man looked like him, that meant there was something more substantial at play, something that couldn't be explained away by Doug wanting to feel a more muscular body or smoother skin beneath his fingers.

How had it happened the first time, Josh wondered. Had they exchanged glances in the showers after their workouts, each sizing up the other while caressing themselves suggestively with soapy hands? Had one of them helpfully offered to spot the other during a routine, being sure to position himself so as to display his jockstrapped crotch to full advantage? Josh knew there had to have been at least minimal courtship, a casual compliment on the shape of a biceps or the strength of a calf that led to something more. After all, you didn't just go from exchanging pleasantries in the locker room to rolling around naked in some man's bed. How had the first suggestion of sex come up? Who had made the first move?

No, he decided suddenly, he wasn't ready to talk it through. A few days away from Doug was exactly what he needed right now. A few days to think—or preferably not think—about what was happening in their relationship. All he wanted to do was sit on the beach and look at the ocean, far away from the distractions of the city, his friends, and the man he was no longer sure he knew at all.

The exit, and the moment of decision, had arrived. Without hesitating, Josh took it.

CHAPTER 2

"Jerry, please tell me you're going to have these walls painted and my place put back together in the next week."

Jackie Stavers stood in the doorway of her restaurant, looking at the two men standing on ladders, paint rollers in their hands.

"Sure, sure, Jacks," Jerry replied, deftly making a blue streak across the wall he was working on. "No problem."

Jackie groaned. "That's what you told me *last* week, Jerry," she said irritably.

Jerry grinned. "But this time I mean it," he said.

Jackie shot him a look and retreated through a doorway to the relative safety of the bar area. Back in the main dining room the two men resumed their banter, their voices a muffled reminder of the chaos that had consumed the club for the past month. Jackie opened a bottle of aspirin and popped two into her mouth, following them with a swig from her water glass.

"Tell me again why I agreed to do this?" she said to the bar's lone patron.

Emmeline laughed. "Because you're not having sex with your girl-friend," she said, lifting a perfectly drawn eyebrow and smiling sweetly.

Jackie sighed. "Can we not talk about that?" she said.

Emmeline lifted both of her hands in a gesture of defeat. Her fingers, the long nails recently painted a deep red, fluttered briefly around her face before returning to rest on the bar. "Then what *should* we talk about?" she asked, the soft drawl of her voice simultaneously teasing and pacifying her friend.

"How about your new act?" suggested Jackie as she began to rearrange the glassware beneath the counter. "What have you come up with?"

"Only the most magnificent evening of illusion and magic you've ever seen," Emmeline purred.

Jackie rolled her eyes. "Sweetie, your entire life is magic and illusion. Could you be more specific? I need to know what to put on the posters."

Emmeline laughed. "I can see you're not in the mood for flattering a girl today," she said. "Fine, I'll tell you. I'm going to do an evening of standards. Ella. Billie. Etta. Sarah. Dinah. All the old greats. And there will be no lip-synching. It's all live. Just me and a piano player."

Jackie, genuinely surprised, stopped what she was doing. "Live?" she said. "And real music? No disco? No drag queen can-can lines? No camp?"

"Well, when you have a boy dressed up as a girl it's always camp, isn't it?" answered Emmeline, brushing some of her luxuriously red hair away from her face. For a moment she seemed tired, sad. Then, as if a light switch had been flipped on, the usual smile returned and she looked up at her friend with a mischievous expression. "I thought this dump could use a little class this season," she said.

Jackie snorted. "Why not?" she said. "It can be part of this makeover I've so stupidly attempted."

Emmeline stood up. Taking her purse from the bar she patted Jackie's hand. "I've got an appointment I have to get to," she said. "Let's talk more about the show tonight, shall we?"

Jackie nodded. "Whenever you want to," she replied.

Emmeline turned to leave, adding as she departed, "And then we'll talk about the sex you're not having with your girlfriend."

When Emmeline was gone Jackie leaned against the wall and rubbed her temples, trying to erase the dull throb that had settled there that morning and refused to leave. The aspirin had done nothing to improve either the headache or her foul mood. What was she doing? The summer season was almost upon her, the place was a wreck, and who knew what was happening between her and Karla?

This wasn't how the summer was supposed to go. On top of everything else, she was going to be turning forty in August. In her daydreams she'd pictured the summer of her fortieth year as being filled with friends, laughter, and a lover. Her goal had always been to have a home, a successful business, and a fulfilling relationship by the time she reached the milestone that forty represented to her.

She had the home, the business, and the relationship. But of the three, only her home was currently in the state that she wanted it to be. Her relationship—which she really didn't want to think about—was somewhere between ending and over. As for her business, it would be fine. She knew that. But at the moment it was driving her crazy, and the cumulative effect of the upheaval was becoming unbearable.

For the first time in twenty years she had started thinking about moving away from Provincetown. She had come there fresh out of college, her degree in business administration clutched tightly in her hand. It was supposed to be a two-week summer vacation, a celebration after four years of hard work. As it turned out, she'd never left. During those two weeks she'd fallen in love with the sand and sea, so different from the asphalt landscape of Detroit, where she'd grown up, and when the time had come to leave she just hadn't gone. That was one of the things she missed most about being twenty, the ability to be irresponsibly impulsive. Now, with two mortgages, a staff depending on her for their income, and roots that went deep into the rock P-Town was built upon, she felt more like a fixture: dependable, stable, and dull.

She thought back to that first year, filled with so much promise. After the raucous party that was summer in P-Town had ended, the quiet of fall had been a welcome respite. She'd gloried in walking on Herring Cove Beach in the early mornings, and in the beauty of the sun on the water. But the bleakness of winter on the cape had almost done her in, and when spring had come she'd been ready to leave. Then summer had wrapped her in its golden arms once more and she'd stayed.

Since then she'd come to love the fall and winter, seeing in them faces of Provincetown that remained hidden to the summer visitors. Plus, she'd become one of the Rounders, the name she'd coined for the community of people who lived in the town all year long. They were diehards who welcomed the tourists with open arms each summer, if only because they provided the Rounders with the financial means to live there during the months when the only faces they saw were each other's. They were the caretakers of the town, watching over it as it slept, preparing to meet its visitors when the days again grew longer.

The first two years she lived in Provincetown, Jackie worked at

Franny's, a restaurant popular with the lesbian and gay crowds that comprised the majority of the town's summer residents. Franny herself was a loud, brassy old school butch who refused to reveal her age but who often regaled her enthusiastic listeners from her position behind the bar with tales of how she and her friends had been jailed during the Stonewall riots for breaking New York's laws against women dressing as men. Later, in the few hours that the restaurant was silent between its closing at two-thirty in the morning and its reopening at six for breakfast, she would sometimes tell Jackie other stories, stories about being beaten up by men who saw something in her appearance that angered them, stories about falling in love with married femmes who always broke her heart, stories about loneliness and despair tempered with defiance and the determination to find or forge a community of her own. Often these stories were accompanied by glass after glass of whiskey or gin and tonics, and it was in those late night, early morning talks that Jackie had begun both to find her own identity and to develop a relationship with alcohol that, several years later, would force her to find herself all over again.

Franny had seen in Jackie a younger version of herself. Despite the differences in their ages, colors, and backgrounds, Franny saw herself as something of a mother figure to the young woman, although, Jackie thought, she would have bristled at being thought of as anything other than a daddy. "You may be a young black butch and I may be an old white one," Jackie remembered Franny saying one night after her sixth scotch, "but we understand each other, you and I."

Jackie worked for Franny for three years, first as a waitress and eventually as a manager. During that time she put her business degree to work, encouraging Franny to expand the place and add entertainment. The popularity of the restaurant—and its profits—grew with each successive summer, until Franny's became the hottest spot in town for vacationers and locals alike. Even in winter they remained open, scaling back the operation to accommodate the tastes and schedules of the Rounders, who used it as a gathering place on cold, dark nights when they didn't want to be alone.

Then, one March night, Jackie had received a phone call. It had been the police, telling her that Franny had been found on the beach. She'd drunk an entire bottle of whiskey and collapsed on the sand, facedown. Unable to breathe, she'd quickly suffocated.

If Franny's death was a shock, Jackie received an even larger one a

week later when she got another call. This one was from a lawyer, in-
forming her that she was the sole beneficiary of Franny's will. While
the money left to her was by no means a fortune, Jackie had also been
left full ownership of the restaurant.

For a month she'd kept the place closed, unable to even think
about it operating under the directorship of anyone but Franny, let
alone under her sole control. Whenever she'd attempted to stand behind the bar, she'd felt sick to her stomach, as if she were playing in
her mother's closet and would be caught at any moment. Instead,
each night she'd drowned the pain in glass after glass of whiskey.
She'd told herself that the drinks were a celebration of Franny's spirit,
but even as she sank deeper and deeper into the comfortable haze of
the alcohol she knew that celebrating a person's life with the same
thing that had killed her was no kind of memorial.

Finally she'd decided that the only way to truly keep Franny's spirit
alive was to keep alive the place that had housed it. The restaurant had
been Franny's temple, and Jackie was determined that it remain open
for business. So come Memorial Day, Franny's welcomed its patrons
back with fluttering rainbow flags and a two-for-one happy hour to celebrate the life of its namesake. News of Franny's death had spread
quickly among the summer people, and the place was packed night
after night as people gathered to talk about her and share stories.

That summer had made Jackie even more determined to remain in
Provincetown. With the money left to her by Franny, she bought a
small house and began fixing it up. She poured herself into the club,
and became even more firmly entrenched in the community, both that
of the gay summer trade and that of the Rounders. Both welcomed
her, and by the time fall had come again she'd known that she would
never leave.

Now, though, she wasn't so sure. The seventeen years that had
gone by since Franny's death had brought many changes to Jackie's
life. The most significant, to her, was the sobriety she'd begun almost
fifteen years earlier. In the two years after Franny's death and her inheritance of the business, Jackie had drunk more and more. The turning point had come on the morning following the celebration of her
twenty-fifth birthday, when she'd woken up in bed with not one but
two women whose names and faces she couldn't recall. After getting
them up and out of her house, she'd looked in the paper for the list-
ings of local AA meetings and had gone to the first available one.

Getting sober brought other changes as well. For one, she'd re-named the restaurant. In her third year as owner, Franny's became Jackie's, and while there was a bit of grumbling from some patrons who found the move insulting to the previous owner's memory, Jackie herself saw it as a symbol of both her newfound freedom and her men-tor's own decision to call the restaurant after herself. "After all," Jackie had told her friends, "the boat should be named after the captain."

Although initially she'd feared working in a place whose very exis-tence depended on the sale and consumption of the one product now forbidden to her, Jackie had found staying away from alcohol relatively easy. It was as if in changing the name of the club, she'd banished the one aspect of Franny's spirit that didn't wish her well. Secretly she also suspected that Franny would have been proud of her for doing the one thing that she herself hadn't been able to. Whenever Jackie looked at the framed photo of Franny hanging behind the bar, she imagined the old dyke giving her a wink and saying, "Good for you, kid. You made it."

The changes since then had been less dramatic, but no less impor-tant. Chief among them was Jackie's introduction to Karla. Like herself, Karla had initially been a summer person, an academic with a passion for Virginia Woolf and a month-long share in one of the town's many guest houses. Jackie had seen her one night, sitting at a table in the restaurant with friends, and had fallen in love immediately, enchanted by her blue eyes, short blond hair, and wild laugh. When she'd gone over to ask the group how everything was, Karla's coy smile in re-sponse had done her in completely.

Their courtship had been relatively slow, at least in summer ro-mance terms. Jackie had waited another week before asking Karla out, and another before taking her to bed. Then Karla had returned to Seattle, where she had a job as an assistant professor, and things had continued by telephone and letter. But when Karla's second summer in P-Town had been even more memorable than the first, Jackie had upped the ante by suggesting that living in closer proximity would not be unwelcome.

The opportunity presented itself when, toward the end of her planned vacation, Karla received word that she would not be offered the professorship she'd assumed would be hers in the fall. With no reason to return, she'd agreed to Jackie's plan to move in together.

That had been ten years ago. During that time, their relationship had settled into a comfortable pattern. After a year of unemployment, during which she'd worked for Jackie at the restaurant, Karla had found a teaching job in Providence. It meant she had to spend three nights a week away from Jackie, but they'd adjusted and things had worked out just fine.

At least until Karla had begun to tire first of the winters in Provincetown and then of Jackie's attentions in bed. At first Jackie had blamed their lack of sex on the natural decline that comes with being together a long time. "We're the latest casualties of lesbian bed death," she joked to her friends. But when she'd discovered what was unmistakably a love note in a pile of term papers Karla had left on the desk, she'd discovered the truth.

That had been six months before. Karla, when confronted with the note, had admitted to an affair conducted during a conference in New York on literature and gender. She further admitted that her interest in the new woman extended to more than just a weekend fling. At first Jackie had insisted on trying to work it out. But when Karla began spending more and more time away from the house, it became clear to Jackie that her partner had already made her choice. Recently they had had the inevitable discussion that with the end of the school year would come the end of their cohabitation. Karla was moving to Providence for good.

That part of the story no one knew but Jackie. Nor did they know that her last-minute decision to remodel the club was her vain attempt to distract herself from thinking about the fact that, as her fortieth birthday neared, she was going to be alone once more.

For all these reasons, she thought, it might even be her last summer in P-Town. If it was, then she wanted to go out with a bang. And she wasn't going to tell anyone about her possible departure. It was her little secret. Not even Emmeline was going to know, and Emmeline knew just about everything about Jackie's life.

Jackie looked at the photo of Franny. "What do you think I should do?" she asked it.

A loud crash emanated from the dining room. A moment later Jerry's face appeared in the doorway.

"Don't panic," he said. "It's nothing we can't fix."

Jackie shook her head and looked at Franny's picture again. "You're right," she said. "I *don't* need this."

CHAPTER 3

"Reid, it's Al Simon."

The voice of Reid Truman's secretary coming from the speaker phone startled him. He put the script he was reading down on his desk and sighed. He'd been avoiding Al Simon's calls for three days.

"Thanks, Violet," he said. "I'll pick it up."

Reid took a deep breath and hit another button on the phone. "Al," he said, feigning happiness. "Good to hear from you."

"Like hell it is," Al responded testily. "Where the fuck have you been?"

"You know how it is," replied Reid. "I've been busy."

"Busy." Al grunted. "Too goddamned busy to talk to the man who writes you checks for eighty-six million fucking dollars so you can make a movie about a washed-up hockey player who falls in love with a stripper?"

"It was eighty-two," Reid shot back, grinning despite himself. "And we came in under budget and on time. Plus, if those latest figures you faxed over are right, that hockey player and that stripper made you another sixteen million this weekend."

"Whatever," said Al. "I still got another ulcer to add to my collection."

"You need to learn to relax, Al," Reid said, as if talking to an unreasonable child.

"Fuck relaxing," Al said. "Look, we want another picture from you."

Reid groaned silently. This was exactly what he'd been afraid of, why he hadn't taken or returned any of Al Simon's calls.

"Yeah?" he said vaguely.

"What was that story you told me about over lunch last time?" Al continued. "You know, the one about the college chick who finds out she's got some fucked-up DNA or something. What does it do, make her psychic or something?"

"She foresees the end of the world," Reid answered. "She tries to get people to listen to her, but they just think she's another nut job. The government sends this assassin to take her out, because the stuff she's telling people is actually true and they want to cover it up. She ends up convincing the guy who's supposed to kill her to help her, and they take on the feds and the media to try and stop Armageddon from occurring. And of course they fall in love. It's your basic boy tries to kill girl, boy falls in love with girl, boy and girl save the world story," he added sarcastically.

"And what was the title?" Al asked, oblivious to Reid's tone.

The Doomsday Code.

"Right," Al said. "As in DNA code. I remember that part. Catchy title. Clever. Works on a lot of levels, and it will look good on a poster. Let's make it."

"I don't know," Reid said. "I'm looking at a couple of things."

"For who?" snapped Al.

"Don't worry, Al," said Reid. "I'm not cheating on you. I just want to see if there's something better out there scriptwise." *Christ,* he thought to himself. *These studio heads are as bad as high school girls afraid their boyfriends are putting the make on someone else.*

"What's better than this?" asked Al. "This is a fucking summer blockbuster. The girls will like the love story angle and the guys will like some hot chick with big tits and lots of explosions. Get it going, Reid. We need at least eight months of lead time for the special effects guys."

"Okay. Maybe. Let me think about it for a week," Reid said, trying to buy a little time.

"Fuck you. Two days. I'm going to make some calls and see if we can get Angelina Jolie. She came to my kid's birthday party last month. Brought that little Asian boy she adopted. You should see the rack on her. I wouldn't mind giving her a titty fuck, I'll tell you that. Anyway, I told her I'd call if we had something good for her."

"You do that," Reid replied, hoping this meant the end of the call.

"We're making this movie, Reid," Al said. "I'll talk to you in two days."

The phone went dead. Reid leaned back in his chair and looked at the ceiling. Unfortunately for him, the image of Al Simon giving Angelina Jolie a titty fuck was playing in his head. He pictured Al, his not inconsiderable backside jiggling as he rode Angelina's chest. He could just imagine the bad porn film dialogue that would spew from Al's mouth in such a situation. Why was it that all middle-aged, fat, unattractive men in Hollywood honestly believed that beautiful actresses half their age would let them shoot a load on their breasts? *Probably because most of them* would *let them,* he thought.

Again Violet's voice interrupted his thoughts. "Reid, Ty Rusk is here to see you."

"Send him in, Violet."

The door opened and a young man walked in, shutting the door behind him. "Hey," he said as he walked toward Reid's desk.

"Hi," Reid answered. "What brings you here?"

Ty smiled as he removed his coat, revealing a tight-fitting white T-shirt tucked into his jeans. "I just thought you might like to see me," he said as he came around to Reid's side and sat on the edge of the desk, putting one leg on either side of Reid's chair and looking down at him with a grin. "Do you? Want to see me, I mean."

Reid looked up into Ty's blue eyes. His short brown hair was arranged in a deliberately tousled way that was supposed to look as if he'd just gotten out of the shower, but which he'd probably paid some Beverly Hills stylist two hundred and fifty bucks to create. He hadn't shaved, and the faint stubble on his chin and cheeks made him look older than he was.

He looks just like he does on the one-sheet, Reid thought suddenly. He glanced at his wall, where the poster for *Hat Trick* hung. It was the movie that was currently topping the charts, the one that had Al Simon up his ass about making another film, and Ty Rusk was its star.

"Of course I want to see you," Reid told Ty. "I've been thinking about you all day."

"Really?" Ty said. "And what in particular were you thinking about?"

"Giving you a titty fuck," Reid said.

"Come again?" replied Ty, looking confused.

"Inside joke," answered Reid, moving his chair closer to the desk so that Ty's crotch was level with his face. "Would you settle for a blow job?"

As his fingers worked the buttons of Ty's 501s, Reid couldn't help but note the irony of the situation. Moments ago he had been thinking of Al Simon and his kind as perverts for thinking they could get it on with actresses half their age. Now here he was about to suck the cock of a twenty-six-year-old actor. True, at forty-six Reid wasn't quite twice Ty's age. Nor was he out of shape, thanks to the time he put in with his trainer. Still, the parallels were unmistakable.

Not that Reid had lured Ty into his bed with the promise of a starring role or anything even remotely like that. In fact, the development of their relationship had been much more old-fashioned. Midway through principal shooting on *Hat Trick* Reid had invited the cast and crew to his house for a cookout, an incentive to get them through the difficult period that always seemed to come when the excitement of starting a new film had worn off and the usual production struggles had taken their toll. The party had been a huge success, and Ty had stayed long after everyone else had left, talking to Reid about his love of film. Reid had been enchanted by the handsome young man—as had legions of fans—but until Ty had unexpectedly kissed him, he hadn't entertained anything but passing fantasies about him.

The next morning, when he'd woken up with his arm across Ty's muscular back, he'd assumed it would be a onetime event, something never again mentioned or perhaps blamed on too much wine. He'd stayed in that position for as long as possible, watching Ty's back rise and fall as he breathed. His arm had gone numb and still he hadn't moved, for fear of waking Ty and bringing their night to an awkward, disappointing close. While he had the chance he wanted to burn the image of Ty sleeping in his bed into his mind so he could keep it as a lovely memory to use later, when Ty disappeared from his life as quickly as he'd entered it.

But Ty had had other ideas, and soon the two of them were seeing each other regularly. They weren't, of course, out about their relationship. Ty still went on dates with popular young actresses and gave interviews to *Entertainment Weekly* suggesting that he might be bedding more than the occasional starlet. Most recently, *People* had named him one of their most eligible bachelors. Ty had read Reid the piece aloud while the two of them had relaxed in each other's arms after a bout of particularly passionate lovemaking, Reid snorting with laughter as Ty quoted himself as saying that he was looking for "a woman with a sense of humor, a sexy smile, and a recipe for killer apple pie just like Mom's."

Reid didn't have to be as circumspect, although he told no one about the fact that two or three times a week he made love to America's newest heartthrob. Most people in the industry knew that Reid Truman was gay, and none of them cared. After all, to the general public a "produced by" credit on a film was simply something to indicate that the director's name was coming up and then, after that final annoyance, the start of the picture. While speculation about a star's sexuality would land her or him on the front page of the supermarket tabloids, a producer could throw the most obscene orgies featuring dozens of gay porn stars and run naked covered in cocaine down the streets of the Hollywood Hills with no one batting an eye. Reid could easily name three who had done exactly that within the past six months, with none of the people who paid to see the movies they produced either knowing or caring.

But things were different for Ty. He was part of the Hollywood machinery that turned gas station mechanics from Alabama into action heros pulling in eight figures per film. While the old studio system made famous by MGM and Paramount had ended years before, there were still rules that had to be followed. Ty was on the brink of stardom, certain to follow in the footsteps of actors like Ben Affleck, Russell Crowe, and George Clooney, but only if he behaved himself. Not even his manager knew of his preference for men, and for the moment things had to stay that way.

"Oh, man, that feels good," Ty gasped, pushing Reid's head down with fingers made strong from years of working on the undersides and innards of cars.

Reid growled a response, concentrating on the taste of Ty in his mouth. He could tell by the way Ty was thrusting against his lips that he wouldn't be able to hold back much longer. He slowed down, not wanting the moment—or Ty—to come to an end too quickly.

Then Violet's voice interrupted Ty's moans, which were growing more frequent.

"Reid, Pamela Hinkle is on the line. She says she needs to talk to you right away."

"Don't take it," Ty whispered as Reid tried to lift his head to reply.

"Reid?" Violet said after a moment. "Are you there?"

Once more Reid attempted to extricate Ty's dick from his mouth, and again Ty pushed his head back down.

"Finish me off," he said wickedly, winking at Reid.

With a tremendous effort, Reid pulled his head away from Ty's crotch. "Put her through, Violet," he said breathlessly as he wiped his lips and gave Ty a menacing glare.

"Reid?" Pamela's shrill voice came through the phone, dripping with both urgency and fake cheerfulness. "How *are* you?"

"Fine," Reid said, slapping at Ty's hand as the young man tried to slip it into Reid's shirt. "What can I do for you?"

"We need to talk about Ty," Pamela answered.

Ty rolled his eyes. He leaned back on Reid's desk and stroked his still-hard dick as his agent continued to talk.

"I'm sure you've seen the latest numbers on *Hat Trick,*" Pamela said. "And I'm sure you know what they mean."

"Let me guess," Reid said, his eyes fixed on Ty's hand as it moved up and down. "You want more money for his next picture."

"It's only fair," Pamela said. "I mean, he *is* the star, right?"

"Sure, Pamela," Reid said.

"And I assume you want to use him again," the agent continued.

"As soon as possible," said Reid as Ty stifled a laugh.

"Good," Pamela chirped. "I'm glad we're on the same page."

"Just out of curiosity, what kind of number do you have in mind?" asked Reid.

"Well, Wesley Snipes got eleven million for his last picture," she replied promptly. "I think Ty is in his league now."

Reid whistled as Ty began pinching one of his own nipples between his fingers and giving Reid a decidedly porn star pout. "That's a pretty high figure, Pamela," Reid said. "I don't think we could really manage that."

"Well, think about it," Pamela said. "After all, you don't want to lose him to someone else, do you? He's out right now talking to people, and I'd hate for someone else to make him an offer."

"So would I," Reid told her. "Let me get back to you."

"Fine," Pamela told him. "But don't wait too long. Ciao."

Reid ended the call and turned his full attention to Ty. "I hate your agent," he said. "And I hate people who say ciao."

"Yeah," Ty said. "But you have to admit, she's good."

"I'm better," Reid said.

"Oh, yeah?" said Ty, looking pointedly down at himself. "Prove it."

Five minutes later, as Ty was buttoning his jeans and tucking in his T-shirt, Reid was thinking. "What's your schedule like for the summer?" he asked.

"I leave for New York in two weeks," Ty told him. "I'm shooting that Kevin Smith film, remember? Pamela says I need to get some indie credibility. Anyway, she made the deal before *Hat Trick,* so I'm stuck with it. Why?"

"I was just thinking," Reid told him. "I think I need a vacation from all of this.

"All of what?" asked Ty.

"This," said Reid, waving his arms around the office. "Hollywood. Films. Scripts. Movie bullshit. I want to spend some time in the real world."

"What did you have in mind?" Ty said.

Reid bit his lip, as he always did while trying to work out a problem. "You're going to be in New York," he said, thinking aloud. That's definitely not the real world. But what's near there?"

"Geography wasn't my best subject," replied Ty. "I was always more of the vo-tech kind of guy, if you know what I mean."

Reid ignored him. He had an idea.

"Violet," he said, pressing the intercom button on his phone, "I need you to look into renting a house in Provincetown for the summer."

CHAPTER 4

Finding the Two Queens Guest House was easy. Even without Ryan's directions, Josh would have been hard-pressed to get lost in Provincetown. Its two main streets, Commercial and Bradford, formed the sides of what was essentially a ladder of smaller streets running between them. It was simply a matter of driving until he saw the sign for Oyster Lane and then making a left.

Number 37 was halfway up the block, a brightly painted Victorian that stood out next to the more traditional white Cape Cod–style houses that flanked it. Josh turned into the driveway and pulled the car into the small parking area beside the house. As he got out, the front door opened and a man came out. He stood on the steps leading up to the house and gave a wave. Tall and heavily built, he had short-cropped silver hair and was dressed in faded khaki pants and a pale green shirt with the sleeves rolled up.

"I take it that you're Josh," the man said as Josh got out of the car.

"And I take it you're either Ted or Ben," Josh replied, walking over and shaking the man's extended hand.

"Ted," said the man. "Ben's out back playing in what passes for the garden. Come on in."

Josh followed Ted through the door and into the front hall, where he was immediately greeted by a large black Lab, who thrust a stuffed toy into his hand and looked up at him with enormous brown eyes, his tail beating furiously against the floor.

"Thanks," Josh said to the dog.

Ted laughed. "This is Brewer," he told Josh. "He's our resident mascot, guard dog, and garbage disposal. And that thing you're holding used to be a stuffed hedgehog named Rupert."

Josh looked at the hedgehog, which appeared to have suffered much abuse, not to mention applications of slobber. He tossed it down the hallway and Brewer scrambled after it, his paws clicking on the polished wood floor.

"How old is he?" Josh asked Ted.

"Five," Ted replied. "We got him at the same time that we bought this place. We like to tell people that every house sold on the cape comes with a Lab thrown in."

Ted followed Brewer down the hall, and Josh trailed after him, admiring the way the house was decorated with a mix of what appeared to be expensive antiques and more casual furnishings, the overall result of which was an atmosphere of hominess, like a summer house crossed with the gleanings from a particularly refined estate sale.

"I know, it's sort of a strange combination," Ted told him, noting Josh's attention to the decor. "Ben and I have very different tastes. His run to what I call the dowager empress school of design, while I'm slightly less formal. We argued for a long time about which look would win out, and in the end we decided to compromise."

"I like it," Josh told him. "It looks like two different people had a hand in it. I suppose that's where the name came from—Two Queens."

"Actually," said Ted, "that was a happy accident. We bought this place from two old spinster sisters, Abigail and Mary Queen. They'd lived here for about a thousand years after inheriting it from their father. When we were going through the purchasing process Ben started joking that at least the house would still belong to two queens. Once we thought of it, there really wasn't any other choice for a name."

They had come to the kitchen. Brewer, having retrieved his toy, was lying on the floor beneath a large table, happily gnawing on what was left of Rupert's head. Ted indicated a chair and said, "I'll get us something to drink."

Josh sat down, relieved to be out of the car. When Ted set a glass of iced tea in front of him, he drank deeply and leaned back in his chair. Ted pulled out another chair and sat across from him.

"So, Ryan said you needed to get out of Boston for a while," he said.

Josh nodded. "The city can get on your nerves sometimes," he answered. He didn't know if Ryan had mentioned his personal troubles to his hosts, and he felt almost as if he was lying to Ted by not telling him the full story. But he just wasn't in the mood to discuss the situation with a man he'd just met, even if he did seem like a nice guy and was letting him stay at his guest house.

Ted nodded, not pushing the issue. Josh waited for him to ask more questions, but Ted just took another sip of his tea. Before he could say anything else, another door opened and a second man came in, wiping dirt from his hands onto the shorts he was wearing. Shorter and slighter than Ted, he wore small round gold glasses and had brown hair. His shirt was pink.

"Did I hear a car pull up?" he asked. Then he saw Josh sitting at the table. "Oh, you're here!" he exclaimed, as if Josh were a much-anticipated guest and not some stranger whose existence he'd only learned of a few hours earlier. Rushing over, he gave Josh an enthusiastic hug. "I'm *so* sorry to hear about your lover," he said consolingly.

So much for that little secret, Josh thought as he returned Ben's hug. *I should have known Ryan wouldn't be able to keep that to himself.*

"Thanks," he told Ben.

"Now don't you worry about a thing," Ben told him. "You can stay here as long as you need to."

"Oh, it will just be for the weekend," said Josh.

Ben ignored him. "Did you tell him about the work?" he asked Ted.

Ted shook his head. "You didn't give me time," he told his partner.

Ben turned back to Josh. "We're having work done on the cottage," he said. "But don't worry, everything works. You still have a bathroom and a kitchen and all of that. Well, part of a kitchen anyway."

Josh looked at him, not quite understanding.

"Didn't you tell him *anything?*" Ben scolded Ted. "Honestly, I swear you've got early Alzheimer's. Josh, you're going to be staying in the cottage out back. It's more private. But we're having some work done on it, so I'm afraid you'll have to put up with a little construction."

"That's no problem," Josh said quickly. He hadn't noticed a cottage when he'd arrived, and had just assumed he'd be staying in one of the regular rooms.

"Now back to this boyfriend of yours," Ben said, sitting down and fixing Josh with a concerned look. "What are you going to do about him?"

"Honey, leave him alone," Ted said. He looked at Josh. "I apologize for my other half. I'm afraid he hasn't had anyone's life to meddle in since our last guests left. You have the unfortunate good luck of being the first new victim he's had in several months."

"Oh, shut up," Ben said, rolling his eyes. "I can't help it. I used to teach seventh grade," he told Ben. "All day long kids would come to me with their problems. Why doesn't this girl like me? Why haven't my breasts gotten any bigger? I haven't been able to shake the habit. Now go on, tell me everything."

"You know what, I think I need to think about it some more before I can talk about it," Josh said.

"Good boy," Ted said, nodding approvingly.

"I knew I should have gotten to him before you did," Ben said to his lover. "Well, okay. But when you're ready, you come to your ancient aunty and tell her everything."

"Ancient my ass," Ted said. "You're younger than I am."

"That's right," said Ben. "And *you're* ancient too, at least in gay years." He turned back to Josh. "He's fifty-seven," he said. "Can you even stand it?"

Josh smiled despite himself. He was enjoying the playful banter between the two partners, and he had a feeling they were playing it up for his benefit.

"I'm only fifty-two," Ben said, as if confiding the most closely held of secrets. "But if you tell anyone I'll only admit to forty-eight. Now come out back and I'll show you the cottage."

Josh stood up as Brewer, sensing an outing, raced to the door and looked expectantly at the doorknob.

"Are you sure you can handle him?" Ted asked Josh. "I'm happy to be your bodyguard."

"I think I'll be okay," Josh said as Ben sighed dramatically.

Ben let Brewer out and he and Josh walked into the backyard. As the dog tore off to sniff some flowers, Ben pointed to a small cottage that sat at the rear of the property.

"There's your home away from home," he said.

Josh couldn't help but laugh. The cottage resembled a smaller version of the main house, right down to the elaborate paint job.

"It looks like someone built an oversize dollhouse based on the big house," remarked Josh.

"Close," said Ben. "It was originally built for the Queen sisters to play in when they were little girls. Weird, isn't it?"

"A little," Josh said as they reached the door and Ben opened it.

"As you can see, only the outside is the same," said Ben as they went inside.

Indeed, inside the cottage looked like any other summer cottage. It was basically two spacious rooms, one a living room and one a bedroom. Each was furnished with comfortable-looking furniture, and a multitude of windows let in the bright summer sun.

"It was in pretty bad shape when we bought the place," Ben said as he gave Josh a quick tour. "We only just renovated it last year, and we're still not done. As you can see, the kitchen is in bits and pieces. We have a local carpenter working on it, but since we weren't planning on renting it out this season we haven't been in any big hurry to get it done."

Josh looked at the cabinets and fixtures scattered around the kitchen. "It's great," he said. "I really appreciate you letting me use it."

"It's our pleasure," Ben told him. "I know how it is to have a cheater for a lover," he added.

"Ted?" Ben said, genuinely surprised. Although he'd only known the men for half an hour, Ted didn't strike him as the type to stray.

"Oh, no," said Ben. "Ted's as monogamous as one of those swans who mate for life. No, before him I was with someone else, this absolutely gorgeous man who had the nasty habit of spending more time in other people's beds than he did in ours. But I was young and in love, and I thought I could change him. I put up with it for a long time, until finally he gave me crabs one time too many and I kicked him out."

Josh shrugged. "Doug's not like that," he said. "In fact, until this morning I would have said that he and I were like you and Ted. Now, though, I don't know."

"Well, you'll have plenty of peace and quiet to think it all over," said Ben when it was clear that Josh wasn't going to say anything else. "In the meantime, I'll leave you to get settled. I'm afraid you can't do too much cooking in this place, but the good news is that I happen to be a fabulous cook. So come on over around eight o'clock and we'll have ourselves some dinner."

Josh smiled at Ben. Despite his nosiness, he seemed like a genuinely kind person. "Thanks," he said. "I'll see you then."

Ben left Josh alone. After another, more thorough, inspection of his living quarters, Josh went to the car to retrieve his luggage. When he returned, he deposited his bag in the bedroom. His laptop he placed on the coffee table in the living room. It was then that he realized that the place had neither a television nor a phone. At first this made him feel lonely, as if without e-mail and the mindless chatter of must-see TV he was somehow cut off from the rest of the world.

Then he remembered his cell phone. Somehow he'd had the presence of mind to pack the recharger, so at least he had that. Besides, whom was he going to call? He didn't even want Doug to know where he was. Ryan could always reach him through Ben and Ted. There was no one else he needed to talk to, at least not immediately. Suddenly, being unreachable took on a pleasant new dimension. He had, for all intents and purposes, successfully run away from home.

This realization brought with it another, less pleasant, one: He smelled bad. In his haste to get away from Doug and his revelation of infidelity, he hadn't showered. He had simply changed out of his running clothes into jeans and a T-shirt. Now, after several hours of sitting in the car, the sweat from his morning run was making itself known.

To make matters worse, nothing in his bag was going to smell much better. He'd basically packed straight from the hamper, as Saturday was laundry day and everything he wore most frequently was dirty. Unless he wanted to arrive at dinner wearing nothing but a T-shirt and a smile, he was going to have to do laundry.

He imagined that Ben and Ted probably had a washer and dryer in the house, but he felt he'd imposed on them enough for one day. Surely there was a Laundromat in town. He picked up his bag, returned to the car, and made the short drive to Commercial Street. After trolling for several blocks, he spied what he was looking for and parked in front of it.

The Bucket of Suds was surprisingly busy. Most of the washers were in use, but Josh found the two he needed and loaded them up. As his clothes washed he went out for a coffee and a quick stroll up and down the street. Oddly enough for someone who had lived in fairly close proximity for many years, he had never been to P-Town before. Although he would have preferred to have made his first visit under different circumstances, that didn't stop him from being curious about what the place was like.

After wandering through the shops for a while, he returned to put his wash in to dry. But when he wheeled his laundry-filled cart over to the wall of dryers, he found them all occupied. Most were on, the clothes inside falling over themselves as the dryers turned. Several, however, were sitting still, their finished loads taking up valuable real estate.

Josh looked at the dryers. He hated it when people were rude like this. How long, he wondered, would the clothes sit there before their owner came to claim them? Was it worth waiting for another dryer to finish, one whose user was more conscientious about things like wasting other people's time? He looked at his watch. It was six-thirty. He still needed to shower.

Deciding that there wasn't time to wait for the other dryers to finish, he opened the ones that had already stopped and pulled their contents into an empty cart. The clothes were barely warm, suggesting that they'd been there for some time. This made Josh even more irritated, and as he threw his own wash in he thought of all the things he'd like to say to the owner of the laundry.

Almost immediately after putting his quarters in, however, he began to feel guilty. He looked at the clean clothes, jumbled in the cart, and he suddenly felt a sense of responsibility toward them. It was stupid, he knew. They weren't his clothes. Their careless owner deserved to have them taken from the warm belly of the dryer by a stranger. But seeing them thrown together in a wrinkled pile upset Josh's sense of order. Sloppiness had always been something he despised, and somehow the untended laundry reminded him that his own life was currently very much not in order.

With a sigh of resignation he wheeled the cart over to a folding table and picked up the first garment. It was a T-shirt, white, Hanes size large, he noted as he turned it right-side-to with a faint sense of irritation that its wearer had compounded his carelessness by leaving the shirt inside out. He spread it out and folded the sides over, lining up the sleeves and smoothing them out of habit.

Not surprisingly, the whites and colors had been mixed together. Josh tried not to think about it as he folded the clothes, mainly T-shirts. But when he reached in and came up with a pair of boxer shorts, white like the T-shirts, he felt a sense of embarrassment. He was holding a stranger's underwear in his hands. He stared at them for a moment, then glanced around, oddly fearful that someone would think he was engaged in some kind of strange sexual act.

He folded the boxers quickly, first in thirds and then once over, like he did his own. There were more of them in the cart, most white but some red plaid and one pair with small blue polka dots. They were all waist size 34, a detail Josh found amusing for a silly personal reason. Someone had once told him that 32 was the most common waist size in menswear. He himself was a 34, and whenever he bought underwear or pants he reminded himself that although he might not be the size 32 he'd been in his twenties, he was at least above average. A 34 waist, he'd decided, was a sign of having grown into himself.

He continued folding, moving from boxers to socks, then more T-shirts and finally onto jeans and what appeared to be the world's largest collection of blue work shirts. He folded all of them with careful attention to detail, and before long he had a pile of clean clothes in front of him, each item neat enough to have been plucked from a display at Banana Republic. Despite the fact that they weren't his, he took some measure of satisfaction from looking at his handiwork. *At least there's one thing I have control over,* he thought.

As he looked at the pile as a whole, he began to wonder more about whom they belonged to. Clearly, it was a man. But what was he like? Who was he? Josh easily fell into one of his favorite games—trying to guess something about a person he'd never met simply by looking at his belongings. He did it in airports sometimes, and on the T while riding around Boston. Sometimes he created whole lives for people he found particularly interesting. Once, after seeing a man in a business suit walking down Newbury Street eating Twinkie after Twinkie from a box he carried, Josh had spent several delicious hours imaging what could possibly drive someone to such behavior.

Now he turned his attention to the person behind the laundry. Who was the man who preferred white boxers? Single, probably, since there were no women's clothes mixed in with his. But what else could Josh tell? Not much, he decided after staring at the clothes for some time. All of it—the T-shirts, the jeans, the work shirts—was impersonal, without any hint of style or character. It could belong to anyone.

He's probably just some stupid eighteen-year-old college kid, Josh thought, annoyed that the clothing wasn't more interesting.

"Did you do this?"

Josh turned around, startled by the voice. Behind him was a man, and he was staring at the pile of laundry.

"Um, yeah," Josh replied. "Is it yours?"

The man nodded.

He wasn't eighteen. He was closer to Josh's own age, and he was incredibly handsome. Slightly taller than Josh, he had short reddish brown hair, blue eyes, and the faint shadow of a two-day beard. His skin was tanned, and he appeared to have a well-built body beneath the jeans and blue work shirt he was wearing. Looking at the shirt, Josh almost laughed at its exact resemblance to the others in the pile, but his surprise at meeting the clothes' owner quickly erased any possibility of making a joke.

"I'm sorry," Josh said finally. "I needed to use a dryer, and they were all full."

The man examined his laundry, as if checking to make sure everything was there. This annoyed Josh, who half expected the guy to accuse him of stealing his underwear or losing one of his T-shirts.

"This is amazing," the man said. "You fold clothes better than my mother."

The comment took Josh by surprise. "Oh," he said dully, all of the comebacks he'd mentally been preparing being inappropriate for the moment. "Thanks."

The man picked up his clothing and turned to Josh. "I'm sorry I left it here," he said. "I was working on a job and lost track of time. I owe you one."

He smiled, revealing white teeth and, even more distracting to Josh, a dimple in his chin. Then, before Josh could reply, he turned and left, the folded laundry cradled in his arms.

"Any time," Josh said to his retreating back. He continued to watch the man as he got into a red pickup truck and pulled away. Then another voice brought him back to the moment.

"Excuse me."

Josh turned around. A woman with a cart full of wet clothes was looking at his dryers, which had just stopped. "Are you going to take this stuff out or what?" she asked accusingly.

CHAPTER 5

"Hey, Mama."

"Mason?"

Emmeline closed her eyes and gripped the phone more tightly. "Yes, Mama. It's me. How are you?"

There was a deep sigh from the other end of the line. "You know how it is," Lula Tayhill said. "I've got some aches and pains. But I don't want to trouble you with my complaining."

Of course you don't, Mama, Emmeline thought. *Talking about things makes them too real, doesn't it?*

"Is everything all right with the house?" she asked her mother.

"The bathroom pipes busted last week, but Petey came by and fixed them up," Lula answered. "It's nice having him living nearby again."

Emmeline decided not to take the bait her mother had thrown out. Ever since her brother had moved back to Louisiana a year earlier, Emmeline had been forced to endure her mother's frequent references to his helpfulness. She understood all too well that the real point of these stories was to underscore the fact that she herself hadn't seen her mother in more than five years, not since the day they'd buried Daddy. What her mother never mentioned, of course, was that Petey hadn't been at the funeral because he'd been locked up in the West Texas State Penitentiary, where he was serving a three-year sentence for robbery and evading arrest. Luckily for Petey, the high-speed car chase he'd led the police on after holding up a liquor store had ended only in a multicar pileup and not in any casualties, thus sparing him tenure on the state's overcrowded death row.

But now Petey was out, and after several years of drifting from place to place doing odd jobs he'd returned home. As a reward, Lula had conveniently forgotten about her prodigal son's past, and Petey had resumed his position as favorite child. Emmeline had once again been demoted, and while on some level she was glad not to have her mother's full attention turned on her, the pattern was all too familiar, and all too painful.

"What about you, son?" Lula asked. "Are you still working at that restaurant?"

"Yes, Mama," Emmeline answered. "I'm still at the restaurant."

"That's good," her mother replied.

Emmeline knew that would be the extent of the conversation about her work situation. Her mother would never ask exactly what she did at the restaurant, preferring to believe that her younger son was a waiter or dishwasher than to know that he performed there dressed as a woman. For Lula Tayhill there was no greater crime a man could commit than to be effeminate. Even Petey's repeated run-ins with the law were preferable, suggesting as they did that while he might be stupid he was at least gifted with an overabundance of manly testosterone.

"Okay, Mama," Emmeline said. "I just wanted to check up on you. You tell Petey hello for me, and I'll call again next week."

"Don't you worry about us," said her mother. "We're just fine."

Emmeline said her good-byes and hung up. How was it that in less than five minutes her mother could make her feel nine years old again? Why did she subject herself to this weekly ordeal?

Because she's your mother, she told herself as she stood and walked to the full-length mirror that occupied one corner of her bedroom.

It was as simple as that, as simple as blood. The Tayhill household had been run on one basic principle—you were to respect your parents. Both of the Tayhill boys had had this law drummed into their heads since they were old enough to comprehend the consequences of breaking it. They had believed it, too, with all their hearts. They'd clung to its truth while their father, drunk on the cheap gin he favored, had held them down and beaten them with his well-worn leather belt for sins they couldn't remember committing. They'd believed it when their mother had told them not to ask questions about the bruises she blamed on her clumsiness. They'd repeated it like a mantra when they'd helped drag their father's unconscious, snoring body from the front lawn into the house early on a Sunday morning before dressing in their best clothes and going to church, where they smiled and thanked Jesus for his blessings.

Emmeline had almost stopped believing the afternoon when she was twelve and her mother had come home early from her job as a Woolworth's clerk to discover her son in her bedroom, wearing her best dress, nylons, and the matching rhinestone earrings and necklace she kept in a tissue-lined box in her top dresser drawer. As her mother had screamed words at her that she'd only ever heard spoken by boys at school, Emmeline had suddenly become blindingly aware that the rule she had been taught to live by did not work both ways. As her mother had torn the dress from her back and chased her down the hallway, sobbing and demanding explanations, she had wondered what other lies about her life she might have accepted as truth.

Later, when her father had come to her room to find out why her mother was sitting at the kitchen table, sobbing and with dinner unprepared, Emmeline had tried once more to put her faith in the strength of family. As her father's hands had slapped her face and shoved her against the wall, however, her ability to believe had slowly crumbled. As he'd screamed his shame and his rage at her, she'd tried to imagine herself as deserving of the punishment. But when he'd finally left her, after extracting a whispered promise to never again venture past the door of the master bedroom, Emmeline had lain in her bed knowing that things had changed forever.

It had taken three more years for her to get up the courage to leave, and another ten after that for her to pick up the phone and call her mother. Her father was by then a feeble ghost of his former self, his liver rotted away and his eyesight gone. When Emmeline had finally gone to see him, he'd barely acknowledged her. Her mother had been more welcoming, pretending that thirteen years hadn't gone by since their last meeting. They'd picked up their relationship where they'd left off, with Lula asking no questions and Emmeline offering no unnecessary information.

Since then another ten years had passed, and now there were changes that neither Emmeline, nor Lula if she saw them, could ignore. Emmeline undid the belt of the pink silk robe she was wearing and let it fall open. Her fingers cupped her breasts, soft and full, and then slid down her stomach. The skin was smooth, hairless, and supple. Even her musculature had changed since she'd begun taking the hormones, and her body no longer felt alien to her. The hardness she'd always felt lurking beneath her skin had been replaced by a sensual softness, a giving in the flesh that pleased her greatly. She no longer felt as if her father were inside her, trying to push his way out.

It was only when her fingers reached the hair below her navel that she stopped. There things became troubling again. She was reluctant to look at what was reflected in the clear glass of the mirror, the panties holding the telltale bulge that reminded her that she still had one more matter to take care of before she would be able to consider herself whole. Although years of performing in drag shows had taught her how to keep her secret from the prying eyes of the world, she had never mastered the trick of fooling her own mind.

Soon, she hoped, that would no longer be a problem. There was a surgeon, a good one, in Boston. She had been to him for consultations, had obtained the necessary psychiatric permissions and endured the questions of therapists who had wanted to know if she truly understood what she was asking. She had wanted to ask them if *they* understood, but instead had been polite and appropriately thankful. She despised most of them for making her beg for what she felt was already hers, but she had long ago learned that it was easier to play their game than it was to make them see that their rules were insulting. Besides, there had been one or two who really had understood, who had gone out of their way to make things easier.

She thought about the money waiting in her bank account. The past few summers had been good ones for her, and she'd managed to save nearly enough. The crowd at Jackie's was appreciative, and generous, and their tips had accumulated rapidly. Now, if all went according to plan, one more summer should find her where she wanted to be.

Emmeline retied the belt at her waist and went into the living room, where she sat on the sofa. On the coffee table in front of her was a pile of sheet music, the songs she and her accompanist had selected for the first shows of the season. She was supposed to have learned them all, but there were a few she was still having trouble with, most notably Cole Porter's "From This Moment On." She had decided to slow the tempo down considerably from the way the song was normally sung, particularly in the version made famous by Ella Fitzgerald, and it was throwing her off a bit.

She opened the music and began singing it softly, keeping time by tapping her hand against the sofa cushions. But after a few minutes she knew that neither her heart nor her mind was in the endeavor, and she put the music down. Going to the stereo she selected a CD and slipped it in. A moment later the opening notes of *The Supremes Sing Rodgers & Hart* filled the room as Diana Ross started in on "The Lady Is a Tramp."

Emmeline stood in the middle of the room, eyes closed, letting the music surround her. She and Diana went way back. As a teenager her musical education had been limited by her older brother's tastes, and as a result she'd grown up listening to the likes of Van Halen, Aerosmith, and KISS. While the peculiar makeup of Paul, Gene, Ace, and Peter had appealed to her in a way she hadn't understood until she'd been in therapy for a number of years, the music itself had never interested her.

That all changed with her first exposure to the gay clubs of New Orleans, where she gravitated to after leaving home. There she discovered a wonderland of sights and sounds she'd never imagined. Some of them, particularly those of the chemical variety, hadn't been particularly good for her. But the music was different. The music became her salvation.

At first she'd only danced to it, finding safety, comfort, and strength on the crowded dance floors where she spent every night. Surrounded by hundreds of others, she came alive, as if their energy filled her and gave her the power to move. Under the twinkling, twirling lights she swayed and laughed as she floated on the voices of angels who went by one name: Madonna, Cher, Bette. Diana had been there too, cooing one moment and demanding the next. Emmeline recalled one particular July night when, while dancing to Diana singing "Upside Down," she looked up and met the eye of the first man who would break her heart since her father had. When he did it, two weeks later, Diana's "Love Hangover" saw her through the tears and got her back into the bars.

Eventually Emmeline moved from the dance floor to the stage, teaming up with two other boys who liked to wear dresses and forming the Gaybor Sisters, a drag queen trio that made its debut during Southern Decadence and swept through New Orleans like a hurricane. They became a family, living together, working together at the clubs as bartenders and bar backs to make ends meet, and performing whenever possible.

Diana had been there then as well. Emmeline had taken her parts when the Gaybors did their Supremes medley, standing front and center while lip-synching "Baby Love," "My Guy," and "Reflections." Sometimes she'd forgotten that she was playing a role, and when the music stopped she'd had to do a line or two of coke to exorcize Diana's spirit from her body.

The Gaybor Sisters ruled the clubs until death—one from AIDS and one from suicide—left Emmeline the sole sister. Not knowing what to do without her companions, she'd retired temporarily. Fleeing the ghosts that crowded the streets of New Orleans even more than the tourists who invaded during Mardi Gras, she went North, to the forbidden land of the Yankees. After a brief stint in New York, where the voracious specter of AIDS only reminded her of what she'd left behind, she continued on to Boston.

There she had rid herself of the ghosts, first by going through rehab and then by returning to performing. This time, though, she began singing live from time to time. She discovered that she was tired of mouthing other people's words, and that she herself had something to say. When she performed Diana's "Missing You," it was no tribute to Marvin Gaye, but instead a farewell to her own past.

The Supremes' Rodgers & Hart album had been a gift from an admirer, an older drag queen named Second Hand Rose who had once been the talk of Boston but who had long since been replaced by a new generation of younger girls. Rose still came to the bars dressed in all her finery, but where once she turned heads for her beauty she now turned them for her ability to tell stories about how things had once been.

Rose had become something of a mother to Emmeline, dispensing advice and offering encouragement. It was to Rose that Emmeline first disclosed her desire to fully become a woman, Rose who helped her begin the long process of achieving her goal, and Rose who helped her remember that there still was something to be gained by trusting someone.

Rose had given the album to Emmeline one Christmas. The original had been a vinyl record, lovingly kept in excellent condition. "It's time you learned some real music," Rose had said, not unkindly, as Emmeline pulled the red bow and shiny green paper from the present.

The original album cover was now framed and hanging on Emmeline's wall. She had replaced the record with the CD when it was finally released, wanting to preserve the original as much as possible. Rose had died several years before, felled by a heart attack. They had played "The Lady Is a Tramp" at her memorial service. The next day, Emmeline had packed up and moved to Provincetown.

Now, in her own living room, dancing to the music, she thought about all of the people who had gone in and out of her life. Friends. Family. Lovers. Enemies. She'd been through a great deal since that afternoon in her mother's room. But she had survived, she had made it on her own terms and in her own way. She was proud of who she'd become, and of what she'd accomplished. She had every right to be.

The music stopped as the song ended, and Emmeline stood in the silence. Suddenly, unexpectedly, the tears began flowing. She *was* proud of herself. Still, she couldn't help but wish her mother could be just as proud.

CHAPTER 6

On Saturday morning Josh woke up with a hangover and what sounded like all eight of Santa's reindeer pawing on the roof overhead. He glanced over at the clock on the bedside table. It was seven-thirty. He'd only gone to sleep five hours earlier. Dinner with Ted and Ben had turned into a late-night talk about boyfriends and the difficulties with having them. Fueled by several bottles of excellent merlot, Josh had let the entire story of Doug's infidelity come out. He couldn't now remember what his hosts' response had been, but he recalled with a growing sense of embarrassment being handed some tissues and given several reassuring hugs. What, he wondered, had he said?

He closed his eyes and turned over, determined to slip back into the oblivion of sleep and not dwell on any possible indiscretions he might have committed. But a series of heavy thumps on the roof erased any possibility of a successful return to unconsciousness. Determined to discover the source of this new irritation, Josh slowly brought himself to a sitting position and then, once assured that he wasn't too hungover to stand up without assistance, got out of bed. Padding to the front door of the cottage, he opened it and stepped out into the cool light of morning.

On the roof a man was lifting a hammer and bringing it down with what Josh thought was undue force for such an early hour. At a pause in the pounding, Josh called up to him.

"Hey," he said, attempting to sound simultaneously friendly and indignant, "do you have to do that right now?"

The man paused and looked over the edge of the roof. "Sorry," he said. "I didn't know anyone was staying here."

Josh shielded his face from the morning sun, which was directly be-hind the man, making it difficult for Josh to look up at him without being blinded.

"I was kind of a last-minute guest," he explained.

The man climbed down a ladder that was leaning against the wall of the cottage. Once on the ground, the sun no longer haloed him, and Josh was surprised to see standing before him the man from the Laundromat.

"Oh," he said. "It's you. I mean, I recognize that shirt," he added, pointing to the denim work shirt the man had on. "I think I folded it."

"Oh, right," said the guy, looking at his shirt and then at Josh. "I didn't recognize you."

Suddenly Josh was very much aware of the fact that he was dressed in only a T-shirt and the old gym shorts he wore for sleeping in. He was sure the effects of all the wine and a night of sleeping with his faced pressed into the pillow weren't helping either.

"I'm Josh," he said finally, holding out his hand.

"Reilly," the man replied, grasping Josh's hand and giving it a single, hard pump. "And thanks for last night."

Josh looked at Reilly blankly. What exactly *had* he done after re-turning to the cottage?

"For folding my laundry," Reilly clarified.

"Oh," Josh exclaimed. "Oh, that's okay. I do that all the time."

He stopped talking. *Why did you say that?* he asked himself. *You sound like an idiot.* But Reilly was laughing. *He has a great laugh,* Josh thought. And there was that dimple again.

"My girlfriend was convinced I was cheating on her," Reilly said. "She didn't think any guy could fold laundry that well."

It was Josh's turn to laugh. *A girlfriend,* he thought. *So he's straight.* Not that it mattered. It wasn't like he was looking for a date or any-thing. He had a lover, after all. At least he might still have one. Doug still hadn't attempted to call him, and Josh wasn't sure what he would say to him if he did.

"The roof can wait," Reilly said. "We're not supposed to get rain any time soon. I can come back when you're gone. How long will you be staying?"

"Oh, just until Monday," Josh said. "I have to get back to Boston."

Reilly nodded. "Well, have a great weekend," he said. "I'll come back on Monday and finish this up."

Josh nodded. Reilly put his hammer into a toolbox sitting on the ground beside the ladder, picked the box up, and gave Josh a nod good-bye.

"See you," he said.

"Yeah," said Josh. "See you."

He turned and went inside. Getting back into bed, he pulled the blanket up to warm himself. The morning air, while hardly cold, had been a little chilly. It felt good to be in bed, alone, far away from Boston and Doug. His headache was starting to fade now thanks to his brief trip outside and the ceasing of the hammering, and he felt more alive.

But how strange it was seeing Reilly there. What were the chances of that? *He must think I'm totally out of my mind,* Josh thought with some sense of amusement. After all, it *was* pretty funny. Josh imagined Reilly telling his suspicious girlfriend about it. "Honestly, honey," he pictured him saying as the woman inspected the piles of perfectly folded clothes, "it really was this guy."

So Reilly wasn't single after all. He'd been wrong about that. Josh found himself wondering what this girlfriend looked like. Reilly was, after all, a good-looking guy. *Who are you kidding?* Josh chided himself. *That guy is fucking hot.*

Suddenly he found himself wondering what Reilly looked like underneath those jeans and denim shirts. How would he look, for example, in just a pair of the white boxers he seemed to like so much? Josh had noticed curls of dark hair poking over the neck of Reilly's T-shirt. He was obviously hairy—one of Josh's particular turn-ons. And he seemed to have a nice body, not overly muscled like one of the gym clones that crowded the bars in Boston, but a normal-looking male body defined by actual work instead of hours with a personal trainer and gallon after gallon of protein drink.

Yes, Reilly in boxer shorts was probably something to see. As he pictured it in his mind, Josh was slightly surprised to feel himself getting hard. The image was undeniably arousing, but it had been quite a while since he'd actively thought of anyone other than Doug in a sexual way. Even when he jacked off he generally relied on images from their own sex life to bring about his orgasm, finding the idea of imagining himself with someone else as being vaguely unfaithful. The few times he had thought of another man it had always been someone famous—an actor or sports figure, someone he could never have in real life. Since there was no chance of his ever getting the opportunity to have sex with those people, he'd deemed it acceptable to imagine being with them, a kind of sexual daydreaming that had nothing to do with reality.

You can't have Reilly, either, he reasoned with himself. *And anyway, Doug cheated on you. Consider this your freebie.*

No, thinking about sex with someone else wasn't the same as doing it. Josh realized that. But maybe, he thought, it was his way of mentally getting back at Doug, of evening the score a little. He didn't have it in him to actually go out and find some one-night stand to take his anger out on, but *thinking* about doing it was something he could manage. He knew that even if Doug could somehow know what he was thinking about, he wouldn't care. It didn't matter to him if Josh fantasized about other men. They'd had that discussion before, after Doug had admitted to thinking about someone else during sex. He'd been surprised at Josh's wounded reaction, had even laughed at how silly it was to be upset about something he considered so trivial. But to Josh it was a big deal. It made him feel unnecessary, as if he'd intruded on Doug having sex with someone else. Ever since that night, he'd gauged Doug's reactions during lovemaking, wondering if when he closed his eyes it was to picture someone else.

He slid his hand into his pants and wrapped his fingers around his dick. What *would* it be like to make love with Reilly? He drove all thoughts of Doug out of his mind and concentrated instead on trying to come up with a suitable scenario. He couldn't just jump right into sex; he had to have a back story, a where and a why and a when. It had to make sense.

First he tried to go with something slightly raunchy, something suitable to revenge sex. He pictured himself in a men's room, standing at a urinal. He imagined Reilly coming in and standing beside him, the two of them secretly checking each other out. They could, he thought, have sex in one of the stalls.

But that didn't work. He couldn't imagine the rest room without also imagining the acrid smell of old urine. The floors, he thought, would be sticky, the walls of the stall covered in graffiti. He would never be able to have sex in such a place, even in his fantasies.

He next tried to make a go of a gym scenario, beginning with him and Reilly undressing after their workouts. He got as far as actually picturing Reilly as he slid his sweat-soaked jock over the mounds of his ass before he remembered that Doug's tryst had likely begun in exactly the same way. This caused his erection to rapidly deflate, and for a moment he considered abandoning his plan. But that somehow felt like giving Doug another victory, so he stroked himself insistently and began again.

This time he stayed closer to home, fishing around in the shallow waters of recent memory to resurrect his morning interaction with Reilly. Only this time Reilly didn't pick up his toolbox and leave. Instead, he came inside, invited by Josh for "a cup of coffee or something."

From there it was relatively easy for Josh to invent a seduction scenario: the casual flirting, Reilly's remarks about a stiff back, Josh's offer of a soothing massage. That was enough to meet his requirements for setting and motivation. Relieved to have passed that hurdle, he quickly got both himself and Reilly down to their underwear and arranged Reilly facedown on the bed, with himself straddling the other man's waist.

What began as an honest massage turned into foreplay as Josh allowed his hands to stray farther and farther past the waistband of Reilly's boxers with each successive pass down his back. When Reilly made no objection to Josh's wandering fingers, Josh went for broke and slid the shorts all the way off, Reilly's ass pushing up into his crotch as he lifted his hips to allow the boxers to be removed.

Before he knew it, Josh had buried his face between Reilly's ass cheeks. Moments later, Reilly turned over to reveal a glorious erection, thick and hard against the fur of his belly. His hands had pulled Josh up so that their bodies were lying against each other. Josh felt the heat rising from Reilly's skin, smelled the scent of him. Reilly slid one hand down to grip Josh tightly.

Josh came. His body was engulfed by the delicious shiver of orgasm, and he felt his muscles contract and release in waves of release. Drops of warmth scattered over his chest and stomach. He held his cock, feeling the blood beating fiercely beneath his fingers, and rested in the warmth as his breathing returned to normal.

As soon as the glow faded he began to reprimand himself. *You didn't even get to the good part,* he thought, irritated. That was just like him, trying to cheat and coming before he'd even had full-on sex. He hadn't even really gotten to imagine what Reilly's cock would feel like in his hand, much less anywhere else.

Disgusted with himself, he pulled his T-shirt over his head and wiped the results of his thwarted encounter from his skin. He wanted to get into the shower. Even after sex with Doug he liked to clean up as quickly as possible. It was almost as if as his orgasms faded so too did his ability to tolerate stickiness. He wondered vaguely if he'd remembered to bring mouthwash with him.

In the shower he let himself reflect on his attempt at mental cheating. Why had he come so quickly? Usually it took him a lot longer. He had to be further along in the story in order to reach the level of excitement required to push him over the edge. Even during actual sex he was always the last one to come, waiting until Doug had climaxed until he did. Coming first seemed rude somehow. Besides, for him sex was about what it took to get the other person off. He came *because* Doug came.

But in his fantasy he hadn't waited for Reilly. He had been unable to control his body's reactions to simply touching the other man. Why? The experience was supposed to have been about sex; instead, he felt as if he'd been on a first date, one that likely wouldn't be repeated because of his incompetence in the bedroom. In his mind he'd left Reilly unfinished, and had thereby failed. *You can't even cheat when you jerk off,* he scolded himself.

When he was thoroughly soaped, shampooed, and shaved, he got out and dried off. Back in the bedroom, he pulled on some shorts and a clean T-shirt. It was time to head out in search of some breakfast. He'd noticed a cute little café while doing his laundry, and he thought it might be a good place to start his day. He was suddenly in the mood for pancakes, perhaps with blueberries.

As he headed out he picked up his cell phone from the table where he'd left it and started to slip it into his pocket out of habit. Then he noticed that his message light was on. *It's probably Ryan checking up on me,* he thought, realizing he'd forgotten to call his friend upon his arrival.

He hit the button to list his calls and felt his stomach knot up. It wasn't Ryan who had called. It was Doug. And he'd left a message.

CHAPTER 7

"You smell like puppy piss."

Reilly Brennan sniffed his girlfriend and made a face.

"Well, don't you know how to make a girl feel sexy," replied Donna, pulling off the latex gloves she was wearing and depositing them in a wastebasket. "Mrs. Chiavetti came in for her bimonthly perm. I'm afraid the results are lingering."

Reilly laughed. "I don't know why she bothers," he said, seating himself in the chair at Donna's station. "She's got to be about a hundred. Who is she trying to impress?"

"She's seventy-nine," Donna said reproachfully as she washed her hands at the shampoo sink. "And it doesn't matter how old a woman is, she always wants to look good. You wouldn't understand. Men don't have to worry about it as much as we do. When you get old you get distinguished, even if you have a belly the size of a Volkswagen Beetle and a bald spot that looks like a lunar landing site. But we girls have to fight the effects of time with everything we've got. She may not have any teeth, but she walked out of here with the hair of a twenty-six-year-old."

"And the scent of an eight-week-old rottweiler," Reilly added.

Donna removed her smock and tossed it into the hamper. "Are you saying that when I'm old and wrinkled you're not going to want to be around me?" she asked.

"That depends," her boyfriend answered.

"Oh?" Donna said. She went over to the chair and sat on Reilly's lap, putting her arms around his neck. "On what?"

Reilly grinned mischievously. "On whether or not you're house-trained."

Donna raised an eyebrow. "Well, then," she said, "maybe we should reconsider this whole wedding thing."

Reilly pretended to think about her comment seriously. "No," he said finally. "Then we'd miss out on all the gifts."

Donna groaned and got off of his lap. "Such a romantic," she said. "Why did I ever start going out with you in the first place?"

"Because our mothers have been planning this wedding since you were born," said Reilly, standing up.

That was true. Reilly was seven years old when Gloria Estoril gave birth to Donna. He remembered vividly his mother hanging up the phone in their kitchen, turning to his father, and saying happily, "Finally, after four boys Gloria had a baby girl. Now they can stop."

Reilly himself was an only child, not because his parents believed in zero population growth but because his mother's pregnancy had been such a difficult one that she'd been advised by her doctor not to risk another. As a result, all of Maura and James Brennan's dreams had been pinned on their only son. And their dreams were not inconsiderable. Through many years of hard work, the Brennans had built a thriving business. Brennan's Fish Market had begun as a small seaside stand in 1937, after Reilly's great-grandfather, Sean Brennan, tired of working in a Boston brewery and moved his family to Provincetown to try his hand at something else.

Since then the business had expanded into a chain of nine stores dotted around the cape. The mini empire, which had been handed down from great-grandfather to grandfather to father, and which most recently had been jointly run by three Brennan brothers and a sister, was now overseen solely by Reilly's father after one of his brothers died fighting in Korea, the other elected to return to Boston to open a pub, and the sole sister declared the smell of fish repulsive to her and became a teacher of mathematics. Determined to keep his great-grandfather's business going, James Brennan had managed to thrive despite increasing pressure from larger chains and decreasing profits caused by ever-tightening restrictions on what could be taken from the region's waters.

The continuing success of the Brennan's Fish Market stores was due in large part to the relationship between the Brennan family and the Estoril clan. This union had begun in 1943, when Gustavo Estoril had arrived in Provincetown with one small fishing boat and a determination to fulfill the American dream. His plan was simple: He would catch fish and sell them to the local fishmongers. Sean Brennan had been one of the first to buy from him. One afternoon, while haggling over the fair price for a day's catch, the two men had recognized in one another a similar ambition. Several beers and much discussion later, they formed a partnership. The Estorils, it was decided, would catch the fish. The Brennans would sell them.

The partnership had immediate and profitable results. With a steady supply of excellent product, Brennan's Fish Market became a favorite with local consumers. With a ready buyer for their hauls, the Estorils eliminated the inconvenience of having to seek out customers. In this way, both businesses had expanded rapidly and the respective families had prospered.

Given the ongoing business ties between the Brennans and the Estorils, it was an inevitability that their partnership would someday be secured as well by marriage. However, for half a century the various women of the families had never managed to produce children of opposing genders at appropriately spaced intervals to make matrimony a possibility. Although on several occasions an Estoril and a Brennan had been pregnant concurrently, each time the resulting births had produced identical results. When one had a boy or a girl, so did the other, until each family had begun to assume the gender of any imminent child based on that of the most recent addition to the other family.

When there *were* deviations from this pattern, something else always prevented any kind of romantic possibilities from flowering. For instance, when Reilly's great-grandmother early on produced a female child three months after the arrival of an Estoril boy, the baby girl's arrival seemed predestined. For years the two families spoke hopefully of yet another union between them, and young Armando Estoril enthusiastically did his part by falling in love with Mary Brennan when the two reached young adulthood.

Mary, however, was in love with someone else, and at the age of seventeen she revealed this relationship when she joined a community of Poor Clare nuns and slipped a thin gold band around her ring finger to signify that she was now a bride of Christ and thereby unavailable to young Armando. It was a crushing blow to both families, and some believed it planted the seed of a curse that plagued them for years despite continuous pleas to the Holy Mother, assorted saints, and any other heavenly figure who might be willing to listen. This was borne out by the string of identical births, until finally the subject of bringing the two families together with the bond of marriage became an unspoken one.

Then had come the fateful phone call on July 3 of Reilly's seventh year. With the arrival of Donna Estoril, the curse had been broken. The following day's display of fireworks had seemed as much to celebrate the country's independence as it was to celebrate the end of the long-endured disappointment. Yes, there was a difference of seven years between her and Reilly, but this was deemed negligible by all concerned. When they reached marriageable age, so it was said in the kitchens over morning coffee, it wouldn't matter at all. In fact, it would give Reilly time to grow up while he waited for Donna to mature. Men, after all, needed more time than women to adjust to the idea of until death do us part.

Both Donna and Reilly grew up knowing what was expected of them. Their families, burned so often in the past, were thankfully less inclined to speak openly about their hopes for the pair. Still, both knew that if they were to one day announce their mutual interest in each other it would be met with much rejoicing.

Interestingly, it was Reilly who seemed more welcoming of this fate than was Donna. Where he obliged by showing her attention, first by teasing her mercilessly when she was five and he twelve, and then later by shyly taking her to the movies when she was nineteen and he twenty-six, Donna had appeared indifferent to the matter. While Reilly seemed content to wait for her, she dated any number of boys, mostly to the horror of her parents, and seemed uninterested in settling down.

Then, when she reached the age of twenty-three and Reilly had celebrated his thirtieth birthday with no sign of a wedding in sight, things had changed. Occasional dates to the movies turned into weekly ones. Invitations offered by other men were refused. Their parents, not wanting to jinx anything, watched hopefully as the two seemed to grow closer. When, on Christmas Eve a year later, Donna and Reilly announced their engagement, a collective cry of delight and relief had risen from the guests assembled at the annual holiday dinner.

That had been five months before. A wedding date had been set for late August. The summer rush would be ending then, and there would be time for a proper wedding celebration. This was, after all, a marriage of no small importance, the culmination of the work of three generations. It was going to be done right.

For Reilly, the marriage meant much more than just the coming together of two families. It also meant an opportunity for him to heal another wound. While he'd been happy to fulfill his parents' dream of seeing him together with Donna, he'd been less inclined to follow his father into the family business. After years of spending his summers working at the market and learning the skills he'd need to one day inherit the operation, Reilly had come to the conclusion that the scent of fish, while most definitely in his clothes and on his skin, was not in his blood. He'd informed his father of this one evening when he was twenty-one.

The reaction, when it came, was less intense yet more painful than Reilly had anticipated. James Brennan admitted to sensing a less than enthusiastic attitude in his son toward the business of measuring out haddock and clams into plastic bags for sunburned tourists and longstanding customers alike. He accepted Reilly's announcement with a minimum of irritation, and refrained from attempting to convince him that he was making a mistake. Yet his silence indicated a sadness and disappointment of enormous depth, like the calm face of the sea could belie the swirling currents beneath. Every time Reilly looked at his father he felt the weight of responsibility for breaking the chain, for being the one to walk away from what his great-grandfather had started.

In the eleven years since Reilly had announced his intentions not to devote his life to fish, his relationship with his father had remained slightly awkward. After working his last shift in one of his family's stores, he had apprenticed himself to a local carpenter. In building he had discovered a passion and a contentment that had grown with each passing week and each new skill learned. The feel of wood under his fingers gave him a thrill that the slipperiness of fish had never imparted. But even as his skills, and eventually his business, grew, he felt he couldn't express his enthusiasm to his father, as it would only make the disappointment he felt in his son more bitter.

As a result, they had spoken less and less. Their conversations gradually became limited to discussions about the weather and about the health of the family's aging dog, Cruller, a happy but arthritic yellow Lab with a fondness for doughnuts. When Cruller had gone to sleep in a patch of sun one summer morning and had not woken up for his afternoon walk, Reilly had mourned both the loss of the dog and one of the only common interests he shared with his father.

The engagement had brought a renewed hope to their relationship, however. It had yet to be decided what would become of the stores once James Brennan decided it was time to retire. He was, after all, only in his fifties. He had no plans on stopping any time soon. Still, the question was there, waiting to be answered, and Reilly knew that his father and Donna's had had numerous discussions about the future of their partnership.

He knew, too, that in the marriage both fathers saw the possibility of Reilly deciding to take the helm of the Brennan half of the operation after all. Perhaps they hoped that Donna would be able to talk some sense into him. Even though she herself had opted to open a salon rather than work in the family office, she remained dedicated to the business. Also, her four brothers remained firmly entrenched in the fishing industry, with none of them showing the slightest interest in leaving either the business or Provincetown. Reilly alone of all the children had turned his back on tradition, and without the benefit of siblings to take some of the pressure off of him, he'd had to bear the resulting accumulation of disappointment on his own shoulders.

His marriage was, in some ways, a way of apologizing to his father. Although that was not why he'd asked Donna to marry him, he was very much aware that it was one of the advantages. He still had no plans to leave carpentry for fish, but if the marriage made his father think that it was a possibility, so much the better. There would, of course, come a time when the issue would be brought into the open again, and Reilly supposed his repeated refusal to take over the business would be met with much more unhappiness than it had been the first time. Until then, though, he was going to enjoy the renewed sense of familial congeniality that the engagement had made possible.

"Are you ready to go?"

Donna's question stirred Reilly from his thoughts. He looked up. Donna was standing in front of the chair, smiling at him. Looking at her, Reilly was reminded of how beautiful she was. Her long dark hair was naturally curly, framing a heart-shaped face. Her brown eyes reflected the afternoon light with glints of gold.

"What's the matter?" she asked, noting his dreamlike expression.

Reilly shook his head. "Not a thing," he said. "But where are we going?"

Donna shook her head. "Don't you remember anything?" she asked. "We have to go meet the caterer to talk about appetizers."

"I thought we already did that," Reilly said.

"That was salads," Donna informed him. "This is different."

Reilly sighed. "Can't we just leave it to her?" he asked.

"Not unless you want spray cheese on Ritz crackers," answered Donna.

"I happen to like spray cheese," replied Reilly, reluctantly getting out of his seat.

Donna kissed him. "That's what I love about you," she said. "You're full of class."

They left the store, Donna locking the door behind them. Reilly started to get into his truck, which was parked on the street outside the salon, but Donna shook her head.

"No way am I getting in there," she said. "We'll take my car."

Reilly shrugged and followed Donna to her car, getting into the passenger side while Donna took the driver's seat. Reilly didn't mind being relegated to passenger status, however, just as he didn't mind participating in all of the preparations for the wedding. He was looking forward to being married to Donna. It was something he'd wanted for a long time. He'd never felt as in love with someone as he did with her. *Not since . . .* he thought suddenly, but he stopped himself before the thought could be completed. He'd promised himself he would never think about that again. Not ever.

"All set?" Donna asked.

Reilly looked at her and smiled. "Let's roll," he said, willing himself to forget.

CHAPTER 8

Josh listened to the message again.

"Hey, it's me. I guess that didn't go so well, huh? Okay, so I guess I'll just wait to hear from you. Maybe this is good, having a little time apart. It will give you time to think about things. If you want to call, you know the number. If I'm not here, just leave a message."

That was it. No "I'm sorry." No "Let's talk things over." No "Come home. I miss you." And what was that "if I'm not here" shit? Where else would he be? Off screwing his trick from the gym? Hanging out in some bar looking for a new one?

Josh had listened to the message at least two dozen times during the past thirty-six hours, analyzing every word, every inflection of Doug's voice, looking for clues. But he didn't need any clues to know what was going on. Doug didn't care if he came home or not, probably didn't even *want* him to come home. What had he said? "It will give you time to think about things." What the fuck was that supposed to mean? It made it sound as if Josh were the one with a problem, the one who had done something to be sorry for and needed time to think about his behavior before things could return to normal.

"Fuck you," Josh said to the phone as he deleted the message. He wanted it gone, both because it irritated him and also because he didn't want the temptation to keep replaying it. As soon as it was gone, though, he wished he could have it back. At least it would give him something to focus his anger on.

What annoyed Josh the most was that Doug had left the message at eleven-thirty on Friday evening. It was almost as if he had been confirming that Josh would be away for the night before he himself went out, or before he had someone come over. There wasn't the slightest hint of remorse in the message.

Josh had spent most of Saturday replaying the message over and over. He'd attempted to distract himself by exploring Provincetown, but ultimately he'd just ended up sitting on the beach, hitting the replay button again and again until finally the battery on his cell phone had worn out and Doug's message had ended with a shrill squeal as the phone discharged. Josh had spent the two hours it took the phone to recharge drinking an entire bottle of wine he picked up on the way home; then he'd started the whole process over again.

He'd woken up on Sunday morning with the phone pressed to his head and the empty wine bottle on the bed beside him, the remnants of the cabernet dripping onto the sheets. He'd been disgusted by both things, and had quickly turned the phone off and tossed the bottle into the trash. After a shower, he'd stripped the dirty sheets from the bed and hurried to the Laundromat to see if there was any chance of saving them. He didn't want Ben and Ted to think he was some kind of lousy drunk, even if the pounding headache he had suggested otherwise.

After two passes through the wash cycle, three aspirins, and four cups of coffee, he'd felt marginally better. Breakfast had helped as well, and Josh had managed to spend a fairly pleasant day wandering around town. Now it was early afternoon, and he had some decisions to make. Or at least one big decision.

He had planned on staying in P-Town only for the weekend. Now, with Monday looming and the words of Doug's message ringing in his head, he didn't think he wanted to go back to Boston quite yet. Although he'd spent a lot of time obsessing over what Doug had said, and particularly what he'd done, he'd devoted surprisingly little time to considering what it all might ultimately mean. He'd been so consumed by the initial anger and hurt that the long-term effects of the situation had been pushed out of the way. Now, though, they were staring him in the face.

He pulled the car into the driveway of the guest house. Ben, who was on his knees busily pulling weeds from one of the flower beds, looked up. He was wearing a big straw hat and oversize sunglasses, looking for all the world like a demented Jackie O, and when he waved enthusiastically, Josh couldn't help but want to call out, "And apart from that, how did you enjoy your visit to Dallas, Mrs. Kennedy?"

He parked the car and got out, trying to hide the washed and folded sheets beneath the copy of the Sunday *Boston Globe* he'd bought, so that Ben wouldn't see them and wonder why his guest had felt the need to do his own laundry. *He'd probably assume there was a bedwetting incident,* Josh thought as he tucked the sheets between the sports section and the comics. *Or that I'd had an overnight guest and was trying to hide the evidence.* He wasn't sure which would be worse.

"There you are," Ben said chirpily, as if he'd been looking all over for Josh. "How was your day?"

"Okay," Josh said, trying to feign cheerfulness. "It's really beautiful here."

"Mmm," Ben said vaguely, looking closely at Josh's face. "Is that why you've been crying, because you just can't take the breathtaking gorgeousness of it all?"

Josh felt himself turning red. He *had* been crying, although only a little bit, and not for a couple of hours. Now he touched his eyes, wondering if they had betrayed him.

"Is it that obvious?"

Ben shook his head. "Ted probably wouldn't notice," he said. "But you're talking to a queen who spends half his life moisturizing and applying cucumber slices to get rid of puffiness. I can tell tearstained skin when I see it."

Josh laughed despite himself.

"Not that it's any of my business—and not that that would stop me from asking anyway—but I take it things haven't resolved themselves with the Total Shit."

"Did I call him that?" Josh asked, surprised. Maybe it was better that he didn't remember much about their dinner on Friday night.

Ben nodded. "Among other things," he said.

"Well, no, things have not resolved themselves," Josh admitted.

"Want to talk?" inquired Ben gently.

"No," Josh said. "But I will anyway."

The two of them went inside, where Ben produced first a pitcher of lemonade and, an hour later, a pitcher of margaritas. When Ted came walking in shortly after, his arms loaded up with grocery bags, he found his lover and Josh laughing hysterically.

"Margaritas," he said, eyeing the half-empty pitcher. "Looks serious."

Josh and Ben both erupted in semidrunken giggles. The truth was, they had been discussing their worst sex experiences. It was a game Ben had suggested to get Josh's mind off of Doug, and it had worked wonderfully.

"Oh, it *is* serious," Ben said, composing himself as much as someone who had downed three margaritas could. "If you consider having a guy ask you to talk like Bette Davis while he bangs your ass serious."

Ted groaned. "Not that story again," he said as he took some tomatoes out of a bag and set them on the counter.

"Josh has never heard it before," Ben protested. He turned back to Josh. "Let me tell you, nothing's more difficult than keeping your hard-on while saying, 'Fasten your seat belts. It's going to be a bumpy night.' I should have won an Oscar."

"The really sad part is that you did it," Ted told him, adding some steaks to the growing pile of food on the counter.

Ben waved a hand at his lover. "I was young," he said. "We'll do anything for a man when we're young."

"I don't think I can beat that story," Josh told him, draining his margarita. "I've never had anything particularly awful happen to me during sex."

"Please," Ben said. "Everyone has had *something* happen."

Josh thought for a minute. "Well, one time Doug was giving me head while we were driving on the interstate," he said. "We passed this bus of high school girls going to a cheerleading tournament. A couple of them happened to look out and see us. The next thing I knew there were pom-poms waving and lots of sixteen-year-old girls cheering us on."

Ted and Ben looked at him, mouths open.

"You're kidding," said Ted.

Josh shook his head. "No. Ever since then every time one of us goes down on the other, the other one says, 'Give me a B! Give me a J!' "

Ben and Ted howled. When they calmed down enough to talk, Ben patted Josh's arm. "Now tell us a story that isn't about *him*," he said.

Josh sighed. "There really aren't that many that aren't about him," he said.

"Surely you weren't a virgin on your wedding night," Ben said.

Josh laughed. "No," he answered. "But in gay terms I was pretty close. There had only been five or six guys before Doug."

"Christ," exclaimed Ben. "You were practically a nun."

"I was just never into sleeping around," Josh told him, the tone suddenly becoming more serious. "I had a couple of one-night stands when I first came out, but other than that I only slept with guys I thought might be long-term possibilities."

"You sound like Ted," Ben said. "I was only the third guy he went to bed with." He looked at his lover, who was tucking things into the refrigerator. "And as far as I *know*, I'm still only the third guy he's ever slept with."

Ted pulled his head out of the fridge and gave Ben an irritated look. "How many times do I have to tell you?" he said. "If I don't know their last names, it doesn't count."

Ben looked at Josh. "It's true, you know," he said. "Neither one of us has been with anyone else since we got together. I expected that from him, but to be honest I wasn't sure I'd be able to do it."

Ted came over and put his arms around Ben's neck, kissing him on the top of the head. "I reformed him," he said. "Besides, once he got a taste of me, no other man could satisfy him."

Ben snorted. "Don't be so sure of that," he said. "I haven't given Ed Harris a try yet."

Josh looked at the two of them, Ben with his head resting casually against Ted's chest as they embraced. That's what Josh wanted, someone he knew would be with him forever, someone he didn't have to share. He knew monogamy was something a lot of gay men viewed as unrealistic, even laughable. His friends, particularly ones in what they thought of as long-term relationships, had often teased him about his ideas on fidelity. "Wait until you've been together a few years" was something he'd heard too many times to count. "You can't expect the sexual chemistry to last forever."

But it *had* lasted for him. No, it wasn't always the way it had been at the start of his relationship with Doug. Familiarity had bred a level of predictability, and there were times when the routine of their lovemaking seemed about as exciting as going to the gym. But that made it even better, as far as he was concerned. Connecting with someone he didn't know, just because he had a great chest, a handsome face, or a big dick, wouldn't be the same. He would be touching a mystery, kissing an illusion. For him it would be like making love to a ghost, trying to give life to an empty shell that would fade away as quickly as the resulting orgasm ebbed. But with Doug, he felt as if he were holding a lifetime in his hands whenever they touched.

For Doug, though, that apparently wasn't enough. To Josh's surprise, his lover had become one of those gay men for whom sex was "just sex," an act separate from love and therefore, presumably, no threat to a relationship. Josh had seen numerous friends come to the same conclusion. "It has nothing to do with how much we love each other." How many times had he heard that? And how many times had he refrained from saying, "Then maybe you don't love each other enough"?

"So, darling, you have some choices to make," Ben said, bringing Josh back to the moment.

He nodded. "I know," he said. "I just wish I didn't have to go back so soon. It's going to be tough being in the same apartment and having to talk about this stuff."

"So don't go," Ted said. "Stay here."

"I can't," said Josh.

"Why not?" Ben asked him. "It's okay with us. We weren't planning on using the back cottage any time soon anyway. Reilly isn't done with the repair work, and we're going to have our hands full with the guests in the main house."

"You're welcome to hang out as long as you need to," Ted said. "No charge. I think we would both like the company."

"I don't know," Josh said doubtfully. "I sort of feel like I need to deal with this. Staying here would feel like hiding."

"Well, think about it overnight," Ted said. "You don't have to rush back tonight, right?"

Josh shook his head. "No. I could leave in the morning."

"Good," Ted replied. "Then let's have dinner and a good night's sleep."

Josh smiled. "You guys have been great," he said. "I really appreciate it."

"Every gay man needs a couple of old aunties to look out for him," Ben told him.

"I'd prefer to be an uncle, thank you very much," Ted said sternly.

Ben rolled his eyes. "He's so butch," he whispered to Josh. "Isn't it exciting?"

Josh grinned. "I'm going to go change," he said.

"Just be back in twenty," Ted told him. "I'm sure this one will have another pitcher of margaritas waiting."

Josh left the kitchen through the back door and returned to the cottage. As he removed his shirt and looked for a clean one, he thought about the offer that Ted and Ben had made him. Could he stay there for a while? He had some freelance work lined up, but there was no reason he couldn't do it from Provincetown. Apart from that, his only real tie to Boston was Doug. But that was a big tie. He felt as if he owed it to Doug—to their relationship—to go back and talk things out.

What if he doesn't want to talk? The thought ran through Josh's mind. *After all, he didn't seem to anxious to hear from me.* That was true. Or maybe he'd just been imagining it, reading something into Doug's message that wasn't there. Maybe playing it cool was Doug's way of hiding how scared he was. He'd never been particularly good at discussing his feelings, Josh reminded himself. Perhaps not asking him to come home was Doug's way of saying he was sorry.

He picked up the phone and dialed their home number. On the second ring Doug picked up.

"Hello?"

"Hi," said Josh, suddenly nervous. The idea of talking to Doug in the abstract had been okay; actually hearing his voice on the other end of the line was oddly disconcerting.

"Oh, hey," said Doug. "What's up?"

What's up? Josh thought, annoyed by the casualness of his lover's response. He started to say something in response, but stopped himself. *Be nice,* he told himself.

"I'm with some friends," he told Doug. "I spent the weekend with them."

"Okay," Doug said vaguely.

Don't you want to know who they are? Josh asked silently.

Apparently, Doug didn't, because he didn't ask. Instead he said, "Can you hang on? I have another call coming through."

He didn't wait for Josh to respond, putting him on hold. Josh was tempted to just hang up, but before he could Doug came back on the line. "Sorry about that," he said. "So, are you okay?"

Who did you just put me on hold for? Josh wanted to say. *Was it your fuck buddy?* He couldn't believe that now that he'd finally called, Doug was treating him as casually as he would a telemarketer calling to ask for donations.

"I'm fine," he said coldly. "I think I'm going to stay here for a while, though."

"Oh," Doug said. "How long do you think you'll be there?"

Once again, his lover had said exactly the wrong thing. *This is where you're supposed to beg for forgiveness,* Josh thought. *This is where you tell me to get my ass in the car and drive home so we can talk.* But no, Doug had said none of those things. All he'd said was, "Oh."

"I'm not sure," Josh said finally, keeping his voice even. "Awhile."

"Okay," said Doug. "I guess that's okay."

Thanks for your permission, thought Josh irritably. "I'll call you in a few days," he told Doug. "Bye."

He hung up, not waiting for Doug to respond. He'd already gotten a response from him, and it wasn't one he'd wanted to hear. But at least it made his decision easy.

He left the cottage and returned to the main house. In the kitchen, Ben was slicing up tomatoes while Ted tended the steaks on the stove's built-in grill.

"I'm staying," Josh said simply.

Ben nodded and handed him a tomato and a knife. "Well, if you're going to be part of the family, you can help get dinner on the table," he said.

"Okay, Mom," Josh told him, and went to work.

CHAPTER 9

Violet came through, Reid thought as he watched the driver carry his luggage into the house.

"Put those in the bedroom at the end of the upstairs hall," he told the man, who nodded and hurried off.

Reid looked around. Yes, Violet had done well. Of course, for what he'd paid the owner for the place, it *should* have been great. She'd already rented it to a group of queens from New York for the summer, and in the end Reid had offered her three times what they were paying to get her to give them some story about burst pipes or the installation of a new septic tank so that he could have it.

Now it was his from Memorial Day through Labor Day. Three glorious months away from Los Angeles. Three months he and Ty could spend together. Well, more or less together. They still didn't travel openly together, and there was no chance of them appearing in public as a couple. But within the walls of the house, they could act like any other lovers.

"The bags are all upstairs, Mr. Truman." The driver had returned.

"Thanks, Evan," Reid said. He stuck his hand into his pocket and pulled out some bills, which he handed to the waiting man.

Evan nodded. "Give us a call if you need anything while you're here," he said as he left.

When Evan was gone and the door was shut, Reid finally relaxed. He was alone. Apart from Violet and Ty, no one else knew where he was. Violet had been instructed to tell anyone who called that he was in Europe at a spa. He knew people would assume that meant rehab, but since everyone in Hollywood was in and out of clinics on a regular basis, he didn't really care. Violet would pass along any truly important messages, and he would have her relay his replies. Since no directors, agents, actors, or producers in town knew how to write their own e-mail or make their own calls, he knew he would be protected by the natural firewall provided by the network of assistants who really kept everything running smoothly. He didn't even know a gaffer who didn't use a publicist these days.

With nothing else to do, he gave himself a tour of the house. He'd seen pictures, but they hadn't done the place justice. Not that the place was anything grand by Tinseltown standards. There were only three bedrooms and two bathrooms. But the living room was big and airy, the kitchen filled with every possible convenience, and there was a small office upstairs where he could set up his computer if he felt the inclination to do any work.

Best of all, the house looked out on the ocean. He could walk out his back door and right down to the beach. The windows of the big bedroom upstairs also looked out on the water, and the smell of the sea filled the rooms. Reid closed his eyes and breathed it in. He was so used to the stink of Los Angeles, with its herds of cars clogging the streets like drunken cattle and its blanket of smog wrapping everything in dirty gauze, that he'd forgotten what the real world smelled like. Now it came back to him in cool, salty drafts that tickled his skin and made him shiver.

He couldn't wait to show the place to Ty. He looked at his watch. Two hours until Ty would arrive from New York. He was in rehearsals for his new film, but the entire cast and crew had been given the long Memorial Day weekend off. Reid and Ty would have four whole days together before Ty returned to the city and the cameras.

Reid's cell phone rang. Hoping it was Ty, he fished it from the pocket of his coat. But it was Violet. Reid hit the answer button.

"Hey," he said.

"Good. You made it." Even Violet's voice radiated efficiency and a love of order. Reid smiled.

"Yeah, I'm all in," he told his assistant. "The house is fantastic."

"There should be enough food for a couple of weeks," Violet informed him. "I sent a list of your favorites to the people who will be doing the housecleaning for you. When you run low, just tell them what you want and they'll get it."

"Thanks," said Reid. It had been so long since he'd prepared food for himself that he hadn't even thought about how that would be handled. It was the one aspect of his vacation he was perfectly happy to have someone else take care of.

"If you want someone to do the cooking, I can arrange that as well," Violet continued.

"No," Reid said, suddenly feeling a rush of independence. "I think I can manage that."

"Are you sure?" Violet's confident tone slipped into surprised uncertainty.

"No," Reid said. "I'm not at all sure. But I'm going to give it a try." He was looking at his summer as a break from his old life, and that meant doing as much on his own as possible. "But I'll take the cleaners. Vacuuming was never my strong suit."

Violet rewarded him with a rare laugh, a sparkle of vulnerability that Reid found wonderfully refreshing. He'd always thought she was much too serious for someone not yet thirty.

"One more thing," she said, the serious demeanor returning.

Reid groaned. "Is it work-related?"

"Could be," replied Violet. "C.J. Raymacher called today."

"Who?" asked Reid, not recognizing the name.

"That shows how often *you* stand in line at the grocery store," Violet said. "C.J. Raymacher. Columnist, if you can call him that, for the *Weekly Insider*. Formerly of *Buzz* and *Vanity Fair*, until he was caught making up sources and snorting a significant percentage of his expense account up his nose."

"You mean that kid who used to hang around with Drew Barrymore and River Phoenix?" Reid said.

"That would be the one," Violet confirmed. "He used to be in all the gossip columns. Now he just writes one."

"What does he want with me?" Reid asked her. "I'm about as gossipworthy as Katie Couric."

"It's not you he's interested in," explained Violet. "Not exactly. It's Ty Rusk."

Reid felt his stomach knot instinctively. Hollywood gossip columnists had never been his favorite species, but he'd always managed to live his life below their radar. Now, it seemed, one of them had set his sights in Reid's direction.

"Ty?" he repeated, trying to sound confused. "What about Ty?"

"He didn't say," Violet answered. "He just said he'd heard some information about Ty that he thought you might be able to confirm."

"But he didn't say what it was?" Reid asked hopefully.

"No," said Violet. "I told him you were out of the country and would get back to him."

"Good," Reid told her. "Don't call him back. Whatever it is, he'll probably forget all about it as soon as Pamela Anderson has her implants enlarged again or Eminem pisses on someone's mother."

"I thought it was a little strange," Violet continued. "I mean they usually just run things whether they're true or not."

"Who knows what the guy is after?" Reid said. "He probably just wants to know who Ty is banging these days."

After a few more minutes of talking, Violet hung up and Reid sank onto the couch to think. Yes, C.J. Raymacher probably *did* want to know whom Ty was banging. Only he probably had some hunch that it wasn't an actress, or any other woman. If he thought Ty was involved with some starlet, he would have called Ty's agent, not the producer of his last movie. The only reason he might have to call Reid was if he somehow thought there was something going on between them.

This was what Reid had feared for most of his life. He'd never had a problem with being gay, at least no more than anyone else who had to go through the coming-out process and live in a straight world. He was even a supporter of numerous gay causes, donating money to the Los Angeles Gay and Lesbian Community Center and several AIDS organizations. But he'd never before had to consider a partner's visibility. Now things had changed. Not even Violet knew that Ty and Reid were an item.

No, he told himself. It wasn't possible that this gossip columnist knew anything. He hadn't told anyone, not even his closest friends. And Ty had certainly kept his mouth shut. They didn't even have dinner together in restaurants unless they were in a group and could pass the evening off as work-related. While Ty was no stranger to persistent paparazzi, regularly finding himself surprised outside of restaurants and events, no one ever saw him arrive at or leave Reid's house.

At least no one they knew about. Reid was almost certain that he and Ty had managed to keep their affair hidden from the world. But what if they hadn't? What if someone *had* seen Ty coming or going? What if that someone had told C.J. Raymacher?

A story like that, even if it wasn't true, could do a lot of damage to Ty's image. Reid had seen it happen to other stars. Once a story was in print, it never died. Even a totally concocted story would eventually become gospel truth when it was told enough times. People would forget that it had originated in a trashy grocery store throwaway. Soon it would become "My friend knows someone who slept with him" and "I hear he hires hustlers to come to his house so no one will know." *Just ask Tom Cruise,* he thought. *Or Ben Affleck, or Richard Gere, or Brad Pitt.* Hell, even Paul Newman was believed by many people to have gone to bed with more than the occasional man. Rumors had surrounded these actors, and many more like them, for so long that even Reid wasn't entirely sure anymore if any of them were on his team.

Although it was true that the gay rumors had done little to affect the marketability of stars like Cruise or Pitt, Reid knew that there were many more actors for whom suspicions of queerness had derailed their careers. He thought immediately of Carter Morris. Two years earlier, Morris had been the actor of the moment, a hunky man's man who earned overnight success starring in a drama for NBC about a rookie baseball pitcher in his first season on a team with World Series chances. Carter's face had appeared on every magazine cover imaginable, and his star quotient went through the roof when he won an Emmy for Outstanding Lead Actor in a drama. Movie offers came pouring in, and it seemed as if Morris would have his pick of roles.

Then he'd been photographed kissing another man while on vacation in Greece. The picture had been on the front page of every entertainment rag in the United States within forty-eight hours, along with statements made by one of Morris's exes, a bitter college boyfriend with an ax to grind and photos of him and Carter together to back up his claims. Although NBC continued to support the show, many viewers didn't, and after its first season finale it was unceremoniously dropped from the fall schedule.

Morris himself had refused to talk about the incident, hoping it would fade from memory. Sadly, it was he who faded from memory. While Reid had tried to help him out by getting him bit parts in some of the movies he produced, other producers and directors were not as kind. To them, Carter's image and reputation as a leading man were tarnished by the fact that he slept with other men, and they chose to go with stars who could more easily provide female viewers with fantasy material and male viewers with someone they could idolize. Eventually Morris had left Hollywood, defeated and broke. The last Reid had heard of him, he was working as a bartender in some state he couldn't imagine people actually lived in—Wyoming, or perhaps one of the Dakotas.

He didn't want that to happen to Ty. His career was at a delicate stage, one where fans would forgive him for certain indiscretions, like a DUI incident or perhaps a violent altercation with a nosy journalist. In a strange way, that would even make him more popular. Like Russell Crowe or Robert Downey Jr., it would lend to him a certain helplessness that would make women want to take care of him and allow men to feel more like him. But it would be difficult for him to overcome something like the revelation of his sexuality, at least for the moment.

The question was how to handle things. Based on what he knew, Reid wasn't convinced that Raymacher was even on the right track. But supposing he was, how much did he know? Reid didn't think it was too much. If he had real proof that Ty was a fag, he wouldn't have bothered to call. He would have just printed what he had and let the shit fly. By calling Reid, he was trying to get something more to go on. But what? It was almost impossible that he would know that Ty and Reid were involved. Was he hoping that, faced with questions about his leading man's bedroom behavior, Reid would somehow accidentally blurt out the truth? It had happened before, he knew, but it was a long shot. Still, Raymacher was a gossip columnist, and there was nothing beneath such a person.

After much thought, Reid still hadn't decided what, if anything, to tell Ty. He could just ignore Raymacher. If the guy actually had any real dirt, he would resurface and they could deal with it then. If not, he would simply fade away. Either way, it wasn't an immediate problem. More pressing was what Reid was going to make for dinner.

He got up and went into the kitchen. As promised, the pantry was well stocked, as were the refrigerator and freezer. *I'll have to remember to give Violet a raise,* he thought as he rummaged around, trying to decide what to make for his and Ty's first night in the house. His assistant had indeed remembered all of his favorites. Now it was just a matter of finding something he could actually cook.

He settled on pasta. As his mother had always told him, anyone could boil water. He proved her right, and before long he had a pot of penne bubbling on the stove. Another pan held sauce from one of the many jars that lined the shelves. And Reid was just making a salad when the door opened and Ty appeared.

"Honey, I'm home," he called out.

Reid wiped his hands on a towel and went to greet his boyfriend. "You look great," he said as he gave Ty a hug and a long kiss.

"That's because I came straight from the set," Ty told him. "Once I shower and wash this makeup off I'll look like my ugly old self."

"Maybe I should shower with you then," Reid suggested, beginning to unbutton Ty's shirt. "That way I can have you before the glamor wears off."

"Can dinner wait?" Ty asked, nodding toward the kitchen, where the pasta sauce was filling the air with its fragrance.

"Yes," Reid replied, sliding a hand inside Ty's pants. "But I can't. Now get upstairs while I turn the stove off."

Ty headed for the stairs, whistling happily, while Reid returned to the kitchen. As Reid watched his lover bound up the steps, he made up his mind. He wouldn't say anything about the phone call from Raymacher.

Why ruin the summer? he thought as he put a lid on the pasta and headed after Ty.

CHAPTER 10

After two full days on a bus, Toby Evans was more than ready to have his feet on the ground again. He'd boarded the Greyhound in Hannibal, Missouri, at eleven twenty-five on Wednesday morning and had left his seat only for a couple of bathroom and food breaks. Now, forty-eight hours and six states later, he'd had enough of the ceaseless hum of the engine and rhythmic thumping of the tires, and he couldn't wait to arrive in Boston. Although the seat was comfortable enough for his six-foot, two-inch frame, he was tired of trying to find ways to amuse himself. He'd exhausted the contents of his CD case before reaching Terre Haute, and was tired of looking at the issues of *Entertainment Weekly, People,* and *Maxim* he'd bought at the magazine stand in Columbus.

A copy of another magazine, *Instinct,* sat unread in the bag tucked in the overhead compartment. Although he badly wanted to read it, he was afraid of his seatmate's reaction if he brought it out. An elderly woman, she'd been with him since Dayton, when he'd awakened from a fitful sleep to find her beside him, knitting a sweater and smiling sweetly. Her name was Genevieve Abernathy, and she was, she'd explained at great length, going east to see her new granddaughter, who was called Patience. "A good old-fashioned name," she'd said happily, adding, "We're a very old-fashioned family."

Genevieve Abernathy, he quickly learned, was very fond of talking about her family, which included seven children (three boys and four girls) and nine great-grandchildren (seven boys and three girls). "Ten now that Patience has arrived," she'd amended. She was also fond of hard candies, a bag of which she carried in her purse. Every fifteen minutes or so she would take one out, remove its cellophane skin, and pop it into her mouth. Her wrinkled little lips would purse ever so gently as she sucked, and Toby was amazed at how long she could make each piece last. She'd eaten nothing but the candies since boarding, telling Toby that she couldn't bring herself to pay the outrageous prices demanded for bus station food. "It's a crime," she'd said more than once, "to ask that kind of money for a ham sandwich."

Toby, moved to guilt by Genevieve's age and vague resemblance to his own grandmother, had offered her half of his own sandwich, which she'd gladly accepted. The half of an hour it had taken her to consume the food was the only time during the trip when she'd been without a candy in her mouth. As soon as she was finished, she'd gone back to her sucking. She had not once offered Toby a piece.

She had, however, offered him something else. In addition to her fondness for family and sweets, Genevieve's other great passion was Jesus. This she did share freely with Toby, dropping numerous references to how "the Lord had blessed her" and to the congregation of her church, all of whom "shined with the spirit of Christ." Toby heard story after story of how Genevieve's life had been transformed by accepting Jesus as her savior, and it was strongly suggested that, should he be interested, Genevieve would be more than happy to make introductions for him with God.

He would have preferred a candy. If there was one thing Toby Evans did not need any more of in his life, it was Jesus. It was Jesus who had caused him to board the bus in Hannibal in the first place. Well, really, it had been his parents, but he blamed Jesus for their behavior, so ultimately it amounted to the same thing. If Jesus hadn't been in the picture, none of what had happened would have happened.

"Oh, we're here, dear," Genevieve said, nudging Toby with her elbow.

He opened his eyes. He'd been feigning sleep, as it was the only thing that kept Genevieve from talking to him. Now, as the bus pulled into South Station, she was too occupied with getting the sweater she'd almost completed into her bag. Toby yawned, stretched, and began to gather up the few items he had brought with him. There wasn't much, and it all fit into a backpack. The small duffel bag overhead was his only other luggage. Everything else he'd left behind, as he'd left behind so many other things.

When the bus came to a stop, Toby helped Genevieve retrieve her suitcase and carry it off the bus. Almost immediately upon setting foot on the asphalt she was greeted by a chorus of squeals as several children rushed toward her. After hugging each of them Genevieve turned to Toby.

"Thank you for a lovely trip," she said. "I hope you have a wonderful time at that college. And remember, God helps those who help themselves."

"Thanks," Toby replied as he picked up his bag and walked away, leaving Genevieve with her family.

He felt a little bad about lying to her. He'd told her that he was going to Boston to take part in a summer program at Boston College before starting school there in the fall. She'd had no reason to disbelieve him, and had therefore not asked too many potentially awkward questions. Toby was sure it was one more thing Jesus would have to hold against him, but at this point he figured he was so far in the hole it didn't much matter.

He looked for the sign for the Plymouth & Brockton bus line. He had one more transfer to make before reaching his destination. He found the bus he needed and boarded, wearily dropping into the first available seat he came to. The bus was crowded, even more than the one from Hannibal had been. But there was something different about the passengers on this bus. Where the Greyhound had been filled with families, the elderly, and the assorted drifter, the bus he sat on now was peopled with a different type of rider.

Toby looked around. Toward the center of the bus a group of women sat, talking excitedly. In front of them was an equally vocal group of men. He looked at them more closely and saw that several of the men wore T-shirts that read BOSTON GAY MEN'S CHORUS. He quickly looked away before anyone could catch him staring.

As more passengers got on, Toby snuck surreptitious glances at them. While most looked like any other people he might see walking around, some earned more than just a casual appraisal: a woman with a rainbow flag pin tacked to her carry-on, two men dressed in almost identical shorts and tank tops who took seats near him and sat with hands clasped, a guy not much older than himself who saw him looking and smiled before passing on, leaving Toby red-cheeked.

This is why you came here, he told himself as he tried to calm his nerves. *This is what you wanted to find.*

"Is this seat taken?"

Toby looked up. A man was standing in the aisle beside him, a bag held in his hand.

"No," Toby said.

"Great," the man replied, putting his bag into the storage compartment and dropping into the empty seat. "I was afraid the bus would be full. Memorial Day weekend can be a zoo. You know, the start of the season and all."

Toby nodded, not sure what to say. Suddenly he was very nervous in a way he hadn't been when it had been Genevieve seated beside him.

"I'm Aaron," the man said, holding out his hand.

"Toby." Aaron's grip was firm, his skin warm as he shook Toby's extended hand. Toby couldn't help but notice that Aaron's muscular forearms were covered in soft brown hair.

"I assume you're going to P-Town," said Aaron.

"Yeah," Toby replied.

"First time?"

Toby nodded.

"You're going to love it," Aaron told him. He crossed one leg over the other, and Toby found himself looking at the man's bare calves. Like his arms, Aaron's legs were hairy. He moved his gaze up and saw more hair poking out above the neckline of Aaron's blue T-shirt. Toby forced himself to look away.

"Do you live in Boston?" asked Aaron.

"Um, no," answered Toby. "I'm from the Midwest."

Aaron nodded. "I thought you had the blond blue-eyed farm boy look," he said, flashing a smile at Toby. "Not to mention the accent."

Toby felt himself blushing. "Is it that bad?" he asked.

Aaron laughed. "Not at all," he said. "In fact, it's almost irresistible."

Toby smiled back nervously. Aaron was looking right at him, and it made him both excited and terrified at the same time. No man had ever looked at him that way except in his fantasies. Now that he was experiencing it in real life, it was almost overwhelming.

"Thanks," he said weakly.

Having no idea what to do next, he opened the copy of *Instinct* he'd been waiting to look at and started perusing it. Aaron took out a book of his own and began reading as well. The two sat in silence as the doors shut and the bus pulled out of the station.

An excruciating couple of hours passed. Although he turned the pages of the magazine at regular intervals, Toby wasn't really reading. He couldn't concentrate on the words, and after attempting to read the same story three times without success he gave up and just looked at the pictures. Even these he had a hard time focusing on.

The cause of his distraction was Aaron's leg, which was pressing against his own. Toby was also wearing shorts, which made the connection more intense, as he could feel the warmth and sense every time a muscle in Aaron's thigh moved. To make everything even worse, Toby had quickly developed a hard-on, which he was now trying desperately to hide with his magazine.

Aaron himself seemed oblivious of what was going on. He continued to turn the pages of his book slowly, never looking at Toby and never moving his leg from its position. His arm rested casually on the armrest between them, and he seemed perfectly at ease.

Toby, however, was in agony. His dick was pressing against his shorts uncomfortably, but no matter how much he willed it to go down it refused. He tried distracting himself by thinking about unpleasant things—gutting fish, cleaning out the garage, his mother naked—but nothing worked. The feel of another man's bare skin so close to his own overwhelmed everything else. Soon he was thinking about what Aaron would look like naked, and then his mind was off and running.

Just move your leg away from his, he told himself. Maybe, if he broke contact, he'd be able to control himself. But he couldn't bring himself to do it. He liked the way Aaron's leg felt against his. He liked looking down and seeing the dark hair of Aaron's thigh mingling with his own, lighter hair. And inconvenient as it was, he even liked the erection that filled his pants. To him it was proof that the feelings he'd had for so long were true ones, that what he needed was to feel the touch of another man.

How far was it to Provincetown? He looked at the schedule tucked into the seat pocket in front of him. A little less than four hours. They had just over an hour to go. How was he going to stand it? He couldn't stay the way he was. For one thing, he was starting to get a cramp in his calf. He needed to move his leg, to stretch the muscle. But he left it where it was, fearful that once he moved away he would never be able to go back.

He felt a touch on his skin and jumped, startled by the unexpected shock of it. When he looked down he saw that the fingers of Aaron's left hand were brushing his leg, resting gently on his skin. He looked over. Aaron was still reading. Was he touching him on purpose, Toby wondered, or did he not notice what he was doing?

He got his answer a moment later when Aaron's hand slipped beneath his arm, continued its journey across his thigh, and disappeared beneath the edge of the magazine in Toby's lap. He held his breath, afraid to look up or do anything else, and waited to see what would happen. When he felt Aaron's fingers playing with the leg of his shorts, he tensed.

Still holding his book in one hand, Aaron gently pulled the leg of Toby's shorts up, then slid his free hand inside. Toby closed his eyes as Aaron's fingers found his cock and squeezed the head gently.

"Nice," Aaron whispered in his ear, his breath hot on Toby's neck.

Aaron pumped Toby slowly, his fingers gripping him tightly. Toby swallowed hard. He wasn't sure he could hold out much longer. Other than himself, no one had ever touched his dick before. Although the sensation of his own fingers around his shaft was familiar to him, having someone else stroke him was completely new. He was surprised to find that it felt totally different from jacking off, and he didn't want it to end.

"I'm gonna come if you keep doing that," he told Aaron softly.

Aaron stopped what he was doing. Giving the head of Toby's dick a final squeeze, he removed his hand and brought it back to his own lap. Lifting it to his lips, he inserted a finger into his mouth and licked Toby's wetness from his skin. Then he cupped his palm around his nose and inhaled.

"Your balls smell great," he told Toby, again whispering in his ear. "I can't wait to see how they taste."

Toby looked into Aaron's brown eyes. He'd often imagined what the first man he made love with would look like. Was this him? Aaron smiled. "Where are you staying?" he asked Toby.

"I'm not sure," Toby told him. His plan only had him getting to Provincetown. He hadn't really thought about what he would do after that. Now that Aaron asked, he realized that he hadn't exactly thought things out. He supposed that was what happened when you ran away from home.

"You don't have a reservation anywhere?" Aaron inquired.

Toby knew he had to think of something to say. Otherwise, Aaron might start asking too many questions, ones that would be harder to answer.

"I'm supposed to meet up with some friends," Toby said quickly. "I'm not sure where they're staying exactly."

Aaron nodded. Apparently the answer was enough for him. "That's okay," he said. "I have my own room. What do you say when we get to town we go there before you meet up with your friends?"

Toby nodded. This wasn't exactly the way he'd pictured his first time happening. But Aaron seemed nice, and he was definitely attractive. *You could do worse,* Toby told himself. *A lot worse.*

CHAPTER II

Here we go again, Jackie thought as she looked around at the sea of faces, all of them smiling.

It was always the same on the Friday of Memorial Day weekend. With the whole summer stretching before them like a magic carpet waiting to take them on the adventure of their lives, the women and men who came to wake the town from its winter slumber were high on the thrill of possibilities. Their voices glittered with hope, creating a swirling wave of sound that swept through the club and left its intoxicating touch on everything. Laughter spilled like champagne from the bar and the dance floor, while the more sedate dining room crackled with the clinking sounds of glassware and silver.

Jackie moved through her kingdom with the practiced grace of a woman who had been in the same position many times. She greeted familiar customers by name and new ones with a smile and a hand on their shoulders. This was what they all wanted, to feel as if they'd come home, and she was happy to provide the illusion. Not that she didn't consider many of them family; she did. But she was finding it more difficult than usual to really care.

Maybe, she thought as she smiled and waved at a couple whose faces were familiar from previous summers but whose names she'd forgotten, it was because she no longer had a home of her own to go home to. She had a house, but that was just a shell that had once housed everything else that was really important to her. Now the house was largely empty. Karla had moved out that morning. With her teaching responsibilities over and her grades handed in, she'd had no more reasons to stay. The boxes had gone into the U-Haul, the cat into her carrier, and Karla had gone, off to her new life in Providence. Jackie had been left with the past and a house that echoed when she walked through it.

The actual leaving had been as civil as she could have hoped for. A quick, sterile hug and the return of her house keys, and Karla was off. Watching her drive away, the huge cheerful sunflower painted on the side of the rental truck to celebrate the beauty that was Kansas growing smaller and smaller until Karla turned a corner and disappeared for good, Jackie had tried to understand how someone whose voice on the phone had once had the power to take her breath away had been reduced to a box of old paperback novels left in a corner of the guest bedroom and a handful of empty hangers dangling in a closet. Where had they gone wrong? At what point had love slipped into indifference?

Maybe June was right. Jackie sighed. June was a whole other issue. Her older sister, June, was the one person in her family who had reacted to her coming out with stereotypical hostility. "It's not right," she'd said, looking across the table at the restaurant Jackie had taken her to lunch at, hoping the public setting might prevent June from having one of her all-too-familiar emotional outbreaks, "two sisters being together."

"I'm not with a sister," Jackie had told her. "Susan is white."

She was nineteen at the time, a sophomore in college and a year out of the house she'd grown up in and the room she and June had shared their entire lives. It was Christmas break, and she'd decided the time had come to tell her sister a thing or two about herself. She'd arrived home with freshly shorn hair, a copy of the poems of Audre Lourde in her suitcase, and the taste of Susan's good-bye kiss still on her lips.

"White?" June had said. "You're doing this with a white girl?"

"She's a woman, not a girl," Jackie had snapped. "And 'this' happens to be love. I'm making love with another woman, and I'm not ashamed of it."

It had all been very political. Thinking back on it now, Jackie had to laugh at the fervor with which she'd defended her relationship with Susan. But June had seen it as both a betrayal of womankind and a betrayal of blackness. "She's just using you to work off some of her white guilt, and you're letting her," she'd said dismissively. Christmas dinner had been an icy affair, and Jackie had returned to school glad to have her family five hundred miles away. When, just before spring break, Susan had dumped her for a Hispanic sociology major, Jackie had been irritated to find herself shouting at her departing ex, "I guess you can check another minority off your wish list now!" She'd waited until she had a new, black, girlfriend to tell June about before bringing up the subject again.

After Jackie's revelation, the relationship between the sisters had cooled. Where once they'd told each other everything, they now rarely spoke. As first their father and then their mother died, they saw less and less of each other, until finally their relationship was confined to the occasional holiday or birthday card, a signature hastily scrawled at the bottom or, more often, absent entirely.

Cancer had brought them back together. At forty-one, June discovered a lump in her breast. A mastectomy failed to eradicate the poisonous tendrils that had curled around her innards, and within a year she was near death. A call from her daughter brought Jackie back to Detroit, and they'd had three weeks together before the cancer launched its final, deadly, assault. Even then, as June had lain in the hospital saying her good-byes, she'd begged Jackie to reconsider her life. "You need a family," she'd said, her voice ragged and her bony fingers clutching Jackie's weakly. "You don't want to die alone."

Jackie hadn't argued, too busy with grieving to try and convince her sister that two women together *were* a family, that there was more to love than the production of children and the leaving of legacies. But now, with Karla and a decade of her life gone, Jackie wondered if maybe her sister had been right all along. No, she didn't think there was any sin in who and what she was. But maybe wanting it all was asking too much. Maybe the energy required to fight thousands of years of heterosexuality was more than she had in her.

The truth was, the last few years she'd been thinking about babies, and this terrified her. Her, a butch dyke, suddenly wondering what it would be like to be a mother? Jackie tried to imagine Franny's reaction to the idea of her in a maternity dress, stomach plumped out like a down pillow and breasts swelling with milk. *She'd never believe it,* Jackie thought, picturing her mentor's shocked expression and smiling to herself.

Still, she'd thought about it. She'd even mentioned it to Karla a few times, as casually as she could. But Karla was too busy with tenure and writing articles for various obscure academic journals to get that Jackie was serious about wanting to start a family, so the subject had died with a whimper. Besides, Jackie getting pregnant would upset the whole butch-femme construct of their relationship that Karla found so appealing. She herself would never even consider motherhood, believing it to be an outdated tradition that kept women confined and raped them of their potential. ("And who exactly gave birth to *you?*" Jackie had asked her once, receiving a long lecture on the lesbian responsibility to overturn the heterosexual ideal in return.) And should her butch lover ever reveal a longing for strollers and tiny booties, Karla would surely have felt it a betrayal of the worst sort.

How ironic, Jackie thought, that Karla had then been the one to bring about the end of their relationship, and not by leaving Jackie for another butch but for a woman even more femme than herself. "I can't live within a definition," she'd told Jackie during one of their breakup fights. "I need to explore other aspects of my being."

Well, let her go exploring, Jackie thought. Maybe it was time for her to do some exploring of her own. Forty wasn't too old to have a baby. Maybe there were a few risks involved, but they were minimal. She was in good health, especially since she'd stopped drinking. Really the only thing she lacked was some good, healthy sperm. *And how hard can it be to find that?* she asked herself. *The stuff is practically flowing in rivers in this town.*

"Jackie!"

Jackie turned and saw three men walking toward her.

"Ted!" she called out delightedly. "Ben! Good to see you."

"Have we ever missed a Memorial Day opening?" asked Ted as the two men embraced and kissed her. "The place looks amazing."

"Thanks," Jackie replied. "I didn't think they'd get it done, but they did. Of course, Jerry was putting the last of the paint on while the staff was setting the tables, but we made it." She turned her attention to Ted and Ben's companion. "And who is this?" she asked.

"This is our fabulous new friend Josh," Ben told her. "He's staying with us for a while."

Jackie took Josh's hand and shook it. "You're a lucky man," she said. "You couldn't ask for better hosts."

"I know," Josh replied, smiling sweetly. "They've been great."

"How about a table for my favorite customers?" asked Jackie. "I have one by the window just waiting for you."

She led the men through the restaurant and to a table situated right in front of one of the big windows that looked out over the ocean. As they sat, she looked again at Josh. He was handsome, not in the way that a lot of the gay boys who came to P-Town were with their overly worked bodies and whitened smiles, but in a comfortable, normal way. He looked like the kind of guy who would go to a ball game without worrying what his hair looked like, or who didn't have to get dressed up just to walk to the store for milk. *Or the kind who would look good pushing a baby stroller,* she thought idly.

"Let me tell you about our specials," she said quickly, pushing the thought from her mind. What was she doing? She wasn't on a man hunt, she was running a business.

Having fully described the Alaskan halibut with dill and capers, the duck breast with fig sauce, and the cioppino with lobster and scallops, Jackie excused herself to allow the men time to peruse the rest of the menu. Ted and Ben had been coming to the restaurant since Franny had owned it. They had quickly become favorites with Jackie upon her arrival, first because of the extravagant tips they gave her as a waitress and later because of the kindness they showed her when she came to know them better. They were her idea of the perfect couple, and she'd often looked at them and hoped that she and Karla would end up as happy as they were.

"So much for that plan," she said out loud.

"Excuse me?"

Jackie turned around and saw Emmeline standing behind her. She was dressed in an elegant beaded black dress, and she was holding sheet music in her hand.

"Oh, not you," Jackie said. "I was just giving myself a hard time."

"Please. Don't you have enough people to do that for you?" asked Emmeline.

Jackie laughed. "More than enough," she said. "How are you doing?"

"Remarkably well, considering I think I've forgotten the lyrics to every song I'm supposed to be singing tonight," Emmeline told her.

"You always say that," said Jackie. "And you're always wonderful."

"I know," Emmeline answered. "But before I only had to remember the lyrics to 'Dancing Queen.' This time I'm singing actual *words.* It takes more than just fabulous hand motions to distract the audience when you screw up Gershwin and Porter."

"Trust me, you'll be great," Jackie reassured her friend. Inside, though, she wondered if it was true. Emmeline had previewed some of her set for Jackie earlier in the day, and it *had* been fantastic. Jackie had been wowed by Emmeline's ability to pull off classics like "Too Darn Hot" and "A Foggy Day." Her voice, a throaty combination of Julie London and Diana Krall with just the merest hint of Tony Bennett to betray her chromosomal heritage, was perfect for the material. If she could manage to stay calm, Jackie knew that Emmeline would give the people who'd come to see her—and those who'd stumbled upon her by accident—something amazing.

But she also knew that this was something new for her star performer. Emmeline was right, lip-synching to Abba was not the same as performing live with just a piano for support. Gone were the campy costumes and the outrageous gags that had made previous shows so popular. This time it was just Emmeline's voice that was responsible for holding the audience captive. Would she be able to do it?

"I need a drink," Emmeline said suddenly.

Jackie wasn't sure what to say.

"I said I *need* one," Emmeline told her, patting her hand. "Not that I was going to *have* one."

"Don't do that to me," Jackie said sternly. "I have enough to worry about."

"Karla?" asked Emmeline.

Jackie nodded. "Among other things," she said. "I just can't help feeling that I'm stuck in a rut. I mean, weren't we doing exactly the same thing last year this time? And the year before that?"

"Not exactly," Emmeline replied. "I had on a different dress." She batted her impossibly long and totally false eyelashes at her employer.

It had the desired effect. Jackie smiled. "You know what I mean," she said.

Emmeline sighed. "Yes, I do," she said. "I also know that sometimes when we think things need to be shaken up what we really need is to just sit back and enjoy what we've got."

"What kind of crazy drag queen Zen moment are you having?" asked Jackie.

It was Emmeline's turn to laugh. "I'm just saying don't go trying to fly over the rainbow just yet," she said. "You might be surprised by what you find in your own backyard."

"I hate that movie," Jackie retorted. "And I hated it even more when Diana Ross did it. You'll have to come up with something better."

"Better than *The Wizard of Oz*?" replied Emmeline. "You are a hard one. I bet you laughed when Bambi's mother died."

"Life is not a Disney movie," Jackie told her. "Even if all the fags in here want to think it is."

"Watch it," Emmeline said. "I'm one of those fags. So are you, when it comes down to it."

"I know," Jackie said. "That's the problem. All my life I've been waiting for the happy ending, and now I don't think it's coming."

"That sounds like Franny talking," Emmeline said, suddenly sounding more serious.

Jackie sighed. "No," she said. "I'm just talking. Everything will be fine."

"All the same, I'll be keeping an eye on you," Emmeline answered.

"Okay, Mom," Jackie quipped. But inside she was grateful to Emmeline. Theirs was a long friendship, and it was good to know that she had something she could count on to remain stable.

"How much time do I have?" Emmeline asked her.

Jackie checked her watch. "It's eight-thirty," she said. "I'll have Robin shut down the music at nine and then they're yours for an hour."

"In that case," said Emmeline, "I have to go powder my nose. I'll see you in a bit."

Emmeline retreated to the rear of the club and her dressing room. Jackie watched her go. If anyone had told her twenty years earlier that on the eve of her fortieth year she would be living on the ocean with no girlfriend and a drag queen for a best friend, she would have laughed herself silly. But there she was, at least for the time being. She still didn't buy Emmeline's assertion that her life didn't need some changing.

First, though, there were customers to seat. Jackie picked up some menus, fixed a smile on her face, and went to greet her guests.

CHAPTER 12

I guess some things do change, thought Devin Lowens as she looked around at the newly redecorated Jackie's. Not that changing the paint was that big a deal. The people were still the same, and it was people that interested Devin. Well, not people exactly, but what they could do for her. She had to admit this even about herself. People were a means to an end, not something with any intrinsic value.

And from the look of things, the people at Jackie's were not going to be much help to her. As she scanned the bar she saw many of the same faces she'd seen there the last time. That had been what, almost a year ago? She'd come for some supposed friend's graduation party. Apparently some of the guests had never left, because there they were, drinks in hand and stupid smiles on their faces. They were probably still having the same dreary conversations they'd been having last Memorial Day weekend, conversations about their boring lives and their boring dreams and their boring plans.

She was tempted to turn around and leave. But where would she go? As much as she hated to admit it, Jackie's was the place to be. *How pathetic,* she thought as she worked her way through the crowd to the bar. *In New York this place would be begging people to come in.*

New York. She wished she were there. Or LA. That would be even better. She could do well in LA. It was a town made for a woman like her. Instead she was stuck in Provincetown again. Why? Because she didn't know the right people. Her family didn't have connections. They didn't have anything. It was her bad luck to have been born to an electrician father and a homemaker mother. "Everyone thinks the traditional family is such hot shit," she'd once told her parents during one of their frequent fights. "What the fuck has it gotten me?" Maybe being the child of a film star or a big-shot power broker wouldn't be the easiest thing in the world, but at least it would have given her a head start. She would gladly trade twenty-two years of birthday parties and perfect Christmases for an uncle who worked at CAA or a cousin who did lunch with Spielberg.

"Give me a gin and tonic," she told the bartender. She hoped a drink would make the evening more tolerable.

"Devin?"

She turned to see a perky blonde behind her.

"Kelly," she said flatly, as if identifying a particularly uninteresting insect she'd discovered crawling across the floor.

Oblivious of Devin's unenthusiastic greeting, Kelly beamed. "It's so good to see you. Are you done with school?"

Devin nodded, looking over Kelly's shoulder as if she were expecting someone else to show up.

"Me too," the girl continued. "Can you believe we're actually out of college? I mean, pretty soon we'll be married with babies and turning thirty."

Like fuck I will, Devin thought. She gladly accepted the drink the bartender pushed toward her and took a deep sip.

"What was your major?" Kelly continued, clearly determined to mine this particularly repugnant topic for all it was worth.

"Organic chemistry," Devin lied, hoping it would be sufficiently intimidating to Kelly to make her pursue another line of questioning or, even better, another victim.

"Wow," replied Kelly. "That sounds tough. I just went for your basic business admin degree."

Devin, who as of a few days before possessed a B.A. in exactly the same field, nodded condescendingly. "That's a pretty standard one," she said.

Kelly shrugged. "I know," she said, sounding guilty for being so ordinary. "But it seemed the most practical. I'm hoping to get a job in Boston. I'm just here for a few weeks to unwind. Me and a friend from school are getting an apartment in the city next month."

The city. Devin cringed. That's what so many of the kids she knew who grew up in and around Provincetown called Boston, as if it were the only major metropolis in the country. To many of them it represented the great unknown, the glorious forbidden city of their dreams where, if they were very lucky, they might escape when they were old enough.

"Sounds nice," she told Kelly.

"Thanks," Kelly said, mistaking Devin's remark for a compliment. "So, how long are you here for?"

"Just a couple of days," answered Devin.

"To see your folks," Kelly said. It wasn't a question, just a statement, as if of course someone would want to come back to town to see her family before setting out to begin her new life.

"Yeah, to see my folks," Devin mimicked.

Before the conversation could proceed, Kelly was surrounded by several more people.

"Hey, Kel, we're going to head over to the beach," said a guy sporting a shaved head and a lip piercing.

"Cool," Kelly replied. "Chad, you remember Devin, right?"

Chad looked at Devin and gave her a lopsided grin. "Sure," he said. "You look good."

And you look like a fish stuck on a hook, thought Devin, eyeing Chad's lip piercing critically. Chad had been their school's football hero, an empty-headed jock whom Devin had looked upon as the epitome of everything that made high school a living hell.

"You want to come with us, Devin?" Kelly asked. "A lot of the kids from school are back for the summer."

Devin shook her head. "No, thanks," she answered quickly. "I'm waiting for someone."

"Later then," Kelly replied as Chad grabbed her hand and pulled her away.

"Not if I'm lucky," Devin muttered under her breath.

She was relieved to have Kelly out of her sight. It was bad enough that she was back in town for the summer. The last thing she wanted was to be reminded of her old life there. During the past four years she'd worked hard to become someone new, someone who hadn't grown up surrounded by people who earned their livings doing work for summer visitors who made more money than they did and thus could afford to have what they wanted. She'd slowly molded herself into something different, a person who wasn't burdened with a blue-collar upbringing and the limitations that came with it.

For the most part, she'd succeeded. The other students at the small college she'd attended knew very little about her. She'd manufactured a family consisting of an architect father and a mother who did political consulting for candidates whose names Devin pulled straight from the newspapers. Details were vague, and she'd allowed stories about her to grow naturally, fueled by the occasional shared anecdote or well-timed introduction of innuendo that could be passed around without fear of being discredited. She'd cultivated no close friends but a large circle of acquaintances and hangers-on, and in this way she'd managed to discard a great deal of what she considered an unwelcome personal history.

One thing she hadn't been able to rid herself of, however, was her educational loans. She now owed various state and federal agencies in excess of $45,000. That's why she was back, living in her parents' home and looking for a way to pay her bills. She'd always assumed that she would find the perfect job, but as time had run out on her senior year she'd discovered that entry-level positions in the fields she thought herself worthy of paid surprisingly little. "For every person who turns us down, there are fifty who will say yes," one recruiter for a New York public relations firm had told her smugly after revealing that the salary of the assistant job she coveted was barely enough to pay for daily lunch at Burger King, much less a studio apartment in Chelsea, dinners in SoHo, and the occasional shopping excursion to Fifth Avenue.

In the end she'd been unwilling to compromise. Scraping by was not her style, and she'd decided to take some time to come up with an alternate plan. Now here she was, newly arrived back in town and wondering if perhaps she'd made a mistake. Her parents, always disconcerted by her disdain for the life they'd provided her, took her return to them as an acceptance of their ideals, and had welcomed her warmly. Ensconced in the upstairs bedroom she'd spent her teen years planning her escape from, she was facing a summer of mindless work at minimum wage, nights listening to her father's snoring in the bedroom below hers, and a steady stream of unwanted parental advice.

I've got to find a way out, she thought bitterly as she lit a cigarette and breathed deeply of the smoke. She couldn't smoke in the house, as her parents strictly forbade the habit. It was yet another reminder to Devin that she was not in control of her own life, and it infuriated her.

Her drink was half gone. Thankfully, the bartender had been generous with the gin, and its soothing touch was beginning to take effect. She leaned against the bar and took inventory of the club. Jackie, as always, was flitting about talking to customers and keeping everything running smoothly. Devin admired Jackie for her ability to run her business, but pitied the woman for what she saw as a lack of vision. The place could be so much more hip, more cutting edge. All it would take was a few changes.

Like getting rid of that tired old drag queen, she thought as Emmeline finished a song and the audience applauded. *Shouldn't she be dead by now?* She hated drag queens. They were an embarrassment, the clowns of the gay community. Why did people like them so much? They were creepy—pathetic men who wished they were women, settling for illusion because they couldn't handle the reality of what they were. *They should all be put in zoos,* Devin thought, laughing at the image of children tossing peanuts at the cages of grotesque creatures as they tapped helplessly on the bars with their fake nails and screamed to be let out.

Yes, if it were her place the drag queen would be out. So would the homely members of the wait staff. Only beautiful people should carry food, she thought. Being handed a plate by a handsome waiter or a girl with a lovely face made its contents taste better somehow. An overdone piece of beef could be forgiven if the hands setting it on the table belonged to a waitress with porcelain skin and full lips, and even the most characterless of salads took on new life when sprinkled with fresh-ground pepper by an Italian man with dark eyes and long, fine fingers.

Devin herself knew all about the effects of beauty. One of the few things she'd inherited from her parents for which she was grateful was her genes. A lovely baby, she'd grown into a charming toddler and then a stunning teenager. Her auburn hair, a gift from her mother's Irish ancestors, glowed like polished wood against her pale skin. From her father she'd gotten eyes the color of dusk, a soft gray that melted into gold at the edges. The combination was breathtaking, and her ability to affect people's moods with her looks was one of Devin's earliest discoveries. Men and women were equally entranced by her, and she'd seldom turned down an invitation from either, particularly when there was something to gain from the encounter.

Not that romance was something that particularly fascinated her. Sex was fine, but the emotional trappings that often came with it were just a distraction as far as she was concerned. Her liaisons were seldom repeated, unless doing so provided substantial benefits, and the notion of something enduring was not an option she was willing to consider. Early in her college years she'd made the mistake of allowing a young man she'd met and bedded at a party to take her out again. The result—a string of pleading phone calls and a final, unpleasant scene witnessed by more people than was necessary—had decided Devin against ever allowing herself to be put in that position again. Since then she'd enjoyed many partners in her bed, or more often in theirs, but had remained blissfully free of the affliction of partnership.

Despite the effects of the gin and tonic, she was getting depressed. There was nothing at Jackie's for her, no one to distract her from her situation or provide some moments of amusement. It was typical Provincetown, and it annoyed her. The residents had nothing to offer, and the summer people were by and large fags. Not that fags weren't interesting; she'd had a lot of fun with gay men over the years. But tonight she was bored by them, irritated by their perfect haircuts and beautiful bodies because she knew that when they left the town most of them would be going back to places she wished she lived, to lives she wished she had.

It was time to leave. She hurriedly finished her drink and put out her cigarette. She found her way through the growing crowd and out the door into the cool air. Even that disturbed her, reeking as it did of nature and the sea rather than the musty scent of a nightclub with its odor of sweat, smoke, and alcohol. Everything was a reminder of the step back she'd been forced to take.

As she walked angrily back toward her parents' house and the cramped twin bed of her childhood room, she spied a fire on the beach. The sound of voices flickered in the night, punctuated by the occasional spark of laughter. *Kelly and the rest of the morons,* Devin thought, looking at the shadows moving around the flames. Probably every single person around that campfire was someone she'd gone to high school with, someone she'd despised. The idea of them all gathered in one spot repulsed her.

Fueled by her bad mood and the drink coursing through her blood, she took the steps down to the beach and walked out onto the sand. If she had to have a miserable night, she thought, she might as well spread the unhappiness. It would at least give her something to do.

"Hey," she said as she entered the circle of the fire. There were five people gathered there. As she'd suspected, she knew them all.

"You came!" Kelly said happily, her voice carrying its perpetual ex-clamation point. "I was just telling everyone that I saw you."

"Well, here I am," Devin said. She settled herself on a log beside Jack Merton. She and Jack had shared an English class in high school. Back then his distinguishing characteristic had been that he wore too much aftershave. Devin was disappointed to discover that things hadn't changed.

"Kelly tells us you're just back for a little while," Jack said.

"Yeah," replied Devin, suddenly wishing she'd gone home instead of detouring onto the beach. "Who could stand more than a couple of weeks?"

"I don't know," said Jack. "It's not such a bad place."

"If you're eighty-five or queer," Devin remarked sharply. In high school Jack had prided himself on his ability to get women into bed, and Devin hoped her gibe would get under his skin.

"Jack's already got quite a gig," Chad said. "Not that he'll tell us anything about it."

"I told you," Jack said, holding his hands up. "I can't say a word."

"What's the big mystery?" Devin asked, intrigued despite herself.

Kelly answered her. "Jack runs a housecleaning business," she said. "He's got some big important client this summer, but he won't tell us who it is."

Big deal, thought Devin, disappointed. *It's probably Martha fucking Stewart or something.*

"All we know is it's someone in the movie business," Chad elaborated.

"I didn't say that," Jack protested.

"Dude, you said it was someone from Hollywood," said Chad. "What else is in Hollywood?"

Devin watched Jack's face. He was looking anywhere but at his friends, making her suspect that he'd already said more than he was supposed to. Was it possible his client *was* someone important? She doubted it, but it was the first even remotely intriguing thing she'd stumbled upon since coming back to Provincetown.

"Come on, Jack," she said, putting her hand on the man's back. "It's not like we're going to tell anyone."

Jack shook his head. "I had to sign a form and everything," he said. "Not even the girls I send out there are allowed to know."

Now Devin really wanted to find out who Jack was working for, not because she thought it was anyone she cared about but because it was a secret that was being withheld from her.

"Okay," she said, employing a new strategy. "That's cool. If this person asked you to keep quiet, you should. We'll just talk about something else."

"Thank you," said Jack gratefully.

"So," Devin said, "what's everyone else been up to?"

For the next hour she listened as her ex-classmates described in excruciating detail the specifics of their pathetic lives. She didn't really pay attention, but she nodded and laughed when appropriate so that they would think she was listening. In reality, though, she was figuring out a way to get what she really wanted.

When, shortly before one in the morning, the party broke up, Devin waited around as everyone left and it was just she and Jack, who had volunteered to put the fire out, left behind. As he spread the coals around, burying the embers beneath a mound of sand, she went to work.

"It's so good seeing you again," she said.

"Really?" Jack replied. "I always got the impression you didn't much like me."

Devin laughed. "You know how girls can be when they have a crush on a guy," she said.

Jack stopped what he was doing and looked at her. "You liked *me?*" he said.

Devin nodded. "Yeah, but you always had some other girl around," she said.

Jack came and sat beside her. "I don't have one around now," he said nervously.

Devin smiled. "Maybe we should make up for lost time then."

As Jack kissed her, she shut her eyes and willed herself not to pull away. Jack's tongue moved eagerly between her lips as he embraced her. Devin allowed him to wrap her in his arms. Jack was clumsy, anxious, his hands all over her. *He probably hasn't gotten laid in forever,* thought Devin. Good. She could use that to her advantage.

She moved her hand to Jack's crotch. Not surprisingly, he was hard. She found the zipper of his jeans and pulled on it. *With any luck,* she thought, *this should only take a few minutes.*

CHAPTER 13

It was going well. She'd remembered all the words. She wasn't nervous. Well, no more than usual. And people seemed to be enjoying it. The only problem was the boy.

Emmeline was halfway through Bernard Ighner's "Everything Must Change," a song she'd first heard sung by Nina Simone on her now-forgotten album *Baltimore*. While Simone herself discounted the record as something she'd been forced by her producers to do, Emmeline thought it was one of her best. Numerous other artists had also recorded the song, including one of the drag world's patron saints, La Barbra, but for Emmeline it was Nina's dark, haunting vocals and spare piano accompaniment that defined the song with its lyrics about the inevitability and, more important, beauty of transformation. It was a message Emmeline could relate to more than most, and she'd built her set around it.

In the middle of the second verse, however, she almost got lost. Having sung the first part of the song with her eyes closed, she opened them and saw at the rear of the room one of the saddest faces she'd ever encountered. It belonged to a young man. He was standing against the wall, watching her with an expression of loss on his otherwise handsome face. At the same time, he watched Emmeline intently, as if seeing something magical for the first time.

He's not even a man, Emmeline thought as she struggled to recall the next words of the song. *He's just a boy.*

She was unable to take her eyes off of the young man, and eventually she gave up and sang the song directly to him. She sent the words out on the stream of her voice, giving them to him as a gift. She didn't know why, but she knew he needed it. Something was troubling him, and although she had no idea what it was, she hoped her song could in some way ease the ache that had taken hold of him. *He looks as if his heart has just been broken,* she thought as she held the final note.

But it was too early in the season for heartbreak. The summer had just begun. Usually those for whom falling in love turned out to be a painful lesson appeared much later, when the intoxicating spell of being in Provincetown began to lose its potency or their supposed beloveds came across more desirable lovers and broke things off. Things were particularly rough around the July Fourth celebration, when many vacations came to an end and a fresh supply of bodies invaded the streets to provide temptation for restless libidos. At such times Jackie's was filled with men and women whose romantic hopes had foundered on the shores of P-Town's beaches.

The young man's heartache was premature. What, Emmeline wondered, had caused it? Had he arrived in town already wounded? Whatever had happened, he was clearly in the grip of unhappiness. For the rest of her set she had to force herself not to look at him too often, and to focus her attention on other faces. Her interest in him was not sexual. Although his beauty was undeniable, particularly as his wounded air heightened the vulnerability radiated by his boyish face, she had never been one to be entranced by youth. No, her interest in him was one of kinship. She saw in him something she'd felt herself far too often, and it made her sad for him.

She managed to avoid looking in the young man's direction for several songs. Finally, when she felt she had to check on him one more time, she looked back to where he'd been standing. He was gone. In his place stood a middle-aged man dressed in a Hawaiian shirt and shorts, an image, perhaps, of what the boy might become in twenty-five years. But for the moment the boy himself had slipped back into the sea of ever-changing faces.

Now, with her set over and the audience expressing their appreciation with clapping and whistling, Emmeline waded through the crowd and toward the bar. She nodded her thanks to those around her and accepted graciously the occasional extended hand. As always, she was sorry that the show was over. Although she often dreaded going onstage, she inevitably missed it immediately when she was away from the lights. Now she wanted to return to her dressing room so she could reflect on her performance.

As she slipped out of the room and headed for the hallway that led from the dining area to the behind-the-scenes rooms of the club, however, she was stopped once again by the appearance of the young man. This time he was seated at the bar. In front of him was a glass, and he was stirring its contents anxiously. He seemed oblivious of the people around him, lost in whatever thoughts occupied his head.

Don't do it. Emmeline's internal warning kicked in. *You're not his mother.* She'd been in this position before. Her natural inclination was to take care of hurt things. Her particular weakness was for dogs and humans, although kittens, plants, and even birds had also found their way into her life from time to time. It was a habit she was trying to break.

Just let him sort it out on his own. It was a logical piece of advice. She didn't know the young man. She didn't owe him anything. Probably he was just some miserable little drama queen who'd just had a fight with his boyfriend of the moment. Or girlfriend. It was hard to tell these days. He'd probably have three or four drinks to kill the pain and then be on his way. Meanwhile, there was a nice pot of mint tea waiting for her back in her dressing room. She should just keep walking.

But she didn't. Even as her mind told her to go, her heart propelled her toward the bar. The seat next to the young man was empty. Emmeline took it.

"Could I have a cranberry juice and tonic, Sammy?" she asked the bartender.

As Sammy prepared her drink, Emmeline glanced over at the boy beside her. He was still stirring his drink, his eyes fixed on the eddies formed in the circling liquid.

"If you keep that up you'll melt the ice and water it down," she said gently.

The young man looked over at her. "That's okay," he said slowly. "I don't really like it anyway. It's whiskey. I only ordered it because that's what people always do in movies. I don't know why. It tastes like crap."

Emmeline smiled. This one *was* a baby.

"Maybe you should switch to something else," she said. "How about Coke?"

The boy looked at her for a moment, as if wondering what accepting her offer would cost him. Then he smiled shyly. "Okay," he said. "Thanks."

"Sammy, a Coke for my friend here," Emmeline called to the bartender. Sammy nodded, and a moment later set both drinks on the bar. Emmeline handed the young man his drink.

"Here's to finishing my first set of the summer," she said, clinking her glass against the boy's.

She took a sip of her cranberry juice. "If we're going to be sharing a toast, we should know each other's names," she said. "I'm Emmeline."

"Toby," the boy said. He paused, as if uncertain of what to say next. "I really liked your singing."

"Thank you," Emmeline replied. "Those are some of my favorite songs. I'm pleased to hear that you enjoyed them, especially considering that most of them were written long before you were born."

She waited for Toby to continue, hoping he would give her some clue as to what had upset him. Now that she was closer to him, she was even more curious. He didn't seem like the usual type who came to town. For one thing, he was much younger. Maybe, she thought, he was here with his family. She'd seen that before, a young man with feelings he needed to explore leaving his unsuspecting family behind in their hotel room while he went in search of adventure, or at least release. Was that what Toby was doing? It was possible, but she suspected there was more to the story.

"Are you here on vacation?" she asked finally, when it became clear that Toby wasn't going to give her any help in unraveling the mystery.

He shook his head. "No. Well, sort of. I don't know. This seemed like a good idea a week ago. Now I think maybe I made a mistake."

Here we go, Emmeline thought. Toby was ready to talk. He just needed a little help getting started.

"What brought you here?" she asked.

Toby sighed deeply. He looked over at Emmeline. His eyes were damp. "My parents found out," he said shakily. "About me, I mean." He looked at Emmeline warily, as if afraid to continue. "I'm gay," he said finally.

Emmeline nodded. "I figured as much," she said. "In case you hadn't noticed, most of us here are."

Toby laughed slightly. "I know," he said. "That's why I picked Provincetown. I figured I'd fit in here. It's small, not like New York or San Francisco. I don't think I'm ready for those places yet. This seemed like a good place to start."

"Sort of like training camp," Emmeline said.

Toby nodded. "I'm from a small town," he told her. "In Missouri. There are no gay people there."

Oh, honey, you have no idea who lives in small towns, Emmeline thought to herself. *Everyone always thinks they're the only ones.* But Toby didn't need to hear that at the moment. He needed to get his own story out.

"How old are you?" she asked instead.

"Eighteen," replied Toby. "Well, I will be in a couple of weeks."

He is *a baby.* Emmeline's heart swelled. Toby was practically a child. *He's not much older than you were when you left home,* she reminded herself.

"So you came here because your parents found out about you?" she pressed.

"They found this magazine," said Toby, sounding embarrassed. "In my gym bag. My mother was washing my baseball uniform. I played for the school team. Anyway, I had the magazine hidden underneath it. It was—you know—a porn magazine."

"Ah," Emmeline said knowingly. "And I take it that it wasn't *Playboy.*"

Toby shook his head. "It had guys in it," he said. "When I came home my parents were in the living room waiting for me. They wanted to know why I had it. I thought about making up a story, telling them that it belonged to someone else. But I was tired of lying about it. So I told them that it was mine and that I was gay."

"And they didn't take it well, right?" Emmeline said.

Toby exhaled sharply. "No," he said simply. "They're really religious. They think it's a sin and that I'm going to hell."

"And is that what you think too?" Emmeline was all too familiar with the threat of God's wrath and the damage it could inflict on people.

"No," answered Toby. "I don't think it's a sin. I can't say why, exactly, but I don't. It's not like I've talked a lot about this with anyone. You're the first person I've really told except my parents."

"Well, I feel very honored," Emmeline said. "Does your family know you're here?"

"They know I'm gone," Toby replied. "But they don't know where. I left them a note saying I was leaving. I'm sure they're freaking out. They've probably called the police. I'm supposed to be graduating this weekend," he added, as if missing his commencement ceremony were the worst part of his running away.

"Well, you're almost legal age, so there's not much they can do about it," Emmeline informed him. "Still, you might want to let them know that you're okay. Despite what happened between you, I bet they're still worried."

"Maybe," Toby admitted.

He sank into silence once more, sipping his Coke. If she was going to get any more out of him, Emmeline was going to have to do some more digging.

"So, do you think you'll stay now that you're here?" she inquired.

"I just don't know," Toby told her. "I didn't really think much past getting here. I don't have a job or a place to stay or anything. I thought I might stay with this guy I met, but that didn't work out."

Emmeline saw a tear slip from Toby's eye and slide down his cheek. *Now we're getting there,* she thought. There was more to Toby's story, and as she'd suspected, it involved a man.

"A guy?" she repeated. "Someone you thought might put you up?"

Another tear slid down Toby's face. "I met him on the bus here," he said. "He asked me to come back to his place with him. We—"

He stopped talking, unable to continue. The tears were flowing freely now, and his shoulders shook with silent sobs. Emmeline reached out and put a hand on his back, rubbing gently. Suddenly she knew what had caused the look of sadness she'd seen in Toby's face.

"It was my first time." Toby was whispering, unable to speak any louder. "I'd never done anything with a guy before. Nothing. And then when we were done he acted like it was no big deal. He just got dressed. I thought he'd want me to stay with him, but he said he was going out and that maybe we could get together again sometime."

It was worse than Emmeline had thought. It was the infamous First Trick. Every gay man had to go through it. Lesbians, too, she supposed. She knew it was a rite of passage, fraught with danger because for many gay people it was an expression of much more than just a first shared orgasm. Like millions of men—and not a few straight women—before him, Toby had probably thought that the first guy he had sex with would become his boyfriend. It likely had never occurred to him that someone would just want to fuck him and then never see him again.

"It wasn't your fault," she said, knowing that Toby had probably spent all night wondering what he'd done wrong.

"But why would he do that?" Toby asked, his voice betraying the truth in Emmeline's thoughts. "Why would he ask me to do that and then pretend like it wasn't important?"

Because it wasn't important to him, Emmeline thought wearily. But she couldn't tell Toby that. Not yet. It was barely his first day as a gay man. He wasn't ready for the hard truth that many men could easily have sex with him and then forget about him as soon as they came.

"Not everyone looks at sex the same way," she said carefully.

"But he seemed so nice," protested Toby. "He seemed to really like me."

How could she tell him that the guy probably *was* nice, that he probably had no idea that he'd just been a scared virgin's first time? How could she explain the complicated dynamics of gay sex to a kid who was barely out of high school and whose mother still did his laundry? Maybe it was best to steer the conversation in a different direction. They could come back to the topic of gay men and their mating habits later.

"What were you planning on doing tonight?" she asked.

Toby sighed again. "I don't know," he said. "I guess I could rent a room somewhere. I took all the money out of my savings account when I left."

"Save your money," Emmeline told him. "You can stay with me."

Toby looked at her, startled.

"Don't worry," Emmeline told him, realizing what he was thinking. "You'll sleep in the guest room. And tomorrow we'll figure out what you're going to do next."

Toby nodded. "Okay," he said. "And sorry about acting weird just now. It's just that after what happened this afternoon I don't know what to think about all of this." He looked around the bar, as if somehow Jackie's was an alien world into which he'd stumbled and was still wary of.

"Well, I hate to disappoint you," Emmeline told him. "But you're not my type." She gave Toby a mock-serious look.

For the first time he rewarded her with a genuine laugh. "That's good," he said. "Because I've never slept with a woman either."

It was Emmeline's turn to laugh. *Oh, boy,* she thought. *This one has a lot to learn.*

CHAPTER 14

"Surprise!"

Josh opened his eyes. He wasn't sure if the voice he'd just heard had been in his dream or if it was real. But when he saw Ryan standing over him, an enormous grin on his face, he realized that his sleep had indeed been invaded by the outside world.

"What are you doing here?" Josh yawned and sat up, stretching beneath the sheets.

"It's nice to see you too," Ryan replied, feigning being insulted. He sat down on the edge of the bed. "I just came to see how my very best friend in the whole world is doing."

"I'm fine," Josh said. "What time is it?"

"It's eleven-thirty," Ryan informed him. "And we're having brunch in half an hour."

"With who?" asked Josh.

"Some friends of mine from New York," explained Ryan. "They're renting a house here for the summer. And some other friends of theirs from Boston are here too. I don't know who they are. Come to think of it, maybe I do. Al didn't tell me their names. Oh, God, I hope I haven't slept with any of them."

"Gee, what are the chances of that?" said Josh as he sat up and tried to muster some enthusiasm for getting out of bed. Boston was, as major cities went, not a very large place. The likelihood of a past paramour turning up in P-Town was about fifty-fifty, especially if, as Ryan had, you'd spent the past five years conducting a random sampling of the sexual habits of Beantown's gay population.

"Just because *your* relationship is on the rocks, don't go mocking my sexual liberation," replied Ryan.

"Sorry," Josh teased. "I didn't realize being a slut made you a candidate for sainthood."

"Please," said Ryan. "Nothing has been in any of my body's openings in months. Well, weeks anyway. I'm practically a virgin again."

"I'll alert the Vatican," said Josh as he stumbled into the bathroom. "When did you get here anyway?" he called out.

"I left town this morning," Ryan answered. "I would have come last night but I got held up at work. Besides, leaving this morning meant I missed the traffic."

"Why didn't you call me?" Josh said.

"I tried," said Ryan. "Your cell is turned off."

Josh returned from the bathroom. "I forgot," he said. "I turned it off. It was too distracting."

"Any more calls from Doug?" Ryan asked.

Josh shook his head. "Not since I told him I was staying away for a while. Frankly, I don't think he cares whether I come back or not."

Ryan cleared his throat. "Well, I wasn't going to say anything," he said. "But I think you should know that I ran into him."

"Where?" Josh asked sharply, not sure if he was more annoyed that his best friend had been planning on hiding something from him or that Doug didn't have the decency to at least stay out of sight while they were fighting.

"Relax," Ryan said. "It was just at the grocery store. We happened to both be in the produce section."

"And?" Josh demanded.

"And he seemed really sad," said Ryan.

"Did he ask about me?"

"Of course he asked about you," Ryan replied. "He knows we're best friends. I told him that I didn't know where you were either, and that he should just give you time to sort things out."

"You could have at least told him he was a cheating bastard," said Josh. "And slapped him."

"If it helps any, he didn't look very happy," Ryan said, ignoring the remark.

"Whatever," Josh answered. "Where are we having brunch?"

"Where else?" said Ryan. "The Shame Café."

"The what?" asked Josh.

"I forgot, you've never been here," Ryan said. "Every Saturday and Sunday morning the place to be is the Same Café, as in 'let's meet at the same café we went to last time we were here.' Only we call it the Shame Café because it's where you sit to watch everyone who went tricking the night before walk back to their own places. It's right on Commercial Street, so you get quite a parade going by."

"Sounds cheery," Josh deadpanned. "I'll be with you in fifteen minutes."

As promised, he emerged a quarter of an hour later showered and shaved. Leaving the car in the driveway, he and Ryan walked to the café, where Ryan quickly spied his friends sitting at a prime table with a view of the street.

"It's about time," called a tall, heavy man with more hair on the expanse of chest exposed by his tank top than on his head.

Ryan hugged the man. "Al, this is Josh," he said.

Al shook hands with Josh, then introduced the rest of the table. "This is my lover, Phil, and this is our friend Aaron and his lover, Eric."

"Ah, the Boston boys," Ryan said. "I'm surprised we haven't met before."

"We don't go out a lot," Eric said as Josh and Ryan sat down. "You know how married couples get."

"Actually, I don't," Ryan told him. "But I've heard. Didn't Bart come with you?" he asked Al.

A collective snicker rippled around the table.

"Bart didn't come home last night," Phil explained. "The last time we saw him was at the Bitter End talking to some guy."

"Making out with some guy is more accurate," Eric said.

"Bart is known as the party favor of the New York circuit," Ryan explained to Josh.

"He has to come out here just to find someone he hasn't tricked with," Al said, earning another round of laughs.

"Did I hear my name being slandered?"

A man arrived at the table and took the empty seat between Josh and Eric. In his early thirties, he had the requisite gym-made body and a face to match. Removing his sunglasses, he set them on the table and leaned back in his chair.

"I need a drink," he said. "Where's the waiter?"

"Aren't those the clothes you had on last night?" Al asked innocently.

"Actually, I only had them on for part of the night," Bart shot back.

"So you did go home with your new friend," Phil remarked.

"For your information, I did not," answered Bart. "I was going to be a good boy and go home early, but as I was walking by the Dick Dock I happened to notice a little after-hours party taking place."

"Dick Dock?" Josh repeated. "Is that a bar?"

"How sweet," Bart said, looking at Josh in wonder. "You mean you really don't know?"

Josh shook his head.

"Dick Dock is what they call the piers over here," explained Al. "You can guess why."

"Well, it certainly lived up to its name last night," Bart told them. "There was so much meat hanging out it was like being in a butcher shop."

"And I'm sure you sampled as much of it as you could get your hands, not to mention other things, on," Phil said.

Bart rolled his eyes. "Honey, there is so much cum in my ass right now, if I fart I'll impregnate half the eastern seaboard."

"You didn't use rubbers?" Eric said, shocked.

"Please. This is not 1992," Bart retorted. "Nobody uses rubbers anymore."

"Actually," Josh said, "new cases of HIV infection are going up again."

"Thank you for the pie chart, Dr. Gloom," said Bart. "I know what they say. But I think that's just a bunch of sex phobics trying to scare us because they didn't get to have any when they were young and pretty enough to enjoy it. Besides, my ass is ironclad. I've never even gotten crabs."

"That's because you shave all the hair off," Al teased. "There's nothing for them to hang on to."

"Let's talk about something else, please," Bart said. "Surely you have other things to discuss than my asshole."

"Not really," Ryan said.

"Well, think of some," Bart told him.

"How was the bus ride from Boston?" Ryan asked Aaron. "Al tells me you came up yesterday to open the house."

"Yeah," Aaron replied. "I got here yesterday afternoon. Everyone else drove up later in the evening after work. It was fine. Boring, actually. There's not a lot to do on a bus. I read the new Clive Barker novel."

"I love public transportation," Bart remarked. "Sometimes you get to sit next to hot guys. One of the best fucks I ever had was on a bus to the March on Washington."

"How could you fuck in that little bathroom?" Phil asked.

Bart grinned. "Who said it was in the bathroom?"

"Well, I didn't sit next to any hot guy," Aaron continued. "It was some bear. All he wanted to talk about was the gay rodeo."

"Hey, some of us are pretty fond of bears," Phil remarked.

"Not me," Aaron said. "Besides, I've got my hot guy right here." He took Eric's hand and kissed it.

"You two make me sick," Bart said. "Trust me, one of these days you'll be looking for action somewhere else."

Eric rubbed a finger along Bart's muscular forearm, then put it in his mouth. "Just as I thought," he said, pulling it out again. "Bitter."

"Love is for children and idiots," Bart said philosophically. "I'm perfectly happy with plain old sex."

"You don't know what you're missing," Eric told him. "I'm so glad I'm not out there in bars looking anymore. I hated that."

"How long have the two of you been together?" Josh asked.

"Three years," Eric answered.

"Do you have a boyfriend?" Aaron asked Josh.

"Yes," Josh answered automatically. Then he caught himself. "Well, I did. I'm not sure at the moment."

"Josh is having a little marital crisis," Ryan said diplomatically.

"You mean one of you cheated," Bart said. "That's what it *always* is. When are you girls going to learn that it is physically impossible for men to be faithful? The sooner you admit that, the sooner you can move on. Monogamy is a myth."

"Not for us," Eric said. "Aaron and I don't sleep around."

"But you probably both want to," commented Bart. "No offense. I'm just saying that men can't be happy with one sexual partner. It's something about needing to mate with as many people as possible to ensure that we have offspring. I saw it on the Discovery Channel."

"Well, since none of the sex any of us are having could possibly produce children, what's our excuse?" Phil asked him.

"We love dick," Bart said simply.

"Well, I can't argue with that," Al said. "Besides, Phil and I have always had an open relationship."

"We figured it was better to just have it all out in the open than to worry about whether each other was doing it," Phil added.

"Doesn't it bother you thinking of each other with other guys?" Eric asked.

"Not really," Phil told him. "Besides, a lot of the time we're with those other guys together."

Al laughed. "We often say we're a living talk show topic. How three-ways saved our marriage."

Josh listened as the other men laughed at Al's joke. *How can they think it's so funny?* he wondered. He looked at Phil and Al. They seemed like a happy couple. But what kind of a couple could they be if they had to look for sex elsewhere? What was the point of being together? It was like they were just friends who happened to sleep together sometimes. He wanted more than that. *Or is there more than that?* he asked himself. Why was sex, and whom you had it with, such a big deal? Why did it mean so much to him that Doug had slept with another man?

"Aaron and I tried a three-way once," Eric said. "It was a disaster. Never again."

"The trick—pardon the pun—is to do it with someone you don't ever have to see again," Al said. "That way it's an adventure. When you have to see the people you have sex with later walking their dogs or picking up their dry cleaning, it ruins the magic. That's why we usually do it out of town or with guys who are visiting the city."

"Let's get back to Josh," said Bart. "Which one of you did the deed?"

"He did," Josh said.

Bart. "So you're the wronged woman. Are you going to dump your boyfriend or what?"

The way Bart said it made Josh think. *Boyfriend. Is that all Doug is after eight years together?* He knew there wasn't really any adequate word to describe two men who had been together longer than most straight marriages, but he'd never really realized before how trivial the word most people used for such relationships sounded. *Boyfriend.* It made it sound as if the two of them were fourteen years old.

"I haven't decided yet," he said finally.

"I say get rid of him," suggested Bart. "There are too many guys out there to waste your time worrying about one."

"And I say give him another chance," said Eric. "Some of us still believe in true love forever." He beamed at Aaron, who smiled back and patted his leg.

"Or at least true love forever with some compromises," said Al. "Maybe you just need to renegotiate things."

Apparently, Josh thought, his options had been reduced to three: settling for sex with strangers, chasing a fairy tale, or working out a deal to save his relationship. None of them appealed to him.

"Are you gentlemen ready to order?" A waiter appeared at their table, notepad in hand. He looked around at the assembled men expectantly.

"Nothing for me," Josh said, closing his menu and pushing it away. "I seem to have lost my appetite."

CHAPTER 15

The weekend had been incredible. For the most part, Reid and Ty hadn't left the bedroom except to make trips to the kitchen for more food and, several times, to shower together in the house's skylit bathroom. Other than that they'd stayed in bed, their clothes still lying on the floor where they'd fallen on Friday evening. Now it was Sunday morning. The sun was slowly working its way from the window to the bed, its golden glow illuminating Ty's bare torso as he slept beside Reid, one arm thrown over his head to reveal the soft forest of hair nestled in the hollow between shoulder and chest.

Reid was tempted to wake Ty by gently biting one of his exposed nipples. He'd woken up half erect, and had been gently stroking himself for half an hour while thinking about the smooth globes of Ty's ass. But something about the way Ty was sleeping, the way he was totally exposed and vulnerable beneath the thin blue scrim of the sheet, had turned Reid's thoughts in a different direction.

He has so much ahead of him, he thought as he watched Ty's chest rise and fall gently. *He's just beginning his life.* It was a thought Reid had had before, and it was usually followed by an intense fear that he would not be part of Ty's future for very long. After all, relationships between stars and the people who largely controlled their careers were notorious for their volatility and, ultimately, their inability to survive the pressures that came with living under constant public scrutiny. Add to that the fact that one half of the pair could never reveal his involvement with someone of the same sex and you pretty much had a blueprint for failure.

Reid had never once been unaware of the impossibility of his situation. He'd always thought of Ty as a momentary gift, a treasure on loan until the demands of career snatched it away again. He'd long ago resigned himself to the knowledge that one day Ty would announce that their last kiss, their last exchange of passion, had occurred, and that everything was over. He'd even practiced his farewell speech, so that his voice wouldn't shake when it came time to deliver it.

In the warm light of the Provincetown morning, however, he wondered if perhaps he hadn't been premature in his assumptions. When he looked at Ty now, he didn't see America's newest star. He didn't see a man separated from him by the flashes of cameras and the screams of adoring fans. Instead he saw a man he could love, a man whose body he'd held in his arms the night before without thought of career or public opinion poisoning the taste of their kisses.

Maybe it wasn't impossible. Maybe it had just never been done. Suddenly, Reid felt that they could do anything they wanted to. He leaned over and very gently pressed his mouth against Ty's. Ty opened his eyes.

"Good morning," he said sleepily.

"Good morning," Reid replied, falling back against the pillows and watching Ty as he stretched and ran his hands through his hair.

"What?" Ty asked, noticing Reid's watchful gaze.

"I was just thinking," Reid said.

"That usually means trouble," said Ty. "What are you thinking about?"

"Us," Reid answered. He rolled onto his side and propped his head up with one hand. "What's your biggest dream?" he asked.

Ty rubbed his eyes. "It's awfully early for a pop quiz," he said.

"I'm serious," Reid continued. "What do you want out of your life?"

Ty sighed. "Couldn't you start with what I want for breakfast?" he replied. He grinned at Reid, waiting for him to laugh. When Reid continued to look at him expectantly, he rolled his eyes. "Okay. Okay. Let me think. I guess my dream is to win an Oscar."

"That's it?" Reid said.

Ty shrugged. "What do you want me to say?" he asked. "Isn't that what actors are supposed to want?"

"If you want an Oscar, you can have mine," Reid said. "It's in a box in the cellar somewhere back home. Trust me, it wouldn't change your life."

"That's because yours was for *producing,*" Ty retorted. "No one cares who produced a movie."

"I'll remember that when it's time to sign your next check," said Reid moodily.

Ty leaned over and kissed his forehead. "What's going on here?" he asked. "Did you have a nightmare or something?"

"No," Reid said sulkily. "I was just thinking that it would be nice if the two of us could do something different."

"You mean like I get to be the top this time?" Ty teased. He ran his hand underneath the sheet and tugged on Reid's balls.

Reid slapped his hand away, annoyed at the obvious attempt to end the conversation. "I meant like maybe we could make a film that means something," he said. "Aren't you tired of all these stupid Hollywood scripts?"

"I'm not exactly Meryl Streep or Robert DeNiro," Ty said. "I pretty much look good kicking butt and kissing Reese Witherspoon."

Reid groaned. "You're much more than that," he said. "Aren't you the one who told *Vanity Fair* that you'd love to do some stage work in New York?"

"Sure," Ty admitted. "But every actor says that. It makes you look cool. You know, like Liam Neeson and Madonna."

"Madonna is *not* an actress," Reid shot back. "Look, what I mean is, don't you want to do films that push you as an actor? Films that have more story to them than just stopping terrorists or getting the girl?"

Ty was quiet for a minute. "I guess so," he said uncertainly. "But who makes those kinds of films anymore?"

"That's exactly my point," Reid said. "No one. But we *could.* I could. You could. We could do it together."

Ty eyed him suspiciously. "Is this about me having to go back to New York tomorrow?" he asked.

"No," Reid said, getting impatient. He sat up and took Ty's hand in his. "Look, I know this is unrealistic. I know I'm supposed to just accept that you're who you are and I'm who I am, and that we work in this ridiculous business. But I don't want to. I can't."

"What are you saying, exactly?" Ty asked him. "Because I'm sort of confused here."

Reid hesitated a moment before continuing. "I love you," he said, unable to believe he was actually uttering the words. "I'm *in* love with you. That's not supposed to happen. There are rules, and I'm breaking them. I'm supposed to act all cool and everything and pretend it doesn't matter when you go off and marry some girl your publicist writes checks to every month, but it does matter. It matters a great deal. So what I'm saying is that maybe it's time to try to change how things are done."

Ty stared at him for a full minute. "You want me to come out?" he asked finally.

Reid shook his head. "No," he said. "That's not what I'm asking. I'm asking you to think about what you want to achieve with your life."

Ty bit his lip. "I'm really confused," he said. "One minute you're talking about making movies and the next you're talking about us being in love. Help me out here."

Reid rubbed his forehead. "It's all the same thing," he said, frustrated that what he understood so clearly in his head wasn't coming out the way he wanted it to. "It's about taking risks. I want to take risks again. I used to, before any of my pictures made money, before the Oscar and the fifty-million-dollar opening weekends. I used to *care* about the movies. I used to care about something."

"And you don't care about anything now?" Ty asked him.

"Yes," Reid said. "I care about you. I care about us. And that makes mc want to care about movies again."

Neither of them said anything for some time. Reid watched Ty's face, looking for any indication of what he was thinking. Ty's own gaze traveled around the room, as if his thoughts were flying like birds from the dresser to the windowsill and back again and he were trying to follow them with his eyes. There was no way of telling what he was thinking, and that, more than his silence, worried Reid. Had he said too much? He forgot sometimes how young Ty was. Did Ty think his remarks were simply the ramblings of an old man jaded by too many years in Hollywood?

"So, you love me?" Ty said finally.

"What?" Reid replied, surprised by the unexpected question.

"You said you love me," Ty repeated, turning to face Reid across the bed. "Did you mean it?"

Reid nervously fingered the sheet that covered his lower body. He was suddenly very conscious of the fact that he was naked. "Yes," he said. "That's what I said."

"Say it again," Ty told him.

Reid, who had been looking down at the lump made by his feet under the sheet, looked up into Ty's face. No, he wasn't laughing. There was no hint of sarcasm in his expression. He was simply watching Reid intently.

"I love you," Reid said haltingly.

Ty cocked his head to one side and smiled crookedly. "Thank you," he said. He leaned across the bed and kissed Reid gently. "And the same goes for me."

Did he just say he loves me? Reid wondered as Ty kissed him again. Ty hadn't actually uttered the words, but he'd implied them. Although he would have preferred to have Ty's feelings expressed more concretely, he could settle for that. After all, actors were really only good at speaking when it was someone else's words they were saying.

"Now what's this wonderful movie idea you have?" Ty asked as they parted from their kiss.

"I don't know yet," Reid said. "I just know I want my next project to be something totally new, something that I can really get into. And I want you to be in it."

"You get the script and I'll do it," Ty replied. "Really," he added after Reid fixed him with a questioning look. "I think you're right. I think it would be great to do something totally different from all the crap out there."

"What if it's gay?" Reid asked.

Ty shrugged. "What if it is?"

"Would you do it? Would you let people see you kissing another guy, for instance?"

"Sure," Ty answered immediately.

"And what about when the *Advocate* interviews you and asks you where your motivation for that kiss came from?" Reid asked.

Ty grinned. "I'd tell them my producer made me do it," he said.

"I mean it, Ty," said Reid. "Are you really ready for what us being together could mean? You haven't even told Pamela that you're gay."

"Pamela will be fine," Ty said. "As long as she gets her fifteen percent she's happy."

Reid wasn't as confident as Ty seemed to be about his agent's possible reaction to the news that her hottest client might one day come bursting out of the closet. Like most people in Hollywood, Pamela Hinkle was tolerant as long as it didn't affect her personally. But he kept his fears to himself. He was too happy about Ty's initial reaction to let something that *might* happen later ruin the moment. Besides, they had time to work out the details. Now that he knew where Ty stood, he was in no hurry to rush things.

"I'm going to take a shower," Ty said, standing up so that the sheet slipped away and he stood before Reid naked. "Want to join me?"

"You go ahead," Reid said, resisting the urge to pull Ty down on top of him. "I'm going to go get breakfast started."

Ty padded off to the bathroom, shutting the door behind him. Reid slipped into a bathrobe and went downstairs to the kitchen. Dirty dishes were piled on the counter, and a pot of now-dried pasta sat on the stove. He ignored the mess, opening one of the cabinets and looking for the coffee.

Once he had the coffeemaker going he turned his attention to the refrigerator, pulling out eggs, a green pepper, mushrooms, and some cheddar cheese. He was about to attempt his first omelette. *How difficult can it be?* he told himself. After all, the people who ran craft services on his sets made two dozen of the things every morning.

Halfway through cutting up the pepper, he decided that maybe it *was* harder than it looked. He'd turned the pepper into smaller pieces, all right, but his chunks were hardly uniform. He fared even worse with the mushrooms, not knowing whether to remove the stems or not.

At least I can do cheese, he consoled himself. That at least looked the way he supposed it should. Now all he had to do was mix it all together with the eggs and throw it into a pan. Once it was all in there it wouldn't matter what the peppers and mushrooms looked like anyway.

He was almost done with the cheese when a buzzing sound startled him. For a moment he thought that some large insect had gotten into the house. Then, when the sound came again, he realized that it was the front doorbell. Someone was ringing it.

But no one knows we're here, he thought as he wiped his hands on a towel and walked to the door. Surely Ty hadn't revealed his whereabouts to anyone. Other than the two of them, the only person who knew where they were was Violet. Since Reid was pretty sure he wouldn't find her standing outside his door, he was puzzled. It must be someone looking for another house, he decided. After all, a lot of them did look alike.

When he opened the door he saw a young woman standing there. She was dressed in jeans and a T-shirt. Her blond hair was pulled back into a ponytail, and thick streaks of blue powder shaded her eyes. By her side was a bucket filled with cleaning products and brushes.

"Are you Mr. Truman?" the girl asked brightly, her jaw working over-time as she chewed the gum in her mouth.

"Yes," Reid said, still confused. "Who are you?"

"I'm from Swept Away Cleaning Service," she said. "I have you down for eleven."

"On a Sunday?" Reid asked. "Who works on Sunday?"

The girl slapped a hand to her forehead. "Oh, shit," she said. "I did it again." She grimaced. "I am so sorry. I thought it was Monday. I do this all the time. I'm really sorry."

The girl fumbled with her bucket, knocking it over. The brushes and bottles scattered on the ground, and she knelt to pick them up. "Sorry," she said again. "I'm such an idiot."

"It's okay," Reid said, kneeling down to help her pick up the mess.

The girl smiled at him. "Thanks," she said. "And please don't tell Jack I came on the wrong day, okay? He'd be really pissed. This is all my fault anyway, not his."

"Really, it's okay," Reid said. The poor girl seemed totally undone by her error, and while he couldn't understand how she could possibly have mistaken Sunday for Monday, he didn't want to make her feel any worse than she already did.

"What are you doing, lover man, bringing in the Sunday paper?"

Reid turned to see Ty standing coming toward him, wearing only a towel wrapped around his waist. He apparently hadn't heard Reid talk-ing to the girl, and thought they were alone. Reid began to motion for him to get back inside, but it was too late. He was at the door.

"Oh, hi," he said when he saw the girl kneeling in front of Reid, still trying to push her supplies back into her bucket.

The girl looked up. For a moment Reid thought he saw a look of surprise cross her face, but then it was gone. "Hi," she said. "Look, I'm really sorry about interrupting your morning. I'll just go."

Reid put the last of the bottles into the bucket and handed it to the girl. "No problem," he said.

"I'll come back on the right day," said the girl. She gave a final wave and turned around, walking away quickly.

Reid went into the house and shut the door. "That was close," he said. "But I don't think she recognized you. For Christ's sake, she didn't even know what day it was."

Ty put his hands on Reid's waist and pulled him close. "Who cares if she did?" he said. "We're risk takers now, remember?"

Reid laughed. "Touché," he said. "All the same, I think it's best if people don't know you're here."

"Fair enough," Ty replied. "Now where's my breakfast?"

"Coming right up," Reid answered. "I was just getting to it."

"Well, hurry up," Ty said. "Otherwise I'll have to tell Letterman that you're a great lay but a lousy cook."

CHAPTER 16

"Long night?"

Josh looked up from his seat on the front porch of the guest cottage. Reilly was standing in front of him, two cups of coffee in his hands.

"Too many beers," Josh answered. "And not nearly enough sleep." One of the more unusual discoveries he'd made since arriving was that he could no longer sleep beyond dawn. It was as if the sun demanded that he be awake each morning to witness what new colors it could coax from the sky as it rose.

Reilly laughed. "Then you really do need this," he said, handing Josh one of the coffees. "It's not Starbucks, but it will wake you up."

"Thanks," Josh said as Reilly sat beside him. "How was your Memorial Day?"

"Well, I spent it with my parents and my future in-laws talking about who's going to sit where at the reception," answered Reilly.

Josh, slightly revived by his first hit of caffeine, nodded sympathetically. "I had to spend the day with a bunch of queens talking about their tans, their personal trainers, and their Botox injections."

"Ooh," said Reilly, grimacing. "I'm not sure which is worse."

"That depends," Josh answered. "Are you looking forward to this wedding?"

"Sure," Reilly said instantly. "I can't wait."

"Then my day was worse," Josh said. "Because I in no way am looking forward to a lifetime of bitterness about the lines under my eyes."

Reilly nodded. "That's one thing I don't get," he said. "About gay guys, I mean. Why are they so obsessed with getting older?"

"Because they think no one will want to sleep with them," Josh told him. "And thank you for saying 'they' instead of 'you,' by the way."

Reilly looked at him as if he wasn't sure if Josh was joking or not.

"I'm serious," Josh said, noticing Reilly's skeptical expression. "When's the last time you saw an overweight, wrinkled, balding fifty-five-year-old in a Calvin Klein underwear ad?"

Reilly shrugged. "I guess I just never thought about it before," he said. "I think people look better as they get older. You know, they have more character."

"What about your girlfriend?" Josh asked him. "Will you still be all hot for her when everything that's perky now is sagging?"

"Sure," Reilly replied. "Why not? I'll probably be sagging too. Besides, by that time we'll have been together so long that I'll love her for a whole lot of other reasons that have nothing to do with how she looks."

Josh sipped his coffee. "You're abnormal," he said.

Reilly looked at him, confused.

"In a good way," Josh clarified. "Most men don't think that way. Especially gay men. They just want young and beautiful."

"Do you?" asked Reilly.

Josh swirled coffee around in his mouth for a moment before answering, letting the sweetness of the sugar and cream that clouded it soak into his tongue. "I like to think I'm not that shallow," he said after swallowing. "Don't get me wrong, I have particular things I find physically attractive in a guy. But I think I'm realistic about it. What I don't understand are these guys who won't even consider dating someone who doesn't have perfect abs, perfect teeth, and a perfect dick. Usually they don't have perfect everything themselves, yet they'll reject a totally nice guy because he doesn't meet their physical standards."

"The Julia Roberts syndrome," Reilly said.

"The what?" asked Josh.

"Sorry," Reilly answered. "It's something Donna and her friends came up with to explain why most of them couldn't find boyfriends. They decided that guys are always afraid that if they settle down with someone, the very next day they'll meet Julia Roberts at the gym or on a bus or whatever and she'll fall for them. Only they won't be able to go out with her because they're already with someone else."

"That's brilliant," Josh remarked. "But what about you? You aren't waiting around for Julia Roberts?"

"Please," Reilly said. "She has a face like a horse."

Josh laughed. He was a little surprised he was having such a conversation with a straight guy, but he was glad he was. In the eleven days that he'd been staying in the guest house, he and Reilly had become friends. Since Reilly was around so much working on the house, they'd naturally fallen into occasional discussions. Now Josh looked forward to the days when Reilly was there. It made him feel as if he had another friend in a town of mostly strangers.

"Did your friends head back to the city?" Reilly inquired.

"Ryan did," said Josh. "The rest of them will be here on and off all summer. I don't think I'll be spending too much time with them, though. They're a little much right now."

"I take it that means you're staying then," Reilly said.

Josh nodded. "Yeah," he said. "I am. At least for a while."

"Mind if I ask what made you change your mind?" asked Reilly.

"Actually, you did," Josh said thoughtfully.

"Me?" said Reilly, surprised.

"It was something you said the other day," Josh explained. "Remember when we were talking about why you became a carpenter?"

Reilly nodded. "Yeah," he said. "I told you that my family was dead set against it, but that I knew if I didn't give it a shot I would always regret it."

"That got me thinking," said Josh. "All my life I've said that I want to write a novel. But there's always been some reason why I couldn't. First I was too busy with school, then I was too busy with work, and then I was too busy doing things with Doug. I kept waiting for the perfect moment to arrive so I could sit down and write."

"Your own Julia Roberts moment," Reilly joked.

"Exactly," said Josh. "Well, there never is going to be that perfect moment. If I'm going to do this, I just have to do it. So I'm staying."

"You're staying to write a book?" Reilly asked.

"Why not?" said Josh. "Here I am with a great place to live and absolutely nothing else to do. What better time is there?"

"What about your work?" Reilly asked.

"I only have a couple of really important gigs going right now," Josh said. "They won't take much time."

"And what about your other little issue?" continued Reilly.

"I'm not ready to go back," answered Josh. To his surprise, he'd found himself telling Reilly about Doug during one of their talks. Even more surprising, Reilly hadn't seemed put off by hearing the details of a troubled gay relationship. He'd listened politely, nodding on occasion and saying, "That sounds rough," when Josh was finished.

"And you're sure you're not using this book thing as a way of avoiding dealing with it?" he suggested now.

"Hey, what happened to not wanting any regrets later in life?" Josh asked sharply.

Reilly held up his hands. "I'm just asking," he said. "I think it's great that you're staying, if that's what you want to do."

"It is," Josh said firmly. "I'm going up to the Arts House later today to talk to them. They have some writing programs going on."

"That's a good place," Reilly remarked. "I built some cabinets for them last summer. You should talk to Marly Prentis. She runs the programs. Great lady. Tell her you're a friend of mine."

"I will," said Josh. "So, you don't think I'm nuts for doing this?"

Reilly drained his coffee cup. "It doesn't matter what I think," he said, standing up. "I'm just the guy who builds stuff around here. But if it's worth anything, it will be nice to have you around a little longer."

"Good save," Josh said. "And thanks for the coffee. If I can manage to stand up I'm going to go take a shower and do something productive."

"Here," Reilly said, extending his hand. "I'll get you started."

Josh accepted the help, and Reilly pulled him up from the porch edge. Josh rose and, unsteadied by the strength of Reilly's assistance, was thrown slightly off balance. He ended up falling toward Reilly, who caught him in his arms and steadied him. For a moment they were face-to-face, and for a brief instant Josh had the confusing thought that perhaps Reilly was about to kiss him. Then it was over, and he was standing on his own again.

"You did have a few too many last night," Reilly said. "You sure taking a shower by yourself is a good idea? I wouldn't want you to get hurt."

Josh looked at him for a moment. *What did he mean by that?* he wondered. Was Reilly coming on to him? He drove the thought from his mind. Of course he wasn't. He was just making a joke. *You've seen too many bad porn films,* he chided himself.

"I'll be okay," he said. "I just need another one of these." He held up his empty coffee cup.

"Okay, then," said Reilly. "I'll see you later."

"Yeah," replied Josh. "See you."

Reilly walked to the rear of the cottage, leaving Josh alone. Josh went inside, shutting the door behind him. He still felt a little unsettled. But why? Nothing had happened. Reilly had simply helped him up. Then why did he feel so embarrassed?

Because you liked being in his arms. The realization came to him suddenly, like remembering the name of a song he'd heard someone else humming but couldn't immediately identify.

Instantly he was angry at himself. Yes, Reilly was attractive. But how pathetic was it, the gay guy having the hots for the humpy handyman. *The next thing you know, you'll be asking him in for a beer so you can get him drunk,* he thought. Okay, he'd jerked off thinking about sex with Reilly. But that had been before he'd gotten to know him. Now it just seemed creepy.

Still, he couldn't deny that when Reilly had been touching him he'd hoped, at least for that moment, that something more might happen.

"Well, it won't," he said out loud. "So get over it."

Besides, he had more pressing things to deal with than his schoolboy crush on Reilly. He'd decided to extend his stay in Provincetown, but he hadn't yet told Doug about it. Although he was still very much irritated at his lover, he knew he owed it to him to explain what he was doing.

He didn't want to make the call. The last contact he'd had with Doug had been a message left on the answering machine when he'd known Doug would be at work and he wouldn't have to talk to him directly. All he'd said was that he was okay and that he'd call in a few days.

He knew he couldn't resort to the answering machine this time. He had to speak to Doug. But he could at least call him at his office, where he would be less inclined to get into any kind of argument. He dialed Doug's number at work and waited for him to pick up. Part of him hoped he'd get Doug's voice mail.

He didn't. Doug picked up after only one ring, surprising Josh with his efficiency so that Josh was momentarily tongue-tied.

"Oh, you're there," he said after Doug had said, "Douglas Stinson," two times.

"You just caught me," Doug replied, his voice neutral. "I have a meeting in five."

"I'm sorry," said Josh instinctively. "I didn't mean to bother you."

Doug gave a short laugh. "That's a little ironic, don't you think?" he said.

"I guess it is," Josh said. "Look, here's the deal. I'm going to stay here for a while."

"Can I at least ask where here is?" asked Doug.

Josh hesitated. Should he tell Doug where he was? He kind of liked the idea of remaining mysterious, but he also knew that was a childish tactic, one he was using to try to provoke Doug into being more upset about their situation than he seemed to be.

"I'm in Provincetown," he said. "I'm staying with some friends."

Doug laughed again. "More irony," he said.

"What do you mean?" snapped Josh. He didn't like the way Doug was treating everything he said as if it were a joke.

"How many times did I try to get you to go to P-Town for a weekend?" asked Doug. "A dozen? Two dozen? Now you finally go, and it's to get away from me."

Then maybe you shouldn't have fucked someone else, Josh wanted to yell into the phone. But he restrained himself. At least Doug was finally having some kind of reaction to his leaving, even if it was to point out one of the few things they'd argued about during their relationship.

"So how long are you staying there?" Doug asked him.

"I'm not sure," Josh told him. "Two weeks. Maybe three." He didn't tell Doug that he was thinking of taking a writing class, and that he didn't know how long they lasted. He knew that would sound cold, and he really didn't want to argue. Not now.

"You'll need some clothes," Doug said. "You didn't take much with you, right?"

"I have enough," Josh lied. The truth was, he was getting tired of wearing the same handful of shirts. Again, though, he wanted to appear self-reliant. He didn't want Doug to think he needed anything from him.

"Do you want to talk about this yet?" Doug continued.

"What, now that you have like two minutes before your meeting?" Josh answered.

"The meeting can wait," Doug told him. "This is more important."

It was what Josh had been waiting to hear from him since their first phone call. But now that Doug had said it, Josh felt the anger inside himself coming out. *Why did it take you so long?* he wanted to scream into the phone. *Why couldn't you have said that eleven days ago?* If he was so important to Doug—if their relationship was so important—why hadn't he done more to save it?

"What's there to talk about?" he said finally, his voice tight with rage. "You slept with someone else. Now I have to decide what to do about it. I'll let you know when I make up my mind."

He hung up, both satisfied and ashamed. He'd said that to make Doug feel bad. But Doug was right. They *should* talk about what happened. Still, why should it be on *his* terms? Josh had a right to be angry. *Or are you just hoping this will force him to try harder?* he asked himself.

"Oh, shut up," he said irritably, and went to take a shower.

CHAPTER 17

Ty Rusk. *Ty Rusk*. Devin still couldn't believe it. At first she'd thought that perhaps she'd been mistaken, that the half-naked guy standing in the doorway had simply been someone who resembled the star. But no, it really had been Ty. She was sure of it. She'd know that face anywhere. After all, he was only on the cover of every magazine around. Besides, she'd seen the small mole on his neck, the one she always noticed in his photos. She found it sexy.

Who would have thought he was a fag? she mused as she twirled the blond wig she'd just taken off around on her finger. There were a lot of men in Hollywood she could imagine sucking cock. Tobey Maguire, for instance. She'd always thought he seemed like he would be good at taking it in the can. She could even see a macho dude like Bruce Willis having an itch for some man-on-man action every once in a while. But Ty Rusk? It had never even crossed her mind. It wasn't that he was so butch or anything, it was just that he seemed so, well, normal. Unlike a lot of celebrities, he didn't come across as having anything to hide.

"Oh, but he does," she said, laughing happily at her good luck. Christ, he'd called Reid Truman "lover man." Devin shuddered. Reid wasn't bad looking, at least for an older guy. But him and Ty together? She didn't even want to picture it. What could Ty possibly see in him?

Maybe he pays him, she thought suddenly. That would make sense. Not that Ty could possibly need the money. She'd just read that he was one of the highest-paid young stars out there. Still, maybe he got off on having someone pay to sleep with him. She'd heard weirder stories. Or, more likely, his pay wasn't in the form of cash but in bigger, more important, roles. Money, she knew, was the least of the currencies available to people with power.

Not that it really mattered. Whether he was gay or just some producer's sex toy for hire, it would be news. And someone would pay for it. That was the kicker to the whole story. She hadn't gone out to the house Truman was renting to see whom he was shacking up with. She'd gone out there to see if she could maybe talk her way into a job. Her plan had been to show up dressed as one of Jack's maids, then charm her way in. The odds of it working had been remote, but how many chances would she ever have to get close to a Hollywood player? It was an opportunity she hadn't been able to pass up. The blond wig and overdone makeup had been last-minute additions, props to help her get into her role as a cleaning woman.

Her act had worked. She hadn't gotten into Reid's house, but she'd struck gold anyway. The question was what to do next. She had some priceless information, and someone would want it. But who? She knew the regular entertainment magazines wouldn't touch a story like this. They'd have too much to lose if they were sued. She had to look lower, and that meant the supermarket tabloids. They didn't care if a story was true or not. If it was, they came out winners. If it wasn't, the worst that could happen was that a star took them to court. Even then, it was the star who came out looking like the bad guy. No matter how innocent a person was, denying a story created an assumption of guilt.

She went downstairs to the kitchen, where her mother was standing in clouds of steam, cooking a batch of her pasta sauce.

"Taste this," Mrs. Lowens said to her daughter as she held out a wooden spoon brimming with marinara.

"No, thanks," replied Devin, looking past her mother to the stack of newspapers and magazines that sat on the dining room table, waiting to be thrown out with the next day's trash. She rifled through the stack, grabbing the occasional paper, and then retreated from the kitchen even as her mother asked for her opinion on what vegetable to have with dinner.

Back in her room she looked at the various magazines she'd snatched from the table. The *Enquirer.* The *Star.* The *Informer.* They all looked the same, with outrageous headlines crowning the most unflattering photos of the stars whose lives they purported to reveal. There was Sarah Jessica Parker, baggy-eyed and haggard, alongside a

banner proclaiming ANOREXIC SEX AND THE CITY STAR'S HUBBY SAYS "YOU'RE
TOO SKINNY TO MAKE LOVE TO." Conversely, Liz Taylor graced the cover of
a different rag, her bloated face plastered in clownlike makeup as the
headline disclosed LIZZY IN A TIZZY AFTER DRUNKEN PLASTIC SURGEON TURNS
HER INTO MONSTER.

But by far her favorite had to belong to the *Weekly World News*'s
Bat Boy. BAT BOY REVEALED TO BE SON OF JFK! exclaimed the cover, which
sported an ingeniously engineered photograph in which a pointy-eared
Bat Boy was shown cradled in the arms of a smiling papa Kennedy. As
if the photo weren't sufficient proof, an additional tagline added DNA
TAKEN FROM JFK JR.'S CORPSE PROVES THEY'RE BROTHERS! OVERJOYED CAROLINE
SAYS, "I HAVE A FAMILY AGAIN."

She flipped through each magazine. Every one of them contained
stories about celebrities, but mostly they were about who'd had breast
enlargements, who had an eating disorder, and who had checked in or
out of rehab. Probably any one of them would be interested in a story
about Ty Rusk being queer, but she wanted to maximize her payout.
What she needed was someone who could take her information and
really do something with it.

She opened the last of the magazines. Like the others, the *Weekly
Insider* boasted of inside scoops and celebrity dish: JEAN CLAUDE VAN
DAMME AND OLSEN TWINS IN X-RATED LOVE TRIANGLE, proclaimed their lead article. She was about to toss it into the reject pile when she turned the
page and saw a column called "Hollywood Hush-Hush." The name intrigued her, as did the subtitle: OUR OWN C.J. RAYMACHER REVEALS THE DEEP-
EST, DARKEST SECRETS OF TINSELTOWN.

A small picture of C.J. Raymacher was placed next to his column. He
was cute, Devin thought. She'd always pictured the writers of tabloid
newspapers to be old men with bad weaves and nothing better to do
than make up stories about Pamela Anderson's tits. But Raymacher
wasn't old. He was probably thirty, she though, with short blond hair
and a sly smile, as if he knew all kinds of things that he would gladly
share, if you would only ask.

She read his column. A lot of it was a rehash of the same stuff she'd
seen in the other papers. But some of it was new, and very interesting.

"What director of Titanic proportions was seen dining out with his
latest leading lady while the star of his last picture (and current wife)
thought he was in the editing room?" she read. "And which recent

Oscar winner for Best Supporting Actress apparently has more than a passing fancy for her golden boy, telling her now ex-fiancé, 'I don't need you in bed. I have him'?"

Oh, please, Devin thought. Still, it was funny. And there was something about C.J. Raymacher that she liked. He was sarcastic, and clearly didn't care if he made enemies of the stars he wrote about. He was, she thought, the sort of person who could help her get what she wanted.

She turned to the front of the paper. There she found the address and phone number for the magazine's headquarters in Los Angeles. Without hesitating, she picked up the phone and dialed.

"Insider," said a voice on the other end.

"C.J. Raymacher, please," said Devin in her crispest, most authoritative voice.

"One moment," the receptionist told her before filling her ear with a tinny Musak version of the Carpenters' "Rainy Days and Mondays."

Mercifully, the song lasted through only half of the chorus before the line was picked up again. "C.J. Raymacher."

"Hi," said Devin. "I have a story for you." She figured the best approach was to just jump in. Hopefully, Raymacher would be intrigued enough to ask her to continue.

"If it's about a certain soap opera star who doesn't want anyone to know his wife is also his cousin, you're too late," responded the columnist. "And please don't tell me you have news about Michael Jackson trying to clone Bubbles, Charlie Sheen setting up a crystal meth lab in his on-set trailer, or Angelina Jolie turning a plaster cast of Billy Bob's wanker into a Christmas tree topper."

"Better," said Devin.

"I'm listening," Raymacher said. "You have thirty seconds. Then I'm going to lunch."

"What if I told you that one of the hottest stars around right now is in the closet?" Devin teased.

"I'm hanging up," answered Raymacher, sounding irritated.

"What if I told you it was Ty Rusk?" Devin blurted out, momentarily losing her cool as she feared Raymacher would make good on his promise.

"Who is this?" Raymacher asked after hesitating a moment.

I've got him, thought Devin, grinning to herself. "Let's just say I'm someone who knows things she shouldn't," she said.

"And what makes you think Rusk is gay?" Raymacher continued.

"I happen to know where he and his boyfriend are staying right now," replied Devin vaguely. She didn't want to give Raymacher too much information, or he wouldn't need her.

"This boyfriend," Raymacher said. "It wouldn't be a big-shot Hollywood producer, would it?"

Devin's heart sank. Did Raymacher already know about Ty and Reid Truman? Was he just trying to figure out how much *she* knew about it? She wasn't sure how to answer him.

"Maybe," she said finally. "I'm not exactly sure who he is. But I saw them kissing." She threw in the little lie to keep Raymacher hooked, suspecting that if she didn't give him more than she really had he would just brush her off.

"Pictures?"

"Excuse me?" said Devin.

"Pictures," repeated Raymacher. "Do you have pictures?"

"No," admitted Devin.

"Look," Raymacher told her, "I get calls from people like you all the time. I don't know who you are or what you might or might not really know, but I can't do anything with this. Thanks anyway."

"You didn't let me finish," said Devin quickly. "I said I didn't have any photos, not that I couldn't get any."

Raymacher sighed. "Don't fuck with me," he said. "Do you know how big Ty Rusk is right now? Do you know how many calls I get every day from people who claim to have something on him? Just this morning some girl called saying she was pregnant with his baby. Last week his high school algebra teacher called saying he had proof that Rusk cheated on his SATs. Everybody thinks they have a story. And you know what, so far every single one of them has turned out to be total bullshit. So stop wasting my time."

"Reid Truman," said Devin.

"What?" asked Raymacher.

"You asked me who Rusk's boyfriend was," said Devin. "It's Reid Truman."

"I thought you said you didn't know who he was?" Raymacher said warily.

"Well, I do," Devin retorted. "I'm not stupid. I know when to keep an ace up my sleeve."

"Well, you played it at the right time," said Raymacher, sounding impressed. "I'd written you off as just another crazy trying to get some attention."

"I'm not crazy," Devin assured him. "And I know it's Reid Truman."

"That makes things a little more interesting," Raymacher said, sounding incredibly pleased with himself. "*That* I can maybe do something with. But I still need more proof."

"I can get it," said Devin confidently. "It will take a little time, but I can do it."

"Who are you again?" Raymacher asked her.

"Just a girl who doesn't want to be stuck in a small town for the rest of her life," Devin replied. "I don't care if Ty Rusk fucks sheep, but I know a good story when I see one."

"And just what do you want to get out of this?" continued Raymacher.

"What can you offer?" Devin asked him.

"Five hundred bucks a photo," replied Raymacher. "A thousand if you can get them nude."

Devin laughed. "The *Enquirer* offered twenty-five hundred each," she said, bluffing.

"All right," said Raymacher, clearly annoyed at being outbid. "Three thousand a photo *if* they're good ones."

"I want more," Devin said.

"That's as high as I go," Raymacher answered.

"Not money," said Devin. "I'll get you photos *and* I'll get you a story. But I want something from you."

"And that would be?" asked Raymacher.

"Introductions," she said. "I told you, I don't plan on being a small-town girl the rest of my life. I want out of here. So if I give you the story of the year, I want you to help me get a job out there. TV. Movies. PR. I don't care what it is. I just want in."

To her surprise, Raymacher laughed. "You're a regular little Eve Harrington," he said when he was done. "Sadly, you remind me a lot of myself a few years back. Tell you what, you get me a story and photos that prove Ty Rusk and Reid Truman are an item and I'll introduce you to whoever you want."

"How do I know I can trust you?" Devin asked him.

"How do I know I can trust *you?*" shot back Raymacher. "I can't," he continued, answering his own question. "And you don't know that you can trust me. But if either of us is going to get what we want, we're both going to have to take that chance."

Devin thought for a moment. He was right. Besides, what else was she going to do with the information? She supposed she could try to blackmail Ty and Reid, but that seemed too dangerous. If she got caught, she would be in a lot of trouble. This way she was just providing information. What Raymacher did with it was his business.

"Okay," she said. "It's a deal."

"Good," said Raymacher. "When do you think you can have something to me?"

"It's going to take a while," Devin told him. "If I'm going to get anything really good, I have to get closer to them."

"And you think you can do that?" asked Raymacher.

"No problem," Devin assured him.

"Call me when you have something concrete," said Raymacher.

"You'll be hearing from me," Devin told him, and hung up.

She picked up the copy of the *Weekly Insider* and looked at C.J. Raymacher's photo. "I think you and I arc going to be *very* good friends," she said. "And I think this is going to be a great summer."

CHAPTER 18

Marly Prentis hated poets. She also hated dancers, spoken-word performers, abstract artists, novelists obsessed with their alcoholic parents and/or bisexuality, science fiction writers, and people who made things out of found objects. But she particularly hated poets. For one thing, they were moody. And they always seemed to be vegans, even the men. Also, they were allergic to everything. The one on the phone at the moment had adverse reactions to dust, wheat, animal dander, sulfites, plastics, grass, synthetic fibers, most cleaning products, artificial sweeteners, paint, paprika, and any shampoo that contained papaya extracts.

"Oh, and latex condoms," he added, giving a little laugh.

That was another thing she hated about poets—they were always horny. *Probably because no one in their right mind would sleep with a poet,* she thought wearily.

"Okay then," she said chirpily. "I think I've got everything. We'll see you on Friday."

She hung up, crumpled up the paper she'd been writing on, and dropped the poet's list into the trash. He was going to complain anyway, so why bother?

After seven years as the director of the Arts House, she knew the routine. Every summer they invited a dozen artists from various fields to the center for summer artist-in-residence appointments. Theoretically, the invitees represented the best in their genres. The Arts House provided them with small cottages to live in, three meals a day, and the opportunity to feel more important than most of them really were. In exchange, they taught classes and workshops, for which the Arts House charged students more than they should and thus raised the money to pay their guests.

It was a perfect system. The students were happy to be able to spend time with people they admired and thought could teach them something, the artists were happy to have adoring audiences and more food than most of them ever saw at home, and the Arts House was happy because they continued to thrive as a popular benefactor of the creative community. Year after year, books, plays, dances, and art-works of every shape, size, and design were created "with thanks to the generous support of the Arts House, Provincetown, MA." Marly herself had been listed on the acknowledgments pages of more novels and programs than she could remember.

The only one who wasn't happy about the system was Marly. She had been happy about it once, when she'd first come to Provincetown fresh off a three-year stint as the assistant director of the Glimmerglass Opera House in Cooperstown, New York. She'd been twenty-nine then, just on the cusp of the milestone she'd always thought thirty would be. She'd had a husband, a two-year-old daughter, and all the enthusiasm in the world.

Now, seven years later, she had a twelve-year-old marriage, a nine-year-old daughter, and a throbbing headache. She still liked her job, at least on some days, but frankly the artists were starting to get on her nerves. She'd endured one too many requests for soy lattes, more than enough complaints about the draftiness of the beach cottages in which residents were housed, and if she had to listen to one more weepy creative-type boo-hoo over a failed relationship she was going to drop dead on the spot. She'd taken the job because of her commit-ment to providing opportunities and support for established artists and to helping new artists get started. But somewhere along the line it had all become tiresome.

Not that there weren't bright spots. She was excited, for instance, about the imminent arrival of Brody Nicholson. She'd loved his work since discovering his first collection of short stories, *After Twilight,* when another visiting artist (a choreographer with bad breath and a seemingly unquenchable desire for cherry yogurt, as she recalled) left it behind in her cottage one summer. Since then Nicholson had pub-lished two novels, *The Tin Box* and *Made by Hand,* to glowing critical reviews, if not commercial success. Marly had offered him a residency three years in a row, and three times he had turned her down. This year, however, he had readily accepted. Marly, having steeled herself for yet another rejection, had been so shocked and delighted by the surprise of his announcement—sent via letter—that he would be happy to come that she hadn't had time to wonder what might have caused him to change his mind.

There were others she was pleased to have with them for the summer as well. Nellie Sa, for example, a video artist whose specialty was convincing people to dress up as the children they wished they'd been, and the composer Randi Colburn, whose work blended traditional African rhythms with the music of the Appalachian Mountains that Colburn called home. Surely Colburn, Sa, and Nicholson would make up for the fact that she would have to endure three months with the likes of Perry Lawrence, the poet who had earlier presented her with his endless list of demands, which included wanting only blue linens on his bed, chamomile soap in his bathroom, and white, not red, grapes on his table.

Then there were the unknown quantities, the names Marly recognized but about whom she knew very little. There were always a handful of these among the invited, generally people who had been recommended by friends or thrust upon her by insistent board members, and they were the ones with the power to make her summer either a good one or a living hell. This year's list of potential spoilers included Rebecca Wilmont, whose memoir about her life among a small religious sect in West Virginia who used bee venom to induce religious ecstasy had gotten her a full page in the *Times* and a National Book Award nomination; Parker Ashbury, a thin, pale girl whose Martha Graham–inspired dances involved the performers undulating beneath red silk sheets and were meant to reflect either the pain of female adolescence or the ongoing war in the Middle East (Marly couldn't remember which); and the singer/songwriter Taney Fuller, whose album *Spirit Gum* Marly played often while working in her own studio but who she'd heard sometimes drank too much and asked whatever woman was nearby if she would like to jerk him off.

And then there was Garth Ambrose. Of all the summer's resident artists, it was Ambrose she was most unsure of. He was a photographer, which in itself was fine. Photographers were generally fairly low-maintenance. But Ambrose wasn't just a photographer, he was a rock-and-roll photographer. She'd seen his pictures first in a copy of *Spin* magazine that Chloe, her daughter, had left lying on her bedroom floor. Marly had opened it to a page featuring a picture of Alanis Morissette, and had been fascinated by the way Ambrose had managed to capture the singer's peculiar combination of beyond-her-years wisdom and childlike sense of wonder.

She'd then looked for more of his work, finding it in many different pop culture periodicals. Unlike most of the photographers whose subjects were the rock-and-roll darlings of the moment, Ambrose seemed genuinely interested in documenting the real people behind the music. A photo of veteran Aerosmith rocker Steven Tyler reaching out to an audience filled with teenagers one-fourth his age became a comment on the enduring power of classic rock, while a seemingly candid shot catching bubblegum diva Britney Spears in her dressing room attempting to apply an impossibly long false eyelash revealed both the girl beneath the image and the industry that created stars out of makeup, hairspray, and glitter.

Marly hadn't expected Ambrose to accept. After all, summer was the busiest concert season of the year, and she assumed that he would be on the road documenting the exploits of America's favorite musicians. However, he had welcomed the idea, saying he needed a break from the music world for a few months. He had, he told her, a project he'd been wanting to work on for some time, and would use his time at the Arts House to make some headway on it.

He'd seemed affable enough on the phone, but Marly was still wary. Often the friendliest artists turned out to be the ones with the deepest stores of emotional unwellness, the ones who agreed to everything and then suddenly came unglued over nothing at all, requiring hours of soothing and, on occasion, the application of medical attention. So until she had actually met Mr. Garth Ambrose in person, she wasn't putting any gold stars next to his name.

She turned her attention to the matter of classes. The first ones would begin on Monday, June 2. Most of the artists had arrived already, and the rest would be there by the weekend. They taught in weeklong segments, thereby accommodating students who could only get a week off from work to come to the Arts House. Most of the classes filled up early, but there were always some that seemed to repel students rather than draw them in. Her particular problem this summer was a sculpture class being offered by a man whose claim to fame was having created a twelve-foot replica of the AIDS virus out of used, dried condoms. She'd hoped the controversy surrounding his work would make him a magnet for hopeful sculptors with $450 to spend on a week with him, but so far only six had plunked down checks. Why was it, she wondered, that sculptors were always so poor?

"Excuse me."

Marly looked up. A young man was standing in the doorway of her office, a schedule for the Arts House clutched in his hand.

"Can I help you?" Marly asked him.

"Um, maybe," he answered. "I was wondering if this writing class is full?"

"The one with Brody Nicholson," Marly said, nodding. "It was, but I had a cancellation yesterday. Something about a cat swallowing some Prozac and needing to be in intensive care for a while."

"Poor thing," the man remarked.

"I'm not so sure," Marly told him. "Its owner lives in a lesbian communal household. I think it might have been trying to commit suicide."

The man nodded. "Death by consensus," he said.

Marly looked at him, not quite understanding.

"I'm sorry," said the man. "It's something I came up with once to describe a group of lesbians. You know, like there are herds of buffalo and parliaments of owls. A consensus of lesbians. It's a plural."

Marly laughed loudly.

"Oh, shit," the man said, covering his mouth. "I hope that wasn't offensive or anything. I mean, if you're a dyke . . ."

Marly held up her hand, still laughing. "I'm not," she reassured him. "But even if I were, it would still be hysterical."

The man grinned. "Well, it does sort of fit. So does this mean I can get into the class?"

"Well, technically you were supposed to apply and send in a writing sample for the instructor to judge you on," Marly told him. "But I think a man who came up with a consensus of lesbians will probably be able to hold his own. What's your name?"

"Josh Felling," the man answered. "Joshua, actually, but no one calls me that except my mother."

"Josh it is then," said Marly, adding Josh's name to the list for Nicholson's class. "Now all we need to take care of is the class fee."

Josh gave her his credit card. As she was running it through the machine Marly questioned Josh.

"So you're a writer?"

Josh shrugged. "Technically, yes," he told her. "I write ad copy."

"That's being a writer," Marly said.

"I suppose," replied Josh. "The same way being Adam Sandler is being an actor."

"You mean you want to write a novel," Marly said, smiling at Josh's self-effacing remark.

"I know," Josh told her, sounding embarrassed. "So does everyone else."

"It doesn't matter what everyone else wants," said Marly, handing Josh his credit card slip and a pen. "It matters what you want."

"Right now I just want to see if I can write a book," Josh said as he signed. "I figured this class will give me a little push."

"Have you read Nicholson's books?" asked Marly.

Josh shook his head. "I am a cultural wasteland," he answered. "To be honest, I hadn't even heard of the guy until I picked up your schedule."

"You should get acquainted with him then," said Marly. She turned to the stacks of books sitting on the floor beside her desk and pulled three volumes out. "Here you go," she said as she handed them to Josh. "No charge. I figure I'm going to use your consensus of lesbians line for the rest of my life without attribution, so consider this your royalty payment."

"Thanks," Josh said. "Now at least I won't be completely in the dark on Monday. What's your name, by the way?"

"Marly Prentis."

"It's nice to meet you," Josh said. "I guess I'll see you around."

"Probably," Marly told him. "I run the place."

"Great job," Josh commented.

Marly nodded. "Most of the time," she said, wishing she were really as convinced of that as she sounded.

"Well, I'll let you get back to work," said Josh. "Bye."

Marly waved farewell as Josh left. He seemed like a nice guy, she thought. Of course, the writing classes at the Arts House were filled with nice guys—and nice girls—who all wanted to be the next Andrew Hollerans and Dorothy Allisons. Probably he'd end up like most of them, stuck on page 120 and facing a cast of characters he'd come to despise. But that wasn't her problem.

Her phone rang and she picked it up.

"Hey, hon." It was Drew, her husband.

"Hey," she said back. "What's going on?"

"Not much," he told her. "I just wanted to let you know that I'm going to have to be in New York all next week."

Marly was used to such announcements from Drew. Her husband was a financial planner. His clients included many wealthy people, and he was frequently away in one city or another, having meetings to discuss stocks and long-term goals and other monetary matters that Marly found incomprehensible but which she appreciated because her husband's knowledge of them allowed them to live in Provincetown during the summers and then, when it got colder, in their brownstone on Boston's Beacon Hill.

Only lately Marly had been spending more and more time in Provincetown, first extending her stay into the previous fall for a month after Drew and Chloe returned to Boston for the start of the new school year, then, that spring, beginning it a month before Memorial Day. While Chloe had been unhappy at losing her mother for those weeks, Drew had seemed perfectly content with the situation. So had Marly, and that troubled her.

"Okay," she told her husband. "We'll have girls' week."

Drew laughed. "Just don't let Chloe guilt you into that piercing she wants," he said.

After a few more minutes of conversation, Marly hung up. She loved Drew. But more and more she felt as if something was missing from her life. It wasn't that they fought, or even that she wasn't attracted to him anymore. She was. But something about her life, like her job, wasn't giving her the satisfaction that it once had.

Maybe you need to have an affair, she told herself. She laughed at the idea. She was four years away from the midlife crisis she'd been planning since she was twenty. She'd always assumed that when she hit forty she would do something drastic, perhaps run away to Italy for a few months or maybe learn how to ski or scuba dive. Just a little something to make herself feel alive.

But four years was a long time to wait, she realized. She needed something now. The question was what.

"Marly Prentis?"

Two visitors in one morning, Marly thought. *It must be my lucky day.* "Yes," she said. "Can I help you?"

Her newest visitor was holding several bags, which he set down.

"I'm Garth Ambrose," he said, stepping forward and offering her his hand.

"Oh," Marly exclaimed. She hadn't been expecting him until Thursday. "Nice to meet you."

"I know I'm early," Garth said. "But I was in New York shooting Pink for *Rolling Stone* and finished early, so instead of flying home and then back again I thought I'd come up and hang out for a few days."

"That's fine," Marly told him. She couldn't help staring at Garth Ambrose. He wasn't at all what she'd expected. She'd pictured a twenty-something kid with lots of tattoos and a shaved head. Instead what she saw in front of her was a fortyish man in khakis and a green plaid shirt, whose eyes sported lines at the corners and whose brown hair was rapidly going gray. *He looks like a schoolteacher,* she thought. For some reason, the idea delighted her. It was an unexpected contrast: the rock photographer who looked like he could just as easily be walking the dog or taking the kids to the park.

"Is something wrong?" Garth asked her.

Marly realized that she'd been staring. "No," she said quickly. "Not at all. Have you had lunch?"

Garth shook his head. "Not yet," he said. "I just got in."

"Good," Marly said. "I'll take you. Then I'll show you where you'll be staying."

She picked up her keys and her purse and prepared to go. As she led Garth Ambrose out of her office she thought maybe the summer wouldn't be as bad as she'd feared. *This one definitely gets a gold star,* she told herself. *Now if I could just get rid of the poet.*

CHAPTER 19

It had been a week of firsts for Toby—his first time running away from home, his first real sex with another guy, his first drag queen. No, he wasn't supposed to call Emmeline a drag queen. She'd given him that lecture during their first breakfast together, right after she'd passed him the syrup for his pancakes and informed him that she wasn't really a woman. Well, not yet, anyway.

He still wasn't really all that clear on the whole thing. When Emmeline had told him that she wasn't entirely the woman he'd taken her for, he'd been surprised. He'd always thought that drag queens were supposed to be sort of scary. The ones he saw on *Jerry Springer* always were. He was always surprised when one of Jerry's guests claimed not to know that the woman he was sleeping with had a dick between her legs. Usually they were so ugly that he couldn't imagine anyone *not* knowing. Yet the men were always shocked.

Emmeline wasn't ugly. She was beautiful. So when she'd first looked Toby in the eye and said, "If you're going to live here, we have to get something straight," he'd had no idea what she was about to tell him. When she'd finished talking, he'd just sat there for a minute, staring at her and wondering if it was all a joke. His response—"You mean like in that movie about the drag queens in Australia?"—had earned him a laugh and then another lecture.

Drag queens. Transvestites. Transsexuals. *Oh, my,* he added, thinking of Dorothy and her friends walking through the forest. Emmeline had carefully explained the differences between them. The nuances of the subject were still a little hazy in his mind, but he thought he understood it a little bit. Drag queens and transvestites were both men who dressed up like women, although for different reasons (Emmeline had deftly glossed over the finer distinctions, not wanting to overwhelm him). Transsexuals were people who were born one gender and were in the process of becoming another. That's where he got confused. From what he could gather, there were no real rules involved. Some transsexuals went all the way, replacing one set of bits with another. Some had only certain areas of their anatomy rearranged, while still others had nothing added or removed but were still considered transgendered simply because they said they were.

Toby couldn't help thinking of Mr. Potato Head. He'd had one as a kid, a gift from his grandmother for his fourth birthday. Mr. Potato Head had come with a wide variety of parts that could be stuck on or pulled off, turning him into any number of different things depending on Toby's mood or the game being played. He understood, of course, that people were slightly more complicated. But somehow thinking of the whole business in terms of little plastic pieces that fit into little holes made it easier for him. Besides, when he thought about it, Mr. Potato Head was always Mr. Potato Head, no matter what nose you stuck on him or which pair of eyes you popped onto his face.

And so Emmeline was Emmeline. He didn't care what she looked like when she took her clothes off. The important thing was that she'd been kind to him. He still couldn't believe his good luck. After the disaster with Aaron, he'd been ready to just get on the first bus back home. But now he had a place to stay.

Even better, he had a job. That was another first. He'd never worked back home, not even over the summers, when his father would load the entire family into the minivan and take off on a long-planned two-week trip to the Grand Canyon, or Six Flags, or perhaps to visit their scattered relatives. They did it every year without fail. The rest of the summer the Evans children spent at the Good News Bible Camp at Lake Muscatooney, where they spent their time swimming, hiking, and learning to love the Lord. It was also where Toby had first discovered the pleasures of touching a dick other than his own, but that had not been one of the camp's planned activities, even though it stood out in his memories as the highlight of his eleven summers there.

So although he had never stood behind the counter at a fast food restaurant wearing a paper crown, thrown newspapers onto front steps early in the morning, or brought diners their meals and asked if there was anything else he could get for them, he was now on his way to his first day of gainful employment. And again it was thanks to Emmeline. A friend of hers was renting his house out to a group of men for the summer, and they needed a houseboy. The one they'd lined up had fallen through for some reason, and they were anxious to find a replacement.

Emmeline had explained his duties to him in detail. He was to straighten up the house, keep the pool clean, do laundry, run any errands the guys needed him to do, and generally make sure the place was kept up. He was *not,* however, required to have sex with anyone. Emmeline had been very firm on that point. "If they try to pull anything, you tell them they'll have to answer to *me,*" she'd said, her hands on her hips.

She'd sounded almost like his mother. But his mother was one thing he did not want to think about. He'd left her and the rest of his family behind when he'd gotten on that bus. He knew they were probably frantic, wondering where he'd gone. Then again, he reminded himself, they'd rejected him for being who he was. Maybe they didn't care where he was.

He pushed the thought out of his mind. He was nearing the house, and he wanted to make a good first impression on his new employers. It wouldn't do to walk in looking depressed. He stopped a few doors down from 138 Myrtlewood Lane and composed himself, much like he used to do before every baseball game he played in. When he was reasonably sure that the smile on his face appeared genuine, he continued on.

His knock on the door was quickly answered by a pleasant-looking blond man dressed in shorts and a New York Gay Men's Chorus T-shirt.

"Hi, I'm Phil," the man said. "You must be Toby."

Toby nodded. "Nice to meet you," he answered, shaking Phil's hand.

"Come on in," Phil told him. "The rest of the boys are anxious to meet you too."

Toby suddenly felt nervous. What if the men didn't like him for some reason? What if they decided he couldn't have the job? Not only would he be out of work, but he'd be embarrassed to tell Emmeline after the trouble she'd gone through to get him work.

"Right in here," Phil said, leading him into the living room, where several men sat talking. When Toby and Phil entered, they stopped and looked up.

"Hi," Toby said cheerfully.

One of the men, a well-built guy wearing a tank top and the smallest bathing suit Toby had ever seen, whistled. "Hi yourself, cutie," he said. Toby felt himself blushing.

"Cut it out, Bart," Phil said. "He's here to work, not to play."

"Yes, but you know what they say about that," replied Bart. "And we don't want Toby here to be a dull boy, now, do we?"

"How old are you, Toby?" Phil asked.

"Eighteen," he answered. "In a week, anyway."

"So you're seventeen," said another man, who then looked at Bart. "That's a little young even for you."

"There's always a first time," Bart said, smiling at Toby and sliding his thumb beneath the waistband of his swimsuit. "You *have* had a first time, haven't you, Toby?"

"And that fellow over there is my lover, Al," Phil informed Toby, nodding at the man who had just spoken to Bart.

Al waved. "Heya," he said.

"And that over there is Eric," continued Phil, indicating a man sitting in a chair beside the couch. "And there's one more of us, but he's out picking up some beer. He should be back in a few minutes. So why don't you sit down and we'll get to know one another?"

"You can sit right next to me," said Bart, patting the empty space beside him on the couch.

"Or you can sit in that chair," suggested Phil. "As far away from that evil queen as you can get."

Toby opted for the chair, sitting down and looking at the four men gathered around him. Apart from Bart, they all seemed really nice and normal. And even Bart wasn't that bad. In fact, now that Toby looked at him, he was sort of attractive.

"We just have a couple of questions," Al said. "For starters, what's a young guy like you doing here for the summer alone?"

"Just hanging out," Toby replied casually. He'd already decided not to tell them too much of his story. "You know, before I start college in the fall." He resorted to the lie he'd begun on the bus ride to Boston, hoping it would work again.

"Where are you going to school?" Eric inquired.

"Boston College," Toby lied.

Eric smiled. "Hey, that's where I went," he said. "And Aaron and I still live in Boston. We can show you around."

"Aaron?" Toby asked.

"My lover," Eric told him.

The front door opened.

"Here he is now," said Eric.

Toby looked up as Aaron walked in, carrying two grocery bags in his arms. For a brief, terrible moment Toby hoped that it was another Aaron. But it wasn't. When Aaron looked over at him and froze, a look of panic on his face, Toby felt his insides knot up.

"Aaron, this is Toby," Eric said, seeming not to notice the tension that had suddenly filled the space between his lover and the young man seated across from him. "He's going to be our houseboy for the summer."

"Oh," Aaron said quietly. "Great."

"Toby was just telling us something about himself," Bart informed Aaron. Then he looked at Toby. "What do you like to do for fun?" he asked.

For a moment Toby didn't answer. He was still stunned by the arrival of Aaron. He was even more stunned by the revelation that Aaron and Eric were lovers. And if Aaron was staying there for the summer, whose house had he taken Toby to on that first night? All kinds of questions swirled around in his head. But they would have to wait. Bart and the others were looking at him, waiting for an answer.

"I play baseball," Toby said, saying the first thing that popped into his mind.

"How perfectly butch," Bart said. "Were you a pitcher or a catcher?"

"Bart," Phil snapped. "Give him a break."

"Second base, actually," Toby said, wondering why Bart cared what position he played, as he didn't seem the sort of guy who was into sports.

"And is that your favorite position?" Bart continued. "Or haven't you tried them all yet?"

"Would you go blow somebody or something?" said Eric. "You're really getting on my nerves."

"Sorry," Bart said, holding up his hands. "I'm just trying to find out what Toby likes."

"I apologize for Bart," Al told Toby. "He's only gotten off three times this morning, so he's a little jumpy."

Toby nodded, unsure of how to respond. The banter between the men was both unsettling and comforting. He knew he was among friends. He just wasn't sure how he fit into the picture. And Aaron was still standing there, holding the bags.

"Why don't you go put those away?" Eric said.

"Right," replied Aaron. "I'll be right back."

He retreated to the kitchen, leaving the others to continue their questioning of Toby.

"You don't do drugs, do you?" Al asked.

Toby shook his head. "No," he said. "I've never even tried them."

"Good," Al said. "We had to can the last houseboy because he got so coked up he set the deck on fire trying to light the barbecue. We don't care what you do when you're not here, but while you're in the house you're clean, okay?"

"Yeah," Toby assured him. "That's fine."

"We're not going to ask you to do anything hard," Phil explained. "Just some straightening up, a little grocery shopping, laundry, and keeping the pool clean. I assume you can do all of that."

"Sure," said Toby confidently. "No problem." Truthfully, he'd never actually cleaned a pool. But how difficult could it be? As for laundry, his mother had always done it, but he was sure it was a piece of cake.

"We won't all be here the entire summer," continued Phil. "Al and I will be here most of the time, but Eric and Aaron will only be up on weekends and occasionally for longer. Bart will come and go. We usually have a couple of parties every summer, and we'll expect you to help out with those. Other than that, it's pretty routine."

"Sounds good to me," Toby told him.

Aaron returned from the kitchen and sat next to Bart on the couch. He was seated directly across from Toby, and Toby had no choice but to look at him. Aaron looked away.

How could he? Toby thought as he looked at Aaron. *How could he lie like that?* He looked over at Eric. He seemed like a really nice guy. And he was handsome, too. Why would Aaron want to sleep with someone else when he had a lover like that? It didn't make any sense.

"You probably want to know something about us."

Toby looked over at Phil, who had just spoken. What had he said?

Toby wasn't sure, so he just nodded, hoping it was an appropriate response.

"Well, Al and I live in New York," Phil said. "I own a coffee shop in Chelsea, and Al works for Barney's."

"It's a clothes store," Bart told Toby when Toby failed to say anything.

"Oh," Toby said vaguely. He'd never heard of Barney's. To him it sounded like one of the many diners that dotted the highways near his hometown.

"Bart works at Barney's too," said Al.

"Only I'm just a lowly buyer," Bart said dramatically. "Men's accessories. Al is one of the corporate suits."

"I'm a lawyer," Al translated for Toby's benefit.

"As you already know, Aaron and Eric live in Boston," continued Phil. "Eric works for the Boston AIDS Foundation, and Aaron does something mysterious involving banking."

"International investments," Aaron said, his voice shaky.

"Do you have any questions for us?" Eric inquired.

Yeah, Toby thought, *do you know your boyfriend fucked me last week?* "Do I have to do any cooking?" he asked. "Because I should tell you that I'm not very good at it." He hadn't planned on mentioning that defect in his repertoire of housekeeping skills, but now he wondered if it might be an easy out. The more he looked at Aaron, the more uncomfortable he became. It was a mixture of anger and the even more disconcerting realization that despite what Aaron had done, he was still attracted to the man. Suddenly he wasn't sure if taking the job was such a good idea after all.

"Don't worry about that," Al told him. "Most of us are pretty handy in the kitchen. The most we'll ask you to do is help chop things up."

"Or marinate our meat," Bart quipped, earning himself a pillow thrown at his head by Phil.

"Oh," said Toby, slightly disappointed that his potential escape from the situation had been so neatly avoided. "Okay."

"Well, then, if that's it, I guess there's nothing left to say but welcome aboard," Phil said. "When can you start?"

"How about now?" said Toby. "Is there anything that needs doing?"

"Besides me?" asked Bart.

"We haven't touched the pool all week," said Al, shooting Bart a warning look. "How about starting there?"

Toby nodded.

"Aaron knows where everything is," Al told him. "He can show you what to do. Okay?"

"Sure," said Aaron. "No problem."

"Okay, then," Al said. "We'll see you later. Phil can make up a list of anything else that needs doing."

The men dispersed, leaving Aaron to show Toby the pool area. When they were outside and alone, he turned to Toby.

"Look," he said, "I hope what happened last week isn't going to be a problem. I'd appreciate it if you didn't mention it to anyone. Especially Eric."

"Just tell me one thing," Toby said. "Why?"

"Why what?" asked Aaron.

"Why did you do it?" Toby clarified. "I mean, you have a great boy-friend. Why did you do that? I thought you liked me."

"I do like you," Aaron replied. "And yeah, I do have a great boyfriend. That's why I'd really appreciate it if you didn't tell anyone about the other night."

"You still didn't tell me why," Toby pressed.

Aaron shrugged. "I was horny," he said. "And you're hot. It's not a big deal."

"Maybe it was a big deal to me," Toby said, getting angry.

"Look," Aaron said, "let's not make a thing out of this. We had some fun. It was one time. No one got hurt, and no one needs to get hurt."

"Whose place was it?" Toby asked. "The place we went to."

"This guy I know," Aaron told him. "He lets me use it sometimes. Why does it matter?"

"You didn't want to bring me here," Toby said. "You didn't want to do it here because this is where you live with Eric, right? How many other guys have you taken there?"

"Look, I don't have to defend myself to you," said Aaron angrily. "You're not my boyfriend. You were just a trick."

Just a trick, Toby thought. *So that's all it was to you. Well, it was a mean trick.*

"I'm sorry," Aaron said, sensing Toby's rising anger. "I know you're young. But you'll understand when you've been around a while. It's nothing personal."

"Right," Toby said tightly. "Nothing personal."

"So we'll keep it between us?" asked Aaron.

Toby nodded. "Sure," he said. "I mean, it was just some fun, right?"

Aaron smiled. He looked relieved. "Great," he said. "Now let me show you where the cleaning stuff is."

As Toby followed Aaron to the shed where the pool supplies were kept, he watched the other man's back. He still found it hard to believe that one night he could be lying in Aaron's arms and a few days later be sweeping dead bugs out of his pool as if nothing had happened.

If this is what it means to be gay, he thought, *maybe my parents were right.*

CHAPTER 20

The book was going surprisingly well. As Josh pecked away at the keys of his laptop, he realized that he hadn't enjoyed writing anything so much since, well, since he'd begun the novel in the first place. When had that been? He thought back. Christ, it was almost seven years now. How could that be right? But it was. He'd begun writing the book after he and Doug had moved in together. Flush with the thrill of love, he'd been determined to channel all of the excess energy he had into creating the Great Gay American Novel. He'd even come up with a schedule: five pages a day for eighty days. He'd figured that was doable for a first draft.

But it hadn't been as easy as he'd thought. The first couple of days were great. He'd come home from work, made dinner for the two of them, and then sat down at his desk to write. The words had flowed, filling page after page as he created what he was sure would become one of the classics of queer lit, destined to sit on shelves alongside Andrew Holleran's *Dancer from the Dance*, James Baldwin's *Giovanni's Room*, and E. M. Forster's *Maurice*, all books that had made him fall in love with writing when he'd read them. He saw his name on the book jacket and imagined himself placing the first copy conspicuously yet tastefully on the coffee table, where visitors would just happen to see it.

And the story had been an obvious one—the tale of two gay men in love making it work despite the odds. Fueled by his unshakable belief that he and Doug would be together forever, he'd poured his enthusiasm into his characters, imbuing them with the same wide-eyed innocence he himself embraced and used to protect himself from the perils of the world. His creations were madly in love and completely devoted to one another, existing in a fairy-tale kingdom where love conquered all and hearts, while bumped and bruised from time to time, were never broken.

It had lasted for all of sixty-three pages. Then, overwhelmed by the unrelenting boredom of people whose lives were perfect, he'd stopped writing. He knew that the only solution to his problem was to saddle his characters with problems of some kind: drug addiction, perhaps, or even terminal illness, anything that could provide a hint of dramatic tension. Infidelity would be the weapon of choice, the fateful blow that would jump-start his sagging plot and give his characters something to react to besides their never-ending love for one another. But that was out of the question. It was something he couldn't bear to inflict upon anyone, even if they were just words on paper.

So he'd stopped writing, closing the file with a click of the mouse while promising himself that he would return to the novel again when he was inspired. At first he'd really believed that he would do it, occasionally making mental notes about possible directions for the plot and even, from time to time, opening the file and working away at it for an hour or two. He'd even dutifully transferred his WordPerfect files each of the three times he'd upgraded his computer, moving them from the clunky desktop model he'd begun on to a smaller one and, later, to first one and then another sleek, Pentium-fueled laptop, as if pouring his ideas into faster, more efficient machines would somehow make the process of writing easier. But as time went on he thought about the book less and less, until eventually it was something he remembered only in particularly gloomy moments when he wanted to torture himself over his lack of success. Even then he attributed his inability to get back to the book to the pressures of his job, the oppressive heat of the afternoon, or the demands of laundry— anything that could possibly be cause for not spending time staring at the screen.

Now, though, things were different. Since returning from registering for the class at the Arts House, he'd churned out another fifty pages. He felt the same way he'd felt when he'd first started writing the book. No, that wasn't true. He felt better. When the first sentences had materialized on the page, he'd been a different person. Then he'd dreamed of writing a novel that proved that what he wanted was possible to have. It had been as if, by writing the story he wanted to live, he could somehow make that story come true.

He had been influenced, largely, by the work of other gay writers. He was convinced that queer authors wrote in cycles. Their first books, generally written in their twenties, were about how wonderful it was to be young, beautiful, and popular in New York, Palm Springs, Paris, or some other gay mecca. The stories concerned the possibilities afforded such men by their endowments, financial and otherwise, and they reflected a world where youth and beauty were tickets to, if not happiness, at least adoration and nonstop sex. The authors' second novels, written perhaps ten years later, were almost always about the disappointment of discovering that with the passing of youth and beauty came the realization that behind the shimmering curtain of the gay stage their characters had once starred on was a world of empty lives and shattered dreams, peopled by men who discovered too late, if at all, that they had wasted a great deal of time. Finally, the third novels would complete the cycle. Composed when their authors were at the tail end of forty or in the opening years of fifty, these books could be counted on to be completely depressing, usually portraying the once-vibrant young men of the earliest novels as bitter old queens who had given up on true love and settled for the occasional hand job in a deserted park.

Josh hated these books. He hated them because the men in them bore no resemblance to himself or to the life he lived. He hated them because they made him feel as if he—along with all gay men—was doomed to end up alone. And he particularly hated them because gay readers seemed to accept them, even to welcome them, as accurate portraits of gay existence. How many times had he picked up a novel after hearing someone say, "I just loved that book," only to find that after reading it he wanted to stay in bed for a week or throw himself from a bridge? How often had he begun to read a book about a gay man "well past the age of being a beauty" and then discovered that the narrator was several years younger than himself? These books infuriated him, and he'd been determined to prove them wrong.

Now those books infuriated him for another reason: He thought they might be right. After all, his book had failed to come to life. The perfect existence he'd imagined for his lovers had been unable to sustain itself, burning brightly for five or six chapters and then toppling over like a too-high wedding cake done in by its own excess of frosting. But since Tuesday he'd gone back in and ripped out the original heart of the story, replacing the romantic candy valentine he'd first created with something more realistic.

But with his anger at discovering that there was more than a little truth in the books he'd once despised came renewed determination. If he couldn't have his fairy tale, he could at least have something that would tell his story. He had decided to put his feelings about Doug, and about their relationship, into his book. The result had been an almost constant torrent of writing. And far from finding it depressing, Josh was finding it invigorating. He'd hardly done anything but write for four days, and each night when he was done he reread his work and liked what he saw.

Now it was Saturday morning. He was giving himself a break, and had taken himself out for brunch at Café Blasé. As he sat at one of the restaurant's sidewalk tables, occasionally taking a bite from the eggs Benedict that sat on his plate, he imagined what Brody Nicholson would say about his work. He had always been hesitant to take writing classes, afraid that the teacher would tell him he had no talent. But he was pleased with what he was doing, and he was confident that Nicholson would like it. Besides, he'd been reading the books that Marly Prentis had loaned him, and he'd decided that Nicholson was a fan of relationships that self-destructed.

"Mind if I join you?"

Josh looked up. For a moment he thought he must be asleep, that he was only dreaming the sun he felt on his skin, the creamy taste of the hollandaise on his tongue, and the smell of the ocean that surrounded him. Because what he saw was not possible.

"Doug?" he said finally, feeling like Scrooge addressing the specter of his late partner, Jacob Marley.

"Shit, it hasn't been *that* long, has it?" said Doug, pulling out a chair and sitting down. "Have you already forgotten what I look like?"

Josh stared across the table at his lover as if seeing him for the first time. There was the familiar half smile, the scar on the chin, the hairline that crept back a little more each year. Doug was wearing a faded blue T-shirt that showed off the tan he'd already managed to acquire, and he looked remarkably relaxed, as if he were on vacation and had just happened to run into an old friend.

"I brought you your mail," Doug said, dropping a pile of envelopes in front of Josh. "It's mostly bills, but there's some good stuff in there too."

Josh looked at the mail blankly, then looked back at Doug. "How did you find me?" he asked. Now that he was over the shock of seeing his partner, he was beginning to feel angry, as if Doug had somehow invaded his private world, ignoring all of the no-trespassing signs and locked gates.

Doug laughed. "It's not a very big place," he said. "I figured if I walked around for a while I'd run into you. And I did," he added, reaching over and taking a piece of fried potato from Josh's plate.

The assumption of familiarity irritated Josh even more. He didn't want Doug to feel comfortable, didn't want him to think he could do the things they had once done without thinking because their relationship permitted it: sharing food, drinking from the same glass, leaving the bathroom door open while they peed. Those things were off-limits to him now as far as Josh was concerned.

"So, how are you?" asked Doug.

"I'm fine," Josh replied shortly. "How's Stephen?"

"Who?" Doug looked at Josh, puzzled.

"Your friend from the gym," said Josh.

Doug closed his eyes. "His name is Pete," he said. "And he's not important."

Josh laughed. "Really?" he said. "He's not important? Then what am I doing here?"

Doug sighed. "I didn't come here to fight," he said. "I came to talk. This is ridiculous, Josh. You can't just run away from me."

"Why not?" snapped Josh. "You just cheated on me. Why do I suddenly need permission?"

Several of the people seated near them turned to look when Josh spoke. He glared at them angrily and they returned to their food. But he knew they were listening. There was nothing queens liked better than an emotional floor show, especially those involving the death of someone else's relationship.

"Not here," he told Doug as he pulled his wallet out and left far more than the cost of his food on the table.

He stood up and walked off, leaving Doug to follow him. He headed for the beach. At least there the sound of the surf and the screeching of the gulls would provide some protection from eavesdroppers. Besides, Doug hated walking in sand, and Josh found some measure of joy in subjecting him to that small torture.

Josh walked in silence. During their entire relationship, he had always been the one to speak first after an argument, the first to break the icy stillness that accompanied harsh words and disagreements. He hated the feeling of tension that arguing left behind, and was always anxious to dispel it with an apology or a comment designed to let Doug know that no lasting harm had been done on either side.

But not this time. This time it was Doug who was going to have to speak first. Josh was determined that he would walk the entire length of the beach without uttering a single word if he had to. He focused his attention on the waves sweeping across the sand, on the people scattered around like a child's discarded toys, on the dogs who ran in and out of the surf barking crazily.

"I'm sorry," Doug said after they'd walked for several minutes.

Josh, who had been watching a little girl in a pink swimsuit let the waves touch her toes and then run away giggling to the safety of her father's arms, didn't look at his lover as he asked, "Sorry you did it, or sorry you told me?"

"I'm sorry I hurt you," Doug answered.

"That's not the same as being sorry you did it," replied Josh.

"Look, if you don't want me to sleep with other guys, then I won't," Doug said.

Josh stopped and turned to face Doug. "Oh, how big of you," he said. "You'd give up other men for me? I thought that's what we were doing when we got together in the first place, Doug."

Doug looked away. "I'm not going to pretend I didn't like sleeping with Pete," he said. "I did like it. It was hot."

"Thanks," said Josh. "Why don't you just tell me how big his dick was, or how he talked dirty when he came?"

"Why do you have to turn everything into a competition?" shot back Doug. "I didn't say I loved him. I didn't say he was better than you. I just said I liked it. Why does that threaten you so much?"

"Why?" repeated Josh. "Why? Oh, I don't know. Maybe because it bothers me just a little bit that my lover is so bored with me that he has to hop into bed with someone else. How's that for a reason?"

Neither of them spoke for several minutes. Josh resumed walking, deciding that moving was better than standing in one spot and hating Doug. Maybe if he kept moving, he thought, Doug would just give up and go away.

"I love you," he heard Doug say.

He kept walking. A moment later he felt Doug catch him by the arm and hold tight.

"I said I love you," Doug repeated.

Josh tried to pull away, but Doug held fast. Josh turned and found himself face-to-face with Doug. Before he could say anything, Doug was kissing him. His mouth was hot, his tongue pushing its way past Josh's lips. Josh put a hand on Doug's chest to shove him off, but Doug pulled him in close, his arms encircling Josh's body.

Josh felt himself slipping, and the two of them tumbled into the soft sand of the dunes. They had wandered away from the beach into a less populated area where the sand rose and fell in gentle hills. They were in one of the depressions formed by the dunes, hidden from view by the clumps of sea grass that managed to take root in the shifting landscape.

Doug slipped a hand inside Josh's shirt, running it up his chest to find one of Josh's nipples. Josh gasped as Doug pinched it. He didn't want this to happen. He didn't want to be aroused by the sudden turn of events. But he was, and when Doug pressed against him and he felt the hardness in his lover's shorts, Josh reached for Doug's belt and with fumbling fingers pulled it free.

Moments later, their shorts hastily removed, the two men were running their hands over each other's bodies. As Josh touched the well-known places on Doug's body, he tried not to think about what he was doing. If he did, he knew he would put an end to it, and as much as he knew that was the right thing to do, he couldn't bring himself to say no. He allowed his fingers to travel through the patch of hair that shaded Doug's groin, his tongue to slip into the hollow of Doug's throat. When Doug brought his fingers to his mouth and a moment later slipped them, wet with his spit, into the cleft of Josh's ass, Josh hesitated only a moment before opening to Doug's hand.

His legs slid over Doug's shoulders as Doug entered him, not gently but with the rush of need. Josh gasped as he absorbed the force of Doug's initial thrust. But Doug didn't wait for him, beginning to pump himself in and out of Josh's ass with full, hard motions. As he moved, sweat slid down his chest and onto Josh's body, where it mixed with the sand and formed a gritty skin.

Josh was surprised to find himself ready to come after only a few minutes. Normally he couldn't come while getting fucked, and had to jerk himself off after Doug had finished. But now he felt the warm ripples that signaled an approaching orgasm creeping up from his balls. A few strokes later and a thick stream of cum erupted from his dick and fell onto his chest in warm drops.

Doug groaned and pushed himself deep into Josh's ass. His hands closed around Josh's thighs and Josh felt several pulses as Doug unleashed his load. Doug shuddered as he came and the low groan Josh had heard so often before came from his half-open mouth.

"Oh, fuck," Doug said as he slid out of Josh and collapsed on his side next to him. "That was great."

Josh didn't say anything. As his orgasm had receded, his common sense had returned, and he was already regretting what had just happened. He reached for his shorts and began to pull them on.

"We shouldn't have done that," he said. "Someone might have seen us." He knew that wasn't the only reason he should have kept his clothes on, but he was too angry at himself—and at Doug—to say more.

"I know," Doug said, grinning mischievously. "That made it even better. Now what do you say, have we made up?"

Josh gathered up his mail, which had scattered when he'd fallen. He stood up, brushing it off. He looked down at Doug, who was still nude, his now-soft dick hanging between his legs as he gazed up hopefully at Josh. He looked like a little boy who desperately wanted to be forgiven for having broken the cookie jar.

Only he wasn't a little boy. He was a man. A man who had hurt Josh deeply. And despite what had just happened—or maybe because of it—Josh wasn't ready to forgive him.

"I'll get back to you," he said as he turned and walked away, leaving Doug to scramble in the sand for his clothes.

PART II

June

CHAPTER 21

"Oh, yeah. Pound me harder. Give me that cock."

Reilly looked down at Donna. Her eyes were closed and her lips were slightly parted. She was making soft little moans of pleasure.

"Fuck me. Make me feel it."

Donna would never say anything like the bad porn film dialogue that was running through Reilly's head. She rarely said anything at all during sex. Even her orgasms were fairly restrained, composed of several long groans while her body shook and she pushed against him.

But in Reilly's imagination, much more was happening. And it wasn't happening with Donna.

"I'm gonna come."

As he erupted inside Donna, Reilly imagined hearing those words whispered in his ear. He surrendered to the shiver that traveled through his body and rode it for the half a minute it lasted before fading away, leaving him wanting more.

When it was over he rolled onto his back. Almost immediately Donna sat up.

"I'll be right back," she said, giving him a quick kiss before getting out of bed and disappearing into the bathroom. A moment later he heard the water running, and he knew she was taking a shower.

Reilly closed his eyes. Now that it was over, now that his dick had softened and the need that had driven him to wake Donna up with his insistent prodding had passed, he was ashamed of himself. But he hadn't been able to help it.

It was the dream that had done it, the dream he hadn't had in a very long time. But it had returned sometime during the night, slipping through some unprotected chink in the armor of his subconscious and springing to life in his head. Once there, it had drawn him into a world he'd long ago turned his back on, seducing him with sights and sounds, smells and tastes, that he'd been unable to resist.

In the dream he had been sitting on the beach. It was night, and the stars filled the sky like fireflies. The summer air still held the heat of the day in its breath, and he was warm despite being shirtless. His bare feet were pushed into the sand, and in his hand was a bottle of beer.

Beside him was Nick Charetti. They were both eighteen, newly graduated from Edward Farrow High School, and half drunk on the six-pack of Budweiser Nick's older brother, Frank, had bought for them at Murphey's Liquors earlier in the evening. They had walked to the far end of the beach, away from the noise of the summer people, and found a deserted stretch of sand they could call their own.

While they listened to the ocean and dusk turned to night, they talked about the things that had long been the topics of their conversations: the cars they would one day own, the lives they would one day have, and the girls they would one day bed. Reilly and Nick had known each other since both were twelve, and the patterns of their friendship were by now very familiar. Their talk flowed back and forth as easily, and as predictably, as the tides.

"A 1968 Mustang convertible," Nick said. "Cherry red."

"A 1957 Nash Metropolitan," countered Reilly. "Sea-foam green and white. Amber taillights."

"That's a fucking sissy car, man," Nick teased. "You're not going to get any pussy in that thing."

"I'm already getting enough pussy," replied Reilly.

"Come on," Nick said. "You can't even get Stephanie to go *out* with you, man. You must be whacking off sixteen times a day just thinking about getting into her pants. I'm surprised you haven't broken your wrist."

Reilly laughed. "Hey, at least the girl I want is real," he said. "Are you still jacking off to that Janet Jackson video?"

"Fuck you," shot back Nick, reaching out and smacking Reilly on the arm.

Reilly laughed even more loudly at his friend's childish reaction. In response, Nick put a hand on the back of Reilly's head.

"You know what you can do?" he said. "You can just fucking blow me."

He pushed Reilly's face into his crotch. It was a routine the two of them performed regularly during their mock arguments, a sign that whatever joking had initiated the event hadn't caused any real emotional damage. As Nick forced Reilly's head between his legs, Reilly continued to laugh.

His cheek pressed against the jeans Nick was wearing, and all of a sudden Reilly was overcome by a barrage of sensations: the smoothness of the well-worn denim, the roughness of the thick hair that covered Nick's bare stomach, the heat that came from his skin where it touched Reilly's, the pressure of Nick's fingers on his neck. And buried beneath all of it was the feeling of Nick's cock against his face. Not hard, it could still be felt below the surface of Nick's jeans, the only thing separating it from Reilly's mouth the buttons of Nick's fly.

Reilly didn't move. He had no idea how long he and Nick stayed like that, but it seemed like hours. He feared lingering, but he feared even more breaking the connection between them. He felt the alcohol in his blood drawing its gauzy curtain across his thoughts, pushing caution aside. *That's it,* he thought. *I'm just drunk. We're both just drunk.*

But still he didn't move. Instead, he gently moved his mouth, tracing the shape of Nick's bulge with his lips. His heart beat wildly as he waited for Nick to push him off, and he busied his mind with thinking of jokes he could make to dispel the disgusted reaction he was certain was about to issue forth from Nick's mouth.

Nick, however, kept his hand on Reilly's neck. Reilly felt the rise and fall of his breathing and, emboldened by Nick's failure to stop him, allowed himself to increase the pressure of his mouth on his friend's quickly hardening shaft. Nick's cock responded eagerly, growing thicker and longer as Reilly coaxed it to life.

Reilly moved his mouth to the bare skin above Nick's waistband, letting his tongue explore the trail of hair that disappeared into Nick's jeans. He breathed in the mix of sweat and sunscreen that covered Nick's skin, and he felt the muscles beneath Nick's skin tense as his breathing quickened.

Although part of him still couldn't believe it was happening, couldn't believe that Nick hadn't brought an end to what Reilly still believed to be nothing more than their usual roughhousing, Reilly brought his fingers to the buttons of Nick's jeans. Moments later, Nick's dick sprang up before him, the head full and round and glistening with the first traces of Nick's excitement. Reilly gazed at it for a moment, wondering if their game would go any further.

He was answered by an upward thrust of Nick's hips. Reilly opened his mouth and allowed Nick to slide between his lips. His tongue slid along the length of Nick's shaft, tasting for the first time another man's hardness. He found it difficult to breathe, but he didn't want Nick to pull away.

He began to move his mouth up and down the full length of Nick's cock, and soon he forgot entirely that he was doing something by which he should—according to all the rules by which friendships between men were conducted—be deeply repulsed. He ran his tongue over the full, ripe head, then down the sides, filling his mouth with the warmth of Nick. When he had become used to the thickness, he managed to push Nick deep into his throat, his nose pressing against Nick's groin. He allowed his hand to slip between Nick's legs, cradling the softness of his balls in his fingers.

When Nick came a few minutes later, without warning and filling Reilly's mouth with several spurts of warm stickiness, Reilly accepted it without hesitation. And as he reluctantly released Nick's softening cock, he licked away the remaining drops, letting them linger on his tongue as he tried to burn the taste into his memory.

That's where the dream ended, before Reilly had to look up into Nick's face and discover that their friendship had come to an end. In the dream he was allowed to remain forever on the beach, perpetually lost in the joy of what had just occurred.

In reality, however, things had not turned out like that. On the night when the events he now remembered only in dreams actually happened, Reilly had sat up, both excited and afraid, and looked at Nick. Nick, however, had refused to meet his gaze, instead hurriedly buttoning himself back up while mumbling excuses for why he had to leave. Reilly, seeing what he had feared unfolding before him, had sat silently as his friend had walked away without looking back.

He'd remained there for the rest of the night, unable to bring himself to leave. The warm air had turned cold, and yet he'd refused to put his shirt back on, punishing himself for not having had the strength to fight what had happened, for being too weak to resist temptation. He'd drunk the rest of the beer, too, trying to rinse the taste of Nick from his mouth, hoping he would make himself sick so that he could empty his insides of the foulness he'd allowed himself to indulge in.

But he hadn't gotten sick. He'd only fallen into a drunken sleep, and in the morning when he woke he was shivering and his head was pounding with both the effects of the beer and the memories he'd hoped would fade with the coming of the dawn but which in reality only became much more clear now that they were illuminated by the rising sun.

He'd tried to talk to Nick, phoned him repeatedly during the first few days following the incident. But Nick always had some reason to avoid him, some job to do or someplace else to be. When, once, Reilly ran into him on the street, Nick crossed to the other side, his eyes averted. Finally the summer ran out and Nick left to attend college in Maine, bringing the matter to a close. They had never again spoken.

Reilly, however, had been left with the memories of that night. For a while he'd played them over and over in his head, sometimes allowing himself the release he hadn't experienced during the actual event. But even as he wiped his chest with the tissues he kept hidden beneath his bed, he knew that he couldn't allow himself to let anything like that happen again. It wasn't what was expected of him. It wasn't what he wanted.

Stephanie Perides was what he wanted, and he began to pursue her even more vigorously. Stephanie, a moon-faced girl with a shy smile and long brown hair she wore in a single braid down her back, was the girl Nick had teased him about liking. And he did like her. She was quiet, and smart. Best of all, after several dates she allowed him to sleep with her. Each time he did, Reilly found the memories of his night with Nick growing more and more faint, as if the joining of his penis and Stephanie's pussy somehow created a magical force that had the power to erase the past. Sometimes he fucked her twice in the same night, hoping to wipe away even more quickly the image of himself bent over Nick, his head moving beneath the guiding force of Nick's hand.

Eventually the memories did fade, and he found he no longer needed Stephanie to keep them at bay. Then there had been a breakup, with the usual tears on Stephanie's part and a feeling of relief on Reilly's. And finally had come the long stretch of years during which he'd waited for Donna. During this time he enjoyed more than the occasional date and several halfhearted attempts at relationships with various women, but always he seemed to know that it was Donna who would eventually share his bed on a permanent basis.

And now that had happened. But along with his engagement to Donna had come something else—the return of the dream about Nick. Shortly after setting a date and making the announcement to delighted families and friends, Reilly had found himself back on that beach, with Nick's hand on the back of his neck and the taste of Nick's cock in his throat. That first time he'd been so convinced that the dream was real that when he'd awakened he'd checked the sheets for traces of sand and, later, gone through almost an entire bottle of mouthwash in an attempt to banish the ghosts from his mouth.

Reilly had convinced himself that the return of the dream was due entirely to the natural stress that accompanied making such a life-altering change, a sudden and unexpected phenomenon not unlike spontaneous combustion or the ability to communicate with the dead that on rare occasions came about as a result of a person being struck by lightning. It was, he decided, nothing more than a side effect of the engagement, much like Donna, now that she saw her future laid out before her, sometimes said that the thought of being called Mrs. Brennan caused her to break out in hives. And just as the infrequent appearance of red blotches on her face did nothing to make Donna doubt the reasonableness of the impending nuptials, so was Reilly determined not to let a bad dream derail his happiness.

At least in theory. The reality was that the dream *was* bothering him. It was especially bothering him at that very moment because, determined to prove once and for all that it meant nothing, he had decided that morning to make love to Donna as a means of proving the dream wrong. However, even as she'd welcomed him into her, he had been thinking of someone else, someone with decidedly different body parts.

Oblivious of the infidelity that was occurring in Reilly's mind even as the body he made love to was hers, Donna had reacted the way she always did when they coupled. Reilly, however, had finally allowed his thoughts to go where he'd forbidden them for so long to tread. In this way, the smoothness of Donna's skin had been replaced by the rough feeling of hair over muscle. The roundness of her breasts and fullness of her hips had become the flatter planes of a man's torso, while the gentleness of her voice had been replaced by heavier, more labored breaths. And most significant, the welcoming tightness that surrounded him, and into which he expelled his desire, belonged not to the soft folds that nestled between Donna's thighs but to the hidden entrance found at the center of a pair of well-muscled ass cheeks.

Once freed to do as it would, Reilly's imagination had leapt head-long into the fantasy. It was not Donna who brought him so quickly to the edge and then pushed him over it, but another man. This alone was enough to alarm him. But even more disturbing was the realization that the man in his fantasies was not, after all this time, Nick Charetti, but someone else, someone who had only recently come into his life. He was still reeling from the shock of the revelation, so that when Donna reappeared, her skin glowing pinkly from the heat of the shower, Reilly barely noticed when she sat on the edge of the bed.

"Just think," she said. "Three months from today we'll be Mr. and Mrs. Brennan."

Reilly looked up at her. Donna was smiling, her wet hair draped around her face as she waited for him to respond. *This,* he thought, *is the person I'm going to wake up to every morning for the rest of my life.*

His stomach lurched. Reilly got up. "I'll be back in a minute," he said as he raced for the bathroom. As the door closed behind him he leaned over the toilet and was spectacularly, loudly sick, as if it had taken fourteen years for the Budweiser to exact its revenge.

CHAPTER 22

"'Brown paper packages tied up with string . . .'"

Jackie couldn't help singing the words, even though she suspected that Trane would be mortified to know that someone was treating his gorgeous rendition of the Rodgers and Hammerstein classic like some kind of karaoke soundtrack.

The Sound of Music was one of those movies for which she had a peculiar fondness. She'd seen it first when she was twelve. Having been only two years old when the film appeared in theaters, she'd had to wait for its debut ten years later on national television. That Sunday evening she and June had sat on the big, comfortable couch in the family's living room, a bowl of popcorn between them and bottles of Dr Pepper in their hands. Their father occupied the Lay-Z-Boy recliner that no one but him was allowed to sit in, while their mother hovered nearby, watching her daughters anxiously in anticipation of the spills she was sure were soon to sully the new shag carpeting she'd had installed only three weeks earlier.

Mr. Stavers fell asleep even before Maria had left the abbey to take up her position at the von Trapp home, and June left not much later, declaring as she went, "That Julie Andrews is no Dinah Washington, I'll tell you *that.*"

Jackie, however, had been completely drawn into the movie, not so much by the story of the family's escape from the Nazis, but because she related to Maria's sense of not fitting in, of belonging somewhere else but not really knowing where. She admired the woman's determination, and her daring. She liked how she stood up to the captain, and how she made her way in a world that threw obstacle after obstacle in her path.

She'd particularly enjoyed it when Maria made clothes out of the family's old curtains. Her mother had done that once, fashioning two identical sundresses out of the draperies that had once hung in the girls' bedroom. Jackie and June had been embarrassed to wear them, and Jackie was both surprised and delighted to see that even rich white children had to endure that sort of indignity.

A few days later she'd gone to the mall and purchased the movie's soundtrack, slipping the album between ones by Patti LaBelle and Peaches & Herb so as not to draw too much attention to herself. At home she'd played it repeatedly on the turntable in her bedroom, pretending she was Maria as she belted out the words to "I Have Confidence" and "Do-Re-Mi."

For years her love of *The Sound of Music* was something she kept to herself, along with other secrets including her lack of interest in black politics and her desire for other women. All three were things she considered strikes against her as a woman of color, flaws in her character that made her undesirable on a number of levels.

In college she discovered that she was only partially right about that. Her desire for other women might have put her at a disadvantage as far as the larger, white-male-heterosexual-dominated world was concerned, but within the Sapphic circles of her school she was most definitely a hot commodity. As for her disinterest in racial politics, whether or not it was a problem depended upon her partner-of-the-moment's attitudes. Her first lover, a white girl, had found Jackie's political ambivalence surprising yet endearing. Susan had taken it upon herself to teach Jackie how to be a young, angry, black woman who knew how to rail at the injustices she suffered because of the color of her skin. She'd done her work well. Unfortunately, when she'd run out of things to change about Jackie she'd left her for someone more in need of an ideological makeover.

It was through her next lover, a black history major named Nina, that Jackie had been introduced to the work of John Coltrane. She'd immediately fallen in love with Trane's sound, and had immersed herself in his classic albums. Chief among these was *My Favorite Things,* a haunting record the centerpiece of which was the song Jackie had learned years before in a much different version. Hearing Coltrane's version, Jackie was tempted to reveal to Nina the effect the other, whiter, rendition had had on her imagination. But after listening to Nina decry white artists who made fortunes releasing bland versions of songs originally recorded by black musicians, she decided to keep her secret safe for a while longer.

In fact, it wasn't until she'd been with Karla for two or three years that her *Sound of Music* affinity had been revealed. It had happened one Thanksgiving, when they'd settled down to watch TV after storing the remains of the turkey in the refrigerator and washing the last of the cranberry sauce from the plates. Turning on the television, they'd been greeted by the sight of Julie Andrews spinning dizzily around atop an Austrian hill. Jackie, lulled into a place of safety by the feeling of Karla's hand on her knee and the tryptophan from the turkey coursing through her digestive system, had told her lover all about her fascination with the musical.

Karla, to her credit, had found Jackie's revelation charming. As a result, Jackie had felt free to occasionally break out into one of the songs from the film without fear of ridicule. It was, she sometimes thought, an odd thing to add to the list of reasons why she loved Karla, but it was there nonetheless.

Now, with Karla gone, there was no one to hear her singing, badly, the words to the song. Trane was long dead, so even if he was somehow listening to her from wherever his soul had ended up when it had flown from his body, he couldn't do anything about it. Jackie had considered playing the actual soundtrack. She had it on CD now, her original vinyl album having worn out long ago. But three o'clock in the morning was jazz time, so she'd slipped Coltrane in instead, letting the sound of his sax fill her house and mingle with the night air.

Now that she thought about it, she'd selected the perfect farewell album to celebrate or mourn (she couldn't decide which) Karla's leaving. In addition to "My Favorite Things," the disc's other three tracks were "Summertime," "Every Time We Say Good-bye," and "But Not for Me." How perfect, she thought, that it should begin with a song she loved for the memories it held and continue on through a series of progressively sadder and sadder pieces that evoked other, less welcome, thoughts.

Not that listening to Trane ever made her sad. Melancholy, perhaps. Maybe even wistful. But never sad. He was too good a player for that, too careful not to let the blues become mere self-pity. That's what she loved about him. He knew how to look at the heart's darker moments without romanticizing them.

She sat down in the big chair near the window, tucking her feet up under her. The window was open, and outside she heard the sound of the sea as it went about its business. It was her favorite time of the night. She had closed up the restaurant, and in an hour she would be asleep. But this was her time, her hour to do as she pleased. And what she wanted to do was read about making babies.

She hadn't dared buy the books at her favorite local queer bookstore, *Now Voyager*. Even though she knew they carried them, she also knew how quickly word would get around that she'd purchased them. It was one of the disadvantages of being part of the tight year-round community; everybody knew your business, sometimes before you did yourself. Finally she'd resorted to using Amazon.com, guiltily typing in her credit card number even as she imagined the local store having to shut its doors as a result of her failure to support them. But the anonymity of it—not to mention the 30 percent off and the free shipping—had been too much to resist.

The books had come that afternoon, and now she sat with them spread out on the coffee table before her, looking at the covers and trying to decide which one to look at first. There were three of them: *The Lesbian Mother Handbook, And Baby Makes Two: A Guide to Single Mothering,* and *The Turkey Baster Baby Book.* The last she'd bought based solely on the title, while the others she'd found listed on a Web site for dykes who were considering motherhood.

Part of her couldn't even believe that such books existed. It would have been unthinkable when she was coming out. Now, though, lesbians having babies was apparently as natural, and as common, as, well, as straight women having babies. A simple search of the Internet had guided her to dozens of sites devoted to the options available to dykes who wanted to dive into the gene pool.

She picked up *And Baby Makes Two* and opened it to the introduction. "Congratulations!" she read. "You've decided the time is right to have a child. Well, just because you're on your own doesn't mean you can't enjoy the rewards of a family."

She skimmed ahead to the how-to section. She didn't need reassurances; she needed directions. She didn't need to read about how women her age were nearing the end of their relatively risk-free child-bearing years and should hurry up and do something about it if they didn't want to die alone. She didn't need to be told that it was *okay* for her to want to have a baby. She needed to be told how to get one of the damn things.

"Too bad it's not like growing an avocado," she mused as she read through the various options available to her. If it were, she could just stick some toothpicks in one of her eggs, pop it into a glass of water, and forget about the whole thing until it sprouted.

Unfortunately, her plumbing was slightly more complicated than that. Her primary problem was that she needed some sperm. "But where am I going to get my hands on some of that shit?" she asked herself. She had to laugh at the irony. P-Town was practically swimming in the stuff, especially with all the queens there for the summer, yet as far as she was concerned she might as well be living all alone on the moon.

There was always a sperm bank, but she was just old-fashioned enough that she wanted to know at least *something* about the potential father of her child. Sure, anything she bought would come with a supposedly detailed report, but somehow it wasn't the same. She wasn't sure she actually wanted the man whose little swimmers she allowed to battle it out in a race through her vagina to be all that involved with the baby after it was all over, but she wanted to have that option.

According to the book, if she wanted to go that route she was going to have to find someone nearby, as sperm, like milk, apparently spoiled quickly. It all involved figuring out when she was ovulating and then having a guy available to hand over some fresh-squeezed juice for her to squirt up herself. Then she just had to hope it took, or she'd have to do it all over again the next time her eggs were in the mood. Thinking about it made her feel like a prize heifer.

Still, she wanted to do it. She was pretty sure about that. And she was equally pretty sure that it had almost nothing to do with Karla's leaving. In fact, she'd realized after much thought that Karla's leaving had made her see how much she'd been repressing her desire for a child. It was as if, along with half the kitchen utensils and the furniture, Karla had carted off an enormous weight that had settled on Jackie's spirit sometime during their relationship, a weight she'd used to prevent herself from saying or doing anything that might upset the balance of power between them. Now, with it gone, she was free to do as she liked.

"But I still need a man to get it done," she said.

She decided to make a list. She knew men. Lots of men. They were coming in and out of her restaurant every day in droves. Surely one of them had sperm that would be acceptable, and that they wouldn't mind loaning her. It wasn't like they needed *all* of it, for Christ's sake. She just had to figure out what she wanted in a man and then find someone who fit the requirements. In other words, she needed a to-do list. This revelation made her happy. She was good at organization. She took up a notepad and a pen and started scribbling.

Color. She looked at the word. Did she care if her baby's father was black or not? The question had honestly never occurred to her. But now that it had she decided that, no, it didn't matter. Frankly, she was relieved. Finding a willing man to donate to her cause was going to be tough enough. Finding a *black* man would have made it all that much harder. While dykes of all shapes, sizes, and colors saw Provincetown as a place where they could be themselves, when it came to men the general population was still pretty much white.

She moved on to religion. That, too, was not an issue. Nor was job, hair color, athletic ability, political leanings, favorite ice cream flavor, or income. In short, as long as he was reasonably good-looking, didn't have any inheritable health problems, and was willing to whack off in a jar and hand it over to her, any man would do.

She put her pad down and sighed. Maybe, she thought, someone would just *give* her a baby and she wouldn't have to worry about any of this. Of course, she could adopt. But she wanted to experience the whole pregnancy thing, swollen ankles and all. She realized that was part of her near-obsessive determination to do everything on her own, but she couldn't help it. She'd never even bought a cake mix. She wasn't about to start taking shortcuts now.

She thought about all of the men she was friends with. They were all great guys. But for some reason the idea of any of them fathering her baby just didn't seem quite right. They were either too old, too young, or just way too—something. She loved flamboyant gay men, for instance, but she had issues with the thought of one day showing her child pictures of her or his father and saying, "That's your daddy— the one in the boa and the Liza wig." Similarly, she couldn't see father-hood potential in any of the many circuit party regulars who populated much of her world.

"How hard can it be to find one normal gay guy?" she asked herself. Then she laughed. How often had she heard that same question uttered by her gay male friends? And what had she always answered them? "He's probably right under your nose. Just keep your eyes open."

Now she was giving herself the same advice. The right guy was out there. She just had to keep looking for him.

"I have confidence the world can all be mine," she sang softly as she stared out at the moon. "They'll have to agree I have confidence in me."

CHAPTER 23

"Have you ever been in love?"

Emmeline looked up from the pot of gumbo she was cooking. She'd just added the filé and was stirring carefully to prevent the brownish green sassafras powder from clumping and turning stringy. Toby, who was sitting at the kitchen table watching her, waited for her to answer.

"Yes," she said, avoiding the temptation to lie and make things easier for herself.

Toby continued to watch her, not saying anything. Emmeline concentrated on the gumbo. The shrimp were just turning pink, and the rich color of the filé had infused the simmering liquid, filling the kitchen with its scent reminiscent of earth and home. Emmeline was making it at Toby's request. He'd never had it before, and after hearing her mention it several times in conversation he'd asked her if she had the recipe for it. She did have it, having copied it years ago from the well-worn handwritten recipe book her mother (who had copied it from *her* mother's book before her) kept on the shelf near her stove.

It had taken her some time to find the recipe, however. Cooking was not something she did a lot of anymore, and her cookbooks were dusty with disuse. But after some searching she'd come across the yellowing notebook in which she'd written the gumbo recipe, along with the others she'd copied at some point, instructions for making things like pecan pie, crawfish etoufeé, and hush puppies. It was the food of her youth, and she'd stopped making it at about the same time she'd decided to let go of her past by changing her name and other, more important, details of her life.

She'd forgotten how much work making gumbo was, and how re-warding the effort could be. The chopping of shallots, peppers, and okra and the peeling of shrimp had taken the better part of an hour, but now that it was all bubbling away in the cast-iron pot she hadn't used in ages, she remembered how comforting making it was for her. She also realized that she was ignoring Toby's question.

"His name was Simon," she said finally. Simon was something else she hadn't thought of in a long time, and recalling the events to which he was connected was not unlike paging through the brittle, faded pages of the old recipe book.

"I was twenty-three," she continued. "I was living in New Orleans and performing every night at a club called Voodoo Daddy's. Simon was a regular. He came in every night around nine, just in time to catch my show. Afterward he'd stay and buy me drinks so that I'd sit and talk with him." She smiled. "I would have talked to him anyway," she con-fided.

"What was he like?" asked Toby.

"He was a welder," answered Emmeline. "Big. Strong. Muscles everywhere. He was typical Cajun—black hair and eyes the color of bayou water at night. When he talked it was like time stood still, wait-ing for him to let the words out."

"Did he know?" Toby inquired. "You know, that you were a guy?"

Emmeline nodded. "He knew," she said. "And that was the best part. He didn't care. At least I thought he didn't."

She spooned some freshly steamed rice into a bowl and ladled gumbo on top of it. She set it on the table in front of Toby along with a bottle of hot sauce and then served herself. After taking her seat she resumed her story.

"We dated for a month before I even let him kiss me," she told Toby. "I just wasn't sure he knew what he was getting into, and I wanted to make sure he wasn't just intrigued by my—difference. Then one night when he dropped me off at my apartment he leaned over and said, 'I might not understand everything there is to know about you, but I know what I want and I want you.' Then he kissed me."

Toby, who was eagerly devouring her gumbo, stopped eating and looked at her expectantly. "And?" he said impatiently.

"And what?" asked Emmeline. Then she realized what he was ask-ing. "No, I did not ask him in to spend the night," she said. "I am a lady, thank you very much." She paused. "I waited until the *next* night for that."

Toby grinned.

"Anyway," Emmeline said, "that was in May. We spent that whole summer together. He stayed at my apartment every night. I cooked for him. Ironed his shirts. I might as well have been June Cleaver. I couldn't wait for him to come home every afternoon. Then after dinner he'd come watch me at the club, sitting right up front so I could sing to him."

She stopped and took a bite of her gumbo. This was the part of the story she would rather forget. But she knew Toby wasn't going to let her get away with ending it there.

"So what happened?" he asked predictably.

Emmeline wiped her lips on her napkin. "One night he came home and told me that he was getting married," she said quietly.

"He'd been seeing someone else?" Toby said, horrified.

Emmeline shook her head. "No," she said, "he hadn't. He'd just decided that he needed to get married. He said he was thirty-five and his family was starting to ask about a wife and children."

"What about you?" Toby asked her. "He could have said you were his wife."

"Maybe," replied Emmeline. "But I couldn't give him children. Anyway, he said he loved me but that he couldn't be with me anymore. Then he left."

"Just like that?"

"Just like that," Emmeline said sadly. "The only thing he left behind was an undershirt. I hadn't washed it yet, and it still smelled like him. I wore that shirt to bed every night for the next three months."

Toby wrinkled his nose. "I bet that smelled ripe."

"I wouldn't have noticed," said Emmeline. "It took half a bottle of bourbon to get me to sleep anyway."

"Did you ever see him again?" Toby asked her.

"Once," answered Emmeline. "The night before he got married. He came by the club and stood in the back. Before I could finish my song and get offstage he was gone. I saw the wedding announcement in the paper the next day."

Toby looked into his bowl of gumbo. "I'm sorry I asked," he said apologetically.

Emmeline gave a little laugh. "Don't be," she said. "It was a long time ago."

"Still," Toby said, "it was none of my business."

Emmeline fixed him with a hard look. "Now don't you *dare* go feeling sorry for me," she said. "I'm not some tragic old drag queen sitting here surrounded by ratty wigs and dresses that don't fit anymore, waiting for some man from my past to come knocking on my door with a bouquet of roses."

"That's not what I meant," Toby protested. "I just feel bad that you haven't been in love with anyone since then."

"Oh, I've been in love," said Emmeline. "Hundreds of times. Just not in the same way."

"I don't understand," Toby said.

"You will," she remarked pointedly.

Toby rolled his eyes. "I know, I know," he said. "Wait until you're older."

"That's right," Emmeline replied. "Now eat your dinner."

Toby laughed. "I always thought there would be just one," he said, becoming more serious. "You know, the perfect guy."

"Maybe there will be," said Emmeline.

"I don't know," said Toby. "I listen to the guys at the house talk. I see what they do. Even the ones in couples."

Emmeline raised an eyebrow. "I take it the gentlemen have been misbehaving?" she asked.

"Some of them," Toby answered. He still hadn't told her that Aaron was one of his employers.

"Everybody has a different idea of what love is," said Emmeline. "Their idea doesn't have to be the same as yours."

Toby nodded in agreement. "So what's your idea of love?" he asked.

Emmeline thought for a minute. "Falling in love means giving someone the power to break your heart," she said. "If they break it less often than they make you happy, then you're okay."

Toby didn't say anything. Emmeline knew he was thinking that she was just being bitter. But she wasn't. She was being realistic. She knew Toby was still hoping the fairy tales would be true. And for his sake she hoped maybe they were as well. But she also knew that people were seldom able to maintain the happily ever after. She blamed this on Hollywood. All the romantic movies ended right at the point where the couples got together despite whatever odds they'd been fighting throughout the film. They never showed what happened after the final triumphant kiss or the "I dos." They never showed the couple two months later, when one got sick of finding the other one's dirty underwear on the floor, or when the bickering over little things started. They never showed people how to keep going after the credits rolled.

The phone rang, interrupting her thoughts. Emmeline answered it.

"Hello," the voice on the other end said. "Is this Mason Tayhill?"

Emmeline, not recognizing the caller, a man, was hesitant to respond. No one but her mother still knew her by that name.

"May I ask who's calling, please?" she said politely.

"This is Dr. Osgood Wickford from St. Elizabeth's Hospital in New Orleans," the man answered. "Are you Mr. Tayhill's wife?"

Emmeline felt a chill wrap its icy fingers around her shoulders. Calls from hospitals were never good news.

"No," she said. "This is not his wife. I am Mason Tayhill."

There was a pause at the other end, and Emmeline knew that Osgood Wickford was trying to decide whether he was being made a fool of or whether he should apologize.

"Mr. Tayhill," he said, apparently deciding to pretend that Emmeline's voice had not thrown him off, "I'm calling about your mother, Lula Tayhill."

"Yes?" said Emmeline vaguely, not wanting to ask the obvious question that was on her mind.

"She's had a stroke," Dr. Wickford told her.

Emmeline gasped. "Is she all right?" she asked.

"She's alive," the doctor said, as if that should be cause enough for rejoicing. "But she's in pretty rough shape. Her right side is partially paralyzed, and it's difficult for her to speak for long lengths of time. She's going to need a lot of looking after."

"Thank God Petey is there," Emmeline said.

"Excuse me?" the doctor replied.

"Petey," Emmeline repeated. "My brother. Peterson Tayhill," she added, in case Dr. Wickford had only been introduced to him by his full name.

"I don't believe I've met him," said the doctor.

"Didn't he come in with my mother?" Emmeline asked, confused.

"No," Dr. Wickford answered. "She was brought in by paramedics two days ago. She called 911."

Emmeline couldn't believe what she was hearing. "My mother didn't ask you to call him?" she inquired.

"No," the doctor answered again. "She only gave us your number. Why? Should we call someone else?"

"No," Emmeline told him. "No, that's okay. I'll call him myself. He lives in the area."

"Good," Dr. Wickford said. "She's going to be ready to go home in a few days, and someone will need to be there with her."

"I'll call my brother and make arrangements," said Emmeline. "Can I have your number so I can call you back?"

Dr. Wickford gave her his phone number. Emmeline thanked him and hung up. As Toby watched, waiting for her to explain what was happening, she dialed Petey's number. She hadn't talked to her brother in years, but she'd asked her mother for his number in case there was ever an emergency.

A woman answered the phone. "Hello?" she asked in a shrill voice, as if annoyed by the interruption.

"Is Petey there?" Emmeline asked.

"Who's this?" demanded the woman. "You the bitch he's been messing around with?"

Emmeline sighed wearily. "No," she said. "This is his sister."

"Petey ain't got no sister," the woman responded. "Now who the hell *is* this, because I got caller ID and I know what your number is. You hang up on me and I'll call you every ten minutes until you tell me where the fuck that lousy son of a bitch is."

"What do you mean where he is?" Emmeline asked. "Isn't he there?"

"No, he's not here, bitch. As if you didn't know. Disappeared two weeks ago saying he had some stuff to take care of. Haven't seen him since."

"Look," Emmeline said, sensing that she wasn't going to get anywhere arguing with the woman, "I'm sorry for whatever my brother's done. But you've got to listen to me. Our mother is in the hospital, and he needs to make arrangements for someone to take care of her."

The woman laughed. "His mother?" she said. "What makes you think Petey'd give a shit what happened to *her?*"

"Excuse me?" Emmeline said, offended by the woman's mocking tone.

"Sweetie, he hasn't seen that bitch since she stopped giving him money."

Emmeline was truly stunned. Her mother had never mentioned a falling-out with Petey. In fact, she'd always implied that he was the most doting of sons.

"Like I said," the woman continued when Emmeline didn't say anything, "Petey never told me about no sister. But if you are, then you're on your own, honey. That bastard doesn't care about nothing but himself."

"Thank you," Emmeline replied. "I'm sorry I bothered you."

She hung up.

"Are you okay?" asked Toby, coming to stand beside her.

"I will be," Emmeline said mechanically. Her mind was trying to process everything she'd been told in the previous ten minutes. She looked at Toby. "But I think we're going to be having a visitor."

CHAPTER 24

"She told you that you should *what?*"

Reid couldn't believe Ty had said what he'd just heard. He stared at his lover in disbelief. Ty looked down at his salad, poking at a candied walnut anxiously.

No wonder Ty had insisted on going out to dinner in public, Reid thought. He knew there was no way that Reid could make a scene, which was exactly what he wanted to do. But given the fact that they were surrounded by a large number of people, at least several of whom clearly knew who Ty was, he had to keep himself under control.

He took a long drink from the tumbler of whiskey in front of him and tried to look at ease. Ty, still busy with his salad, risked a quick glance up.

"It's not like I'd really go through with it," he said quietly. "It's just for the publicity."

Reid set his drink down and folded his hands. "So tell me. Just who does Pamela think you should become engaged to?"

"No one in particular," Ty answered.

Reid nodded. "I see," he said. "So just anybody is fine?"

Ty shrugged. "I guess," he replied. "Like I said, I don't really have to go through with it. I'll just stay engaged for a while and then break it off in a year or so."

Reid picked up his knife and fork and stabbed at the chicken breast on his plate. "It sounds like it's all worked out," he said evenly. "Now you just have to find the perfect girl."

"I don't like this any more than you do," Ty said as Reid angrily chewed his food, barely tasting the delicious sauce it was covered in.

"But Pamela says people don't want to see me going from woman to woman. It makes me look like a bad boy."

"She's right," Reid said. "She's absolutely right. We don't want you to turn into the next Robert Downey Jr. or Charlie Sheen. You should settle down."

Ty twirled some pasta around his fork. "So you're okay with this?" he asked doubtfully.

"Absolutely," Reid said. "Get engaged."

"Now you're just being sarcastic," Ty retorted irritably.

"And how would you like me to respond to this little announcement?" Reid asked, spearing a piece of broccoli with a vengeance.

"You know the game as well as I do," Ty told him. "I didn't make up the rules."

"No, but you're playing by them," snapped Reid. "I thought the whole point was to break them."

"We will," Ty said. "Just not now. My career is really taking off, but I'm not there yet. I need to be more settled before I can rock the boat. Look what happened to Anne Heche when she came out."

"She went straight again," Reid replied.

"I meant with her movie roles. Everyone talked about how she didn't lose any, but you know that isn't true."

Reid couldn't respond. He knew Ty was right. Even he had debated using Heche in a movie after all the press surrounding her relationship with Ellen Degeneres. Thankfully, she'd taken another offer and the choice had been made for him. He liked to think he would have used her, but when he was honest about it he wasn't sure he would have. How could he ask the man he cared about more than anyone else in the world to put himself in the same precarious position while he remained safely in his behind-the-scenes position?

"You didn't tell Pamela about us, did you?" he asked Ty.

Ty gave a short laugh. "No way," he said. "She may have my best interest at heart, but she also has one of the biggest mouths in Hollywood. Give her three martinis and my name would be all over one of Ted Casablanca's 'Awful Truth' columns. No, she still thinks I'm just a typical Hollywood playboy who needs a little image tweaking."

Reid had to smile when he thought about just how much of a tweaking Ty's image would get if he came out. He'd love to see Pamela's face when she discovered the real reason her star client kept going out on the town with one new beauty after another. It was one of the great ironies of Hollywood, he thought. The whole town was basically run by queers, yet they still expressed shock when one of the stars who populated the world they created turned out to be just like them. He wondered what kind of damage control Pamela would do if Ty revealed his sexuality publicly. *You mean* when *he reveals it,* he reminded himself.

"How is everything?"

Reid looked up to see the woman who had seated them earlier standing beside the table. Jackie, she'd said her name was. He'd assumed she was the owner.

"Everything is great," Reid told her.

"Yes," Ty echoed. "Fantastic."

"Wonderful," Jackie told them. "Don't forget to leave room for dessert. We have an amazing coffee crème brûlée tonight that isn't to be believed."

Jackie left them alone again. For a moment Reid sat there, looking at his food. Then he looked at Ty.

"Did you hear that?" he asked.

Ty shrugged. "What?" he asked. "Crème brûlée? I can't have any. My trainer would kill me."

"No," Reid said. "I mean the way she treated us like normal people. She didn't fawn. She didn't gush. She didn't do anything."

"She probably doesn't recognize me," Ty said casually.

"That's exactly my point," Reid told him. "In LA everyone recognizes everyone. We all live for seeing people. Dinner isn't dinner there; it's a premier. When's the last time you ate in a restaurant where someone didn't either ask you for an autograph or try to talk business?"

Ty thought for a moment. "I can't remember," he said.

"It's so nice to be around normal people," Reid remarked.

"No one's normal," replied Ty.

"You know what I mean," said Reid. "No one is talking about deals or options or grosses. Don't you find that refreshing?"

"Actually, I find it a little depressing," Ty answered.

"Depressing?" repeated Reid. "Why?"

"These are the people we *make* movies for," explained Ty. "We make them for the so-called normal people, the ones who go to movies so they can get away from their lives for two hours. Having to see them all the time just reminds me that what we do is provide fantasies for people who don't have any of their own. At least back in LA I can pretend what we do is important."

"It is important," Reid argued. "Or at least it *can* be. It *should* be. What about the film you're making now?"

Ty shook his head. "Pretentious indie crap," he said. "The script *was* great. The director *is* great. But somewhere along the line the money people got their hands on it. Now one of the producer's nieces has a costarring role and all the good stuff has been edited out. We might as well put a Faith Hill song in it and pretend it's a *Coyote Ugly* sequel."

Reid stifled a smile. He'd been keeping an eye on the film's progress, and he knew things weren't as bad as Ty was making them out to be. Still, he knew what his boyfriend meant.

"Look on the bright side," he said. "It will still make you the next Parker Posey."

Ty groaned. "Anything but that," he said.

"Let's get back to this engagement thing," said Reid.

"Do we have to?" asked Ty. "I was kind of happy that we'd moved on."

"No such luck," Reid informed him. "If you're going to do it, I think it should be on of these 'normal' girls, not another celebrity. It will make you look obtainable. And then when you dump her all your female fans will think *they* have a chance to get you."

Ty gazed at him, openmouthed. "For someone who was pissed off twenty minutes ago you seem to have this all worked out," he commented.

"Oh, I'm still pissed off," said Reid. "But I know what I'm up against, so I figure the best thing to do is make sure you get what you're after."

"I'm not sure whether I should thank you or be afraid," Ty said.

"Both," answered Reid.

"Excuse me."

Reid looked up, expecting to see their waitress standing beside him. Instead what he found was a young woman holding a pen and a napkin.

"I know this is incredibly rude," she said. "But could I ask you to sign this?"

She was looking at Ty. Reid saw him look around quickly. He knew Ty was hoping that no one else saw the girl approach them. If they did, they might consider it an open invitation to do the same.

"Sure," Ty said, reaching out for the pen and the napkin. "What's your name?"

"Devin," the young woman answered. "I don't normally do things like this. But it isn't often that we get anyone really interesting coming to town, and I really do love your work. I hope you'll excuse the interruption."

"No problem," Ty said as he handed the napkin and pen back to Devin. "It's always nice to meet a fan."

"And I'm a big fan of yours too," Devin said, addressing Reid. "Would you mind?"

"Me?" Reid said, genuinely surprised. "I think you must have me mistaken for someone else."

"No, Mr. Truman, I know who you are," said Devin. "I'm sort of interested in film. I studied it in school. I know it's nerdy, but I almost know more about the people who make the movies than the ones in them."

"Really?" Reid asked. "Well, that's a nice change from what I usually hear." He took the pen and scribbled his name on the napkin right beneath Ty's.

"Thank you so much," Devin said. "And again, I'm very sorry for interrupting. I'll leave you to your dinner now."

"Wait a minute," said Reid, stopping her. "You mentioned something about no one interesting ever coming to town. Do you live here?"

Devin nodded. "Most of my life," she said. "I just graduated, so right now I'm trying to figure out what to do with the rest of my life. Any suggestions?"

She laughed again, a natural, carefree laugh that Reid found irresistible.

"I don't know about the rest of your life," he said. "But I'm staying here for the summer, and I might need some help on occasion. You know, administrative stuff. Would you be interested?"

Devin's eyes went wide. "Would I?" she said. "Oh, my God, that would be amazing."

"Why don't you give me your number?" Reid suggested. "If I find myself needing someone, I'll call you."

Devin hastily scribbled her name and number on another napkin and handed it to Reid.

"It would be so cool to work for you," she said. "I can't even tell you."

Reid smiled. "Okay, then," he said. "You might just be hearing from me."

Devin thanked him again and then left. When she was gone, Ty fixed Reid with a look.

"I thought you didn't want anyone around while you're here," he said. "What's with telling her you might hire her to work for you?"

"She's a nice girl," Reid answered. "And I really might need someone to help out. You know, do some filing, make copies, that sort of thing."

"Mmm-hmm," Ty said suspiciously. "Well, I wouldn't be too quick to let her into the house," he said. "You never know what people want."

"How'd you get so jaded so fast?" asked Reid. "I think you've seen *All About Eve* a few too many times."

"I'm just saying," Ty told him. "I mean really, how many people know who *producers* are?"

"People who are smart enough to know that actors aren't the ones who make the movies," said Reid. "That's who. And don't worry, *if* I hire her to do any work I'll be sure she's not around when you're running all over the place in your underwear."

"It was a towel," Ty said. "And I didn't have any underwear on. And seriously, if you want someone to help out, why not just fly Violet out here?"

"Because I need Violet where she is," Reid explained. "And I don't need a full-time assistant. I just think it would be good to have someone I can call on if I do need anything."

"Sounds to me like you've got a project in mind," Ty suggested.

"No," said Reid. "Not yet, anyway."

"Ah-ha. So you've been thinking about one," said Ty triumphantly. "Now it all makes sense."

"Maybe I've been thinking of *something*," admitted Reid. "But nothing definite. It's just that being here has made me think about all the things I've wanted to do but haven't. And stop trying to change the subject. I'm still mad at you."

"I was hoping you'd forgotten about that."

"Not likely," Reid said. "So, when does Pamela want you to make your big announcement?"

"She hasn't set a time line," said Ty defensively. "Look, it's just something she threw out as an idea. I didn't mean for it to turn into a huge thing."

Reid didn't reply. He wasn't sure what to say. Everything about the summer had seemed perfect, and now Ty had thrown him a curve ball. The worst part was, if it had been anyone but Ty making the suggestion he probably would have been supportive of it. But it *was* Ty, and it was their relationship that was caught in the middle. There were decisions that would have to be made, maybe not immediately, but soon, and those decisions could affect both of them in ways Reid didn't want to think about.

The arrival of the waitress, however, spared him from having to make any of them right then.

"Can I interest you gentlemen in any dessert?" she asked, oblivious of the situation she'd walked into.

Reid looked at her and nodded gently, thankful to have at least one choice he could make easily.

"We hear the crème brûlée is out of this world," he said. "Let's have one of those." He looked over at Ty. "And two spoons," he added.

CHAPTER 25

Predictable.

Josh looked at the lines of words crawling across his laptop's screen like little electronic ants marching in formation, the cursor blinking at the end like some kind of sergeant piloting them on an endless game of follow the leader. He was tempted to hit the backspace button and send them all to their deaths, his finger a cosmic force capable of obliterating the literary landscape he'd so painstakingly created. And it had taken him much longer than seven days.

Predictable. He still couldn't get the word out of his head. There were lots of other words, too, some of them nice ones. But the only one that Josh could focus on was the one he'd been so shocked to hear coming from Brody Nicholson's mouth. He'd gone to his first class filled with enthusiasm and looking forward to hearing what his teacher and his fellow students had to say about his work.

That had lasted until Wednesday. That was the day they'd discussed the sample chapter he'd dutifully made twelve copies of and eagerly distributed to the others. And things had gone well at first. By and large the other people in the class had praised Josh's writing. But then it had been Nicholson's turn to pass judgment, and things had taken an unexpected and demoralizing turn.

True, he had spoken kindly of Josh's style, and had enjoyed many of the characters. It was the plot he'd found fault with. And that's where the charge of predictability had been leveled. Josh had left the classroom under a cloud of disappointment that over the following forty-eight hours had turned into a full-blown hurricane of self-doubt and unhappiness.

Now he was sitting at a table on the deck at Jackie's, alternately staring out at the ocean and down at his computer and wondering if maybe he should just forget the whole thing. The afternoon crowd was getting larger as newcomers arrived for the weekend and vacationers who were starting on their second weeks in P-Town gathered at what had quickly become "their" meeting place of choice.

"You don't look like you're having a good time."

Josh looked up and saw Jackie standing beside him, a drink in her hand.

"I thought you could use this," she said as she set a margarita in front of him and sat down in the chair across from him.

Josh grinned. He and Jackie had gotten to know each other a little better since their first meeting during his dinner with Ben and Ted. This was due largely to the fact that he spent almost every afternoon there writing and frequently stayed on into the evening, when things picked up and he could unwind.

"Is it that obvious?" Josh asked Jackie as he took a sip of the drink, the salt on the glass's rim mixing with the bitterness of the tequila.

"It's either that or boyfriend trouble," replied Jackie. "It's basically the same look."

"In my case it's both," Josh said. "But after two or three of these I imagine things will look a lot better."

"Or worse," Jackie remarked knowingly.

"Not possible," said Josh, taking another drink. "My book is predictable and my relationship is most likely over."

"Then look at the bright side," Jackie told him. "It can't get any worse."

"It can *always* get worse," said Josh.

"There you are."

Suddenly the table was surrounded by more bodies as Ryan and his friends arrived en masse and seated themselves.

"See?" Josh said to Jackie, who smiled.

"I'll send out a pitcher of those for you guys," she said as she left.

"Make it two!" Al called out after her.

"Put that thing away," Ryan ordered Josh as he pushed the laptop closed. "It's now officially the weekend. No work."

Josh complied, stowing the laptop in its case and putting it under his chair. There was no point in arguing with Ryan and his gang when they were in the mood to party. Besides, he was tired of reading his own words over and over, especially when he couldn't find any way to make them less predictable.

"So, how are the Merry Men?" Josh inquired, using the name he'd recently coined for Ryan, Al, Phil, Bart, Aaron, and Eric.

"Horny," answered Bart immediately.

"He was watching our houseboy clean the pool all afternoon," Eric explained. "He has a terrible case of perpetual hard-on."

"Fuck you," Bart snapped. "That kid is walking sex, and you know it."

"Please," said Eric. "He's so uptight I don't think you could get inside him with a crowbar and a gallon of Elbow Grease."

"He does seem a little edgy," agreed Phil. "What do you think is up with that?"

"He's probably terrified that Bart is going to deflower him," Al joked. "As he has so many other young men."

"I don't do anything they don't want me to," Bart said defensively, and they all laughed.

"What about you?" Ryan asked Josh. "Have you talked to the Cheat lately?"

Josh shook his head. "No," he said. "I don't think there's a whole lot to say."

"You need to forget about him," Bart said as the pitchers of margaritas arrived. "Fuck him out of your system."

"What?" Josh asked.

"Fuck him out of your system," repeated Bart. "It's a proven fact that when you break up with someone you need to go out and have sex with someone else as soon as possible. It rids your system of whatever emotional toxins the old guy left behind. Sort of like having a colonic." He took a sip of his drink and looked thoughtful. "Actually, if you're lucky it's a *lot* like having a colonic."

"He's right," Al said. "Sleeping with someone else breaks that bond and lets you move on."

"I'm not sure I want to move on just yet," replied Josh. "But thanks for the suggestion."

For the next two hours the conversation, and the margaritas, continued to flow. As the tequila worked its way through his body, Josh found himself growing more and more relaxed. Content to listen to the others talk, he sat back and allowed himself to be surrounded by the warmth of the summer night and the soft buzzing of the voices around him. Little by little his concerns about his writing faded away and he became lost in the mood of the evening.

He looked around at the people gathered on the deck. Some were having dinner, others were sipping cocktails, and a few had come onto the patio simply to enjoy the evening. Josh could easily have sat there for hours, lost in the dreaminess of it all. But a hand on his knee startled him back to reality.

"Come on," said Ryan. "We're going to Milky Way."

"Where?" Josh asked, confused.

"Dancing," Ryan elaborated. "Let's go."

Josh began to protest, but found himself being lifted up by Ryan on one side and Aaron on the other. He hastily fumbled for his laptop as they dragged him away from the table and toward the door.

Fifteen minutes later he was standing in the middle of Milky Way, surrounded by a crowd of men. His laptop had been handed over to a smiling young man at the coat check (Why did they need a coat check in summer? he'd wondered vaguely) and a drink had been placed in his hand. He took a sip from it. Gin and tonic. He was going to have a headache later.

"Look at all these guys." Bart was standing beside him, his head moving first one direction and then the other as he scanned the crowd. "How can I pick just one?"

"Knowing you, you won't pick just one," said Al. "Just be sure to leave a few for the rest of us."

"How about you, Josh?" asked Phil. "If you had to pick one, who would it be?"

"Oh, I don't know," Josh answered uncomfortably.

"Come on," coaxed Bart. "You're allowed to look."

Josh sighed. Bart was right; he *was* allowed to look. But he'd always been uncomfortable playing the "who would you sleep with?" game, even in jest. It made him feel as if he were cheating on Doug. Worse, it made him feel like one of those gay men who only ever thought about other guys in terms of whether or not they'd make good sex partners.

But maybe it was time to lighten up a little, he thought. He was, after all, on a semivacation from his life. He took another sip of his gin and tonic and looked around the bar.

"Okay," he said as he scanned the crowd, "I'll tell you who I'd do."

Bart and the others waited expectantly while Josh made up his mind. He hadn't done this in a long time, and as he took in all the different men he realized that deciding on one was more difficult than he thought. He'd been with Doug for so long that his sexual ideal had more or less settled on one particular type. Except for his brief—un-successful—fantasy about Reilly he hadn't much thought about what might turn him on. Now that he let himself think about the possibilities, he found that he was a little surprised by the men who caught his eye.

He first considered a tall, dark-haired guy standing against the wall with a beer bottle nestled casually in the crotch of his jeans. He liked the brooding look. But then he realized that with a couple of minor modifications the man could easily pass for Doug, and he moved on. His next choice was almost a polar opposite, a thin blonde in an Aber-crombie & Fitch T-shirt and cargo shorts. Josh, however, firmly be-lieved that no man over twenty-five should go out in public wearing anything with the A&F logo on it, so he passed the blonde over and briefly settled on a latino powerhouse whose bulging arms and chest filled out his white tank top to the point of bursting. What would such a man be like in bed? he wondered, until he remembered what one of his gym rat friends had once told him about most muscle guys being on steroids and, as a result, having more than a little difficulty in the erection department.

He was about to default to the beer-bottle-in-the-crotch guy when he spied a man leaning against the bar, talking to some friends. Dressed in jeans and a plain white T-shirt, the guy wore a San Francisco Giants baseball cap. His face was ruggedly handsome, with a dark dusting of five-o'clock shadow, and Josh was immediately taken in by his smile, which was slightly crooked and gave him a boyish look despite his very masculine appearance.

"That one," he said before he could change his mind.

The others immediately looked in the man's direction, as if trying to catch a glimpse of a shooting star.

"Nice," Aaron remarked.

"Sort of an overgrown frat boy," Al suggested.

"Do you think he's a top or a bottom?" mused Bart.

"It doesn't matter, because I'm not going to find out," answered Josh.

Bart sighed. "Must I do everything myself?" he asked.

Before Josh could stop him, Bart walked across the bar and directly up to the object of Josh's interest. Josh watched, horrified, as Bart spoke to the man, turning once to indicate Josh with his glass. He was even more horrified when, a moment later, Bart returned with the guy in tow.

"Josh, this is Ed. Ed, this is Josh. Begin."

Ed smiled. "Hi," he said as Josh's friends watched with amusement.

"Um, hi," replied Josh, feeling like some wallflower schoolboy who was being set up at the junior high dance.

"We're going to let you boys get acquainted," Bart announced. "We'll be on the dance floor if you need us."

"Wait . . ." Josh began, panicking, but the others just waved at him and moved toward the dance floor, leaving him alone with Ed.

"Sorry about that," he said.

"Why?" asked Ed.

Josh looked at him. *God, his smile is hot,* he thought involuntarily.

"Want another?" Ed asked, holding up his empty beer bottle. Josh noticed that his forearms were covered in hair—another of his turn-ons.

"Why not?" he replied. "But no more gin. I'll take a beer."

Ed returned to the bar and came back a minute later with the drinks.

"Cheers," he said, tapping his bottle against Josh's.

"So, you're from San Francisco?" Josh asked after taking a long sip from his bottle.

Ed nodded. "It's my first time out here," he said. "You?"

Josh shook his head. "I live here," he replied. "Well, not *here.* I actually live in Boston."

He'd forgotten what bar small talk was like. He'd always hated it, trying to learn something about a man while really wondering what he looked like naked. His one-night stand history was relatively small, almost inconsequential by gay standards, and mostly because he found the conversational foreplay unbearable. How many times could you ask what someone did for a living, or what his favorite Cher song was?

To his surprise, talking with Ed was easy. He was funny, and their back-and-forth banter flowed easily. The alcohol helped, of course, and Josh was thankful for its assistance. As rusty as he was with the whole business, he found he was enjoying his time with Ed. It made him feel more alive than he had in some time, since, well, the first time he'd met Doug.

"How'd you like to get out of here?"

The question took Josh by surprise. A moment before, they had been discussing movies. But now Ed was looking at him, that sexy smile on his face, waiting for an answer.

Josh's mind raced. Suddenly the music and the voices seemed to swarm around him, making it difficult to think. No, he didn't want to go home with Ed. Yes, he wanted it more than anything. His will was pulled first one way and then another, his conscience wrestling with the decision he had to make.

"Sure," he found himself saying.

Ed took his beer from him and set the two empty bottles on the bar.

"Let's go," he said, taking Josh's hand.

Fifteen minutes later they were in Josh's bed. Their clothes were scattered on the floor, Ed's Giants hat was on the dresser, and his tongue was tracing a line down Josh's stomach. Josh, his eyes closed, tried not to think about what was happening. The warmth of Ed's mouth on his skin, the touch of his fingers on Josh's body, were drowning out everything else. When Ed ran his tongue under Josh's balls and darted into the soft pucker of his ass, Josh forgot everything else as he ran his fingers through Ed's hair and pushed him deeper.

As they made love Josh thought only briefly of how different Ed's body felt from Doug's. He was bigger, for one thing, and softer. He moved differently, too, taking his time as if Josh's body were a new, unexplored world. It wasn't at all like Doug's familiar patterns, the pattern of who touched whom where and when set in stone after years of practice and design. Free from the routine, Josh found himself remembering just how enjoyable it could be to experience another man's body, and when he finally came, with Ed gently sucking on his nipple while stroking him firmly, it was almost as if it were for the first time.

He fell asleep almost immediately afterward, lulled into a stupor by the combination of alcohol and sex. When he awoke, it was to the sound of pounding. He opened his eyes, saw Ed sleeping beside him, and groaned. Then he got up to see where the pounding was coming from.

When he opened the door he found Reilly on the porch, hammer in hand as he laid a new board down.

"Hey," Reilly said cheerfully. "Did I wake you?"

"What time is it?" Josh asked sleepily.

Reilly looked at his watch. "Almost eleven," he answered.

Josh nodded stupidly. His head was killing him. It hurt even more now that he was remembering the events of the previous evening. What had he been thinking?

"Rough night?" asked Reilly.

"Just a late one," Josh lied. "I was writing."

He started to say more but was interrupted by the touch of a hand on his shoulder. He turned as Ed stepped out onto the porch. He was dressed in his clothes from the night before, the wrinkles in them revealing their time spent in a heap on Josh's floor.

"Hey there," he said. "Sorry to run off, but I'm supposed to meet some friends in half an hour."

"Oh," said Josh. He noticed Reilly looking at Ed with an expression of barely disguised curiosity. "That's okay."

"I guess I'll see you around," Ed remarked as he adjusted his Giants hat.

"Sure," replied Josh casually. "See you."

Ed nodded at Reilly and walked away, not looking back. Josh watched him go, wishing he could just disappear. *He didn't even ask for my number,* he thought.

"Friend of yours?" Reilly asked him, looking at Ed's rapidly retreating figure.

"Yeah," Josh lied. "He stayed over last night. We know each other from Boston."

Reilly nodded. Josh prayed that he believed the story. He didn't know why, but he didn't want Reilly to know that he'd just tricked with some guy he'd never seen before and probably would never see again.

"Well, I should get back to work," said Reilly, not looking at Josh. "I have a lot to do."

"Me too," Josh told him, wanting very much to be inside.

He stepped back into the house and shut the door. Then he leaned against it. Reilly hadn't believed him. He knew what had happened in Josh's bed. But so what? Why did Josh care? He didn't have to answer to the handyman.

But he did care. He cared very much what Reilly thought of him. And suddenly he was deeply ashamed of himself. But why? It wasn't a crime to have sex. He was a grown man. He wasn't hurting anyone. He could do whatever he wanted to. Yet he still felt disappointed in himself for reasons he couldn't quite put his finger on.

Suddenly the words of Brody Nicholson came back to him. Predictable. That's what it was. He'd done exactly what he hadn't wanted to do, what he so often complained that gay men did too often. He'd done the predictable, and worse, Reilly had been there to witness it.

CHAPTER 26

"Theresa Marie, are you awake? We're leaving for Mass in twenty minutes."

Devin closed her eyes tightly and tried to keep her breathing even. She could feel her mother in the doorway, watching her closely. *I'm not Theresa Marie anymore,* she thought, drowning out the sound of her mother's plaintive voice.

"Theresa Marie?" her mother repeated, a little more loudly.

Devin let out a sharp snore, an ugly explosion of a sound that would have disgusted her had it come from someone else, particularly someone with whom she was sharing her bed.

Mrs. Lowen waited another minute before closing the door. Devin listened for the footsteps on the stairs that signaled her mother's retreat, then opened her eyes. The sun was pushing its way through the curtains at her window, the cool yellow light sliding across the floor like water. The slowly expanding pool had almost reached the foot of her bed, but for the moment she remained safely within the shadows, wrapped in a cocoon of blue cotton sheets.

How many times had she been in this situation before? She thought about the many Sunday mornings when she'd attempted to escape the torment of Mass at St. Timothy's by feigning either sickness or sleep. Her mother, who as a girl had taken to Christ the way some of her peers would later take to John, Paul, George, and Ringo, had dutifully made her way to Mass every Sunday of her life, beginning during the reign of Pope Pious XII and seeing out John XXIII, Paul VI, and John Paul I. She was particularly enamored of John Paul II, and seemed to think that the pontiff remained more or less alive due solely to her continued prayers for his well-being. Devin's father often joked that he was the only man in town whose wife was having an affair with a celibate.

Unfortunately for Carlotta Lowens, her daughter had not inherited her passion for the Church. Although Reggie Lowens reluctantly accompanied his wife to her weekly soul-cleansing, believing on some level that simply walking into St. Timothy's was enough to ensure his entrance into whatever paradise awaited those who went through the motions on a regular basis, Devin—or, as she had been called then, Theresa Marie—had defiantly refused to accept the notion that she had been born sinful and needed to make up for it by not squirming through Father O'Leary's sermons. Or rather, she had decided at an early age that if she was going to be made to pay for something she hadn't even done, she was going to make damn sure she got her money's worth.

For many years Devin's mother had prevailed in the weekly battle over going to St. Timothy's, a loss Devin revenged by surreptitiously removing bills from the collection plate when it came her way and using them to buy gum and, later, cigarettes. But when Devin turned fifteen, she announced that she would no longer be going to Mass. It was also at this time that she insisted that she be called Devin, a name she'd come across while devouring a forbidden Jackie Collins novel and decided fit her better than the pitiful Theresa Marie, which to her reeked of piety, knee socks, and virginity, all of which she'd abandoned at the first opportunity. Reeling from the shock of the first announcement, her mother scarcely noticed the second, and thus Devin had been introduced to the usefulness of distraction.

When she'd left for college, Devin had been more than happy to leave St. Timothy's, and all it symbolized, behind her. She hadn't set foot in a house of worship since, and among the many things that irritated her about having to return home following her graduation was her mother's renewed attempts to get her up on Sunday mornings. Particularly when combined with the use of her hated former name, it made Devin feel fifteen again.

When she was sure her mother had left for church, she sat up and reached for the pack of cigarettes she'd hidden in her bedside table drawer. Lighting one, she took her first puff of the day and exhaled the smoke in the direction of the sunshine, as if she could put a protective nicotine barrier between herself and its cheerfulness. She wished she had a glass of water. Her head pounded, the price for all the drinking she'd done the night before at Jackie's. She'd been hanging out there every night, hoping that Reid Truman would return, with or without Ty Rusk. Ty was, of course, an interesting development, but it was Reid who could offer her what she wanted. Yet he hadn't called her, and that was a problem. It had been two weeks since her conversation with C.J. Raymacher, and as yet she had nothing to offer him.

She got up, pulling her robe from the hook on the back of the door, and went downstairs. In an act of defiance she took her cigarette with her, even though her mother strictly forbade smoking in the house. As she sat at the kitchen table, drinking the glass of water she hoped would tame her headache, she looked around at the room she'd spent so much time in growing up. Now it felt like a prison, one papered with bright yellow flowers and decorated with smiling cow salt and pepper shakers and a cookie jar shaped like a ladybug. And there, presiding over everything like a watchful, scapula-topped jailer, was the weary-eyed photo of John Paul II that hung above the stove, where her mother could gaze upon it as she scrambled her eggs. Devin gave the picture the finger and stood up. A shower would help, she thought, and then maybe an hour or so on the beach.

As she left the kitchen she noticed a note scribbled on the pad that hung beside the telephone. There, in her father's nearly illegible hand, she read "Reid Truman for TM. 555-8752."

Devin ripped the paper from the pad and stared at it. Reid had called her. But when? Not only had he not told her of the call, but her father had put neither date nor time on the note. It could have come any time in the preceding four days.

She snatched up the phone and began to dial before remembering the time. In all likelihood, she thought, Reid didn't have a mother who woke him at ridiculous hours to get him to go to church with her. She would have to wait. She returned the receiver to its cradle and went upstairs to shower.

When she emerged an hour later, clouds of steam billowing from the bathroom door as she walked back to her room, she felt much better. And when another half hour saw her dressed and made up, she picked up the phone and dialed Reid's number with confidence.

"Reid," she said when she heard his voice. "Devin Lowens returning your call. I hope I didn't keep you waiting too long."

"Not at all," replied Reid. "I just called last night."

Devin breathed a sigh of relief and forgave her father. "So what can I do for you?" she asked.

"Why don't we talk about that over lunch?" said Reid. "Can you meet me at Jackie's in an hour?"

"Sure," Devin answered, trying not to betray the disappointment she felt at not being asked to come to Reid's house.

"I'll see you then," said Reid, ending the call.

Devin looked at the clock. Her parents would be home any minute, and if they found her there her mother would want her to stay around for lunch. Having already avoided Mass, she didn't want to press her luck. She needed to be out before their return.

Grabbing her purse, she left the house and got into her car. Given the limited options provided by Provincetown on a Sunday morning, she decided her best bet was to simply head straight to Jackie's and wait for Reid to arrive. At least, she thought, it would suggest punctuality on her part.

It took her all of ten minutes to make the drive, and soon she was seated at a table in the main dining room, sipping a Bloody Mary and taking stock of the crowd that had already gathered.

Fags. They were all fags, she thought, as she looked around the room. What was it about queens that they all loved brunch so much? A gay friend in college had told her once that brunch was to gay men what breakfast was to the rest of the human race, the most important meal of the day. "Besides," he'd added, "after fucking all night you've got to eat *something.*"

Not that she minded. She liked gay men. They were usually better to look at than straight guys, and definitely more interesting. Especially if you could get them into bed. She hadn't done *that* in a while, she reminded herself as she looked at the handsome faces talking and laughing over their eggs Benedicts and mimosas.

"Am I late?"

Devin looked up to see Reid Truman pulling out a chair and seating himself across from her. She flashed a smile at him.

"Of course not," she said. "I'm early. I'm afraid it's one of my bad habits."

Reid laughed. "I wish more people had such abominable manners," he joked. "I spend half my life waiting for people who think noon means any time between twelve and two. It's like Hollywood is run by UPS."

Summoning the waitress, Reid ordered a scotch on the rocks. When the girl went to get it he leaned back in his chair and looked at Devin.

"So, you studied film in school?" he asked.

Devin nodded. "Yes," she said. "I had this idea that I wanted to be a film critic. Then I found out they make no money and everyone hates them, so I changed my major to business."

"Smart move," remarked Reid. "What are your five favorite films?"

Devin was taken aback by the unexpected question. She'd expected Reid to ask her more mundane things about herself. She hadn't planned for this line of conversation. But she had a feeling her answer might be important, so she switched gears and thought for a moment.

"Well, to paraphrase the Miss America contest, I guess the fourth runner up would be *Casablanca,*" she said. "I know it's an obvious one, but you can't beat it for a love story. Next would have to be *Pulp Fiction,* and then *Life Is Beautiful*—I thought Roberto Begnini was *amazing.* First runner up would be *All About Eve.*"

She looked at Reid, who was watching her with an unreadable expression.

"And the winner?" he asked her.

"Definitely *Independence Day,*" answered Devin.

"The Will Smith movie?" Reid said, looking at her oddly.

"Absolutely," Devin replied firmly. "I saw it when I was fourteen and it changed my life."

She paused a moment as Reid clearly struggled with his response.

"I'm kidding," she said. "My real favorite is *A Beautiful Mind.* I know it's not a classic yet, but I think Ron Howard did a fantastic job making an esoteric subject into a commercial film."

She sat back and waited for Reid's reaction. *Thank God for* Entertainment Weekly, she thought. Every single thing she'd said had come right out of their "100 Best Films of All Time" issue, which she'd conveniently just finished reading. The truth was, out of all the films she'd mentioned, she'd only seen *Independence Day,* and it really was her favorite.

"An interesting list," said Reid as the waitress returned with his drink. "Especially your remarks about the Howard film. I totally agree with you on that one. He did a fucking kick-ass job."

Devin breathed a silent sigh of relief.

"I notice you didn't list any of my films," Reid continued. "Not that

I blame you. They make a shit load of money, but they're pretty much all crap."

"I wouldn't say that," objected Devin. "Didn't Ebert and Roeper call *Hat Trick* the *Dirty Dancing* of the year?"

"I believe they did," Reid said, smiling. "I guess I probably should have sent them bigger Christmas baskets, eh?"

"So what are your favorite films?" asked Devin.

"Fair enough," Reid said, nodding his head. "And easy to answer. *Chinatown, Close Encounters of the Third Kind, Secrets and Lies, Philadelphia Story,* and anything by Robert Altman but particularly *Nashville.*"

"An interesting list," said Devin.

Reid laughed. "Touché," he replied. "You have a good sense of humor. I like that. It's something else no one in Hollywood has. I think that's why I like it here so much."

"I know what you mean," Devin remarked. "It's sort of nice, isn't it?"

"It must have been interesting growing up here," said Reid.

"It was," Devin said. "I feel really lucky."

"So look," said Reid, "like I told you the other night, I need someone to help me out while I'm here. I wasn't planning on doing any work this summer, but I'm feeling inspired."

"Is there anything in particular you're working on?" Devin asked.

Reid shook his head. "Not yet," he said. "That's part of what I need help with. I want to find something, something *not* Hollywood."

"You mean like a script?" suggested Devin.

"No," Reid answered emphatically. "That's exactly what I don't want. I'm tired of reading scripts. Writers just send me what they think a Hollywood movie should be. I want something different."

"Not that I want to talk myself out of a job here or anything, but how can I help you find something?" Devin asked.

"Do you know the Arts House?" asked Reid.

Devin nodded. "Sure," she answered. "Why?"

"They hold performances and stuff there," explained Reid. "Readings. That sort of thing. I want you to go to them. Check out the people they have there. If anything—or anyone—is interesting, I want to know about it."

"Okay," Devin said slowly. "But couldn't you just do that yourself?"

"I could," Reid acknowledged. "But eventually someone would figure out who I am and everyone would try to impress me. But if you go, you're just another audience member."

"Now I get it," said Devin. "But what makes you think there will be anything interesting at the Arts House?"

Reid shrugged. "Maybe there won't be," he said. "But it's worth looking into. But that's only part of your job. I also need help with basic stuff like running to the post office, reading some books I'm thinking about optioning, maybe a little shopping. Can you handle that?"

"Let's see," said Devin. "Licking stamps, reading, and shopping. I think I've got those covered."

"There's one more thing," Reid said. "It's very important that you don't talk about this job—or about certain other aspects of working for me—with anyone. For example, from time to time I may have guests at the house. Guests who are coming here to get away from being famous, if you understand what I mean. It wouldn't make them—or me—happy if people knew about their visits."

"Got it," Devin said. "Believe me, I know how gossip can spread in a small town. I can keep my mouth shut."

Reid looked at her for a moment, and for a brief second Devin feared that perhaps he saw in her face something that reminded him of a certain forgetful cleaning woman. But then Reid nodded and held up his glass.

"Here's to your new summer job, then," he said. "I hope it's everything you want it to be."

Devin clinked her glass against Reid's and smiled happily. "Oh, I think it will be even better than you can imagine."

CHAPTER 27

"Buy you a drink?"

Toby looked first at the man standing next to him and then at the empty beer bottle in his own hand.

"Sure," he said.

The guy was hot. Early thirties, Toby guessed, with a nice build and a handsome face. When he handed Toby the beer he smiled.

"You looked like you needed someone to buy you a drink," he said.

"That bad?" asked Toby.

The man laughed. "Let me guess," he said. "You just broke up with your boyfriend."

Toby shook his head. "Nope," he answered. "It's my birthday."

The man grimaced. "Even worse," he said. Then he clicked his bottle against Toby's. "Well, happy birthday."

"Thanks," said Toby, drinking deeply from the bottle. The buzz in his head deepened, like the sound made by water when you sank to the bottom of a pool. Toby welcomed it, allowing himself to float on the gentle rocking that had started after his third beer, and which was intensifying with every new sip.

He'd come to the bar immediately after finishing up work at the house. The bartender hadn't even asked him for ID, which was a good thing considering that despite his birthday he was still three years away from being allowed to drink freely. *I can join the army and blow the heads off terrorists in the Middle East,* he'd thought as the bartender slid his drink across the bar to him, *but I can't get drunk in my own country. Something is very fucking wrong with that.* Earlier in the day he'd dutifully gone to the post office and filled out his selective service registration card, which conveniently had not included a box to check for sexual preference among the many other pieces of information he'd been required to provide.

"So, what are your big birthday plans?"

Toby returned his attention to his new friend. The man was leaning against the bar, looking him up and down. His gaze moved to Toby's crotch, then back to his face.

"I didn't really make any," replied Toby. Technically, this wasn't true, as Emmeline was making dinner for him. But he didn't feel like sharing that information with his companion.

"Maybe we can change that," said the man.

"Oh, yeah?" Toby said. "What did you have in mind?"

"How about we go back to my place and you can blow out my candle?" suggested the guy, leaning in closer. "I can guarantee whatever you wish for will come true."

Toby looked at him. The man was waiting for an answer.

"You don't even know my name," Toby said.

A look of confusion crossed the man's face. "So what's your name?" he asked.

Toby didn't answer. Instead, he reached into his pocket, pulled out some bills, and slapped them on the bar.

"That's for the drink," he said angrily.

"What the fuck?" exclaimed the guy, looking from the money to Toby. "What's your problem?"

"My problem is that I don't want to turn into you," snapped Toby, turning around and heading unsteadily for the door.

He walked as quickly as he could down the sidewalk away from the bar. Why had he gone there? What had he been hoping would happen?

Exactly what did happen, he told himself. And that was the problem. He wanted someone to find him attractive, to desire him. But not like that. He wanted someone to *really* like him, not just for one fuck or one night, but for a lifetime. He wanted to fall in love. And that wasn't going to happen in a bar.

No, he corrected himself. *It's not going to happen in a gay bar.*

Why did gay men have to be like that? Why did they have to go to bars and get drunk to meet each other? It made him angry, and sad. He hated looking around at all of those men—handsome men, men he was attracted to—and seeing them all trying to work up the courage to talk to each other. They were all there because they wanted the same thing. So why couldn't they talk to one another like people instead of like . . . ? He couldn't think of the right word to describe how he felt.

Then it came to him. Competitors. That's what they all reminded him of. It was like watching the opposing team before a baseball game, when you checked out the other guys and tried to figure out what their weaknesses were, made a mental list of which ones you could probably strike out easily and which ones were going to put up more of a fight. That's how he'd felt back in the bar, as if they were all playing some game where who won and who lost depended on how many hits you could get.

He was going to be sick. He could feel it rising up inside him. He willed it down again, but it was no use. Dashing to the nearest bushes, he leaned over and heaved. His stomach lurched, emptying itself of the beer and pretzels he'd consumed in the bar. His mouth filled with the stale taste, and he spat, trying to clear it away.

When he was done he continued home, walking more slowly. His head hurt and he wanted badly to brush his teeth. But he felt slightly better, and the evening air cooled his overheated skin and dried the film of sweat that had formed on his face.

When he entered the house, Emmeline was there to greet him.

"Happy birthday!" she crowed, opening her arms and enfolding Toby in an embrace.

When she released him she eyed him suspiciously. "And just where have you been, young man?" she asked.

Toby groaned. "Don't ask," he said. "Can I take a shower before we eat?"

"I insist on it," answered Emmeline. "Be down here in twenty minutes."

When Toby entered the kitchen, with two minutes to spare on Emmeline's deadline, he found her taking a roast chicken out of the oven. The shower had done much to rid him of the bar's ill effects, and the smell of the chicken made his mouth water.

Emmeline placed the chicken on the table, which already contained a mountain of food. Mashed potatoes, corn on the cob, salad, and corn bread were spread out on the tablecloth, enough for five people, let alone the two of them.

"I went a little overboard," Emmeline said, surveying the meal. "But a boy only turns eighteen once, right?"

"If he's lucky," said Toby.

Emmeline sat down and faced him across the table. "That doesn't sound like someone happy to be able to vote," she remarked.

"Right," Toby said. "Like voting means anything anyway. That last election really went well, didn't it?"

"Point taken," admitted Emmeline, spooning potatoes onto her plate.

Toby picked at his chicken. It was delicious, but somehow the dinner didn't feel like the celebration he'd always thought his eighteenth birthday would be.

"Do you know any happy gay couples?" he asked suddenly.

Emmeline looked at him as she chewed the food in her mouth and swallowed. "Why do you ask?" she said.

"Do you?" pressed Toby.

Emmeline put her fork down. "Yes, I do," she said. "I know a lot of them."

"How many?" Toby inquired. "I mean compared to the fags you know who aren't happy?"

Emmeline looked at him seriously. "I'm going to assume by your use of that vile word that something is upsetting you about the state of the gay world," she said.

"I'm serious," protested Toby. "Just look around this town. How many really happy people do you see? They're all drunk, or drugged up, or horny—usually all three."

"Is that you talking or your parents?" Emmeline asked him.

Toby looked down. "All right, so maybe all of them aren't like that," he said. "But a lot of them are."

"You keep saying 'them,'" noted Emmeline. "Are you implying that you're not gay?"

"No," said Toby quickly. "But I don't want to be like the guys I see here."

"So don't be," Emmeline replied.

Toby sighed. "That's just it," he said. "Sometimes it doesn't seem like there's any other way *to* be. I mean, why do so many fags—I mean gay guys—end up so messed up?"

Emmeline resumed eating, not speaking for a minute as she sampled her own cooking. Then she took a drink of iced tea.

"It's not like there's a class or anything," she said.

Toby looked at her, confused.

"What I mean is that no one ever teaches you how to be gay," she continued. "Straight people grow up in a world that encourages them to be straight every step of the way. They see other straight people dating, and getting married, and having children. They go to dances in school and on dates with people they're interested in. They see films and TV shows about what it's like to be straight. Gay people don't get that."

"There are gay magazines and movies," countered Toby.

"It's not the same thing," Emmeline replied. "When's the last time you heard about a father sitting down with his son to talk about what two guys do in bed? And how many teenage lesbians can go talk to their friends about the crushes they have on other girls? Gay people don't have those opportunities."

"I don't get where this is going," Toby said.

"My point is that gay people have to figure it all out on their own, and usually a long time after their straight counterparts have figured it out. So is it really any surprise that so many gay men act like they're sixteen when they're twice that age? They're scared. They don't know how to have relationships because they've never been allowed to. So they do it the only way they know how."

"I never thought about it like that," Toby said. "I always thought that when I finally got away from my parents and our town, things would be different."

"You mean perfect," Emmeline corrected him. "You thought everything would be perfect."

"I guess," Toby said.

"We all did," Emmeline told him. "We all thought we were going to run away and find Oz. But the truth is that even when you find that family you're looking for, you still have to work to make your life what you want it to be."

"You never answered my question," Toby said. "How many really happy gay couples do you know?"

"Six," Emmeline answered.

"Six?" Toby repeated. "That's it? And I'm supposed to feel like this is all worth it?"

"How many happy straight couples do you know?" asked Emmeline.

"Lots," Toby said quickly.

"Really?" asked Emmeline. "Are they really happy? Or do they just look happy because they have what we've been brainwashed into believing is the perfect life?"

"All right, so maybe a lot of them have problems," Toby said reluctantly. "But six?"

"That's five more than I knew ten years ago," Emmeline replied. "And it's six more than I knew growing up."

"I just don't want to end up like the guys in the bars," Toby said sadly.

"Why are you acting like it's a foregone conclusion?" Emmeline asked him.

Toby shrugged. "I guess because that's what I see," he said.

"We'll have to fix that," said Emmeline. "In the meantime, we have a birthday to celebrate. Finish your dinner and we'll move on to the good stuff."

Toby did as she suggested, wolfing down his food until the chicken was nothing but bones and his plate was fair near licked clean. He helped Emmeline put the dishes in the sink, and then the two of them retreated to the living room.

"We'll have dessert in a little bit," Emmeline said. "But now it's present time."

"You didn't have to get me anything," protested Toby as he sat on the couch and Emmeline produced a stack of boxes, which she set on the coffee table.

"I know I didn't have to," Emmeline told him. "But I wanted to."

She handed Toby the first gift, which he quickly unwrapped. It was a gray T-shirt that had PROPERTY OF P-TOWN ATHLETIC DEPT. printed across the front.

"There's a theme to this birthday," Emmeline explained as Toby held the shirt up to his chest. "You're sort of a gay boy in training, right? Well, these gifts are all things to get you started in your new life."

Toby laughed. "A homo starter kit," he said, grinning. "Cool."

He reached for the next gift, tearing the paper off eagerly.

"*Tales of the City,*" he read, looking at the cover of the book in his hand. "Never heard of it. Is it good?"

"It reminds me of you," Emmeline explained. "Of us," she added thoughtfully. "Consider it your handbook."

"Thanks," Toby said, laying the book down and moving on to the next present, which was a small envelope.

"Must be a card," he said as he ran his finger under the seal and opened it. Then he reached inside and pulled out what at first glance appeared to be a passport. He flipped it open and stared at it, confused. When he realized what it was, he looked up at Emmeline in amazement.

"You opened a bank account for me?" he said incredulously.

"A man needs a bank account," said Emmeline simply.

"But you put all this money in there," Toby stammered. "You didn't have to do that."

"There you go again with that 'have to' nonsense," Emmeline scolded. "If you have to do it, then it's not a present, is it?"

Toby looked back at the bankbook in his hands, not saying anything.

"I expect you to add to that every week when you get paid," Emmeline said firmly. "No wasting it all on cheap booze and loose men."

Toby laughed. "I don't know what to say," he told her. "I just don't know what to say."

"Then open your last present," said Emmeline. "That way you don't have to say anything."

Toby put the bankbook on the table, giving it a last, bewildered glance. He picked up the final package and hefted it in his hands. "It feels like a picture frame," he said.

A few pulls of the paper later and he was looking at his gift. It was indeed a picture frame, and inside it was what looked like a diploma. "Provincetown Summer School," Toby read.

"It doesn't really exist," Emmeline said. "I didn't know the name of your high school, so I made one up. Appropriate, don't you think?"

When Toby looked up he had tears in his eyes. He stood up and went to Emmeline, giving her a long hug.

"Thank you," he whispered, his voice choking.

"See?" Emmeline said as she put her arms around him. "You knew exactly what to say."

CHAPTER 28

"Okay, that's great. Now lift the nutcracker up and look at him." Marly dutifully lofted the big wooden nutcracker, staring up into his wide, painted eyes. His chin was bearded in fuzzy white fur, and his enormous teeth appeared ready to turn any walnut placed between them into dust. She felt like an idiot.

"Now turn slowly."

Marly attempted to pirouette, and immediately felt her knees sag.

"I'm sorry," she said to the woman watching her from behind the video camera.

Nellie Sa laughed. "Don't be sorry," she said easily. "The whole point is to be natural. Why don't we take a break and start over this afternoon?"

Marly nodded. She was grateful for the break. Nellie had been videotaping her for almost half an hour, and she was sore. Besides, the tutu was starting to irritate her with all of its flounciness.

"You make quite a prima ballerina."

Marly looked up and saw Garth Ambrose standing in front of her, his camera in his hands.

"Please tell me you didn't get any of that on film," she said.

"Every twirl and every knee bend," the photographer replied.

Marly groaned. "I may have to confiscate that," she said.

Garth laughed. "Personally, I can't wait to see how they come out. But would you mind telling me exactly what you were doing?"

"Yes, I would," answered Marly. "It's completely embarrassing."

"It can't be any more embarrassing than Courtney Love trying to explain why I caught her in the men's room smearing herself with melted peanut butter cups after a Madison Square Garden show," Garth countered. "And *those* photos were amazing."

Marly laughed. "Okay," she said. "Nellie asked me to take part in one of her videos. You know, where she gets adults to act out what they wish they'd been like as children."

"And you wanted to be a ballerina?" Garth asked, sounding surprised.

"I *was* a ballerina," explained Marly. "Just not a very good one. The Lakewood Academy Ballet School," she continued when Garth raised an eyebrow and leaned against a nearby table, clearly waiting to hear the rest of her story. "Miss Gilruddy's. Three years. I went every Tuesday and Thursday. I also practiced at home."

"And were you good?" Garth asked her.

Marly nodded. "Yes," she said. "But I was painfully shy. As soon as I got around the other girls, it was like my feet were made of stone. I always stayed in the back, never stood out. My particular nemesis was one Julia Sayres. Julia was tall and thin and perfectly blond. She did all the moves perfectly, and on top of everything else her father was an orthodontist, so she had perfect teeth."

Garth smiled. "Let me guess. She was also really mean and had a pony."

Marly shook her head. "That would have made it easier to dislike her," she said. "In reality Julia was as nice as could be. But I was intimidated by her. I wanted the roles she got. Specifically, I wanted to be Clara in the annual production of *The Nutcracker.*"

"But Julia got it," Garth said, shaking his head. "How tragic."

"It *was,*" Marly said, faintly annoyed at Garth's teasing. "I couldn't even bring myself to audition for it. I ended up being Mouse with Big Ears. No one even knew it was me."

"So now you're finally getting your chance to be the star," Garth said. "I get it."

"Yeah, well, I'm not so sure my knees are up to it anymore," said Marly.

"Well, you look great in that outfit," Garth remarked. "Where did you get it?"

"Nellie practically brings a whole wardrobe department with her," explained Marly. "In fact, I bet we could find something in there for you. What did you want to be when you were a little boy?"

"A photographer," Garth answered firmly. "A middle-aged photographer."

"Come on," Marly said. "I told you my hideously embarrassing story. Now out with it. What did you want to be? A cowboy? An astronaut? What?"

"A rodeo clown," Garth said.

"Come on," said Marly, laughing.

"Really," Garth protested. "We lived in Montana. The rodeo was a huge deal. When I was a kid I thought the rodeo clowns had the best jobs in the whole world."

Marly looked at him skeptically, not sure if he was kidding or not. "So what stopped you from putting on the big shoes and the red nose?" she asked.

"I heard the Rolling Stones," Garth answered. "Rock and roll stole me away."

"I'm sure there are some bulls out there right now who wish you'd never heard 'Satisfaction,' " Marly told him.

Garth laughed. "There are some bands that wish I hadn't either," he said. "So, are you free for lunch? I don't have another class until two."

"Sure," answered Marly. "Let me just get out of this tutu."

She excused herself to change and returned ten minutes later wearing a much more comfortable outfit. Then she and Garth took a walk into town, where they decided to eat at the Post Office Café.

"So, what do you think after three weeks here?" Marly asked Garth as she bit into her turkey on rye.

"It beats sleeping in a tour bus and having thirteen-year-old girls offering you blow jobs for backstage passes," he answered.

Marly wiped some mustard from her mouth. "I would think most guys would find that completely thrilling," she commented.

"A lot of them do," Garth said. "I just don't happen to be one of them. Frankly, a boring summer is exactly what I needed right now."

"Boring?" Marly said. "Is it that bad?"

"You know what I mean," Garth replied.

Marly nodded. "It's not exactly life in the fast lane here," she said. "I guess that's why I like it. But I've been meaning to ask you, why did you agree to come this year after turning me down so many times? I'd almost given up for good."

Garth put his mozzarella and tomato on sourdough down. "I didn't want to die without doing something worthwhile," he said.

Marly looked at him, unsure of whether he was making a joke or not.

"I was diagnosed with MS last November," Garth said gently. "I was on a shoot and had some trouble making my hands work. I thought it might be arthritis or whatever it is everyone complains about now. Carp-something."

"Carpal tunnel," Marly said.

"That's it. I figured the doctor could just give me a pill and make it go away. As it turned out, she couldn't. She made it so I can work more or less pain-free, but she can't stop it forever. So after I finished being pissed off and wondering why it had to happen to me, I sat down and decided to do something with my life. This seemed like a good place to start."

Marly looked down at her half-eaten sandwich. She wanted to say something comforting, or at least profound. A revelation of degenerative illness seemed to her to warrant some sort of deep response. But all she could think of to say was, "That really sucks."

Garth paused a moment. Then he laughed loudly. "Yes," he said. "Yes, it does suck. It sucks big time. And thank you for saying it. I'm so tired of people looking at me with wet eyes, or grabbing my hand and patting me like I'm a dog. I'm sick of well-meaning friends sending me articles about macrobiotic cures and green algae shakes and who knows what the fuck else. Why do you think only my doctor and my business manager know where I am right now? Everyone else thinks I'm touring with Ozzfest."

"Well, I'm glad you're here," Marly told him. "Even if this is what it took to get you here."

"I figured it was time I started sharing a little of what I've learned with other people," Garth said. "And so far, it's been great."

Marly paused a moment before finally asking, "You're not really dying, though, are you?"

Garth smiled. "That was perhaps a little too dramatic," he said. "No, I'm not dying. At least not yet, and probably only at a slightly faster rate than other men my age. But there's a chance that the disease will take away my ability to work, and to me that's almost the same thing as dying."

"I can't imagine it," Marly said softly.

"Neither can I," Garth told her. "That's why I try not to think about it too much."

"And here I am making you talk about it," Marly said, turning red. "I'm sorry."

"No, it's okay," said Garth, patting her hand. "I'm glad someone here knows."

He left his hand on top of Marly's. She felt it there, Garth's finger tips pressing against her skin. The warmth of his touch soaked into her, making her heart beat more quickly. She didn't want to move, for fear that he might remove his hand. Nor could she look at him directly.

"Thank you for telling me," she said.

Garth left his hand on hers for another moment before pulling away. Only then could Marly look at him again. But then it was his turn to be looking elsewhere, not meeting her gaze. Marly wanted to say something—anything—to break the tension that had suddenly descended on them, but everything she thought of sounded artificial and forced.

"I guess we should head back," Garth said finally, still not quite looking at her directly. "I'm going to have fifteen would-be Annie Lebowitzes wondering where I am."

Marly nodded as she collected her purse and they both stood up. She was relieved to be getting out of the restaurant and back into the world, where as they walked back to the Arts House she could remark on things like the heat of the noontime sun and the beauty of the clouds, and not have to think about how nice it had been to have Garth touch her so gently.

When they'd returned and Garth had gone to meet his class, Marly went to her office and shut the door. She sat in her chair and held her hands in her lap. Why was she so freaked out? All he'd done was touch her. It was just a friend touching another friend's hand.

No. It was more than that, and she knew it. Since meeting Garth Ambrose, she'd more than once thought about him in—that way. She couldn't even bring herself to say it. But the truth was that she'd fantasized about making love to Garth. She'd even thought about it while she and Drew were together, closing her eyes and imagining that it was Garth's body thrusting against hers, his mouth covering her neck in kisses.

Oh, it was all completely ridiculous. She was a grown woman, not a teenager with a crush on the new boy in school. Especially not with a boy who had just told her—as a *friend*—that he had MS. It was stupid, she told herself, stupid and just plain wrong, for a woman her age to be having fantasies about a man who first of all wasn't her husband and second of all was sick. That was far too Valerie Bertinelli television movie-of-the-week to be acceptable. Almost as foolish, she thought, as dressing up like a ballerina and trying to recreate a perfect childhood.

She sighed. She had to get Garth out of her mind.

But even as she turned back to her laptop and started answering the morning's e-mail, she found herself staring at the place on her hand where Garth's fingers had been.

CHAPTER 29

"Well, it's about time."

Reilly looked down from his position on the ladder. Josh was standing below him on the grass, his hand shielding his eyes from the glare of the midmorning sun.

"Hey," Reilly said casually.

"Where have you been?" Josh asked. "I haven't seen you around in two weeks."

"I've been busy on some other projects," replied Reilly. "Can't spend all of my time here."

"Oh," Josh said. "I guess you can't. Well, it's nice to have you back on the job."

"I'll try not to make too much noise," Reilly told him as he quickly ascended the ladder to the roof.

Once he was perched on the wide expanse of bare tarpaper, the sheath of shingles by his side, he relaxed a little. As long as he was on the roof, Josh couldn't talk to him. At least not easily, and he doubted Josh would risk climbing the ladder to come up there.

He felt badly about lying. He *had* been working other jobs, but they were ones he'd deliberately scheduled to avoid going back to 37 Oyster Lane, mostly small repairs that hadn't been worth his time to do. Finally, when he'd found himself fixing the squeaky step on his parents' back porch—the one his mother had been complaining about for almost a dozen years—he'd decided that enough was enough.

He spilt open the package of shingles, the smell of cedar filling the air as his utility knife sliced through the plastic covering. *Just think about doing the job,* he told himself. *Don't think about the other stuff.*

The other stuff was Josh. Specifically, it was how upset he'd been to see that strange guy coming out of the house that morning two weeks earlier. At first he'd tried to accept Josh's thinly veiled story about the man being a friend in need of a place to sleep for the night. But he knew that wasn't true. He knew a one-night stand when he saw one, and the guy who'd walked out the door that morning had definitely been all about sex. He practically stank of it.

Reilly picked up his hammer and drove a nail through the first shingle, giving it three hard whacks and sending it deep into the wood beneath the tarpaper. He'd expected more from Josh. Picking someone up and taking him home for a screw was something he expected his drinking buddies to do. He was used to hearing about the supposedly hot chicks they bagged when no one was around to contradict their stories. He was more than familiar with the post-fuck recaps, the elaborately detailed descriptions of perfectly round tits, pussies that couldn't get enough, and blow jobs that went on for hours. Sometimes he even liked hearing the stories, if only because he knew they were more about his friends' fantasies than about what really happened when they got home, too drunk to get it up, and passed out on the bed after a few halfhearted attempts at getting an equally drunk girl to go down on them while they fantasized about the women in the porn videos they jacked off to.

He'd heard, too, all the stories about how much sex gay men had. Such talk was common among the locals, who delighted in sharing the scandalous accounts of the sex between men they sometimes caught glimpses of, as if they had managed to snap photographs of rare and exotic birds. Dotty Moffat, who ran one of the cheapest and most popular of the summer motels, even kept a collection of unusual items she found in her gay guests' rooms after they'd checked out. It was housed in a cardboard box in her office, and counted among its holdings two sets of handcuffs, a dozen dildos in a range of shapes and colors, an entire shoe box full of nude Polaroids, a videotape containing footage of six men engaged in an orgy of Roman proportions, and an item none of them had yet been able to identify that resembled a metal dog bone with clamps on either end.

It was items such as this, along with the more public displays that frequently occurred when the summer guests had had a little too much to drink and acted out their courtship displays on the streets or, more commonly, on the beaches and beneath the piers, that had created an aura of almost mythic proportions around the sex that took place between P-Town's gay visitors. As a result, many of the residents were convinced that gay men lived only to drink, dance, and exchange as many bodily fluids as possible before dying. Donna, discussing some of the gay men who wandered into her shop looking for touchups on their already-perfect haircuts, had once said to Reilly, "It's a good thing queers can't have kids, because if they could those boys would have more children than Catholics."

Reilly added another shingle to the row he'd made along the roofline. Despite everything he'd heard and some of the things he'd seen with his own eyes, he didn't believe that gay men were any more sexual than anyone else. Okay, so maybe a lot of them seemed more than a little preoccupied with the subject. But surely there were guys who weren't all about how much dick they could get, just like there were straight guys who were content to be with one woman and didn't need to stick it to any willing girl who came along.

Like you, he told himself.

"Yeah, like me," he said angrily and brought the hammer down on the nail he was holding. He missed, striking his finger. A burst of pain shot up his arm.

"Holy fucking mother of Christ!" he shouted, shaking his hand vigorously, as if the pain could be brushed away like an annoying bee. "Goddamned son of a bitch in hell."

"You all right up there? Sounds like you've just told off the entire holy family." Josh's voice rose from below, filled with concern.

"I'm fine," Reilly snapped.

A minute later Josh's head appeared over the edge of the roof. He looked at Reilly, who was sitting nursing his quickly swelling finger.

"You don't sound fine," he said. "And I think your tab adds up to about three hundred and seventy-eight Hail Marys."

"You shouldn't be up here," barked Reilly. "You could get hurt."

Josh ignored him and climbed onto the roof. He sat down and cautiously peered over the edge.

"It's not *that* high," he said. "The treehouse my dad built for us when I was a kid was higher than this, and I fell out of that at least once a week playing cops with Mickey Royal from down the block. We'd be partners and I'd pretend some bad guy shot me while I was covering Mickey."

He turned and looked at Reilly. "Of course I only fell so he'd have to pretend to perform CPR on me," he said, grinning.

Reilly grunted, not looking at Josh. Why did he have to come up there? Why couldn't he have stayed on the ground? Now there was no graceful way for Reilly to get away from him. All he could do was sit there and look at his hand.

Josh inched his way closer to Reilly and sat down beside him.

"Let me take a look at that," he said, reaching for Reilly's hand.

Reilly jerked his arm away.

"Don't be a baby," said Josh. "I want to make sure you didn't break anything."

"I said I was fine," Reilly said, forcing himself to ignore the pain that was consuming his hand and picking up the hammer he'd dropped on the roof. He could barely stand to bend his finger around it, but he gritted his teeth and held on.

"Okay," Josh said. "I guess you are fine."

Reilly picked up a shingle and a nail as further evidence of his well-being. He held them up, not saying anything. Josh nodded.

"I see my work here is done," he said. "I'll leave you to it."

He inched his way back to the ladder and turned to go, giving Reilly a final wave. Reilly replied with a curt nod of his head.

When Josh had disappeared down the side of the house, Reilly dropped his tools again. His hand was killing him. It wasn't broken, he could tell, but it was badly swollen. He was going to have to get some ice on it, and quick. But that meant getting down the ladder, and he wasn't sure he could do that.

He crawled slowly to the edge of the roof. Turning himself around, he stretched his foot back until he felt a rung. He gripped the edge of the ladder with his good hand and tried to keep the other tucked into his chest as he began his descent.

Everything went fine until he was halfway down. Then, as he put his foot on what he thought was the next rung, he missed by a fraction of an inch and slipped. His good hand slipped, and he instinctively reached out with his injured one, grabbing on to the closest rung. The pain made him see stars, and the next thing he knew he was falling backward.

He woke up with Josh bent over him, his mouth hovering inches from Reilly's own. Reilly could feel Josh's breath on his face.

"What the hell are you doing?" he asked, pushing Josh away and sitting up.

"I thought you were knocked out," Josh said defensively.

"Well, I'm not," said Reilly. "And I'm not Mickey whatever his name was. And I'm most definitely not one of your little sex buddies."

Josh stared at him, confused, as Reilly stood up. Now his head hurt along with his hand, but he needed to get away. He was starting to realize what he'd just said to Josh, and how it must sound, and he didn't want to look at Josh's wounded expression.

He turned and walked to his truck, leaving his ladder, his tools, and Josh behind. He didn't look back as he got in, slammed the door, and started the engine. He pulled out of the driveway as quickly as he could, using one hand to steer, and drove off.

Once home, he sat at the kitchen table with his hand plunged into a bucket of ice and tried not to think about what he'd just done. He hastened the onset of forgetfulness by taking frequent sips from the bottle of beer he'd pulled from the refrigerator while getting the ice.

But even this couldn't stop him from replaying the scene in his mind. He saw Josh looking down at him, lips parted. He saw himself push Josh away. And he heard the words that had poured from his throat before he could stop himself. Each time he replayed them they sounded more hateful.

As the ice numbed the pain in his hand, the pain in his head grew more intense. No, he thought, it wasn't pain in his head. It was pain in his heart. He felt terrible, both about what he'd said to Josh and about the reasons he'd stayed away from the house for two weeks. It wasn't because he was disappointed in Josh, or because he felt somehow that his expectations hadn't been met. After all, what right did he have to expect *anything* from Josh? They really weren't anything more than friends, and accidental ones at that.

And that, really, was the problem, wasn't it? Reilly finally admitted what he'd been fearing all along. He and Josh were just friends. But part of him wanted something more. He wanted to be Mickey Royal. He wanted to be the man who walked out of Josh's bedroom in the morning. But not as just a one-night visitor.

CHAPTER 30

"This is the last of them."

Toby set the two large light blue suitcases next to the three smaller ones he'd already brought in. Sitting at the foot of the stairs, they looked like a group of curious children waiting for permission to go explore the upper reaches of Emmeline's house. But Emmeline had decided to give her mother the downstairs bedroom. Her bedroom. Only now she was ensconced in the upstairs room next to Toby's, and the big bed she'd slept in for so many years awaited her mother's tiny body.

And tiny it was. Emmeline had been shocked upon seeing her mother wheeled off of the plane by the smiling flight attendant. At first she'd thought that there had been some mistake, that her mother had been switched with someone else's. The frail woman seated in the chair, her pocketbook clasped firmly to her chest like a shield, bore little resemblance to the mother she remembered from her last visit. It was as if all but the last few drops of life had been drained from her, leaving behind a pale, shaking ghost in green polyester slacks and a food-stained sweatshirt.

"What happened to you?" she'd wanted to ask. "Where did you go?"

But she knew what had happened. Dr. Wickford had warned her, albeit inadequately, she now saw, in the few phone conversations they'd had before Lula Tayhill had been placed aboard Delta Airlines flight 138 and sent north. "She's going to need a lot of help," he'd said. "The stroke took a lot out of her."

Emmeline looked at her mother, who was now seated in the big armchair near the window. She still clutched her purse in the way a child might hold on to a stuffed bear, for comfort or protection from unseen dangers. She'd said very little on the drive from the airport.

"Mother, do you want something to drink?" Emmeline asked. "Some tea?"

Lula turned her head. "Get me out of these," she said slowly, looking down at her clothes. The stroke had, fortunately, not completely taken away her voice. It had, however, made speaking difficult.

Emmeline was only too happy to grant her mother's request. The cheap clothes made her look like one of those people on the news, interviewed moments after a tornado had swept their trailers into the sky and left them standing in the road, barefoot and dazed, clutching the broken bits and pieces of their lives that had been left behind. She supposed Binny had chosen them. Petey had never called, and Emmeline had finally resorted to contacting her mother's closest neighbor and asking her to pack up her mother's things and put her on the plane. Binny, nearly as old as the dirt of Louisiana itself, was one of those remarkable old women whose minds seemed to become sharper with every passing year, but her fashion sense clearly had suffered the effects of time.

"I think we can find you something better," Emmeline said as she stood. "Toby, can you help me?"

Together they transferred Lula to the waiting wheelchair, a procedure the elder Tayhill responded to by closing her eyes, opening them again only when she was safely ensconced in the safety of the padded vinyl seat. Her reaction was so slight as to make Emmeline feel as if she had merely shifted some knickknack from one place to another on a shelf to dust it instead of aiding a human being possessing life and spirit.

"Do you need me to help you in there?" Toby asked Emmeline, nodding meaningfully at the bedroom door.

Emmeline, sensing his discomfort at the idea of having to handle an old naked woman, shook her head gently. "I'll be okay."

She wheeled her mother into the bedroom, then returned for one of the suitcases, which sported along its top a piece of masking tape marked with the words GOOD CLOTHES in Binny's spidery scrawl. Emmeline placed the suitcase on the bed and snapped open the latches, praying that Binny had sent along at least one thing that didn't look as if it had been snatched from a Goodwill bin.

"Who is the boy?"

Emmeline was still startled by the sound of her mother's voice, a faint rasp that chilled the air like a winter's breeze. It was the voice of someone closer to death than to birth, someone whose body was fighting a losing war against time and disease. It was accompanied by a muted cough, as if speaking came only at the risk of suffocation.

"Toby is a friend, Mother," Emmeline said as she pawed through the pile of blouses and pants in the suitcase. "He's staying with me for a while."

Mrs. Tayhill had said almost nothing since being picked up by her daughter. Emmeline wasn't yet certain whether this was a good or a bad sign. They had never actually spoken about the turn of events that now brought them together; too weak to speak on the phone, Lula had been informed of her change of residence by her doctor and by Binny. But Emmeline knew full well that her mother resented having to be taken care of, and so the issue of Petey's abandonment had not yet been raised between them. Lula was, Emmeline felt sure, embarrassed to have been caught in her lie regarding her eldest son's devotion to her, a lie that had clearly been perpetrated to make Emmeline feel inadequate. And now that her mother was living in her house, Emmeline chose not to use that particular weapon against someone so fragile, even if she did deserve it. *Break the chain,* she kept repeating to herself, a phrase her therapist had helpfully provided just for the occasion.

The clothes in the suitcase were frighteningly threadbare and of dubious cleanliness, making Emmeline wonder exactly what her mother's life had been like for the past few years. Still, she managed to find both a blouse and some pants that were neither dirty nor offensive, and these she laid out on the bed.

Getting the old clothes off of her mother proved more difficult. The sweatshirt was relatively easy, involving as it did simply lifting her mother's arms and pulling the shirt over her head. But the pants were more problematic, requiring a lot of lifting and tugging, until finally Lula Tayhill sat naked in the wheelchair, her skin wrinkled and blotchy, a pair of thin white cotton underpants all that remained of her privacy and dignity.

Emmeline tried not to stare at her mother's breasts as she dressed her, but she couldn't help it. Never large, they now looked like those of an adolescent girl, as if she were aging backward and becoming once more a girl of thirteen. Only the skin, milky and blue-veined, seemed old and tired. Emmeline thought of her own breasts, the products of excellent surgery performed by one of Boston's most skilled doctors. Would they age as her mother's had? Most likely not, thanks to the wonders of space-age polymers. Oddly, this was one of the things that disappointed her about the woman she'd become, one of the few reminders that her identity was in some ways manufactured.

She had a friend, a man named Jesse, who had made the transition from female to male at the age of forty-two. The biggest shock, he told Emmeline, was discovering that the body he ended up with wasn't the boyish one he'd fantasized about having all those years but rather that of his middle-aged father. "Even my chest hair has come in gray," he said wistfully after the hormones had given him the hirsute body to match his deepened voice. "All this time I've imagined myself becoming the eleven-year-old I'd always wanted to be—the one who climbed trees and played baseball and went on camping trips with the Scouts. Instead, I've become my dad. All I need is a Budweiser and a Barcalounger."

Emmeline felt differently. She liked aging, liked seeing the changes that took place in her body with the passing of the years. As she helped her mother put on the clean clothes, she felt the old skin beneath her fingers, smelled the mixture of powder and age that emanated from Lula's body like the fragrance of a summer flower in the last days of August. Underneath it she smelled the sickness, too, and that saddened her. But even the sickness couldn't erase the scent of a body grown ripe with life, and that was comforting.

When Emmeline had wrestled the pants onto her mother's body and Lula looked more or less refreshed, Emmeline decided she needed to do something about her mother's hair. Already disheveled from the long trip, it had been completely undone by the removal of the sweatshirt, and now the pale wisps stuck out like a ball of cotton candy that had been picked apart by dozens of greedy fingers.

Emmeline located a hairbrush in the bathroom and sat on the bed beside her mother's chair. Gently she pulled the bristles through the tangles, bringing them into alignment and smoothing Lula's hair into something more orderly. As she brushed, she found herself humming out of habit.

" 'Lavender Blue,' " Lula said suddenly.

Emmeline nodded. "Yes," she said. "It's one of my favorites."

"I used to sing it when I was brushing *your* hair," Lula said slowly. "After your bath."

Emmeline paused for a moment, remembering. Suddenly the image of herself at the age of four or five popped into her head. She was seated on the floor, wearing pajamas patterned with cowboys and horses. She was warm and sleepy from the effects of the bath she'd just stepped out of, and her mother was combing her hair while she sang.

"I haven't thought about that in years," she said.

"Brushing your hair," Lula repeated dreamily, as if she and Emmeline were sharing the same memory. A faint growl came from her throat. At first Emmeline thought that she was having difficulty breathing, but then she realized that her mother was attempting to sing. Only the words caught in her throat and drowned there.

Lula made a fist and beat it feebly against the handles of her wheelchair. With a surprise, Emmeline realized that her mother had begun to cry. Tears were running down her cheeks as her body shook silently.

"Mother," she said, dropping the brush and kneeling, "what's wrong? Do you need something?"

Mrs. Tayhill just shook her head, not replying. Finally she whispered, "Different. Everything is different. I hate it."

Emmeline understood. Everything *was* different. The stroke had rendered her mother's body helpless in many ways. It had altered her entire life, forcing her from the safety of her routine into the uncertainty of life with Emmeline. Perhaps more important, it had forced the two of them to switch roles. Now it was Emmeline who was the caretaker. And of course there was the larger change that had taken place in Emmeline's life, one that had also rearranged the nature of their relationship. The child who inhabited both of their memories had been replaced by another one, and on some level Emmeline knew that her mother was only now facing the death of her youngest son.

She held one of the old woman's trembling hands for a minute, letting her cry. Then she picked up the brush and resumed combing her mother's hair.

"'Lavender blue, dilly dilly,'" she sang softly as her mother's sobs subsided. "'Lavender green. When you are king, dilly dilly, I'll be your queen.'"

CHAPTER 31

"How's the book coming along?"

Josh tossed the papers he was reading onto the table. "Let me put it this way," he said to Jackie. "If you have any busboy positions open, I might just apply."

Jackie laughed as she sat down. "It can't be that bad," she remarked.

"Not quite," replied Josh. "But close. This week Nicholson told me that my main character sounds too much like me."

"Does he?" Jackie asked.

"Yes," Josh said. "But that's the whole *point*. I'm writing what I know."

"Well, that's what they always told us to do in freshman comp," Jackie said sympathetically.

Josh sighed. "I'm starting to think maybe the real problem is that I don't know myself as well as I thought I did," he told her.

Jackie snorted. "Who does?" she said.

"Apparently Brody Nicholson," Josh answered. "If he wasn't such a good writer, I'd tell him to fuck off. But his stuff is brilliant."

"Yeah, but he probably has a really small dick," Jackie said thoughtfully. "Whenever God gives someone talent like that, she makes sure she takes something else away, just to keep us humble."

"That would explain stupid porn stars," said Josh, taking a drink from his glass of iced tea.

"Exactly," Jackie agreed. "Big dicks, little brains."

She looked out at the ocean. It was a perfect June day, sunny and clear. The impossibly blue sky melted into the sea and the breeze was just strong enough to make the heat comfortable. The lunch crowd had pretty much cleared out, and she was enjoying the hour or two lull until the dinner rush plunged her back into chaos for the evening. It was, she thought, as good a time as any to bring up what had been on her mind for some time.

"So," she said before she could change her mind, "you ever thought about being a daddy?"

Josh set his glass down. "I don't think I'm old or heavy enough for that," he remarked.

"Not that kind of daddy," Jackie said as Josh grinned. "You know what I mean—a father."

"I don't know," said Josh. "I can't even keep a plant alive. I don't think trusting me with a kid is a good idea. Besides, you sort of need to be straight for that, don't you?"

"Not these days," Jackie told him. "Lots of queers are doing it."

Josh nodded. "I know," he said. "What I meant is that I'd need a woman."

"I'm sure that could be arranged," Jackie said cautiously.

Josh gave her a look. "Why are you asking me this anyway? I'm not even sure I have a lover anymore, why would I be thinking about having a kid?"

"It's just a question," Jackie answered quickly. "I just wondered, you know, if the right woman came along you'd consider having a kid. Or helping her have one," she added.

"Oh," said Josh. "Um, well, I'd have to think about it, I guess."

"Well, think about it, okay?" said Jackie.

Josh stared at her for a moment. "What are you saying?" he asked slowly.

"I want a baby," Jackie blurted out. Now that she'd said it, she found she couldn't stop. "I know we don't know each other all that well," she continued. "But I like you, and I think you're a good guy. So I was wondering if maybe you would think about, you know, loaning me some of the stuff you have that I don't."

She stopped, suddenly feeling incredibly foolish. She glanced at Josh, who was still staring at her. His expression was unreadable.

"Oh, shit," Jackie said. "Look, I'm sorry. I'm just all fucked up from breaking up with Karla and turning forty. Just forget I said anything, okay?"

She started to stand up, but Josh reached out and grabbed her hand. She paused, then sat down again.

"No," Josh said. "I mean, it's okay. It's just that no one has ever asked me something like that before. Sure, my friends have asked me to dog-sit when they went on vacation, but that's about it. Having a kid—that's different."

"It's just something I've been thinking about," said Jackie, still feeling the need to explain herself. "And like I said, you're a nice guy and everything."

"Me. A father." Josh said the words to no one in particular, as if trying them out.

Jackie hesitated, wondering if she should continue or just get up and let them both forget she'd ever said anything. Josh still seemed dazed. She was ready to let him off the hook.

"How would something like that work?" Josh asked before she could say anything.

"Oh," Jackie said. "Well, basically, you would, um, give me some of your sperm."

Josh grimaced. "You make it sound like I'd be loaning you a cup of flour to make some bread," he said.

"It's a little more complicated than that," Jackie told him. "But basically, yes. I mean, I wouldn't expect you to be involved or anything. With the baby, I mean. I'd raise it."

Josh scratched his head. "It sounds so clinical," he said. "I'd have this kid running around but wouldn't be in its life?"

"You can be if you want to," Jackie told him. "I just assumed it would be easier if—" She stopped.

"If I wasn't," Josh said, finishing the sentence.

"I guess maybe it's not as easy as it was in my version," Jackie told him. "Not that I wouldn't *want* you involved or anything. It's just that most men don't seem all that interested once they've, you know, made the deposit, so to speak."

Josh looked at her and started to laugh. "This is a really weird conversation," he said.

Jackie, glad to have the tension broken, laughed along with him. "Yeah," she said. "Again, this isn't exactly how it went in my version."

"But you're serious?" Josh asked. "You want to have a baby?"

Jackie nodded. "Yes," she said. "I want to have a baby. I really do. I know it sounds completely insane, but I do. And not just because I'm turning forty and Karla left me. I want it for me. I want to give something to someone else, bring a life into this world."

"But me?" Josh asked. "Don't take this the wrong way, but we aren't even the same color or anything."

"I don't care about that," Jackie told him. "But if it's an issue for you—"

"No," Josh said quickly. "It isn't. I'm just saying."

"You don't need to come up with an excuse to say no," Jackie told him. "If you don't want to, you don't want to. It's okay."

Josh leaned back and ran his hands through his hair, not saying anything. Then he began laughing. Jackie watched him, not sure what was happening. Finally Josh stopped and wiped his eyes.

"I'm not laughing at you," he said. "I'm just remembering how when I told my mother that I was gay, the first thing she did was cry because she thought she'd never get any grandchildren out of me. I can just imagine what she'd say if I called her and told her she was going to be a grandmother."

Jackie thought about that. In all of her planning, it had never occurred to her that her plan might involve more people than just herself and the man who donated his sperm to her cause. With her family almost entirely gone, she really had no one to think about telling if she became pregnant. But Josh apparently did.

Maybe, she thought, she hadn't considered all of the possible complications thoroughly enough. In her midnight fantasies it had all seemed so straightforward: Josh would help her get pregnant, she'd have the baby, and then . . . It was the "and then" that she'd never really gone beyond. Certainly she'd never pictured grandparents being involved. Why, that would involve visits, and holidays, and family photos.

Unless, of course, Josh just wanted to help her out and then disappear. But judging from his reaction, Jackie didn't think he was willing to just provide the contents of a turkey baster and then move on.

"I shouldn't have asked you," she said quickly.

"It's okay," Josh said, thinking he was reassuring her but actually adding to her growing sense of panic. "I'm glad you did. But you're right that it's all a little too much to take in right now. Can I think about it for a while?"

"No problem," Jackie answered. "No problem at all."

She stood up. "I should go check on dinner," she said. "We'll talk later, okay?"

Josh nodded, and Jackie escaped to the safety of the restaurant's bustling kitchen, where the staff was busy getting ready for the evening's guests. There, surrounded by the sounds of pots rattling, knives chopping, and voices filling the air, she leaned against a counter and took a deep breath.

She'd thought that Josh would be the one who was taken aback by their conversation, but now she discovered that she herself was the one who was realizing what having a baby might actually mean. No, she wouldn't be married to the man who fathered her child. But they would be family nonetheless. There would be people other than herself and the child involved.

Could she do that? She wasn't sure. She'd never been particularly successful with families. *Wait,* a voice in her head told her. *That isn't entirely true. You just weren't so good at the family you were given. You did pretty well with the one you made.*

It was Franny's voice she heard, the throaty sound filling her ears. Jackie smiled. She could just picture Franny standing in front of her, giving her that look that meant she'd better listen up if she knew what was good for her. Jackie had been on the receiving end of that look many, many times.

"You're right," she said, causing the assistant chefs who were chopping up carrots nearby to look up. "We did make a good family."

Except for Karla. She couldn't forget that. She'd tried to make a family with Karla, and look how it had turned out. What if the same thing happened again? Worse, what if she did have a kid and it turned out bad? She'd always wondered about that, about how parents with truly awful children managed to love them anyway. It wasn't like a puppy or a kitten that you could take to the pound. A kid you were pretty much stuck with, whether it was a bad one or not. There was no returning it for a nicer one.

You're not marrying the guy. Franny's voice cut through her doubts, wiping them away. *And you're going to love any kid you have. You just do. Besides, you don't get what you want if you don't take some risks.*

"Okay," Jackie said, putting her hands up in defeat and earning another bewildered glance from her staff. "I give. I'll do it."

She looked out toward the deck, where Josh still sat, staring at the ocean. He was lost deep in thought, and Jackie was pretty sure she knew what was weighing on his mind.

"I'll do it if he will," she said.

CHAPTER 32

A father.

Josh tried to imagine himself holding a baby—his baby—in his arms. He couldn't picture it. He'd held babies before, ones belonging to friends, anyway. But he'd never thought about what it might be like to hold one that was *his*. The closest he'd ever come to being a parent was sharing his first apartment with a cat. Tabasco had been a hand-me-down, left in Josh's care by a former roommate who promised to come back for the animal once he was settled into his new place. When a week and then a month went by with no call from Tabasco's erstwhile master, Josh had resigned himself to the role of cat owner. Tabasco himself hadn't seemed the least concerned with the transition, simply moving his favorite sleeping spot from Eric's bed to Josh's, where he settled down on the pillow as if he'd been born there.

But a cat was one thing. A baby was an entirely different matter.

Josh replayed his conversation with Jackie over and over. It still felt more than a little surreal. One minute he'd been sitting in the sun wondering whether he should forget all about writing and go back to school for a degree in something more practical—computers, maybe, or accounting. The next he'd been asked if he would consider helping someone create a life.

The way Jackie explained it, he really wouldn't have to do much more than whack off in a jar. *That* he could do. Hell, he usually did it at least once a day anyway. The only difference would be that instead of wiping the results off with a tissue or flushing it down the drain, he'd be handing it over to Jackie.

Was it really that easy? Josh was a little unnerved by the realization that yes, it was. The fact was, making babies wasn't much more complicated than making a good martini. Actually, it was probably easier in many respects. It was the end result that was slightly more difficult to deal with. A martini you could sleep off; a baby was around for a good long time. And if you didn't like it, you couldn't send it back.

No responsibility. That's what Jackie had said. He wouldn't have to have any role in raising the kid. He was just a sperm donor. He shuddered. He hated that word—*sperm*. It sounded like some kind of jellied meat product, something you'd find on a grocery store shelf in Japan with one of those weird mangled-English labels. HAPPY MILK BABY DANCE! it might say on it, or TANGY LOVE SAUCE DELICIOUS.

Sperm. It was just nasty. Cum wasn't much better, but at least if you had to say it, "Eat my cum" was slightly less revolting than "Eat my sperm." He'd read that sentence once in a jerk-off story, and instantly his hard-on had disappeared. It was just too clinical. Then again, he thought, cum donor didn't sound exactly right, either.

The problem, really, was that what Jackie was proposing wasn't sexual. It was purely science. And sex words and scientific words just didn't mix. No one, Josh thought, would ever in the heat of passion say something like "Lick my testicles" or "Stick it in my vagina." Similarly, a lab technician would probably not lean over a woman whose legs were in stirrups and whose stomach was covered by a paper sheet and say reassuringly, "I'm going to pump your cunt full of cum now, Miss Archibald."

Basically, Josh decided, he was being asked to participate in a medical procedure. He just had to separate that notion out from the usual baby-making activities of lovemaking and passion. Parenting, too, had to be redefined. This wouldn't be so much his baby as it would be a science fair project, like making a potato clock or a saltwater battery.

He looked out at the ocean. He'd been wandering around town for several hours, thinking about Jackie's request. Now he'd come to the waterfront, where he'd wandered out to the end of the pier. Dusk was falling, and the shadows were creeping in around the edges of the boats that bobbed on the water. The surface of the ocean ran with black and gold as the sun descended, and the air had taken on a coolness that soothed the faint burn on the back of his neck.

Josh sat at the end of the pier, his legs hanging over the edge, as twilight wrapped the world in its gauzy arms. There was a moment as day slipped away and night took its place when he felt as if he were in the most magical place on earth. He breathed in the air and smelled the scent of summer, filled with surprises and possibilities.

He stood and walked back to the beach. But halfway back, he stopped, his attention caught by noises coming from somewhere beneath him. He paused, trying to hear, and was drawn to the edge of the pier. There the noises grew louder, soft grunts barely distinguishable from the sound of the waves washing up onto the sand.

Josh knelt down, the planks of the pier rough against his knees. Below him, he knew, men were having sex. He listened as the grunts became louder. Peering between the cracks in the board, he could just make out two shadows, one leaning against a piling and another on its knees in the sand.

They must have been waiting until the sun went down, Josh thought. Maybe they'd spent the afternoon drinking in one of the nearby bars, slowly increasing the suggestiveness of their conversation as the beer made them bolder. Perhaps they'd come to the spot separately, each looking for the same thing and finding it in each other. However it had occurred, the men were lost in the moment. The grunting sounds grew louder and deeper, and were accompanied by the occasional "suck it" and "fuck, yeah." Again, Josh thought, the dialogue of bad porn films. But somehow, in this place, it seemed neither silly nor inappropriate.

He was tempted to stay, to prolong his voyeuristic enjoyment. Perhaps even, unknown to the shadow men, he would join them in their pleasure. He could feel his dick pressing against the fabric of his shorts. It would be nothing to free it, to stroke himself to the accompanying soundtrack coming from below until he spilled his load on the dock.

But despite the publicness of their sex, there was something private about the moment being shared by the two men beneath the pier, and Josh decided to leave them to it. Instead, he suddenly decided he would go home and call Doug. The decision surprised him. He hadn't been thinking about Doug at all. But for some reason he was overcome with a desire to talk to his boyfriend.

He walked home quickly, but without rushing, trying to understand what had made talking to Doug a sudden priority. Was it hearing the faceless men having sex that did it? Had that triggered some memory of Doug's infidelity? Josh didn't think so. It was more, he thought, his thinking about fatherhood that had done it. Ironically, thinking about helping Jackie create a family had triggered his own desire for the same thing. Maybe he didn't want a child, but he did want a home and someone to share it with. It's what he'd always wanted. And Doug, despite his recent transgression, was as close as he was likely to come to having that. Maybe, he thought, it was time to forgive him and work on rebuilding their relationship.

When he reached the house, he picked up his cell phone and dialed Doug's number. *Their* number, he corrected himself. To the phone that sat in their shared apartment, that was connected to the answering machine with both their voices on it. *All those connections,* Josh thought as the phone rang once, then again. *They must be holding* something *together.*

On the third ring, the phone was picked up. "Hello?"

"Doug?" Josh said, confused. It didn't sound like Doug.

There was a pause. "He's in the bathroom. Can I take a message?"

"Who is this?" demanded Josh, realizing that he wasn't talking to his boyfriend.

"Can I take a message?" the man on the other end repeated.

"Yeah," Josh answered. "This is his boyfriend."

"Oh, shit," the man said. "I'm really sorry."

"Sorry?" repeated Josh. "Sorry for what?"

"I hope you're ready for round two." Josh suddenly heard Doug's voice in the background. Then there was silence.

"I thought it was Mr. Ning's calling to confirm our order," said the unknown man's voice apologetically.

"Fuck." Doug again. Then Josh heard the phone being snatched up. "Hello?"

"Hi," Josh said, still a bit stunned. "It's me."

"Oh, hi," replied Doug, the forced cheerfulness in his voice telling Josh everything he needed to know. "What's up?"

"Who is it?" Josh asked sadly. "Anyone I know?"

"What?" Doug asked. "Oh, just a friend. We're having dinner."

Josh laughed. "Come on, Doug," he said. "I deserve better than that."

There was a long pause. Then Doug cleared his throat. "It's not like I've heard from you or anything. I wasn't sure where we stood."

"So when in doubt, fuck whatever moves, right?" said Josh.

"You're the one who left," countered Doug.

"You're right," Josh said. "I was the one who left. And I think I can safely say that as of now, I'm the one who's not coming back. Enjoy your sweet-and-sour shrimp."

Josh hung up. He expected to start crying, but he didn't. Instead he sat in the chair, looking out the window at the stars. He wasn't sure what he felt. He tried to picture the man Doug was with right at that moment. What had Doug said to him when he hung up, what had he done? Had they gone back to bed for a little action before their dinner arrived? Had Doug chided his trick for picking up the phone?

Josh thought back to the two men under the pier. He'd been aroused by their faceless actions, turned on by the sounds of them getting each other off in the darkness. But what if there was more to their story than just simple fucking? What if one or both had lovers sitting at home, oblivious of the fact that the men they were in love with were underneath a pile of seaweed-choked logs with their mouths and hands wrapped around someone else's cock?

Suddenly he felt sick. He pictured one of the men with Doug's face, the muscles strained in ecstasy, the lips mouthing the words Josh had found so exciting when they'd drifted to him through the darkness. Now those words, and the actions attached to them, repulsed him. There was no longer anything erotic about the action going on beneath the pier, nothing appealing about the possibilities roaming in the shadows. Instead, there was only sadness and disappointment.

Josh took a deep breath. It was over. It was really over. He knew that now. He wouldn't go back to Doug, would probably see him again only when he returned for his things. Already he was referring to Doug as his ex-lover. Ex. He imagined not the word but the letter, a huge red X covering Doug's face. Blotted out. Removed. Stricken. He'd been removed from the list of possibilities, discarded as unacceptable.

Just like that, his life changed. He was no longer one half of a couple, one half of a linked pair. No one would say "Josh and Doug" again, unless it was to say "Did you hear what happened to Josh and Doug?" or "Josh and Doug split up." Now he was just Josh.

Just Josh. It sounded like a bad sitcom title. *A sitcom about a formerly partnered man who, suddenly single, finds himself living in a small town and trying to figure out what to do next,* Josh thought. *All we need is the wacky next-door neighbor and we're all set. We'll be number one in our time slot.*

He almost laughed. He really could see it on TV. He pictured the execs sitting around a conference table talking about it. *You know what would make it even better?* he imagined one saying excitedly. *Let's give him a baby. People love babies. They're funny.*

This time he did laugh. "Why not?" he said out loud. "Why the hell not?"

CHAPTER 33

"Oh, excuse me. I didn't know anyone was here."
Devin stood in the doorway of Reid's house. The key was still in the lock, and she clutched a stack of folders to her chest as she faced Ty, who was sitting in a chair in the living room, looking annoyed.

"It's okay," Ty told her, sounding irritated. "I'm not supposed to be here. I'm supposed to be on my way to the airport. But my car hasn't shown up."

Devin shut the door. "I was just bringing Reid these script reports," she explained, walking into the living room and putting the files on the coffee table. "I thought I'd do it while he was out on his morning run. That way I wouldn't interrupt him."

"Well, now you can keep me company until my car shows up," Ty told her, smiling.

Devin took a seat across from him. So far, everything was going as planned. But things were just getting started, and she didn't want to rush. She needed Ty to trust her.

"So, have you and Reid found anything to work on yet?" she asked. The story Reid had given her to explain Ty's frequent appearances at the house was that they were going over scripts for possible film projects. And in fact he *had* given her a lot of scripts to look over and make notes on, a ruse she went along with because it helped support the notion that she really was simply interested in learning more about the film business.

Ty shook his head. "No," he said. "There's a lot of crap out there."

"That's something I don't understand," said Devin. "I mean, everyone talks about how hard it is to get a film made, but I see tons of really bad movies coming out every week."

Ty laughed. "That's because the suits who run the studios know they can make the most money by making films that appeal to the lowest common denominator," he told her. "They don't care if people come out of a film thinking. All they care about is getting asses into seats. Everything else—the story, the dialogue, the meaning—comes second. Not even second. Special effects come second. Then the title and how everyone involved is credited. The movie actually ranks about fifth or sixth on the list of what they think about when they make this shit."

"But some good films get made," Devin said.

"Yeah, by accident," Ty replied. "I swear to God, if something good comes out of Hollywood it's because most of the people involved were so high on coke they didn't notice."

He waved a hand at Devin. "I'm sorry," he said. "I don't mean to sound so down about it all. It's just that you're right—there *are* excellent scripts and ideas out there. But they make it so hard for anyone to do anything different, anything special, that most people give up."

"Haven't you liked any of the films you've made?" Devin asked him.

Ty nodded. "A couple," he said.

"And now that you're a star," Devin added quickly, "I bet you can do whatever you want."

Ty sat up. "See, that's the problem," he said. "When no one knows who you are, you *can* do things that are risky. But once America loves you, you're stuck with this image, and nobody wants you to do anything that might change how much everyone loves you. And why? Because then the profits go down."

Devin nodded. She'd gotten Ty to start opening up, and she wanted him to continue. "Like Meg Ryan," she said.

"Exactly," Ty replied. "Look what happened when she left Dennis Quaid for Russell Crowe. Suddenly she went from being everybody's sweetheart to being this huge slut, a homewrecker who ditched the nicest guy in Hollywood for a bad boy. You can bet her publicist and manager went through a dozen bottles of Prozac a day while that was going on. And what has she done since?"

"Not much," Devin admitted.

Ty leaned back in his chair. "The truth is, we make movies so that other people can escape their lives. Look at who goes to them. It's not the CEOs and the people with fantastic lives. It's people who make minimum wage, live in little towns, and wish they were somebody else who really pack the multiplexes every weekend. *Those* are the people Hollywood makes movies for. And those people want to pretend that if things were just a little bit different, they could *be* in the movies. They want that fantasy."

"What about you?" Devin asked. "Is it true that you were discovered when a casting director saw you working at a gas station?"

Ty nodded. "And the guys who come to see me in movies want to think *they* could get discovered working at a gas station. Or at Home Depot. Or McDonald's."

"And the women who come like to believe they could meet a guy like you working at a gas station," Devin added.

"That too," Ty agreed. "It's all about fantasy."

"I always figured that's why Madonna was popular," Devin continued. "You know, because underneath it all she's just a sort-of pretty girl from Detroit with an okay voice and lots of attitude. She's this amazing star, but really it was kind of an accident."

Ty smiled. "Don't say that to all the queens who think everything she does is magic," he said.

"The gay community loves its icons," Devin said, pleased that the conversation had veered in this particular direction.

"Well, they've resurrected Cher on more than one occasion," said Ty. "That woman is like Dracula in drag."

"So why don't more actors come out then?" Devin asked. "I mean, if the gay community supports celebrities so much, you'd think more people would be open about who they are."

"Ah, but that's the thing," Ty answered. "How many gay icons are actually gay? Think about it. Bette Davis. Judy Garland. Joan Crawford. None of them were gay. And none of them were men. Gay men might as well be straight women when it comes to the actors they love. They want the big, butch heros too. They don't want the sissy queens or the old men whose careers couldn't possibly be damaged by their coming out. They want Bruce Willis and Colin Farrell and Vin Diesel, not Danny Pintauro and Rupert Everett and Nathan Lane. It's only the dykes who throw their cash at someone just because she eats pussy. Melissa and k.d. owe their whole careers to lesbians. But even in Hollywood you won't find many lesbians who are out of the closet."

"Yeah, well, we can probably thank Anne Heche and her amazing disappearing lesbianism for that," joked Devin, earning a big laugh from Ty.

"I wish things were different," Ty said. "But right now they aren't."

"What do you think it would take to make things change?" Devin asked.

Ty sighed deeply. "Somebody big coming out," he said. "Someone everyone really likes. I think that would probably do it."

He stopped talking and looked out the window. "Yeah, that would do it," he repeated.

"But you don't see it happening," Devin prodded.

"Not for a long time," replied Ty. "Not as long as the weekend gross is the bottom line."

He looked at his watch. "If I don't get to the airport I am going to be so screwed," he said. "Maybe I should call the car service."

"Why don't I just drive you?" Devin suggested, as if the idea had just that moment occurred to her. "My car is right here."

Ty looked at his watch again. "You're sure you don't mind?" he asked.

"Not at all," said Devin.

Ty stood up. "Okay," he said. "You've got a deal. Let's go."

He picked up his bag and followed Devin outside to her car.

"Buckle up," Devin told him. "I'm going to have to break a few traffic laws if you want to make your plane."

Ty did as she asked, and Devin took off. She'd made sure to check the departure time for the Cape Air flight before calling the car service to cancel Ty's pickup, and she knew exactly how much time she had and how long it would take her to get to Provincetown's tiny airport. They were fine. But she wanted Ty to think she was saving his ass.

"So, it's great that you and Reid are such good friends," she remarked after they'd been driving for a minute.

"He's a great guy," Ty said. "I owe a lot to him."

"I can't believe I'm getting to work for him," Devin continued.

"I know he's really impressed by the work you've been doing," Ty told her.

"Really?" Devin said happily.

Ty nodded. "He's so used to the players in Hollywood that having someone normal around is really good for him."

"You seem pretty normal," remarked Devin.

"Compared to some of the freak shows in La-La Land, I'm totally normal," Ty replied.

"You remind me a lot of my ex-husband," Devin said casually.

"Ex-husband?" Ty said, sounding surprised. "What'd you do, marry him when you were thirteen?"

Devin smiled. "I'm not that young," she said. "Besides, we were only married for two years."

"You don't sound too broken up about being divorced," said Ty. "I'm not sure I like the fact that I remind you of this guy."

"It's okay," Devin reassured him. "It's a good comparison. Zane is a really great guy."

"Then why the divorce, if I'm not being too nosy?" asked Ty.

"It's sort of a strange story," Devin answered. "Actually, it would make a good movie, now that I think of it. Zane and I were in college together. We met in a film class and became good friends. To tell the truth, I had a major crush on him. One night I had a little too much to drink while we were watching *Chinatown* in his dorm room, and I kissed him."

"And one thing led to another, you got pregnant, and he had to marry you!" Ty said excitedly.

"Sadly, no," said Devin. "He told me he was gay."

"Ah, a plot twist," remarked Ty. "So how do you get from kissing a gay guy to marrying him?"

"Zane was from a wealthy family," explained Devin. "A family that wouldn't exactly be thrilled if they knew that he was gay. He stood to inherit a lot of money, but only if he got married to someone the family approved of. So he asked me if I'd be his wife for a little while."

"You're kidding," Ty said incredulously.

Devin shook her head. "Really," she said. "We came up with this whole plan. We would get married and live together for a while. Zane would get his inheritance. Then there would be this nasty breakup caused by Zane finding me in bed with his best friend. We'd divorce, everyone would feel sorry for him, and when they found out that *he* was really the one sleeping with his best friend, it would be too late for anyone to do anything about it."

"Get out," said Ty.

"I'm serious," said Devin. "You should have seen the wedding. There were swans."

Ty laughed. "This is the weirdest thing I've ever heard," he said. "Did you pull it off?"

"Yes and no," said Devin. "Everything was going fine until one afternoon Zane's parents came over for a surprise visit and found him and his boyfriend going at it in the pool house. His father had a massive coronary and dropped dead on the spot. Other than that, though, it pretty much went off the way we'd planned it. Zane's mother tried to get him disinherited, but by then he'd gotten all of the money anyway. We got divorced and he and his boyfriend bought a house in Palm Springs."

"You have got to be shitting me," Ty said. "That did not happen."

"Here we are," Devin said, pulling up in front of the airport terminal. "Now run. You have five minutes."

Ty got out and retrieved his suitcase from the backseat. "Thanks again," he said, pausing beside Devin's window.

"No problem," Devin told him. "That's what I'm here for. Anything you need, just ask."

"I'll keep that in mind," Ty told her.

He gave a final wave and then walked quickly into the building. When he was out of sight, Devin put the car in gear and drove away. As she pulled out of the airport she turned on the radio. The Stones were playing.

"You can't always get what you want," Mick growled.

Devin smiled. "You can if you know how to tell a good story," she said.

CHAPTER 34

"Would you like some more applesauce?"

The old woman pushed Toby's hand away and made a face. Toby sighed and put the spoon he was holding back into the bowl. He was tired of trying to get her to eat anyway. It was like trying to feed a baby. Sometimes she would turn her head and purse her lips tightly; other times she would open her mouth and accept the spoon willingly, slurping the applesauce greedily.

Now Lula Tayhill collapsed against the couch cushions wearily and pointed to the television. "Turn it up," she said.

Toby picked up the remote, which was inches away from Lula's hand, and increased the volume. *You could have done that yourself,* he wanted to say. The old woman was getting lazier and lazier since she'd moved in. He didn't mind helping Emmeline take care of her, but sometimes her refusal to help herself made him angry. After turning up the sound, he placed the remote just out of her reach.

"I'm going to go wash these dishes," he told Mrs. Tayhill. "I'll be back in a few minutes."

Lula didn't respond. Her eyes were fixed on the television screen, and she seemed to be devoting every ounce of her concentration to understanding what the actors were saying. Her brow was knit up, and her watery eyes blinked slowly in the glow of the set.

Toby carried her tray to the kitchen, where he scraped the remains of her dinner—a pork chop, green beans, and the applesauce—into the trash and turned on the water in the sink. He squeezed a drizzle of blue dish detergent into the water and watched it foam up into soapy clouds.

Suddenly an image of his mother standing at their kitchen sink flashed across his mind. How often had he seen her there after dinner, washing up while his father sat in the living room watching whatever sporting event happened to be on and he, Ruth, and Jacob sat around the kitchen table, doing their homework? He'd enjoyed those hours, secure in the heart of the house with its warm light, the lingering smells of dinner, and the sound of his mother humming as she washed up.

But all that was gone now, left behind when he'd fled the house, determined to escape his parents' shame. Now he was in a new kitchen, one where he once again felt safe. As he plunged his hands into the water and began to wash the supper dishes, he thought about his mother, and about Emmeline. Really, they weren't all that much different. His mother, he thought, would probably even like Emmeline if she knew her, at least as long as certain facts weren't revealed.

And that, of course, was the problem. His parents couldn't face facts, not about someone like Emmeline, and not about someone like himself. They'd made that very clear to Toby. There was no room in their lives for someone like him.

Like him. Gay. It sounded so ugly. He was "that way." He remembered how his father's face had contorted when he'd said, "I won't have a son who's that way." He couldn't even say the word *gay*. It was as if it were poisonous, or bitter, too awful to hold in his mouth.

Another image came to him. A boy. A thin boy with hair the color of corn and eyes that always looked down. Stewart Perkins. The school fag. Toby winced just thinking the word. But that's what everyone had called him. It's what Toby himself had called Stewart on more than one occasion, usually when he was with his baseball team buddies and Stewart had the bad luck to walk within twenty feet of them. Then the routine would begin, like a well-rehearsed play.

"Hey, Stewart," one of them would call out, "want to go to the prom with me? I bet you already have your dress all picked out."

The others would laugh and make kissing sounds in Stewart's direction. Always, he would ignore them, walking by without acknowledging their taunts, as if they—or he—were invisible.

Once one of them had tripped him. Stewart had stumbled, dropping his books and falling to his knees. As he'd knelt on the ground, frantically trying to gather up his papers, Dean Kelly had grabbed him by the head and pushed Stewart's face into his crotch.

"Hey, Stu, while you're down there why don't you help me out?" he'd said, pumping his hips against the other boy's face while Stewart had beat futilely against Dean's legs and Toby and his friends had laughed. When Dean finally let Stewart go, the boy had scrambled to his feet and run off, leaving his books behind.

Was Stewart gay? Toby wondered. Certainly he seemed gay. But looks were deceiving. After all, none of Toby's friends ever suspected his secret. But what did they think now that he was gone? Surely they must have asked his family where he'd gone. What lies had they told to cover up the truth? He knew his parents would never tell anyone the truth. Even his brother and sister, he suspected, didn't know the real reason behind his sudden departure.

He was ashamed of how he and his friends had treated Stewart. At the time, he'd told himself they were just having some harmless fun, that Stewart wasn't being hurt by their words. But he knew now that sometimes words could be worse than any physical hurt, could leave bruises and scars that took far longer to heal.

He finished the dishes, rinsing the last plate and setting it in the drainer to dry. Wiping the counter, he returned to the living room to check on Mrs. Tayhill. She was sitting in exactly the same position he'd left her in, only he noticed that the channel had been changed and the remote was now clasped in her hand.

"When will Emmeline be back?" Lula asked him, never taking her eyes off the television.

"Not until late," answered Toby. "Her weekend shows aren't over until midnight."

Lula Tayhill nodded slowly, as if keeping time to a song only she could hear. Then she turned her head and looked at him.

"Is she any good?"

Toby looked at the old woman. "You've never heard her sing?" he asked, surprised.

"Not in front of people," Mrs. Tayhill replied, looking away.

"Yes," Toby told her. "She's good. She's very good."

Lula nodded again and went back to watching her show. After a few minutes she spoke again. "They don't hate you, you know."

"Excuse me?" said Toby, not understanding.

"The people you ran away from," Lula continued slowly, as if she was growing more and more tired.

Toby didn't reply. It was the first time Emmeline's mother had ever said more than a few words to him. She'd never asked him about himself, and as far as he knew, she didn't really know anything about him.

"I guessed," the old woman said unexpectedly, as if reading his mind. "She didn't say anything. But I'm right, aren't I?"

Toby nodded. "Yes," he said softly.

"They don't hate you," Lula repeated. "Just don't understand you. Blame themselves."

Toby cleared his throat. "Is that how you felt about Emmeline?" he asked.

Mrs. Tayhill didn't say anything, but she nodded gently. Toby wasn't sure she was answering him or if she'd slipped back into her television-watching mode. He thought about trying again, but Lula seemed to be finished with talking. So he sat there, watching television with her and thinking about what she'd said. Was it true that his parents just didn't understand him? He didn't think that was possible. They knew what being gay meant, and they knew it was what he was. That's all there was to it. If they couldn't accept him, then they couldn't accept him. It wasn't about understanding anything.

Then he thought about Stewart again. Why had he and his buddies picked on him? Because he was different, yes, but there were lots of kids who were different: the goths, the math nerds, the stoners. Sure, they'd made fun of those kids, too, but not in the same way. Something about Stewart had provoked them to unusual levels of hostility. What was it?

Fear. Toby saw that now. In his case, he'd feared his friends discovering that underneath his letterman jacket he was just like Stewart was, or what they thought he was. He also feared admitting the truth to himself, that although he didn't look or act like what he thought a fag looked and acted like, he was one nonetheless. As for his friends, maybe they had feared that if someone their own age, someone really not all that much unlike themselves when it came down to it, could be gay, maybe they could too.

What other explanation was there? Stewart posed no threat to them, either socially or physically. He never even went out of his way to bother them. All of their animosity toward him came from within themselves. Stewart himself was almost irrelevant. It was what he represented to them that mattered. Apart from how he looked, Toby and his friend knew absolutely nothing about the guy.

Was it the same with his parents? Could it be that they were so afraid of what he represented to them that all their other feelings for him were buried under an avalanche of misunderstanding? Would they, maybe, be able to accept him if they could just have some time to see who he really was?

He looked at Lula Tayhill. Was she right, or was she just a sick old woman whose medications made her say crazy things? He knew she'd rejected Emmeline for years, refusing to accept her for who she was. What had she missed out on during those years? *She's never even heard Emmeline sing,* Toby thought sadly.

Lula's eyes had closed, and she seemed to be sleeping. Soon he would carry her to her room and put her to bed. But for right now she was fine where she was. Toby got up and went into the kitchen.

It took him several false starts before he remembered the number. And when finally he heard the phone ring, he almost hung up. But then he heard his brother's voice. "Hello?"

"Jacob," Toby said, his voice catching in his throat. "It's me."

"Toby!" his brother said. "How's summer school?"

"Summer . . ." Toby began. Then he realized his parents must have made up a story to explain his absence. "It's fine," he said, trying to compose himself. "How's everything there?"

"Okay," Jacob said happily. "I got a new skateboard, and we're going to Great Adventure next week."

Jacob's voice cut out for a moment and Toby heard him say, "It's Toby." Then there came the sound of someone taking the phone from his little brother.

"Toby?"

It was his mother.

"Hi, Mom," he said hesitantly.

"Where are you?" Mrs. Evans asked.

Toby hesitated. Did he want her to know where he was? Or did he just want her to know he was okay?

"I'm staying with a friend," he said finally.

He heard his mother sigh, in relief or irritation, he couldn't tell. "Are you all right?" she said.

"I'm fine," he told her. "I just wanted to let you know I'm fine."

Before his mother could say anything else, he heard the sound of his father's voice in the background.

"I'm sorry," Mrs. Evans said, her voice suddenly icy. "I'm afraid you have the wrong number."

The line went dead.

PART III

July

CHAPTER 35

"What the hell are those?"

Josh stared at the plate Bart was holding out to him. It was covered in triangular cakes frosted a garish pink.

"They're urinal cakes," Bart replied, grinning broadly.

"What?" said Ryan, staring hard at the plate.

"You know," Bart said. "Urinal cakes. That's what they call those awful pink disinfectant things they stick in urinals. Only these are made out of pound cake."

Josh grimaced. "You're the Martha Stewart of the men's room set," he remarked.

Bart laughed. "Aren't they fabulous? I thought they'd fit the theme of the party perfectly."

"I'll give you that much," said Ryan, picking up a cake and looking at it closely. "What's with the licorice whip curled on the top?"

"Pubic hair!" Bart exclaimed before turning to offer the tray to another guest.

Ryan and Josh exchanged a glance; then Ryan set his urinal cake on a nearby table. "I just can't," he said.

"Especially not when lemonade is the beverage of choice," Josh agreed, holding up his cup of yellow liquid.

"Leave it to Bart to come up with the Tea Room Tea Party," said Ryan.

It was the afternoon of the Fourth of July, and 138 Myrtlewood Lane was filled with a great many of Provincetown's gay male population. All of them had come to get into the mood for the big event of the holiday weekend, a beach dance that culminated in a spectacular fireworks display that took place over the ocean. For the Fourth, the number of visitors to the town swelled to outrageous numbers, and somehow most of them had found their way to Bart's party.

"Can you believe the amount of queenage in this place?" said Phil, coming to stand beside Josh and Ryan. "I swear to Christ there's an Obsession haze hanging over the pool."

"It wouldn't be the Fourth without one of Bart's parties," Ryan said.

Phil nodded. "I know," he replied, then laughed. "Remember the year he got that stripper from Rounds to dress up as the Statue of Liberty?"

Ryan laughed. "It was great," he told a bewildered Josh. "Instead of a torch, the guy was holding a huge fucking dildo spray-painted silver."

Josh gave a halfhearted laugh. *I knew I should have stayed home,* he thought miserably. The last place he felt like being was at a party, especially one overflowing with fags.

"Have you guys seen Aaron?"

Josh looked up to see Eric standing in front of them. He was holding a half-eaten urinal cake and looking annoyed.

"No," Ryan answered. "I haven't seen him in about half an hour."

"I sent him to get me a beer," said Eric testily. "Now I can't find him."

"Try the pool," suggested Phil. "Everyone else seems to be out there."

"Thanks," Eric replied, heading for the door.

"So, are you coming to the dance with us tonight?" Phil asked Josh.

Josh shook his head. "I don't think so," he said.

"He and Doug broke up," explained Ryan. "For good this time."

Phil made a face. "Sorry," he said.

"Yeah, well, these things happen," said Josh. "But thanks," he added.

"Sometimes I wonder what I'd do if Al and I ever broke up," Phil continued. "It's been so long since I was single, I don't think I remember what it's like."

It's lonely, Josh thought to himself. *That's what it feels like.*

"Sure you do," Ryan told Phil. "It feels like being a kid at Christmas and looking through the Sears catalog. There are all these things you could have, and every time you turn the page you find something else to add to your wish list."

"I can't relate," said Phil. "I was one of those kids who always got sweaters. My mother knitted a new one every year."

"Poor you," said Ryan sympathetically.

"No," Phil replied. "I liked them. They were warm, and I knew my mother made them just for me. Sometimes a sweater is better than a toy you play with for a while and then forget about."

"Someone should have told Doug that," Josh said quietly.

Before either Phil or Ryan could say anything, there was a commotion from the pool area. Then Eric came flying through the door, with Aaron behind him.

"I want him out of here!" Eric screamed. "I want him out *now!*"

A moment later, Toby entered the room. He looked angry and frightened. "But I told you—" he started to say.

"Shut up!" Eric yelled savagely. "Just shut the fuck up."

"Eric," Aaron said, putting his hand on his boyfriend's arm, "he's just a kid. He made a mistake."

"I made a mistake?" Toby said angrily. "You're the one who stuck his hand down my pants."

"He's lying," Aaron said to Eric, ignoring Toby. "You know I would never do something like that."

"Right," Toby said. "Just like you never slept with me before your boyfriend got here."

"I knew you were a whore the minute you walked through that door," Eric said.

By now a group had gathered to watch the entertainment. Some looked on, not bothering to conceal their amusement at the unfolding drama. Others were more discreet in their voyeurism. Toby looked around at the men encircling him.

"You're all fucked-up," he said. "All of you." He looked directly at Aaron. "Especially you," he said before turning and heading for the front door.

"Don't you ever come back here!" Eric called after him. "Never!"

The door slammed as Toby left the house. Aaron put his arms around the now-weeping Eric and began to console him. "It's okay," he said. "He's gone. Nothing happened. It's all okay."

"All right, folks," Phil called out. "It's all over. Back to the party." He turned to Ryan and Josh. "Excuse me while I go direct traffic," he said. "You know how everyone wants to stare at an accident."

When he was gone, Ryan looked at Josh. "Aaron or the houseboy," he said with mock seriousness. "Who do *you* believe? Tune in today for another episode of *As the Summer Share Turns.*"

"I'll be right back," Josh told his friend.

He set his drink down and left the house. He could see Toby walking down the street a few blocks away. Breaking into a fast jog, he quickly caught up with the young man.

"Hey," he said, "wait up."

"Why?" Toby said. "So you can tell me what a whore I am too?"

"No," Josh said, trying to catch his breath. "I'm pretty sure I know who was to blame for whatever happened."

Toby looked at him suspiciously. "Why's that?" he asked. "You don't even know me."

"No," Josh admitted, "I don't. But I know queens, and that little scene had all the makings of a classic drama. Let me guess. Aaron was trying to get you into bed. Eric walked in. Suddenly *you* became the one who was all over Aaron. Am I close?"

Toby looked at him again. This time he smiled a little. "Pretty close," he said. "But there's a little more to it. I still don't get why you care though."

"I've been there. Sort of," Josh told him.

Toby looked at him warily.

"My boyfriend cheated on me," explained Josh. "Let's just say Aaron looked like he was trying a little too hard."

"That seems to be his specialty," Toby said. "What a jerk."

"Want to talk about it?" Josh asked. When he saw Toby's expression grow wary again, he added, "Don't worry. I'm not looking for anything. It's just that I think we both needed to get away from that party."

"Okay," Toby said after a moment.

"Great," said Josh. "How about we get some drinks and go down to the beach?"

Fifteen minutes later, armed with some sodas and chips picked up at a little grocery near the beach, they were sitting in some dunes. They'd taken their shoes off, and their feet were plunged into the warm sand.

"I can't believe he did that," Josh told Toby, having just heard the story of his first encounter with Aaron. "Wait. I *can* believe he did that. What I can't believe is that he'd keep trying to do it once you started working there."

"What I can't believe is that Eric doesn't know," Toby said, munching on a chip.

Josh laughed. "It's called Gay Alternate Reality," he said. "You just pretend that your life is exactly the way you want it, despite all evidence to the contrary. Eric doesn't *want* to know that Aaron isn't the perfect boyfriend he thinks he is."

"That's sad," Toby said simply. "Really sad."

"Yes, it is," Josh agreed. "Unfortunately, it's how a lot of queens live their lives."

Toby shook his head. "One more reason why it's easier to be straight," he remarked.

"That's not true," said Josh. "There's Straight Alternate Reality too. Do you really think all of those hetero couples are happy?"

"Not all of them," Toby answered. "But more of them."

"Not really," countered Josh. "They're just better at hiding things. Gay men like drama. We do everything on a huge scale, especially when it comes to romantic shit. Straight people prefer to keep it all hidden away so nobody will know that they're just as fucked-up as we are."

Toby laughed, making Josh smile. The kid seemed nice. Josh wondered how he'd ended up in P-Town, but now wasn't the time to ask. Toby just needed someone to talk to, and Josh had nothing but time.

"My parents seem pretty happy," Toby said, sounding a little sad.

Josh didn't say anything. Most likely, he thought, Toby was wrong. Probably his mother frequently wondered how her life would be different if she'd married someone else, and his father fantasized about screwing the checkout girl at the Safeway. But saying so wasn't going to make anything any better. Instead he said, "So, how was Aaron in bed?"

The unexpected comment seemed to shock Toby out of his gloominess.

"Um, well, I don't have anyone else to compare him to," he said. "But he seemed a little small."

Josh laughed loudly. "Size queen!" he said.

Toby blushed. "It just seems to me that if you're going to have something, you know, *up there* it should be worth it," he said. "Is that mean?"

"Not if it's true," replied Josh. He put his arm around Toby's shoulders. "You're going to be just fine," he said. "Just fine."

CHAPTER 36

"Your wiener is on fire."

Reilly looked at the stick in his hand. At the end of it, burning brightly, was the hot dog he'd been carefully grilling in the flames.

"Oh, shit," he said, pulling the hot dog out of the fire, but not before its skin had blackened and charred.

"Hey, watch your mouth in front of Mom," said Donna. "You know she doesn't like swearing."

"Sorry," Reilly told his fiancée.

He was angry, not about the hot dog but that he'd let his concentration slip. What had he been thinking about? He couldn't even remember now. He'd just been staring into the flames, watching the colors change.

"I'll go get you another one," Donna told him, standing up and wiping the sand from her jeans.

As soon as she was gone, one of her brothers took her place. It was one of the twins, Peter or Paul, Reilly couldn't tell which. He'd never been able to tell them apart, and in the dark it was even more difficult.

"Hey, Paul and I were just talking."

Peter, Reilly thought. Not that it mattered. As soon as Peter was gone he'd have them mixed up again. Only Donna was able to tell with any certainty which twin was which. Even Mrs. Estoril sometimes got it wrong. "Their mouths are totally different," Donna said every time someone complained about mistaking one twin for the other. "I don't know why you can't see it."

"So Paul and I were talking," Peter said again. It was one of the twins' more annoying habits, repeating things, as if their thoughts, like the egg from which they'd come, had doubled. "About your bachelor party," he continued. "You know, before your wedding."

"That's generally when they're held, yes," said Reilly, gently teasing Peter.

"Okay, well, you know how normally for a bachelor party the guys go to a, you know, strip joint or something."

Reilly nodded. "Uh huh," he said vaguely, wondering where the conversation was going.

"We think maybe that's not such a good idea," Peter continued. "First on account of how there aren't any titty bars around here, and second because if Donna found out she'd kick our ass."

You mean asses, Reilly wanted to say. *You don't have one between you.* Instead he said, "Yes, she would."

"Right," Peter agreed. "So instead, we thought we'd just have a poker night or something. You know, all the guys."

"I think that sounds like a great idea," Reilly told him.

Peter grinned and nodded, clearly pleased that his idea had gone over well. "Good," he said. "Great."

"What's great?" asked Donna, returning with a fresh hot dog.

"Oh, the fire," Reilly said quickly, knowing that if it was left to Peter to make up an excuse, things would go terribly wrong. "And being here together."

"That's what the Fourth is all about," Donna said, sitting down beside him on the log. "Being with family."

She took Reilly's stick from him and skewered the hot dog before handing it back to him. "Now don't burn this one."

"Yes, dear," said Reilly as Peter stood up and disappeared into the shadows.

"Let me guess," Donna said when her brother was gone. "He wanted to talk about the bachelor party."

"How do you always know what those two are up to?" Reilly asked her, genuinely surprised.

"I ran into Paul at the picnic table," answered Donna. "He tried to stall me by talking about the deviled eggs I made. It wasn't hard to figure out."

Reilly laughed. One of the things he enjoyed most about Donna was the relationship she had with her family. His own family, while very loving, weren't nearly as outgoing as the Estoril clan was. Donna and her brothers always seemed at ease with one another, even when they were fighting. His family, in contrast, was the model of repression. Issues were rarely discussed, and feelings were almost always kept in check. Even fun was discouraged, as it might lead to an embarrassing outpouring of emotion.

So while he sat on the beach with his soon-to-be in-laws and their brood, his parents were tucked safely into their house, away from the Fourth of July festivities. Even their dog, easily upset by the sound of firecrackers being set off by neighborhood kids, was most likely hiding under the bed.

"As long as there are no titty whores around, I don't care what you boys do," Donna told Reilly.

"Titty whores?" he said.

"Strippers. Exotic dancers. Whatever. Girls who take their clothes off for money," she elaborated.

"Do I look like the kind of guy who would be into titty whores?" Reilly asked, feigning seriousness.

"No," replied Donna instantly. "But my brothers are."

"Don't worry," said Reilly, removing his perfectly roasted hot dog from the fire. "It's just going to be cards."

"Good," Donna said.

"What about you?" Reilly asked. "How do I know your girlfriends aren't dragging you off to some male strip show?"

"Please," Donna said. "My girlfriends' idea of a hot time is eating hot-fudge sundaes and not listening to their husbands complain about their jobs."

"And you still want to get married, huh?" said Reilly.

"Strangely enough, yes," Donna answered. "Now finish your hot dog. There are s'mores waiting to be made."

As they were talking, Reilly heard a high-pitched whine. It was followed a few seconds later by an explosion of blue stars that swirled out into the night sky like out-of-control rockets and then fell toward the ocean in great glittering arcs. Almost immediately, a second explosion—this time in red—lit up the surface of the sea. The fireworks had begun.

"This is my favorite part," Donna exclaimed as she took Reilly's hand and settled back to enjoy the show.

As Reilly watched the fireworks, he thought about the few times he had been to Fourth of July celebrations as a little boy. He had stood, mesmerized, the first time he'd held a sparkler in his hand. The tiny sparks sizzling and crackling from the burning stick had seemed like pure magic to him, and he'd run along the beach laughing with joy. Later, when he saw his first real fireworks display, he had been afraid to even blink, lest he miss one single explosion of color. The shooting stars, whirling rockets, and zigzagging streaks of gold, blue, red, and white had taken his breath away with their fierce, wild beauty. When the show ended, with a grand finale consisting of one burst of light after another, he'd refused to leave the beach until he was absolutely sure that no more surprises awaited him.

Later, as a teenager, he'd spent his Fourths with his friends, sitting on the beach drinking beer. Even then, when it was no longer cool to find such things overly exciting, he'd watched the fireworks with the same sense of awe. To him they were an exclamation of happiness, a way to celebrate not patriotism but the crowning moment of summer, the time when the sun was at its warmest, the days their longest, and the possibilities their fullest.

"Come on," he said, standing up and pulling Donna with him. "Let's go for a walk." Suddenly he wanted to tell her about holding that first sparkler, wanted to watch the fireworks together, away from the crowd.

"But the family . . ." Donna protested.

"They'll still be here when we get back," Reilly told her. "Come on. Just a short walk."

"I want to stay by the fire," said Donna.

Reilly looked at her. Should he ask her again to come with him? Or should he just sit back down? It really wasn't that big of a deal, he thought. It was just some fireworks.

"I'll be right back," he said, turning away before Donna could say anything.

He walked quickly down the beach, away from the fire. Part of him expected Donna to get up and come after him. But she didn't, and when he looked back he could see her still seated by the fire, surrounded by her family. He almost went back, but instead he forced himself to keep going. It wasn't important, he decided, if Donna was with him or not. This was something he wanted to do for himself, not for her.

He kept walking, moving away from the large groups of people and into the dunes, where the clumps of viewers were fewer and there was more room to be by himself. Finally he found a spot where he couldn't see his nearest neighbor. He stopped there and stood, looking up at the sky.

He heard a loud whoosh, then watched as corkscrews of green and yellow cascaded through the air, like confetti tossed by a giant hand. These were followed by a huge, spreading fountain of blue, out of which rose first a smaller bloom of red and then, finally, a crackle of white stars that burned hot and fast high above him. With each new boom and pop he waited to see what colors would emerge from the night, and what form they would take.

"My mother used to tell me that fireworks were caused by star giants lighting matches," said a voice in the darkness close by.

Reilly turned to find Josh standing beside him.

"Sorry," Josh said. "I didn't mean to scare you. I was just walking along and saw you standing here."

"Oh," Reilly said. "Okay."

"When I was a kid I used to wait all year for the Fourth," Josh continued. "We weren't allowed to have fireworks where I lived, but somehow my dad always got some. All I really wanted was sparklers. I liked to write my name in the dark with them. Luckily, it's a short one. My name, I mean."

"I used to hold one in each hand and pretend I was a rocket ship going to the moon," said Reilly.

Josh laughed. "I used to pretend I was Tinkerbell from *The Wonderful World of Disney*," he said. "Remember how she used to write the title of the show with her wand? I even gave it that little extra tap at the end. I guess I was the gay version of you."

"Yeah," Reilly said quietly, "I guess you were."

He had barely spoken to Josh since the awkward moment at the house a few weeks before. He'd managed to go over there when Josh wasn't around, and he'd tried to push the events of the past month out of his mind. But now, with Josh standing beside him, they all came back.

"I wonder why they always use fireworks in movies to symbolize falling in love," said Josh. "I mean, think about it. They're really beautiful, and they make your heart beat faster when you see them, but when they fade out they're gone. There's nothing left of them."

"You remember how they made you feel," said Reilly, surprising himself. "You remember. Until the next time. Then you experience it all over again."

Josh looked at him. "I guess you're right," he said. "I never thought about it like that. Who would have thought you'd be such a romantic?"

"Right," Reilly said. "Who would have thought?" He paused a moment, then faced Josh. "Look, there's something I need to say—" he began.

"Look," Josh said, interrupting and pointing up to the sky. "The finale is starting."

Reilly looked up. A series of fireworks was going off, filling the sky with thunderous retorts and flashes of color. His heart was racing. But it wasn't because of the lights.

"I need to tell you something," he began again.

Josh looked at him, waiting for him to continue. Before he could stop himself, Reilly put his arms around the other man and kissed him.

CHAPTER 37

There were too many chairs.

Marly looked around the room and counted. Forty-seven. That was way too many. Why did the people who helped set up the readings always seem to think that Stephen King or Anne Lamott was going to be appearing instead of a gaggle of student writers? It wasn't as if these people actually had *fans.* For Christ's sake, most of them didn't even have friends.

She chided herself for that unkind thought and blamed it on the cramps she'd been fighting all morning. As if having to listen to nine nervous would-be novelists wasn't torture enough, she had to pretend she actually enjoyed it. And now there was the chair problem.

"Annalisa, could you take out about fifteen of these?" she called out to one of the numerous volunteers who were scurrying around with plates of cheese and stacks of photocopied programs, choosing the girl merely because she was the only one whose name Marly could remember at the moment.

As the chairs began flying out of the room under Annalisa's care, Marly turned her attention to the table at the rear of the room. That was where the copies of the instructor's books were supposed to be sitting, waiting to be purchased by the people who ostensibly came to hear the student readers but who generally only wanted to meet their teachers and get signed copies of their work, either for their own collections or to give to friends who would be impressed by such things.

Only the books hadn't arrived. They were, according to UPS, somewhere between the warehouse in Weehawken and Marly's desk. "But we'll get them to you as soon as we can," the customer service rep had assured her brightly, right before Marly had told her exactly where she could put the books once they were located. She had then grabbed yet another of the fidgety assistants and sent him down to the local bookstore to buy up whatever copies they had left of Brody Nicholson's books. They would have to pay retail, of course, which would completely defeat the point of selling the books in the first place, but at least Nicholson would be appeased.

"This is all they had."

Marly turned to see the assistant standing behind her with a disappointingly small stack of books in his hands. She counted.

"Seven," she said dully. "That's it?"

The assistant nodded. "They cleared him out to make room for the new E. Lynn Harris," he said.

Marly groaned and took the books from the young man. She carried them to the table and attempted to make something resembling an attractive display out of them.

"Need some help?"

"No, thanks," Marly said automatically, then realized that it was Garth standing behind her, and not one of the assistants. "Oh, hi," she said, relieved.

"How's it going?" Garth asked. "Or shouldn't I ask?"

"Well, we have too many chairs, not enough books, and about ten minutes before people start showing up," answered Marly. "Oh, and my period arrived this morning with a vengeance. So all in all, I'd say everything is just about perfect."

Garth laughed. "In that case, maybe I should leave you alone."

"Don't you dare," replied Marly. "I need you here for moral support. Especially since Brody just arrived with the ducklings."

Marly waved at Brody Nicholson, who had entered the room with his students in tow. Walking over to where Marly and Garth stood, he surveyed the table.

"This will look good when the other books are put out," he remarked.

Marly and Garth exchanged a glance, but before Marly could come up with something to say, Nicholson continued.

"Are there enough chairs?" he asked, frowning. "I expect there to be quite a crowd."

"We can always add more," Marly said, falling naturally into the voice she used when dealing with potentially difficult artists. "Let me show you where you'll all be standing."

She led Nicholson and his students to the front of the room. As she explained how the sound system worked and showed them where the pitcher of water was conveniently placed inside the podium, she kept one eye on Garth. She was glad he'd come.

"I will go last, of course," Brody said, drawing her attention back to the matter at hand.

"Of course," Marly agreed. She didn't care when Nicholson read, or even if he read at all. She loved the man's writing, but he'd turned out to be something of a prima donna. She'd agreed to an afternoon reading by his students only because she felt the people who'd paid so much to have their writing torn apart by the man should get *something* more for their money than just bruised egos.

Nicholson turned to his students, who looked at him nervously. "Don't forget what I told you," he said seriously. "This isn't about *you;* it's about the *work.*"

"Excuse me," Marly said with practiced experience. "I see some guests arriving."

She slipped away, leaving Nicholson to pontificate. The students would be fine. They would each read for fifteen minutes and then it would be over. Neither they nor anyone who heard them would remember what they'd read. But it was good experience for them, and for whatever reason it made them feel like real writers. She knew many of them, irrationally flushed with excitement after their reading, would sign up for the next round of classes. They were like kids at summer camp who, after writing plaintive letters home describing the bad food, tormenting bigger campers, and disastrous hiking experiences, begged to be allowed to stay for another two weeks following the final night bonfire and talent show. She herself had been one of those campers, many years ago at the Lake Simpiwanna Girls' Camp, and she retained not a little empathy for the students who came to her office on the day following the student performances, credit cards in hand, and extended their stays.

"Do my students look that frightened?" Garth asked her when they reunited at the door to the room.

"Worse," she said seriously, then rolling her eyes when Garth seemed to believe her. "They *love* you," she told him. "Now go sit down."

She pointed to a seat in the rear of the room and Garth obediently went to it. Marly turned and, fixing a welcoming smile on her face, began to greet the people who were starting to come in. As always, she thanked them for coming and encouraged them to partake of the refreshments before settling down for the reading. The wine and cheese, she knew, would be of immeasurable help in keeping the listeners satisfied during the hours to come.

From a quick survey of the people coming in, it looked to be a fairly typical reading. There was a scattering of the elderly, most of them familiar faces from past readings. Marly was careful to be particularly nice to them, as many of them were much wealthier than their outdated clothing suggested, and their donations in large part paid her salary. Then there were the guests invited by the participants, identifiable by their unfailing habit of waving encouragingly to one or more of the anxious readers sitting in the front row.

The rest were a mystery, and these were the ones who interested Marly most. Without either a financial or a personal connection to either the Arts House or the afternoon's readers, their presence at the event was inexplicable. Who, after all, would want to spend upwards of three hours listening to the end products of a summer writing workshop? *Masochists,* Marly thought evilly. *That's who.*

She continued making her rounds, saying hello to those who needed to be acknowledged and smiling politely at those who didn't. Finally, when most of the thirty or so chairs were filled and the trickle at the door had stopped, she decided it was time to begin. Walking to the front of the room, she began her introductions.

"Good afternoon," she began. "And welcome to the Arts House."

The rest of her speech was given by rote. She thanked a great list of people, enumerated a much smaller list of writers who had graduated from the summer writing program to larger literary success, and ended with an only slightly manipulative plea for continued financial support for the arts. "And now," she concluded, "I will turn the afternoon over to the marvelous Brody Nicholson."

As the audience applauded, Marly returned to her seat beside Garth in the last row. As she settled in, he leaned over and whispered, "Very nice. I'm sure no one even noticed your cramps."

Marly giggled and playfully slapped his knee. When she went to move her hand away, Garth reached out and covered it with his, returning it to his knee and holding it there, his fingers intertwining with hers. Marly looked around, worried that someone might see them and fighting the impulse to pull away. Then, realizing that everyone around was listening intently to whatever Brody Nicholson was saying, she gave in to a deeper desire and allowed her hand to remain where it was.

She watched as the first reader, a young woman with strawberry-blond hair and a large birthmark on her right cheek, stood up and began to read. The story had something to do with an anorexic girl who returned to the scene of a brutal rape that had occurred when she was eleven. But even as Marly watched the woman's mouth move, she heard very little. Instead, a story of her own played out in her head, a story narrated by the sensible side of her that stopped her—on occasion—from doing incredibly foolish things, like purchasing yet another pair of navy pumps or eating an entire cheesecake.

What are you doing? the voice asked her harshly. *What if somebody sees you? Get your hand off of his knee. You're supposed to be a professional, for heaven's sake.*

For heaven's sake. It was a phrase Marly's mother had used frequently to express her displeasure at something Marly had done. Marly had always wondered what heaven had to do with any of it, as if staying up past her bedtime or forgetting to hang up her clothes was somehow going to bring catastrophe and ruin on God's kingdom. Now, as an adult, whenever she heard the phrase she imagined a chorus of distraught angels wringing their hands and waiting for the sky to fall.

Still, it was a good question. What *was* she doing? There she was, thirty-six years old and a married woman, holding hands with someone who wasn't her husband.

You're not really holding hands, she reassured yourself. *He's just a friend.* It was a good try, she thought. But not good enough. She and Garth were most definitely holding hands, just as she and Drew had first held hands at the movie he'd asked her to all those years ago. And just as she'd had to decide whether or not to let Drew kiss her later on in the evening, she now had to decide what to do about Garth Ambrose.

Either you're going to have an affair with him or you're not, she told herself. *You're not some twelve-year-old playing games with the boys in school.*

"Excuse me."

Marly jumped, startled by the sound of someone speaking to her. She looked up to see an unfamiliar man standing next to her.

"May I?" he asked.

For a moment Marly didn't know what he was asking. Then she noticed him looking at the vacant seat beside her.

"Oh, of course," she said, feeling herself redden in embarrassment. "Please."

The man gave her a kind smile and sat down. Distracted from her daydreaming, Marly was once again very conscious of the fact that her and Garth's fingers were knotted together. She hoped she wasn't sweating. Suddenly her own hand felt alien to her, completely disconnected from her body. Her wrist seemed leaden and graceless, hanging against Garth's leg like a broken tree limb in need of cutting. She was afraid to move, and she was afraid not to.

Luckily, the choice was made for her as the woman with the birthmark stopped reading and the audience burst into scattered, polite applause. Garth released her hand and clapped with them, freeing her from one problem and presenting her with another: When she was done clapping, would she return her hand to his knee? She felt that if she did, she would be committing to something larger, something with potentially dangerous consequences.

"And now we'll hear from Mr. Joshua Felling," she heard Brody Nicholson say.

Marly looked at the young man taking his place behind the podium. *That's that nice guy who told me the consensus of lesbians joke,* she thought vaguely as she clapped. Then, too quickly, the applause ended and it was time for her to find a resting place for her hand. Would it be her lap or Garth's knee?

Garth solved the problem for her by putting his arm around the back of her chair. She felt it against her shoulders, barely touching her skin. Her hands rested in her lap. And, she noted with some small horror, they *were* sweaty.

CHAPTER 38

His ass was already hurting, and it had only been ten minutes. Reid sighed. Why did they always have to have such hard chairs at these things? he wondered. How difficult would it be to find comfortable ones?

He shifted a little, trying to alleviate the stress on his backside. The woman next to him glanced at him nervously. She seemed tense, as if she were waiting for something bad to happen. But she seemed to settle down when the guy she was with put his arm around her. Probably, Reid thought, she just needed to get laid.

At least the guy reading now was better than the girl with the weird splotch on her face. What the fuck had *that* been about? Granted, he'd come in on the last couple of minutes, but from the brief bit he'd heard he could tell her story was a real downer. Rape? Nobody wanted to hear about that. Jodie Foster had been damn lucky to get an Oscar for that rape movie she'd done, he thought. But at least it was a good performance, a hell of a lot better than that mute girl she'd played, the one who lived in the woods and talked like a hillbilly who'd had a stroke. Where was her manager when that script had come in?

He tried to focus on the guy reading. After all, that's why he'd come to the reading in the first place, to listen, to hear fresh new voices. After reading one awful script too many, he'd needed to hear something else, something not written with Hollywood in mind. Something happened to writers when they tried to write for Tinseltown. They turned stupid. They forgot how to write real dialogue. They forgot how real people felt and acted. Everything turned into car chases and computer-generated monsters that were apparently designed to make audiences ignore the nonexistent stories.

That's what he wanted: stories. He wanted to hear about characters whose lives were changed, who bounced off of one another and came away with new perspectives on the world around them. He was tired of government conspiracies, alien invasions, and kids who saw ghosts. He wanted to hear something about people he actually could imagine knowing.

"'Joe looked at Kirk,'" the guy reading said. "'If it didn't mean anything, then why did you have to fuck him?'"

Reid sat up and started listening more closely.

"'I never said I could be monogamous,' Kirk replied. 'You said you loved me,' Joe said sadly. 'I thought that was the same thing.'"

Something about the lines caught Reid's attention. They sounded real, which was a refreshing change from the stilted lines he'd been reading lately. More than that, they were being spoken by two men.

He listened intently for the next ten minutes, surprised at how quickly he became engrossed in the story. He found himself laughing loudly at several points, and shaking his head in recognition at others. The writer had captured beautifully the painful and sometimes comic moments of a couple breaking up. When it was over, Reid clapped enthusiastically, disappointed that it was over.

He sat through three more readers, all of them adequate but none of them as interesting to him as the first young man had been. When it was announced that there would be a twenty-minute break before the second half of the program, he got up and looked around for the man whose work he'd enjoyed so much. When he couldn't find him, he instead went up to the man who had done the introductions.

"The young man who read the piece about the couple breaking up," Reid said. "Who is he?"

"Josh?" the man asked, sounding a bit surprised.

"Yes," Reid said, recalling the name once he heard it. "Where is he?"

"Over there, by the cheese."

"Thanks," Reid said, turning and making a beeline for Josh, who was attempting to spread Brie on a cracker, not too successfully.

"Hello," said Reid, extending his hand.

"Oh, um, hi," Josh replied as the cracker broke in his hand, leaving him with Brie on his fingers. "I'd shake, but I seem to be all cheesy."

"I really enjoyed your work," Reid told him.

"Really?" Josh said, as if not believing him. "Thanks."

"It's part of a book, right?"

Josh nodded. "A novel," he answered.

"Is it finished?" Reid inquired. "I'd love to read it."

"Well, no, it isn't finished," Josh told him. "Not quite yet. I'm afraid you'll have to wait awhile. That is if it even gets published."

"I can't wait that long," said Reid firmly. "How much of the manuscript do you have?"

Josh looked at him with a bewildered expression. "I'm sorry," he said. "Who are you?"

Reid laughed. "No, *I'm* sorry," he said. "Sometimes I forget I'm not in Los Angeles. I'm Reid Truman."

Josh looked at him blankly.

"I make movies," Reid elaborated. "I'm a producer."

"Oh," Josh said. "I'm afraid I don't know much about movies. Should I know who you are?"

"Apparently not," answered Reid. "But that's okay. The point is, I like what I heard you read. What was the title again?"

"'Regular Joe,'" Josh answered.

"Great title," said Reid.

"Well, the whole point of the book is that it's about a gay guy who is just a normal guy. He isn't part of any particular gay clique. He just wants to have a regular life. And that's the problem—no one will let him. They all think he has to be a certain way because he's gay. So *he* starts thinking he has to be a certain way, only every time he tries it backfires on him."

"It's like the anti–*Will and Grace* or *Queer As Folk,*" suggested Reid.

"Right!" Josh said excitedly. "You get it. Those shows are okay, but they don't really reflect how most of us live. I'm sorry, how most of us gay guys live. I didn't mean to imply that you—"

"Don't be sorry," Reid interrupted. "I am. Gay, I mean."

"I hope I didn't just insult one of your shows," said Josh.

"No problem," Reid said. "I don't do television." He gave a mock shudder, as if the idea of working for TV were the most horrifying thing he could be accused of.

Josh laughed. "I still can't believe you like what I read," he said. "Brody keeps telling me it's too melodramatic and unrealistic."

"Fuck Brody, whoever he is," Reid said.

"He's my instructor," explained Josh, indicating Brody Nicholson, who was engaged in answering questions from two elderly women who nodded vigorously as he talked.

"What the fuck does he know?" remarked Reid. "Teachers never want their students to be better than they are."

"I don't know if I'm better than—" began Josh.

"Life is melodramatic and unrealistic," Reid proclaimed, cutting him off. "At least any life worth watching on-screen. That jerk probably thinks the only worthwhile art is the kind that imitates life's most boring moments. He probably writes novels about people who spend six hundred pages agonizing over the death of their favorite cat."

Josh laughed. "You're not far off," he said. "But to be fair, he's a wonderful writer."

"So are you," Reid said. "And that's what I'm interested in. Have you thought about turning this thing into a script?"

Josh shook his head. "No," he said. "I don't know anything about writing movies."

"Neither do ninety-nine percent of the people who write them," said Reid. "It's not a problem. The question is, are you interested in trying?"

Josh shrugged. "I guess I could give it a shot," he said.

"Good," Reid replied. "So here's what you do. Print out everything you have written and bring it to my house tomorrow night. We'll go from there. Do you have a pen?"

Josh fished in his pocket and produced a pen, which Reid used to write his name and address on a napkin. He handed them both to Josh. "Tomorrow night, seven-thirty," he said. "You'll be there?"

"I'll be there," Josh said.

Reid nodded and left the room. He couldn't take hearing any more pretentious literary crap. The kid had been the only good one in the bunch, despite what his teacher apparently thought. Well, screw him. Reid couldn't stand people who thought everything had to be all highbrow and artsy.

"What the hell is wrong with entertaining people?" he asked aloud, earning a confused look from a couple sipping wine near the front door.

Besides, he couldn't waste the whole afternoon at a reading. He had other things to think about, namely Ty's latest suggestion. Ty had brought it up the previous evening, as they'd been lying in bed after making love. Reid, drowsy from the wine they'd had at dinner and the effects of two orgasms in the space of an hour, had listened in a kind of hazy dream state, hearing what Ty was saying but not really taking it all in.

In the morning, however, he'd woken up clearheaded, and then the conversation had come back to him in its totality. It was a skill he'd developed over the years, storing information away while in an altered state and then recalling it with perfect clarity when he was in a more sober attitude. It had helped him avoid making bad deals while drunk or stoned, and on more than one occasion had meant the difference between attaching himself to a box office flop and passing on what, under the influence of alcohol or chemicals, seemed like a sure thing.

Ty's proposal, however, was of a more serious nature than the making or losing of several million dollars. It was also more intriguing. The more Reid considered it, the more he thought it just might work. That is, as long as the girl could be trusted.

And he thought she could. At least more than some Hollywood starlet could, some power-hungry bimbo who would be more than happy to betray him and Ty if it meant a bigger salary or an over-the-title credit. He'd seen them do worse for a walk-on in a pilot or a chance to costar in some straight to cable movie with the likes of Emilio Estevez.

Anyway, the girl would make things a lot easier. Nobody knew who she was. It would make the whole thing appear even more authentic. Plus, it would play into the whole image of Ty as a man of the people, someone who would rather pair up with one of his own than some movie industry princess.

Yes, it was a good idea. Reid chuckled as he thought about it. Two great ideas in one day. It was good to be king. He took his cell phone out of his pocket and hit speed-dial.

"Devin," he said when the call was answered. "Can you come by the house tonight? I have a little project you might be interested in."

CHAPTER 39

Emmeline looked down at her penis. It was resting on the blue paper sheet that covered the examining table in Dr. Tulevitch's office, cradled on the wrinkled water bed of her testicles. She had shaved the whole lot, to make them look more ladylike, but still they exuded maleness.

Not that they could help it. That's just what they did, and it didn't bother her. She had never actively disliked her dick. In fact, she'd had a lot of fun with it over the years. But now it was becoming a nuisance, a constant reminder that she hadn't quite achieved the goal she'd set for herself.

"So, basically, we core it out and invert it," Dr. Tulevitch was saying.

Emmeline gave a little laugh, covering her mouth as her doctor looked at her over his glasses. Dr. Tulevitch was what Emmeline liked to refer to, not unkindly, as "a middle-aged, straight, white guy with humor issues." But he was good, and that's what mattered. At the moment he was showing her some pictures of his handiwork.

"I'm sorry," Emmeline said. "It's just that you make it sound like we're making a jack-o'-lantern or something."

Dr. Tulevitch blinked but didn't smile. "Many people mistakenly think that we just cut the penis off," he said seriously. "It's much more complex than that."

Emmeline nodded and took the photo that the doctor held out to her. It didn't bother her that Dr. Tulevitch was taking it all so seriously. *After all,* she thought, *talking about coring out a penis probably makes him a little nervous.* She'd wondered about that before. What was it like for a man to turn another man's dick into a vagina? Did he see it as a colossal waste of perfectly good cock, or was it simply another opportunity to practice his surgical skills? It was an interesting position to be in, caught between playing God and protecting the supremacy of the phallus.

She pushed the thought to the back of her mind and looked at the photo in her hand. It showed a young woman with her legs spread. Her labia folded back like the proverbial flower petals, and between them Emmeline saw a crush of pink. The picture could, she thought, have been torn straight from the pages of a *Playboy* magazine.

"As you can see, the results can be quite good," Dr. Tulevitch said calmly, as if he were discussing the new paint job on a Buick or the recovering of a sofa. He handed Emmeline another photo, this one showing a before and after. In the before photo, one of the biggest dicks Emmeline had ever seen was hanging between the subject's legs. In the second, a neat little pussy was in its place, the hair around it shaved into an almost heart-shaped mantle.

"Very nice," Emmeline said, genuinely impressed. "You got all of that stuffed up inside her?"

She said it just to see what the doctor would do. Without a pause he replied, "The larger the penis and testicles are, the easier it is to fashion the new vagina," he explained. "Even her gynecologist didn't know until she told him."

Emmeline handed back the photos. "So what do you think mine will look like?" she asked.

Dr. Tulevitch hefted her balls in one latex-gloved hand, as if he were handling fruit at the market. "I think you'll be very pleased," he said. "And with a little luck, the neurological results will be excellent as well. I expect you'll have full sensation."

"It's hard to believe you can do that," said Emmeline. "I mean, it just seems like it should be more complicated."

"Don't get me wrong," the doctor said. "It's not a simple procedure, and the results are not guaranteed. Each person is different. But you're fortunate in that you're going from male to female. The reverse is much more difficult. Although structurally the genitals of both men and women develop from the same types of cells, building a penis is much harder."

Building a penis, Emmeline repeated to herself. *He says it like it's the same as erecting a monument or something.* It was an all-too-typical male view of the bits of flesh between their legs. Suddenly she pictured thousands of Egyptian slaves pushing and pulling great chunks of marble to construct a pinnacle that towered over the desert, a permanent celebration of the glories of the cock.

"And it will really feel natural?" she asked, hoping Dr. Tulevitch understood her meaning.

"I don't have any firsthand experience to back this up," he said, surprising her. "But I'm told that the effect is most convincing—for both parties."

He turned away to remove his gloves and make some notes on Emmeline's chart, leaving her to collect herself. When he turned back, he said, "We can schedule the surgery any time you're ready."

Emmeline nodded. She was ready. Unfortunately, her bank account wasn't. The surgery was expensive, and most definitely not covered by her insurance.

"I'll let you know soon," she told the doctor. "And thank you." She hesitated a moment before speaking again. "May I ask you a personal question?"

Dr. Tulevitch nodded.

"Why do you do this?" asked Emmeline. "This kind of surgery, I mean."

The doctor removed his glasses and slipped them into his pocket. "My daughter, Sarah," he said quietly. "She was always what we used to call a tomboy. She wanted to do everything her brothers did. When she was young, my wife and I thought it was her way of asserting herself in a house filled with boys. Then, when she was fourteen, she told us she didn't want to be a girl, that she felt she *wasn't* a girl. We didn't understand. We thought she was saying she was a lesbian. I sent her to talk to a colleague, a psychiatrist. He prescribed medication. But Sarah became more depressed."

He stopped and took a breath. "One morning my wife went to wake Sarah for school and found her dead. She'd overdosed on some pills she'd taken from my office. She was fifteen."

Emmeline ran a hand through her hair distractedly. "I'm sorry," she said. "I shouldn't have asked."

Dr. Tulevitch raised one hand, as if stopping her. When he looked into her face, he was smiling wistfully. "You asked why I do this," he said. "I do it for the daughter I lost and the son I never got to know."

He stood up and put his glasses back on. "You call me when you are ready," he said.

Emmeline nodded. "Thank you," she said as the doctor left, shutting the door behind him.

She dressed quickly and left. As she drove home, she couldn't help but think about what Dr. Tulevitch had told her about his daughter. What must it have been like, finding her dead like that? How must he have felt? Emmeline knew how the girl probably felt: frightened, confused, alone. Most likely she had simply been unable to understand who she was. Emmeline had seen that happen before. She understood it all too well.

But what about Sarah's parents and siblings? They probably hadn't understood her, either. Faced with her death, had they blamed themselves? How could they not? How could they not wonder what they might have done differently? How could they not feel guilt of some kind?

She thought then of her mother. All of the years they'd gone not understanding each other. Had her mother simply not known what to say? Had she somehow blamed herself for what she saw as her baby's illness and her inability to successfully cure it?

It seemed too simple, too obvious. Her mother had never even tried to understand who Emmeline was, despite Emmeline's numerous attempts to show her. She'd refused every invitation to Emmeline's shows, changed the subject whenever Emmeline had tried to discuss it with her. She was the one who had rejected Emmeline, not the other way around. Why, she'd even preferred to keep Petey in her life, covering up his behavior with lies to make Emmeline feel inadequate. Even now she wouldn't admit that he'd abandoned her and that, once again, it was Emmeline who was picking up the pieces.

She's just lucky I was brave enough to leave instead of killing myself, she thought angrily. *If I'd done that, she'd be sorry.*

With a shock, she realized what she'd just done. With that one thought, she'd blamed Sarah Tulevitch—and everyone like her—for their own deaths. Yes, perhaps Emmeline had been brave for knowing that she needed to leave home for her own good. But was Sarah any less brave for leaving in her own way? Was she somehow weaker because she didn't understand that she was okay as she was? And was Emmeline any stronger because she was still here?

No, she told herself. *You're not stronger. If anything, you're the weak one because you're still running, still blaming, still angry.*

Although she wasn't supposed to, she pulled the car to the side of the highway. As traffic rushed by her, the occasional face peering out of the window to see why she'd stopped, she sat with her hands on the wheel, staring out at the afternoon sun while tears began their slow journey down her cheeks. She'd wasted so much time. So much time being angry at her mother for not being smarter, or less stubborn. Emmeline had been unable to forgive her for her faults, while demanding that Lula accept *her* as she was. It had been unfair of her, yet somehow she'd managed to convince herself that she was in the right, was the one who deserved to feel betrayed.

Maybe, she thought, it was time to accept her mother the way she was, even if it meant accepting that she would never understand, couldn't understand, who Emmeline was. Emmeline had spent her whole life telling the people around her that real love meant accepting the whole person, not just the pleasant parts. Hadn't she said as much to Toby?

A line from *Alice in Wonderland* popped into her head. "I give myself very good advice, but I very seldom follow it." She couldn't recall to whom, or under what circumstances, the demented little heroine of Lewis Carroll's book had uttered those words, but they seemed aimed directly at her. And wasn't she quite a bit like Alice anyway, she thought, making her way through an ever-changing world in an attempt to find her way home.

She wiped the tears from her face and looked in the rearview mirror to check her makeup. When she did, she saw the unmistakable flashing lights of a police car. A moment later, there was a knock on her window. She hit the button and the glass retreated into the car door.

"Is everything all right, ma'am?" asked the officer.

"Yes," said Emmeline. "I just dropped my lipstick and didn't want to have an accident while I looked for it."

The officer nodded curtly. "You do know the tag on your plate is expired, don't you?" he asked.

"No," Emmeline said, genuinely surprised. "I'm afraid I didn't."

"Could I see your license and registration, please?"

Emmeline opened the glove compartment and located the paperwork. Then she fished in her purse for her wallet. She handed the requested documents to the policeman, who looked at them for a moment and then looked at her with a puzzled expression.

It was only then that Emmeline realized he was confused by the information on her license. Although she'd had her name legally changed, the small matter of her sex was something else. She and the Massachusetts Registry of Motor Vehicles disagreed strongly on that point.

The officer continued to look at first the license and then her. Finally he handed both back and said, "All right Mr., I mean Mrs., Tayhill. I'm going to let you off with a warning. But make sure you get that tag renewed right away."

Emmeline nodded. "I will, Officer," she said. "And by the way, it's *Miss* Tayhill."

The policeman walked back to his car as Emmeline rolled the window up and started the engine. As she thought about what had just transpired, she began to laugh. And as she pulled her car back onto the highway and headed for home, she began to feel a sense of happiness. Unlike Sarah Tulevitch, she was still alive. So was her mother. And it was time they had a nice, long talk.

CHAPTER 40

"Mrs. Ty Rusk." Devin said it out loud, seeing how it sounded. "Well, you'd never actually get married," Reid corrected her. "You'd just be dating. And even that would just be for the press."

Devin nodded. "I get it," she said. "It keeps all of those tabloid types off your back."

"Right," Ty said. "All you have to do is go out with me to a few dinners, a few premiers, a couple of parties."

"We'd pay for your expenses, of course," Reid added. "And when Ty is done shooting in New York it would mean you'd need to move to LA. You could work for me, so you'd have a job. It would be a good way for you to get into the business."

I'll say, Devin thought to herself. She looked at Ty and Reid, seated across from her on the couch in Reid's house. "Okay," she said. "I'll do it."

"That's my girl," Reid said happily as Ty broke into a grin. "I had a feeling we could count on you."

He retreated to the kitchen and returned with three glasses and a bottle of champagne. Deftly removing the cork, he poured the bubbly out and handed glasses to Ty and Devin.

"To the two of you," he said. "May your love never die."

Devin and Ty laughed at the joke and they all clinked glasses.

"I can't thank you enough for doing this," Ty told Devin. "It will make life so much easier for me. I can focus on my work instead of on who to take to the Oscars."

"We're going to the *Oscars?*" Devin said excitedly. "No way."

Ty nodded. "As long as you promise not to slap Joan and Melissa on your way in," he said.

"We'll have to come up with a good back story," said Reid. "You know, to explain how you two got together."

"Always the producer," Ty joked. "How about this? You hired Devin to do some work for you while you were here for the summer. I came out for a weekend, met her, and fell in love. It's pretty much the truth, so we'll both sound genuine when we talk to *Entertainment Tonight.*"

"Now how are you going to break this news to Pamela?" Reid asked Ty.

Ty cringed. "I hadn't thought of that."

"Who's Pamela?" Devin inquired. "A girl you're supposed to be seeing?"

"Eew," said Ty, making a face. "What a horrible thought. No, it's even worse than that. She's my agent."

"She'll be pissed that he's not shacking up with some Hollywood name," Reid explained. "But frankly, I think this is even better. Devin could be any girl in America. Your fans will eat it up."

"Once they stop hating me," Devin said.

Ty took her hand and kissed it. "They'll just have to accept our love, darling," he told her. "There's no other woman for me."

I'll bet there isn't, Devin thought as she smiled back at him. How dumb did he and Reid think she was, anyway, pretending that Ty needed her to pose as his love interest so he could concentrate on *work?* If they had any balls, they'd tell her it was because they were fucking each other and needed a beard.

Ultimately she didn't care. She had what she wanted. Or at least she would once she was in LA and working with Reid. Her plan had actually worked out much better than she'd hoped. She'd thought that if she gave Ty the bullshit story about having married a fag, he might decide to spill the beans about himself and Reid. But this was even better. She would just play dumb and collect the payoff.

What about Raymacher? The question popped into her head, dampening her mood somewhat. She'd promised the columnist proof that Reid and Ty were ass bandits. But if she delivered it, they wouldn't have any need for her. Suddenly, the irony of her situation dawned on her. Ty and Reid were only good to her as long as they *weren't* exposed. If everyone knew they were queer, she'd be out of the picture.

This was going to require some thinking. But she could pull it off, she was sure of it. After all, hadn't she managed to fool Ty and Reid so far? Now she would simply have to use the same cleverness that had gotten her this far on Raymacher.

"We should start slow," Reid said, drawing her attention back to the moment. "Devin, you should go into New York next week and have dinner with Ty. Go somewhere romantic but out of the way. I'll pull in a favor or two and make sure a photographer from the *Post* just happens to snap some shots of you two together. I guarantee you you'll be all over Page Six the next morning. We'll let it go from there."

"Should I warn my publicist about any of this?" asked Ty.

Reid shook his head. "Absolutely not," he said. "We want him to be just as surprised as everyone else. It will make it look more realistic if reporters call him for comment and he has no idea what they're talking about."

Ty looked at Devin. "You're sure you're ready for this?" he asked her.

She laughed. "Please, if I could handle Zane's mother, I can handle some reporters," she said. "Trust me, Greta Mulholland was one tough bitch."

"Besides, we'll be there to help her," added Reid. "Just think of it as an acting job. You're starring in your very own life."

"I just hope the reviews are good," remarked Ty.

Devin stayed for another hour, then excused herself on the pretense that she was tired and needed to get to bed. After saying good night to Reid and her new boyfriend, she got into her car and drove home. As she drove, a plan began to form in her mind, and by the time she pulled into the driveway of her parents' house, she knew what she was going to do.

"Hi, honey," her mother said when Devin walked into the kitchen. "How was your night?"

"Fine," replied Devin shortly.

Her mother was sitting at the kitchen table, clipping coupons from one of the numerous supermarket circulars she collected each day. Already a tidy pile of slips sat in front of her, papers she would exchange later for ten cents off of toilet paper and a dollar off three cans of select Progresso soups for Devin's father's lunches. Her thriftiness angered Devin. She didn't need to use coupons, she just liked to. As a child, Devin had shuddered each time her mother had handed her bundle of perfectly trimmed coupons to the checkout girl at the local

A&P, convinced that the pimply faced teen who listlessly punched in the savings would think them poor. They were, she thought, just a step away from food stamps.

Devin left the room quickly. Her father was in the living room, where the sound of the Red Sox game he was watching filled the air with a false sense of excitement. A quick glance at the screen and at her father's closed eyes and open mouth showed that at the bottom of the sixth inning, both the Sox and her father were out. She passed through and made her way upstairs to her room.

She picked up the phone and dialed C.J. Raymacher's office.

"Well, it's about time," the columnist said when he heard her voice. "I was beginning to think you were turning out to be a dead end."

"You shouldn't assume anything," Devin said coyly.

"What have you got for me?" Raymacher asked her. "Photos?"

"Better," replied Devin. "The inside story on Ty Rusk's new mystery girl."

Raymacher groaned. "What girl?" he said, sounding irritated. "And who gives a fuck? The guy's a homo. *That's* what you're supposed to be getting the dirt on."

"Relax," said Devin. "The girl is me."

Raymacher paused a moment. "What kind of shit is this?" he said. "I sent you to out the guy, not fuck him."

"Oh, I'm going to fuck him, all right," said Devin. "But not the way you think. Just listen."

She told Raymacher about her new deal with Reid and Ty. When she was finished she concluded by saying, "So what do you think? How much would the story of the woman who was hired to protect Ty Rusk's image be worth to you?"

Raymacher chuckled. "You're an even bigger bitch than I thought," he said. "You want me to pay you for your story?"

"If you don't, I imagine the *Star* or the *National Enquirer* would be more than happy to," answered Devin coolly.

"How much?" Raymacher said.

"Two hundred and fifty thousand," said Devin.

"No fucking way," snapped Raymacher.

"Why not?" Devin said. "You offered Monica Lewinsky twice that for her story."

"She blew the goddamned president of the United States," said Raymacher.

"And I'm giving you the hottest story in Hollywood," Devin retorted. "Do you know how many copies of that magazine you'll move when this comes out? You'll make your money back just on your sales at Seven-Eleven alone."

Raymacher sighed. "Fine," he said. "I'll see what I can do. But you'd better come through on this one."

"Don't worry about me," Devin said. "I'll do my part."

She hung up. *Always make sure you have the last word,* she thought happily as she took off her shoes and lay down on the bed. It had been a good day, especially now that Raymacher was playing into her hands. At first she'd considered telling him that they were wrong, that Ty wasn't queer after all. But she knew a longtime muckraker like Raymacher would be on to her as soon as he saw pictures of her and Ty together. Her only option had been to let him in on her secret. That way, not only would he feel he could trust her, but she could get more money from the deal. With both Raymacher and Reid paying her off, she was going to be sitting pretty.

Coming home for the summer, she thought, wasn't turning out to be so bad after all. With a little more luck, she would be out of Provincetown by fall and would never have to set foot in it again. Good-bye, boring house. Good-bye, boring family. Good-bye, boring life. It would all be behind her.

"And hello, Hollywood," she said happily.

CHAPTER 41

"He *kissed* you?"

Ben looked at Josh in astonishment. They were sitting in the kitchen, having coffee and blueberry muffins that Ben had just pulled from the oven.

Josh nodded. "And then he took off," he said. "I didn't even have a chance to say anything."

"Was he drunk?" Ted asked. "That would explain it."

Ben waved a hand at him. "Just because *you* were drunk the first time you kissed a man doesn't mean everyone has to be," he said.

"He wasn't drunk," Josh said. "At least I don't think so. He seemed fine."

"I always said that boy had it in him," said Ben happily.

"Let's not get all excited now," Ted told him sternly. "We don't know what got into Reilly."

"I do," replied Ben. "He decided he'd had enough of pussy." He made a face. "Nasty," he added.

Josh sighed. "It's just so weird," he said. "And now I don't know what to do."

"What do you *want* to do?" asked Ben.

Josh leaned back in his chair and groaned. "I don't know," he said miserably. "I guess I want him to do it again."

"Then tell him," Ben said instantly.

"Do *not* tell him," Ted countered. He tapped Ben lightly on the wrist with his spoon. "You're causing trouble," he told his lover.

"The trouble has already been caused," said Ben. "I'm just trying to clarify things."

"What you're trying to do is butt in," Ted warned.

Ben ignored him, turning back to Josh. "Have you seen him since the Fourth?"

Josh shook his head. "He hasn't been here all week," he said. "I think he's avoiding me."

"Of course he is," said Ted. "He made a mistake. He's embarrassed."

Ben gave Ted a stern look. "And what makes you think he made a mistake?" he demanded.

Ted rubbed his forehead, as if Ben's voice were giving him a headache. "He's *engaged,*" he said, as if explaining to a child why it was a bad idea to run with scissors.

"Oh, I see," Ben said sarcastically. "I'm sorry. I forgot that men who are engaged aren't allowed to kiss other men."

"You are such an old queen," Ted said, laughing softly. "Look, I know you think it would be the most wonderful thing in the world if Reilly turned out to be gay. But I don't think it's going to happen."

"Well, excuse me for being the only romantic around here," said Ben. "But if you ask me," he said to Josh, "there's no harm in trying."

Josh picked at his muffin. "This summer is just weird all the way around," he said. "First the thing with Doug, then Jackie asking for my sperm and this producer liking my book. Now this."

"That's Provincetown," Ben informed him. "It likes to shake people up."

"I thought it was supposed to be quiet here," said Josh.

Ted laughed. "That's what the town wants you to think," he said. "But really it's just waiting for you to let your guard down."

"Oh, and I didn't tell you about the kid," Josh continued. "The one from the party."

"You didn't kiss him too, did you?" asked Ben.

"No," replied Josh. "I think that's the last thing he needs. But he does need a job, and I was wondering if you guys could use any help around here." He told them about Toby, and what had happened to him at the other house. "What do you think?" he asked when he was finished.

Ben looked at Ted, who shrugged. "Why not?" Ted said. "We're booked through Labor Day. We can always use another pair of hands."

"Thanks," Josh said. "I'll have him come over later today and meet you. He seems like a good kid."

He stood up. "And now I'm going to go work on this script," he said. "Thanks for the coffee and the advice."

He left Ben and Ted at the table and returned to the cottage. He'd met with Reid Truman a few days earlier, and Reid had given him some ideas on turning his novel into a script. Josh had promised to work something up to show him, but so far all he'd managed to get down was the title. Writing scripts, he'd discovered, was no easier than writing novels.

He sat down and tried to concentrate on his computer screen. But his eyes kept moving from the screen to the hammer sitting on the coffee table. Reilly had left it behind on his last visit to the house. Josh had been waiting for him to return, so he could give it to him, but now it was collecting dust.

I could return it to him, he thought. *I mean, he might need it.*

It was a stupid excuse, and he knew it. But he ignored that fact and snatched the hammer from the table, leaving the house before he could change his mind. Getting into his car, he drove toward town. He had no idea where Reilly might be, but he went anyway, thinking he might see his truck parked somewhere.

He found it outside a hardware store. Parking his car, he got out and went into the store, carrying the hammer with him. Inside, he wandered the aisles until he saw Reilly. He was halfway down the tool aisle, looking intently at the wall.

"Can I interest you in this fine hammer?" asked Josh, walking up to him nervously.

Reilly looked at him with an unreadable expression, but didn't say anything.

Josh waved the hammer at him. "You left it at the house," he said.

"Oh," said Reilly, making no move to take the hammer from Josh. "Thanks. I've been looking for that. Actually, I was just about to buy another one."

"Now you don't have to," Josh said, putting the hammer in Reilly's hand. "Bye now."

He turned to walk away, but Reilly reached out and touched his shoulder. "Wait," he said.

Josh turned around. Reilly looked at him. "I'm really sorry," he said. "About what happened."

"It's okay," Josh told him. "You were probably drunk."

Reilly looked at the floor and moved the hammer from one hand to the other. "I wish I had been," he said. "Then I'd have an excuse."

"Really," Josh told him. "It's okay. You don't need an excuse. It just happened. Now it's over. Forget about it."

He didn't know why he was practically forcing a way out on Reilly. Hadn't he just told Ben that what he really wanted was for Reilly to kiss him again? So then why was he acting as if it didn't matter? He didn't know.

"No," Reilly said. "I owe you an explanation. I just . . ." He stopped, looking around the store as if perhaps there were a sign somewhere that would tell him what to say next, a list of step-by-step directions for dealing with the situation hung beside the ones for creating faux marble finishes and grouting a bathtub.

"You just did it," Josh said, finishing the sentence for him. "That's all."

Reilly looked at him. His eyes were sad, all the life drained from them so that he looked worn out and in desperate need of sleep. "Yeah," he said, nodding resignedly. "I just did it."

Josh nodded. "Okay then," he said. "I guess I'll see you around the house."

This time he didn't give Reilly a chance to call him back. He walked out of the store as quickly as he could, almost knocking over a display of rakes in his hurry to get out the door. He was opening his car door to get in when Reilly came running down the steps.

"I didn't just do it," he said as Josh paused, his fingers on the handle. "I wanted to do it."

Josh let go of the handle and slipped his hands into the pockets of his shorts. "So why then?" he asked hesitantly.

"I don't know," Reilly answered. "No, I do know. It was the fireworks."

Josh cocked his head. "The fireworks? What, they made you go temporarily insane or something?"

"I liked sparklers the best too," said Reilly. "I know that sounds completely stupid. But when you said that, all I could think about was how right at that moment I wanted to be with someone who knew what that was like, that feeling of being totally excited about something as dumb as a sparkler on the Fourth of July, just because it was totally amazing and beautiful."

Josh nodded silently. "You're right," he said after a moment. "That *is* completely stupid."

Reilly looked away.

"But what's even stupider is that I know exactly what you mean," Josh finished.

Reilly met his eyes. "You do?"

Josh nodded. "I do," he said. He hesitated before continuing. "But now the question is, what do you want to do about it?"

Reilly didn't answer. Josh watched his face, his heart racing and his thoughts jumping from one thing to the next as he waited for an answer. Reilly cleared his throat.

"I—" he began.

"Hey, handsome. What are you doing here?"

A young woman appeared seemingly out of nowhere and walked over to Reilly, giving him a kiss on the cheek. He looked at her for a moment, as if trying to figure out who she was.

"Hi," he said. "I was just . . . um . . ." He paused as the woman waited for an answer.

"Picking up a hammer," Josh said, feeding him the line.

"Right," Reilly said quickly. "Picking up a hammer." He held up the hammer in his hand. "This one. Right here."

"So he can finish work on the cottage," Josh suggested when Reilly paused again.

"Yes," Reilly said. "So I can finish work on the cottage."

"Well, I just ran out for a quick lunch," the woman said. "Want to join me?"

Reilly nodded. "Sure," he said, a little too brightly. "Lunch would be great." He turned to Josh. "I'll see you later," he said.

Josh nodded. "Later," he echoed.

The woman smiled at Josh. "I'm Donna," she said. "Reilly's fiancée." She extended her hand to Josh. "Since he's not going to introduce us," she said lightly.

Josh took her hand. "Josh," he said. "Nice to meet you. Reilly is working on the cottage I'm staying in."

"Oh, over at Ben and Ted's place," Donna replied.

Josh nodded. "That would be the one," he said.

"Tell them I said hello," said Donna. "I haven't seen them in ages. But I'm sure they'll be at the wedding."

"I'm sure they will," Josh said. "You guys have a good lunch. I'll see you later," he said to Reilly.

Reilly nodded, and Josh got into his car. As he drove off, he saw the couple in his rearview mirror. Donna had taken Reilly's hand, and they were walking down the street away from him, growing smaller and smaller as he sped toward home.

CHAPTER 42

"Here," said Jackie.

Josh looked at the container in his hand. "What is this?"

"A baby food jar," Jackie answered as she sat down on the couch. "It's what you put it in."

"A baby food jar?" Josh repeated, looking at her with a sleepy expression, and not only because she'd gotten him up at three thirty-five in the morning.

"I *sterilized* it," replied Jackie a little defensively. "I used to help my grandmother put up jam. I know how to sterilize a jar."

"Jam?" said Josh, making a face. "You're comparing this to making jam?"

Jackie sighed. "It's the perfect size," she said. "Now go fill it. I'll wait here."

"Excuse me?" asked Josh. "You'll wait here?"

Jackie nodded. "What did you think I was going to do?"

Josh laughed hoarsely. "Oh, I don't know," he told her. "Maybe leave it here and let me bring it over later."

"Josh," said Jackie gently, as if speaking to a distraught child, "according to my temperature chart and vaginal mucus production, we have to do this *now.*" She nodded at the jar in his hand. "I'm taking that thing home with me, and I want it filled with your best swimmers."

Josh winced. "Well, using terms like 'vaginal mucus production' isn't going to help!" he exclaimed.

Jackie rolled her yes. "It's not like you're actually sticking your dick in it," she said. "Just go squirt a little something into that jar and I'll be on my way. It's no big deal."

"Right," said Josh. "No big deal. Apparently *you* never tried to jack off while your parents were in the next room watching *Hart to Hart.*"

He went into the bathroom and shut the door behind him. Dropping his boxer shorts, he sat on the toilet and looked at the jar. The round smiling face of the Gerber baby stared back at him, squealing in delight at the thought of being given strained peas or beef puree. *I can't believe I'm doing this,* Josh thought. When he had agreed to donate his sperm to Jackie, he'd envisioned clinics and plastic cups, not him sitting in his bathroom jerking off into a baby food jar.

You might as well get to it, he told himself. After all, it couldn't be that difficult. He'd whacked off thousands of times. How many? he wondered idly. *Let's say four times a week,* he thought as he tried to tease his dick to life. *That's roughly two hundred times a year. Let's round up to two hundred twenty-five just to be safe. And I started when I was about twelve. So two hundred twenty-five times twenty-one years. No, almost twenty-two. That's what? Shit, almost five thousand times!*

He looked down at his cock. Had he really beat off almost five thousand times? Had he had five thousand orgasms? And that didn't even count ones he'd had during sex with other people. If he added those in, he was probably somewhere around seven thousand five hundred. If he were a car, he'd be long overdue for an oil change. *That's a lot of cum,* he thought, impressed by himself. *A lot of babies. Well, it would have been a lot of babies if that cum hadn't gone down a toilet, into a trash can, or all over someone else's chest.*

He'd never thought of it that way. But when he did, it was sort of staggering. All those potential children, just flushed or wiped away with no particular thought to who they might have been or what they might have grown up to become. It was sort of weird, really, to imagine it. Of course, thinking that an actual human being could grow out of his cum was a little weird, too.

His attention was drawn back to the jar in his one hand and the dick in his other. He wasn't getting hard. *You have to focus,* he told himself. He shook his head to clear it and tried to think about something sexy. His mind considered and discarded several images: his junior high gym teacher, Mr. Rigby, who used to shower with the boys after class and who had been his first real crush; an oddly appealing William Shatner as a cop in *T.J. Hooker;* the smooth chest he'd displayed in *Star Trek* now covered in hair; the Giants' David Bell, whom he'd seen in a game on televison the evening before and who had provided an excellent presleep fantasy.

But David and the other guys weren't working for him now. Nor were any of the other stock fantasies he relied on to get him off when he lacked any more immediate stimulation. Somehow, knowing that Jackie was sitting outside, *waiting* for him to come and waiting to use the product of his time in the bathroom to fertilize one of her eggs, made it far more difficult to do so.

He whacked his uncooperative cock against his leg several times, as if to wake it up. This only succeeded in dampening his arousal even further. He'd never been into pain of any kind, and couldn't imagine what guys into S&M found attractive about it. The one time he'd done anything even remotely kinky—allowing Doug to tie his hands behind his back—he'd been more concerned with getting lube on the necktie Doug had used to secure his wrists than about any thrill that might be gotten from the experience.

"Are you okay in there? Do you need me to get you a magazine or something?"

The sound of Jackie's voice startled him. "I'm fine," he called out, horrified that Jackie actually seemed to be timing him. It made him feel like a contestant on the *$25,000 Pyramid*, sitting in his chair trying to guess what the clues provided by the celebrity guest had in common before the clock ran out. He imagined Dick Clark standing near the sink, looking on encouragingly while Valerie Harper or Bob Crane perched on the side of the tub and tried valiantly to describe Things That Make You Come.

Quit it, he ordered himself, banishing the image of Valerie shouting, "Falcon videos! The dad in *Flipper*!" He closed his eyes and stroked his cock, trying to think about anything other than the fact that just outside his bathroom door Jackie was sitting, waiting for him to emerge with a baby food jar containing more than air. He had to wipe that from his mind and think about something that would make him hard.

He decided to go with the plumber fantasy. It was one he'd developed years ago, while living in his first apartment. One day the pipes beneath the kitchen sink had burst, and he'd been forced to call a plumber. The man who had come had not been particularly handsome or well built, but Josh had found him incredibly sexy. His name was

Sam. In his early thirties, he'd had the body of a man who had proba-bly once been the star of his high school football team, but who had gone slightly soft thanks to too many Budweisers and too many hours in front of the televison watching games he dreamed about playing in himself. He'd worn a blue short-sleeved work shirt over a white T-shirt, and he'd had the Superman logo tattooed on one biceps. He'd smelled of cigarettes and oil.

As Sam had lain under the sink, his lower half sticking out into the room, Josh had watched surreptitiously from the other room. The more Sam moved, the more his T-shirt had ridden up, slipping from the waistband of his jeans and revealing more and more of his hairy stomach. The hair had been thick and dark, blooming up from the man's crotch in a soft swirl.

Josh had seen enough porn videos to know that in a perfect world, he would have dropped to his knees, unbuttoned Sam's jeans, and gone to work on his undoubtedly huge cock. In reality, he had done nothing until Sam, finished with his repair, had left him with a $487.61 bill and a magnet to put on his refrigerator to remind him to call Colluci & Sons Plumbing the next time he needed his drains snaked or his furnace serviced. Only then had Josh been able to entertain his fan-tasies, jacking off right there onto the linoleum floor of the kitchen, where the smell of cigarettes still lingered.

He'd revisited the scenario many times since then, until it was so fa-miliar that he could reliably predict where in the fantasy he would shoot his load. It generally happened a minute or two after Sam, aroused by the ministrations of Josh's tongue, told him to get on all fours and prepare to be fucked good and hard.

He was relieved to find that the fantasy was once again doing its trick. His dick had stiffened almost immediately upon picturing Sam, his work-boot-clad feet scuffing up the kitchen floor and his rough grunts issuing from beneath the sink as he attempted to remove a stubborn nut. Now his hand moved quickly up and down the shaft, coaxing an orgasm from his balls. Josh, with practiced skill, imagined the taste of Sam's dick as he began to suck him off, felt the weight of the plumber's fingers on his head as Sam, realizing what was going on, accepted the offer of release.

Josh was almost there. His breathing quickened, and he felt a tight-ening in his groin. Pushing his dick down, he aimed the head at the opening of the baby food bottle.

"Daddy, tell me about how you and Mommy made me."

Out of nowhere, he heard a child's voice. *His* child. The voice was very young, too young for it to reveal the speaker's gender. But he knew it was his.

Do you want your little girl or boy to owe its existence to a fantasy about a plumber? he asked himself, his orgasm retreating quickly. *Is that how you want to become a father?*

He stopped jacking off and groaned. He'd been so close. But now he leaned back against the toilet tank and sighed. *I can't do it this way,* he thought miserably. *I just can't.* He couldn't imagine seeing Sam's face every time he looked at his child. He wanted more than that. He wanted to think of someone he really cared for, someone who was more than just a jack-off fantasy.

Someone like Reilly. The thought came suddenly, naturally, as if it had been waiting all this time to be noticed. And now that it was, it took over Josh's thoughts completely.

He was making love with Reilly. Not the way men did in porn movies, detached and interested only in getting off, but in the way lovers did, with deliberate slowness so that the pleasure lingered and release was the happy by-product and not just the end result. He felt Reilly's mouth move over his skin, his hands and tongue working together to coax joy from Josh's body. He heard his breath, and smelled his sweat.

Again he felt himself getting close. But this time no small voice interrupted him. When he came, he came hard, his cum hitting the glass walls of the jar in a thick spray as his body tensed. For a moment he lost his breath as he emptied himself into the container.

When he was done, he held the jar in his hands. It was warm. Inside, his milky stickiness barely covered the bottom, looking completely inadequate for the job it was going to be asked to perform. But there was nothing he could do about it now. If only Jackie had *told* him that he was going to be expected to produce, he wouldn't have allowed himself to jerk off the night before bedtime. Now she was going to have to make do with what he had.

He pulled his shorts on, opened the door, and walked out. Jackie was flipping through a copy of *Vanity Fair.*

"It's about time," she said when she saw him standing there. "Shit, and I thought girls took a long time to come."

Josh handed her the jar. Jackie gave it an appraising look.

"You're sure that's the right stuff?" she asked. "It's not conditioner or something?"

"It's certified grade A," replied Josh.

Jackie made a face. "It's not very appetizing," she remarked.

"You're not spreading it on crackers," replied Josh. "But since we're on the subject, exactly how *are* you going to use that?"

Jackie waved a hand at him. "Don't worry about that," she said. "My doctor gave me all kinds of stuff. And if there's one thing dykes like, it's tools."

They both laughed, then fell into an awkward silence. It was Josh who spoke first.

"This is a little weird," he said, rubbing his chin.

Jackie nodded. "I know," she said. She looked at him. "You can still back out if you want. We can always toss this into the recycling."

Josh shook his head. "No," he said. "I want to do it. I really do."

Jackie smiled. She leaned forward and hugged him. "I should get going then," she said as Josh hugged her back. "I don't think this stuff has a very long shelf life."

Josh let go of her. She put the jar into the pocket of her jacket and turned to leave.

"Wish me luck," she said.

"Good luck," Josh said obediently. "To both of us."

CHAPTER 43

"Look at this wicked cool shirt I got at Don't Panic," Toby said. He put his hands on his hips and modeled his purchase for Emmeline, who was standing at the kitchen counter pulling apart a head of lettuce for salad.

Emmeline glanced at the shirt, which read GLINDA THE GOOD'S FINISHING SCHOOL, and smiled. *They all have to go through their Oz phase,* she thought to herself as Toby sat down and reached for one of the rolls she'd placed in a basket on the table.

"Don't fill up on that," she warned. "We're having lasagna."

"I'm *starving,*" Toby said. "I think I cleaned every room in that house today."

"Find anything good?" asked Emmeline cautiously. The day before, Toby had come home with a pair of nipple clamps someone had left behind in their room. Ben and Ted, amused that he hadn't known what they were, had told him to, in effect, go ask his mother. Emmeline had found herself oddly discomfitted at having to explain their use to the boy. She hoped today hadn't brought any additional surprises, at least not of the erotic variety. She was feeling surprisingly domestic and housewifely, and she wasn't sure she'd be able to handle a discussion of, say, butt plugs or ball stretchers.

"Nothing," Toby replied. "Just the usual dirty underwear and condom wrappers."

Emmeline breathed a sigh of relief. *Only in a gay vacation town would dirty underwear and condom wrappers be considered "the usual,"* she thought, not without a trace of amusement. Equally amusing was how quickly Toby was adjusting to such facts of gay life.

The doorbell rang.

"Could you get that?" Emmeline asked Toby. "I'm covered in tomatoes."

Toby got up and bounced into the living room. She heard him open the door. Then there was silence.

"Who is it?" Emmeline called out.

There was no answer from the other room. "Toby?" Emmeline called. "Who is it?"

When again there was no answer, Emmeline wiped her hands on a towel and went to see for herself what was going on. When she stepped into the living room, she saw Toby standing in the doorway. Outside, a man and woman stood on the steps. Their glances shifted from Toby to Emmeline.

Good Lord, Emmeline thought when she saw them. *The Mormons have finally reached P-Town.* The woman was dressed in a plain pink dress and white cardigan straight out of the latest J.C. Penney catalog, while the man was wearing what looked uncomfortably like knit slacks. Emmeline scanned their hands for Bibles, but found none.

"We're just about to have dinner," she said. "You'll have to excuse us."

Toby turned and looked at her, his face drained of color. "Emmeline," he said softly, "these are my parents."

Emmeline was used to keeping her emotions in check, and although her heart began to race more quickly, she remained outwardly calm. Stepping forward, she put her arm around Toby's shoulder and faced his parents.

"It's nice to meet you," she said evenly.

Mr. Evans stared hard at her, his eyes dark and his lips pressed tightly together. Mrs. Evans blinked nervously. "It's nice to meet you," she said as if on autopilot.

"What are you doing here?" asked Toby, sounding like a little boy caught doing something he knew his parents wouldn't approve of.

"We came to get you out of here," his father said stiffly.

Mrs. Evans looked at Emmeline. "Your number was on the caller ID," she said, as if apologizing for her husband's behavior.

"I'm not going anywhere," Toby blurted out angrily.

"You're coming with us," his father replied. "And we're going to fix this little problem of yours."

Emmeline tightened her grip on Toby's shoulder. "And what prob-lem would that be, Mr. Evans?" she asked.

"That's none of your business," he snapped. "I don't know who you are or why my boy is here with you, but it's ending now. Toby, get your things and let's go." He looked at the shirt Toby was wearing and frowned. "And leave that here," he added.

Toby shook his head. "I'm not going with you," he said. "You threw me out, remember? You said you didn't want me around. But Emmeline wants me. She's my family now."

Mr. Evans's face reddened. "Don't speak to me that way," he said.

"Please, Toby," said Mrs. Evans more softly.

Toby looked at his mother. "You hung up on me," he whispered.

Emmeline cleared her throat. "Mr. and Mrs. Evans," she said, "I should remind you that your son is eighteen years old. Legally, he can do what he likes. If he doesn't want to go with you, or if he doesn't want to talk to you, that's his decision."

"Just who do you think you are?" Mr. Evans asked, clearly enraged.

"Who I am is someone who cares for your son very much," Emme-line replied. "And although I'm sure you don't believe it, I understand exactly what you're going through. Now, if you'd like to come inside and talk instead of standing here fighting, that can be arranged."

"Emmeline—" Toby began.

"It's all right," Emmeline reassured him. "Now, are you coming in?" she asked his parents.

Before Mr. Evans could say anything, Mrs. Evans entered the house, briefly pausing as if she wanted to hug her son but continuing on with-out touching him. After a moment, Mr. Evans followed her. Emmeline shut the door behind them.

"Please sit down," she said, indicating the couch.

Toby's parents sat down, while he took a chair as far away from them as possible. Emmeline sat in the closer chair.

"Did she make you come here?" Mr. Evans asked Toby, nodding at Emmeline.

"No," Toby said. "She's why I stayed here."

"Don't tell me you're . . ." Mr. Evans began, his question left unfin-ished.

"Your son is living with me as a *guest,*" explained Emmeline.

"Are you okay?" Mrs. Evans asked her son, sounding worried.

"I'm fine," answered Toby. "No thanks to you."

Emmeline wished she could tell Toby to soften a little. But she understood his rage. She'd felt it herself once, and if anyone had told her then that her rage should be tempered, she would have ignored them the way she knew Toby would surely ignore her.

"Do you know what you've put your mother through?" demanded Mr. Evans predictably.

"Do you know what *I've* been through?" Toby shot back.

Good for you, Emmeline thought proudly as she remained silent.

"Do you know what it's like to have your own parents tell you they can't stand who you are?" Toby continued. "Do you know what it's like to run away because nobody wants you?"

"We want you, Toby," his mother said, her voice shaking. "We want you back."

"Under what conditions?" Toby asked. He looked from his mother to his father. "There are conditions, right?"

Mr. Evans coughed. "Your mother and I think you need some help," he started.

Toby laughed. "I thought so," he said. "Let me guess, as long as I'm not gay anymore, I'm welcome in the house."

"You never were gay," his father said.

"Really?" replied Toby. "I'm not? Then why do I like sucking dick, Dad?"

Mr. Evans flushed as his wife looked away.

"What? You don't like hearing about what gay guys do?" Toby continued. "You don't like knowing that I take it in the ass?"

Mr. Evans stood up. "Don't talk that way in front of your mother!" he yelled. "Don't you ever!"

Toby stood up, and Emmeline realized that he was actually taller than his father. Toby pointed his finger at Mr. Evans. "That's the problem," he shouted. "You don't ever want to hear the truth. It's always been the problem."

Mr. Evans and Toby stared at each other. For a moment, Emmeline was certain they were going to rush at each other. Then Mr. Evans turned to his wife. "Come on, Hope," he said. "We're leaving."

Mrs. Evans stood up, looking sadly at her son.

"We're staying at the Seaside Motel, and we're leaving tomorrow morning," Mr. Evans said to his son. "That's your last chance."

"It's yours too," Toby told him.

Mr. and Mrs. Evans walked to the door and let themselves out. Emmeline stood and closed the door behind them. When it shut, Toby fell into her arms and began sobbing.

"It's all right," Emmeline said, stroking his back as she would a child's.

"Why did they come?" Toby asked between sobs.

"Because they love you," Emmeline said, knowing he wouldn't believe her.

"I don't want to see them," said Toby. "Not ever."

Yes, you do, Emmeline thought to herself. *You just can't admit it yet.* She continued to hold Toby while he cried. When he was finished, she wiped his hair from his eyes.

"Go wash your face," she said. "It's time for supper."

Toby went upstairs and Emmeline returned to the kitchen, where she resumed slicing tomatoes. Part of her felt as if she should be making a bigger deal out of the fact that Toby's parents had just flown two thousand miles to try and save him from the evils of homosexuality. But for some reason she felt incredibly calm about it all. The best thing she could do under the circumstances, she thought, was to keep everything as normal as possible for Toby.

A tinkling sound interrupted her thoughts. It was her mother, ringing for something. Emmeline had given her the bell so that she could summon them whenever she needed anything. So far, she had yet to use it. The fact that it was ringing now filled Emmeline with apprehension.

She again wiped her hands and went to her mother's bedroom. The old woman was propped up on her pillows. She'd been sleeping for most of the afternoon, and Emmeline had been only too happy to let her sleep. In all the excitement surrounding the unexpected appearance of Toby's mother and father, she'd momentarily forgotten about her own.

"Is everything all right?" she asked.

"The yelling," Lula said hoarsely.

"It was nothing," said Emmeline. "Nothing to worry about."

Her mother waved one wrinkled hand at her. "I'm not deaf," she said. "I heard it all."

Emmeline wasn't sure what to say. She and her mother had never really discussed Toby's situation, mainly because it was too close to what had happened between them and Emmeline feared reopening old wounds.

"I'm sorry, Mama," Emmeline said, beginning to apologize.

"You did right," Mrs. Tayhill said, interrupting her.

Emmeline looked at her mother. Had she heard correctly?

"You did right," repeated the old lady. "The boy, too. Both of you."

Emmeline was speechless. Not once had her mother ever told her that she'd done something she approved of. Maybe, Emmeline thought, it was time to have the talk she'd been planning ever since her drive home from Dr. Tulevitch's office. She'd rehearsed a lot of it in her mind, but had yet to find the right moment to deliver it to her mother.

"I'm hungry," said Lula suddenly.

Emmeline hesitated. Now that her mother had presented an opening, she wanted to go further. But perhaps it wasn't the right time. Her mother seemed tired, despite her long nap. And surely there would be another time, one when things weren't so hectic, when the lasagna and Toby weren't waiting for her attentions.

Finally Emmeline nodded. "I'll bring you a plate," she said.

CHAPTER 44

"This is good. Really good."

Reid put Josh's first attempt at script writing on the coffee table and leaned back into the couch.

"Really?" Josh asked. He still wasn't convinced that Reid Truman's interest in him wasn't some kind of joke.

Reid nodded. "You write like you've never been to a Hollywood pitch meeting," he remarked.

"And that's a good thing?" said Josh.

Reid laughed. "A *very* good thing," he replied. "The last thing I want is a script written by committee. This is, for lack of a better word, a virgin script. Keep it up."

There was a knock on Reid's door, and a moment later a young woman stepped inside.

"Oh," she said when she saw Josh sitting in the living room. "I'm sorry. I didn't mean to interrupt."

"Devin," Reid called out, "come meet Josh."

The young woman walked into the room. Josh rose and extended his hand to her. "I think I've seen you before," he said. "Don't you work at Jackie's?"

"No," Devin answered. "I just spent a lot of nights there drinking and trying to figure out what to do with myself."

"But now she works for me," Reid informed him.

"It's all very *Charlie's Angels.* You know, girl gets saved from dead-end existence and starts a whole new life."

"Devin is my assistant this summer," Reid elaborated. "She's been a big help."

"Well, it's nice to meet you," said Josh.

"Josh is writing a script for me, and hopefully for Ty," Reid told Devin.

"I still can't believe it," Josh said. "Ty Rusk. In a movie *I* wrote."

"You have to finish it first," said Reid.

Josh nodded enthusiastically. "Absolutely," he said. "I'm planning on having the first draft done by the end of the summer."

"Good boy," said Reid. "Now if you'll excuse us, Devin and I have a little work we need to do this evening."

"Oh, sure," Josh said, getting up and taking his script pages from the table. "I should go write anyway."

Reid escorted him to the door as Devin took his place in the chair.

"It was nice meeting you," Josh called to her, earning a wave in return.

"We'll talk in a couple of days," said Reid as Josh left. "And again, great work."

The door shut and Josh was left standing in the early summer evening. The sun was doing a slow fade into the ocean, and the stars were just visible beyond the purple haze separating day from night. He was, Josh thought, in the most beautiful place on earth.

Now if you could just straighten out your romantic life, everything would be perfect, he thought. But he couldn't let that ruin his good mood, so he pushed the thought to the back of his mind. Besides, there was nothing he could do about what was troubling him personally.

He could, however, celebrate his newfound fortune. Getting into his car, he made the quick drive to Jackie's. The dinner crowd was there, and there was a line to get in, but he wasn't interested in food. Pushing past the people waiting on the deck, he made his way to the far less crowded bar. Jackie was standing behind it, making a martini for an overly suntanned woman who stood talking to her equally tanned companion.

"Hey there, little mama," Josh said, taking one of the vacant stools.

Jackie shot him a look as she added an olive to the woman's martini and slid it across the bar, accepting a five in return. "Not so loud," she told Josh as she made change. "I haven't exactly mentioned our agreement to anyone."

"Agreement?" Josh said, pretending to be hurt. "Is that what you're calling the fruit of my loins?"

"The only fruit around here is you," Jackie shot back.

Josh looked around the room. "Looks to me like there's a whole fruit *basket* in here," he countered. "So, are we pregnant?"

"No," Jackie answered irritably. "I mean, I don't know. It's too soon to tell."

"But everything went okay?" Josh continued. "You know, with the—" He pantomimed squeezing a turkey baster.

"I think so," answered Jackie. "It's my first time with this too."

"Suddenly you don't sound so thrilled about it," suggested Josh.

Jackie sighed. "I'm *fine,*" she said firmly. "Really. It's just that . . ." She trailed off, shaking her head. "Never mind."

"What?" said Josh. "Come on. If we're going to be parents, you have to learn how to share. Now spit it out."

Jackie looked up. "I'm forty," she told him flatly.

Josh looked at her, not understanding.

"Today," said Jackie. "I'm forty *today.*"

"Oh," said Josh, finally getting her meaning. "It's your birthday. Well, why didn't you say so?"

"I didn't want anyone making a big thing out of it," Jackie said.

"Right," Josh replied. "So you decided just to pout until somebody asked. Got it. You are *so* a Leo."

"Fuck you," said Jackie, suppressing a smile.

"Technically, you sort of already have," Josh told her. "But now you're blowing me off, just like all the others. You never call. You never write." He feigned a crying jag until Jackie started laughing.

"That's better," said Josh. "So, what are we doing for your big day?"

"Nothing," Jackie said. "I have too much to do here."

"Bullshit," said Josh. "You have an entire staff to run this joint. You're coming with me."

He went behind the bar, grabbed Jackie by the hand, and dragged her away.

"What the hell do you think you're doing?" she demanded, swatting at him with her bar towel.

"Kidnapping you," he said. "Don't make me throw you over my shoulder."

Jackie relented and let him lead her out of the restaurant to his car.

"Get in," he ordered, and opened her door.

"Where are you taking me?" Jackie asked as they left the parking lot.

"It's a surprise," answered Josh. "Just sit there and look pretty."

He drove until they came to a grocery store, then stopped. "Wait here," he ordered Jackie.

Ten minutes later he emerged with a paper bag, which he put into the backseat. Then he continued driving until they reached the beach, where he parked and got out. Jackie followed.

"Come with me," he said, removing the bag and a blanket from the backseat and taking Jackie's hand.

He led her through the dunes until they came to a spot nestled between two hills of sand. Josh spread the blanket on the sand and motioned for Jackie to sit. Then he knelt and opened the bag. Reaching in, he removed a candle, which he pushed into the sand and lit. The flame flickered in the gentle breeze blowing in off the ocean, but it held.

Next he took out some pears and a wedge of blue cheese. "Salad," he said. This was followed by two plastic containers, one holding half a roast chicken and the other pasta with vegetables.

"Dinner," Josh declared before reaching in and bringing out an enormous chocolate chip cookie.

"And dessert," he said dramatically.

Jackie looked at the food and smiled. "This is quite the birthday dinner," she said.

"It took me forever," Josh said as he handed her plastic utensils, a paper napkin, and little packets of salt and pepper. Then he took out two bottles of water and handed her one.

"It was either this or Gatorade," he said apologetically.

"It's perfect," Jackie said reassuringly.

They began eating. After a minute or two Josh said, "So, how does it feel to be so old?"

Jackie took a bite of chicken and chewed slowly. "Strange," she said finally.

"Strange how?" Josh asked. "Strange as in I can't believe I'm this old, or strange as in it's not as bad as I thought it would be?"

"My sister was only a little over forty when she died," Jackie said. "Breast cancer."

"And you're worried that you—" Josh began.

"No," Jackie said. "I'm fine. I get myself checked out every year. It just reminds me is all. She and I didn't part on such good terms. I sort of wish she could see where I am now." She looked out at the ocean. "She told me to get myself a family," she said softly.

"Is that why you want a baby?" asked Josh.

Jackie shook her head. "I want a baby for me," she said. "Not for June. Not for my mama. For me. If there's one thing I've learned in forty years, it's that you can't live your life for other people. Still, I wish June could know."

She turned and looked at him. "Why'd you agree to help me?" she asked. "I mean really."

Josh sighed. "I'm not entirely sure," he answered. "I think because I saw it as a way to finally do something good with my life."

"Atoning for past sins?" Jackie asked.

"No," said Josh. "No sins. Just wasted time." He paused. "And maybe because it would be nice to have someone around who didn't want me to be something I'm not."

"Sounds to me like you have some ghosts to get rid of yourself," said Jackie.

"Maybe," Josh said.

"Just one thing to remember," Jackie continued.

"What's that?" Josh asked.

"You don't make a child because you want someone to love you."

Josh looked down at the pasta on his plate. Jackie's words surprised him, not because she'd said them, but because of his reaction to them. He felt as if he'd been thrown into cold water. Was what she'd said true? Had he really been thinking, on some level, that helping her have a child would give him someone to love and someone to love him back?

"You have to find love on your own," Jackie said. Only now it seemed she was speaking as much to herself as to him. Then she turned to Josh. "Dance with me," she said.

"What?" asked Josh.

"Dance with me," Jackie repeated. "Here."

"There's no music," Josh protested.

"There's the ocean and the wind and the stars," said Jackie, standing up and holding out her hand. "Now dance with the birthday girl before she kicks your skinny white ass."

Josh allowed her to pull him to his feet.

"I'm the butch," Jackie said as she wrapped her arms around him. "I'll lead."

Holding each other, they danced in the sand. The last heat of the day was still contained in the tiny grains, and it warmed Josh's bare feet. He closed his eyes and listened for the music Jackie had spoken of. He heard the waves and the sighing of the wind. The stars he was less sure of, but he felt something undeniably magical about the moment.

Her words ran through his mind. Was he helping her have a baby because he wanted someone to love? Was it just a reaction to what had happened between him and Doug? He told himself it wasn't. No, he thought, she was wrong. But he would let her think she wasn't. It didn't matter. He and Jackie weren't lovers. They weren't even in love. But at that moment, dancing together beneath the moon, he felt that maybe it could be enough.

CHAPTER 45

"Where's your bag?"

Toby stood at the doorway to his parents' room. Inside, his mother was folding the last of her things and putting them into the single suitcase that contained both her and her husband's clothing. His father blocked the door, looking impatiently at his son.

"I don't have a bag," answered Toby. "Because I'm not going with you."

His father nodded. "That's your choice, then," he said. "We gave you a chance."

Toby shook his head. "No," he said. "You didn't. You never gave me a chance. That's the problem."

"The problem is that you refuse to act like a man," snapped Mr. Evans.

Toby started to speak, then stopped himself. He'd promised Emmeline that he wouldn't get into a screaming match with his father. He'd been up all night wavering between coming to the hotel and just letting his parents leave. Now that he was there, he saw that he'd made the wrong decision.

"I'm more of a man than you'll ever be," he said softly, watching as his father turned red with anger. "At least I know who I am."

He turned and walked away, striding purposefully down the hallway away from room 129. It was over. Soon his parents would get on a plane and return to their lives, leaving him to get on with his. That was fine with him. If they couldn't accept him, then he didn't need them.

He was halfway down the stairs to the lobby when his mother caught up with him.

"Toby," she said, "please."

He stopped and turned to face her, saying nothing. Her eyes were wet, and he could see her mouth trembling. She was going to cry.

"He doesn't mean what he says," she said, sniffling.

"Yes, he does," Toby replied.

"He loves you," his mother said.

"He loves the person he thought I was," said Toby. "Not the one I am."

His mother shook her head. Tears had begun to roll down her cheeks, and she wiped them away with a wadded-up tissue clutched in her hand. Had she already been crying that morning? he wondered. It would explain her worn look.

"Just come home," Mrs. Evans said shakily. "Just come home with us."

Toby hated seeing her like that, and he felt himself begin tearing up as well. Stepping forward, he hugged her tightly. She felt so small, like a little girl. She leaned her head against him and wept.

"I can't," he said slowly, trying not to break into sobs. "I can't come with you."

Mrs. Evans looked into his face, not understanding. Toby let go of her.

"I know you want me to," he said. "But I can't. Not for Dad. Not for you. You want it to be like it was, and it can't be."

"We can talk to someone—" his mother said plaintively. "We can get help."

Toby nodded. "You should talk to someone," he said. "But not with me. This isn't about me. It's about you." He bit his lip as he saw his mother's face collapse into sorrow. "I love you," he said. "I really do. But until you can love me the way I am, I can't be around you. I'm sorry."

He turned away and continued down the stairs, leaving his mother standing on the landing looking after him. He almost turned and ran back to her. Part of him wanted her to hold him, the way she had so many times when he was little and had skinned a knee or suffered some seemingly unendurable childhood calamity. But he wasn't that little boy anymore, and she couldn't kiss the hurt away. Not this time.

He left the motel and emerged into a brilliant morning that knew nothing about the misery he felt. The street sparkled in the morning sun, and the men and women he passed as he made his way into town laughed and talked and smiled as if no one could possibly be unhappy in such a place. Toby looked at them and hated them for their joy, but at the same time he welcomed what had become the familiar sights and sounds of Provincetown. He was, he thought as he walked to his job, home, where he belonged.

When he reached 37 Oyster Lane, he was met at the foot of the stairs by Ted, who had a stack of towels in his arms.

"Just the man I wanted to see," Ted said, handing him the towels. "Take these up to number nine."

Toby nodded and started up the stairs. He was relieved to have work to do. It would take his mind off of his parents.

He walked to the door of number 9 and knocked. A man's voice called out, "Come in."

Toby pushed the door, which had been left open a little bit, and walked into the room. A man was lying on the bed, a newspaper open in front of him. He was wearing a white bathrobe, which provided a stark contrast to the tanned brownness of his skin. He lowered the newspaper and looked at Toby.

"You called for some towels?" Toby said.

"Actually, I did," said another man as he emerged from the bath-room.

The second man was slightly taller than Toby, with a muscular build and smooth skin. His blond hair was cut almost to crew-cut length, and he had a trimmed goatee. A white towel was wrapped around his waist.

"Thanks," the man said, taking one of the towels from Toby. He casually let the towel he was wearing fall to the floor, where it puddled around his feet. Using the fresh towel, he began to dry himself. Toby couldn't help but look as the man ran the cloth between his legs, where a large cock hung over a pair of smooth balls.

"Like it?" the man asked.

Toby looked away.

"It's okay," said the man. "You can look."

"I should go," Toby said.

The man stepped forward and gently shut the door to the room. Then he faced Toby. "Stay awhile," he said.

The man's cock had begun to harden, growing even larger as he stroked it with the towel. It stood out from his body, the head pulling it down in a heavy arc. The man's hand was slowly moving up and down the length, squeezing it.

Toby glanced over at the man on the bed. He hadn't moved. The newspaper still covered his lap, but his eyes were on Toby and the blond man.

"What's your name?" asked the blonde.

"Toby," Toby said quietly.

"I'm Alan," the blond man told him. "That's my lover, Jay."

Alan stepped closer to Toby. He took one of Toby's hands and placed it on his dick.

Toby closed his eyes. He could feel the heat of Alan's cock beneath his fingers as blood rushed through it. Alan pumped his hips slightly and Toby felt his hardness slide against his palm. Then his fingers touched Alan's close-cropped bush for a moment before being pulled back.

"That's it," Alan whispered. "Play with it."

Leave, Toby told himself. *Just get out of here.* But he couldn't. The feeling of Alan's cock in his hand had aroused him. When Alan reached for the buttons on Toby's jeans, Toby let him undo them, let him push the pants and the underwear beneath them to the floor.

"Nice," Alan said as he began to stroke Toby's rapidly growing dick. He ran his other hand up Toby's flat stomach, pushing his T-shirt up. He leaned over and gently bit one of Toby's nipples, making the boy groan.

Toby opened his eyes. On the bed, Jay had discarded his newspaper and opened his bathrobe. He was playing with his cock while he watched his lover and Toby.

Alan, seeing Jay, took Toby by the hand and led him to the bed. Putting a hand on Toby's shoulder, he pushed him down toward Jay's cock. Toby opened his mouth and ran his tongue over the dick in front of him while Alan stood behind him, watching.

Jay made very little sound as Toby sucked him, grunting occasionally and every so often pushing himself deep into Toby's throat. When he suddenly pulled away and brought his knees back, Toby wasn't sure what he was doing.

"Fuck him," Alan said.

Toby looked down at Jay's exposed asshole. He didn't know what to do. Finally, Jay grabbed Toby's cock and guided the head toward himself. Toby felt himself pressing against warm flesh. Then, unexpectedly, his cock was surrounded by heat as he entered Jay's ass.

He gripped Jay's legs, steadying himself. He pulled out slowly, then pushed back in. Jay moaned as if in pain, and Toby stopped. But Jay pushed against him, plunging him deeper. Looking down, he saw that he was buried all the way up to his balls in the other man's ass.

He started to move in and out, finding a rhythm. The sensation was unlike anything he'd ever felt, and not at all what he'd expected. As he grew accustomed to the feeling of being inside another man, he thrust harder, his stomach slapping against Jay's butt.

Alan was behind him. He had been rubbing Toby's ass while watching him fuck his lover. Now he slid a finger between Toby's ass cheeks, penetrating him with practiced skill. Toby was too caught up in what he was doing to protest, and when next he felt the head of Alan's cock taking the place of his finger, he only momentarily thought to stop him. Even the pain of being entered couldn't distract him, the discomfort nothing compared to the exquisite feeling that had taken hold of him.

Alan pushed up into him, matching Toby's own strokes. When Toby pulled out of Jay, he felt himself in turn filled with Alan's thickness; when he thrust forward, he was emptied again. The three of them had become a machine, pistons moving in and out in well-oiled time.

Toby was going to come. He could feel it. He tried to ward off the approaching climax, but it had already begun. Then he was pushed forward by the weight of Alan's body against his, and he fell forward. His hands grabbed at Jay's legs and he cried out, his load exploding into the warmth of Jay's ass.

As the waves of release surrounded him, he felt Alan grow even harder. Alan gave several hard thrusts and then he too gave a loud groan. Toby felt himself filled with a sticky heat as Alan's cock pulsed once, twice, and then a final time. Then Alan pulled out, leaving him empty.

Toby himself pulled out of Jay, his dick now soft. He saw then that Jay had come, too, his chest covered in thick white spatters. He turned away and looked for his underwear on the floor.

"Fuck, that was hot," said Alan.

Toby didn't respond as he pulled his briefs back on and followed them with his jeans. Suddenly the realization of what he'd just done hit him. He'd allowed someone to fuck him without a rubber. It was something he'd sworn he would never do. But now he had. And what scared him most was how easily it had happened.

"Why don't you come by later tonight?" Alan asked him as Jay got up and disappeared into the bathroom.

Toby, who was putting his sneakers on, shook his head. "I can't," he said. He wanted to get out of room 9 before he did anything else stupid.

"Well, if you change your mind, you know where we are," said Alan.

Toby opened the door and slipped out without answering him. He wanted to take a shower.

When he got downstairs, Ted was just finishing up the breakfast dishes.

"Did you take care of room nine?" he asked.

Toby nodded. "All taken care of," he said. *But the real question,* he thought as he started to wash his hands in the hot, soapy water, *is, can you take care of yourself?*

CHAPTER 46

"I got a bigger smile out of Patti Smith. What's wrong?"

Marly pulled nervously at the edge of the shirt she was wearing. Garth put down the camera he was holding and looked at her, waiting for an answer.

"I feel like an idiot," Marly said finally. "And I hate having my picture taken."

"You posed for Nellie," Garth reminded her.

"Yes, and I felt stupid then too," said Marly.

"You look fantastic."

"No, I don't," Marly snapped. "I look like a fool. This shirt is too big and these earrings are horrible and my hair looks like rats just moved out of it because it was condemned."

Garth set the camera down on a table. "Okay," he said. "You're just giving me excuses. If you were a supermodel or a singer, I'd tell your assistant to get you some aromatherapy oil or some coke. What's really the problem?"

Marly looked at him and sighed. "Are we having an affair?" she blurted out. "Because if we are, shouldn't we be having sex or something? I mean, the summer's almost over and we haven't even kissed."

She stopped talking and put her hands to her mouth. "Oh, God," she said. "I didn't mean to say that."

Garth regarded her for a moment without speaking. Then he said carefully, "Do you *want* to have an affair?" he asked.

"Yes," said Marly. "I mean no. I mean I don't know. Can we forget I said that?"

"That would be very difficult," replied Garth.

Marly groaned and ran her hands through her already distressed hair. "This is so *not* what I had in mind," she said.

"You had something in mind?" asked Garth. "You mean you've been planning this affair and just now got around to mentioning it to me?"

Marly pointed a finger at him. "Don't mock me," she said.

Garth smiled and gave a small laugh. "I'm not mocking you," he said. "I'm just surprised is all."

"Why?" Marly asked. "Because I'm a respectable married woman?"

"Hardly," Garth answered. "I've had plenty of respectable married women want to have affairs with me. But usually it's because their rock-star husbands are ignoring them and they're bored."

"Well, I'm bored," said Marly. "And maybe I'm tired of being respectable, okay? Maybe I want to do something nobody would expect. What's wrong with that?"

"Nothing," Garth said, shaking his head. "Absolutely nothing." He began unbuttoning his shirt. "So, shall we go at it? Here? Is this good?"

It was Marly's turn to laugh. Garth pretended to be wounded. "You haven't even seen me naked yet," he sad mournfully.

Marly flopped down on the couch that was pushed against one wall of the photo studio. "I'm so sorry," she said as Garth came and sat beside her. "I don't know why I said all that. I didn't mean to make you uncomfortable."

"I'm not uncomfortable," said Garth. "I don't think I've ever been *more* comfortable with someone."

Marly took his hand and held it. "Thank you," she said.

"And I'd be delighted to have an affair with you," continued Garth. "But I really don't think that's what you need."

"No?" Marly said. "Why not?"

"Because despite what you may think right now, I think you like your life the way it is," he told her.

Marly raised an eyebrow. "Oh, really. So tell me, Dr. Ambrose, on what do you base this diagnosis?"

"Mainly on the fact that it's taken you this long to mention going to bed with me," Garth said matter-of-factly. "If you really wanted to have an affair, you would have jumped me *way* before now."

"You think a lot of yourself, don't you?" Marly said sharply but affectionately.

Garth nodded. "I do indeed," he replied. "But I think more of you."

Marly looked into his face for a moment. Then she leaned in and kissed him. He kissed her back, their lips touching for a long moment. Then they pulled apart.

"Thank you," Marly said.

"Any time," said Garth. He paused. "I should probably tell you that I thought about having an affair with you too. Only since I'm not married, I guess technically I'd just be having sex with someone else who was having an affair."

"So why didn't you?" asked Marly.

Garth sighed deeply. "I came here this summer to sort out some things," he said. "To figure out what I want from my life from here on out. You just happened to be an unexpected surprise. I decided I didn't want to fuck up a friendship, so to speak."

Marly leaned back against the couch. "I think probably affairs are overrated anyway," she said.

"Not if you're a divorce lawyer," Garth remarked thoughtfully. "But when you're a mom and a wife, I think probably you're right."

"Is that what I am?" asked Marly. "A mom and a wife?"

Garth nodded. "Among many other things," he said. "I, on the other hand, am just a photographer."

"No," Marly said, squeezing his hand. "You're a lot more than that."

"Maybe," Garth said. "Maybe not. So, have we gotten this whole affair thing over with?"

"For the time being," answered Marly.

"Good," Garth said. "Now we can get back to taking your picture."

"Oh, no," said Marly. "Not after I came up with this whole affair thing to distract you."

"It's either have your photo taken or have sex," Garth said firmly. "Your choice."

Marly rolled her eyes. "Christ, you're a bastard," she said, standing up. "Okay, let's get this over with."

"Not so fast," said Garth.

Marly looked at him, confused.

"This setup clearly isn't working," Garth told her. "I want to try something else."

Marly narrowed her eyes. "Something else?" she repeated warily.

"Trust me," Garth said. "You'll love it."

Ten minutes later Marly was pushing open the door to a small barn that stood behind the Arts House main building. Situated where the grass gave way to sandy dunes, and after that to beach and ocean, the barn had once been used for the repair of fishing boats. Now it was Marly's personal painting studio, although she'd spent less and less time in it over the past year or two. Now, entering it, she saw that cobwebs and dust had formed a soft gray layer over many of the barn's surfaces.

"I'm not sure this is a good idea," she said. Seeing all of her painting tools and the canvases stacked against the walls was making her stomach knot up with anxiety.

Garth ignored her, walking into the center of the single huge room and turning around.

"The light in here is fantastic," he said, looking at the sunshine that streamed through the rows of windows set high in the barn's walls.

"I know," Marly said. "It's one of the things I liked best about it."

"Liked?" repeated Garth. "As in the past tense."

Marly leaned against the beat-up wooden table she used to hold her cans of brushes and tubes of paint. She wrapped her arms around herself in a protective gesture.

"I'm not sure anymore," she answered.

Garth walked over to the paintings stacked against the wall. They were all covered with sheets to protect their surfaces from the dust. Taking the corner of one, he pulled it off, revealing the work beneath. It was a large canvas, perhaps five feet on each side. The background was blue, and there were abstract swirls of purple-black paint dipped in a graceful arc across the top. Garth looked at Marly.

"Seabirds," Marly explained. "One day I saw a flock of them flying over the ocean. They kept skimming the waves, playing with them. I liked the way they moved."

Garth nodded. He pulled the sheet from another painting, this one bursting with reds, pinks, and oranges.

"Don't tell me," he said as Marly started to explain the piece. "Let me guess." He stared at the painting for a moment, tilting his head from side to side. Then he looked back at Marly. "Sunset?"

Marly shook her head.

"I'm bad with real art," Garth said apologetically.

"It's a little girl running on the beach," Marly explained. "She was wearing this bright pink swimsuit and trying to fly a kite. Only she was holding the string too short and it just fluttered along behind her, like it was chasing her. But she didn't care. She was just running. That's all."

Garth looked around the room. "Why did you stop?" he asked.

"Oh," Marly answered, "that's hard to explain. I guess the simplest answer is that I didn't see any point in it anymore."

"What was the point in the first place?"

"I suppose I thought I'd be famous," said Marly. "Or at least make my mark on the art world. Then I got married, had a kid, took this job. I guess I realized it was never going to happen."

"Running wasn't enough, eh?" Garth asked.

"Excuse me?" replied Marly, not understanding.

Garth nodded toward the picture of the little girl. "Running wasn't enough," he repeated. "You wanted to see the kite soar."

"It's not the same thing," Marly said, seeing where he was going.

"Why?" said Garth stubbornly.

"Would you take pictures if you didn't get to see them in magazines?" Marly said. "If the only person who ever saw them was you?"

Garth shrugged. "I don't know," he said. "I honestly don't."

"Then don't tell me it should be enough for me," said Marly.

"There's a difference, though," said Garth. "I'm *just* a photographer, remember?"

Marly laughed. "One of the most famous photographers in the world," she said.

"That's not such a big thing when it comes down to it," Garth replied. "You have much more than that." He looked at her. "Paint for me," he said.

"Paint for you?" Marly said.

Garth nodded. "Paint something. Anything."

"I can't just paint something," Marly protested.

"Paint me then," Garth said.

Marly regarded him suspiciously. What was he up to? She hadn't painted in months. She couldn't just produce something because he said so. Still, part of her wanted to go along with the game Garth had begun.

"Okay," she said finally. "Fine."

She walked over to a stack of blank canvases and pulled one out. Setting it on an easel near the table, she began pulling out brushes and paints.

"This isn't going to take just a couple of minutes," she told Garth, who was playing with his camera.

"That's fine," Garth said. "I have all day."

Marly removed her shirt so that she was wearing just a simple white T-shirt over her jeans. She jumped as Garth snapped a photo of her.

"What are you doing?" she demanded.

"Just paint," he said.

Marly turned to the blank canvas. Looking at it made her feel sick to her stomach. It was a feeling she remembered all too well, one that had first hit her several months before she stopped painting altogether. It was a feeling of not knowing where to begin, of the overwhelming unimportance of beginning because whatever came after was going to disappoint. Now, sensing it again, she wanted nothing more than to just put the paints and brushes away and go back to her office, where she knew a pile of paperwork awaited her attention.

Instead, she forced herself to pick up a brush. Garth had, in a completely unfair manner, challenged her. She might, she knew, very well fail that challenge. But she was going to try, if only to prove him wrong. She heard him off to the side of her, his camera whirring and snapping as he recorded her progress. Shutting her eyes, she blocked out the sound and pictured Garth in her mind. How did she see him? What image flashed across the screen of her memory when she conjured him up?

After a moment, she opened her eyes. Choosing a color from the jumble of tubes on her table, she squeezed some out, dipped her brush into it, and began to paint.

CHAPTER 47

Devin read the caption again. HOLLYWOOD HUNK TY RUSK AND AN UNIDENTIFIED GAL PAL SHARE MORE THAN APPETIZERS LAST NIGHT AT SOHO'S POMELO. Above it was a photo of her and Ty, caught midkiss.

The accompanying article was even better. "Ty Rusk, star of the recent blockbuster *Hat Trick* and in town lensing Kevin Smith's latest, was spied having a late-night supper at decidedly low-key Pomelo. The heir apparent to Russell Crowe and George Clooney reportedly was so taken with his stunning date that he only picked at his panfried catfish and sweet potatoes, while the mystery gal was spotted feeding him Hog Island oysters straight from the shell. The cozy couple only had eyes for each other, making us wonder if Tinseltown's most eligible bachelor might not be on the market much longer."

"That photo couldn't be better," Ty said.

"I don't remember feeding you oysters, though," remarked Devin.

Ty laughed. "You didn't," he said. "They make all that shit up."

Ty walked to the living room window, drew the curtain back a little, and looked out. He turned to Devin and grinned.

"Just as we thought," he said happily. "Reporters."

Devin jumped up and ran to see for herself. When she looked down, she saw several people standing on the sidewalk in front of Ty's building, a couple of them toting cameras.

"This is perfect," she squealed with excitement. "Reid said they would show up."

"Good old Page Six," said Ty. "It works every time. I'm going to have to buy Richard Johnson a nice fucking Christmas present."

"So, what now?" Devin asked him. "Do we just wait for them to go away?"

"Absolutely not," Ty replied. "We want them to stick around. I guarantee you some of them have been out there all night waiting for you to come out. Now that you've spent the night, we'll get an even bigger column out of Richard tomorrow."

Devin plopped onto the couch and hugged a pillow to her chest. She was thoroughly enjoying herself. Not only was New York absolutely amazing, but she was quickly becoming the hottest thing in Gotham. She picked up the *Post* and looked at her photo again.

"Wouldn't they love it if they knew I slept on the couch last night?" Ty said, going into the apartment's tiny kitchen and pouring himself some orange juice.

Before Devin could say anything, the phone rang. Ty went over to it, looked at the number flashing on the caller ID, and groaned. Picking up the handset he said cheerfully, "Good morning, Pamela."

Devin could practically hear the screaming from fifteen feet away. Ty hit the speakerphone button and stepped away as Pamela's hysterical voice filled the room.

"Who the *fuck* is that girl?" she said. "Because I don't remember having a conversation about you kissing anyone besides Gwyneth, Tara, or that skinny Brazilian bitch who's all over the goddamned Calvin Klein ads. So fill me in, if it's not too much trouble, and let me know just what the fuck you think you're doing. Because frankly, I don't have a fucking clue, and apparently neither does your publicist, who just happens to be sitting here feeling as in the dark as I am."

"Hey, Jeremy," Ty said.

"Go fuck yourself," a man's voice said gruffly. "What's with the girl?"

"What can I say?" Ty told them, grinning at Devin, who covered her mouth as she began to laugh. "I'm in love."

"The fuck you are," Pamela said, clearly well beyond irritated. "Who is she anyway? Some slut you met at a bar?"

"Hey," said Ty, "don't be talking that way about the woman I intend to marry some day."

There was total silence for all of ten seconds. Then Pamela and Jeremy began speaking at once.

"What—"

"Bullshit—"

"Who the fuck—"

"Ty, listen to me," Pamela said, winning out over Jeremy for the right to speak. "This is very important. I'm sure this girl is a hot piece of ass."

"She's more than that," Ty countered. "She's sweet, and smart, and . . . and . . ." He looked at Devin for some help with the ruse. Devin mimed patting the air a few feet off the ground.

"And she likes dogs," Ty said doubtfully.

Devin shook her head.

"Dogs?" Jeremy shouted. "You think you're in love with her because she likes dogs? Christ, Ty, bang her if you want to, but give us something to work with here."

"Just tell anyone who asks that we're very much in love," said Ty. "I'll talk to you guys later."

He hung up before either Jeremy or Pamela could continue, bursting out laughing as soon as the line went dead.

"I like *dogs?*" said Devin. "What was that?"

"You were pretending to pet a dog," said Ty.

"I was saying I want *children,*" replied Devin, laughing.

"Dogs, children, it doesn't matter," said Ty. "Right now Jeremy and Pamela are trying to figure out what to tell the papers."

"Don't you think maybe you should have told them the truth?" Devin asked.

Ty shook his head. "It always looks better when a star's agent and publicist really don't know what's going on. The only time they sound believable is when they're lying."

"That takes care of them," Devin said. "Now what about the jackals outside?"

"Easy," Ty answered. "I'll leave first. Most of them will follow me, trying to get information out of me. A car will come for you at ten to take you to the airport. Don't say anything to anyone. Just get in and go."

"Got it," Devin told him.

"The papers will spend all week speculating about who you are," Ty continued. "Next weekend we'll do it again, only we'll give them a little more. We want people to be fascinated by you."

Yes, Devin thought. *That's* exactly *what we want.*

As Ty showered and prepared to leave, Devin kept going to the window and peering out. She loved seeing the little knot of paparazzi hanging around the steps of Ty's brownstone. She loved being in New York. And most of all, she loved that she was now someone everybody wanted to know.

She didn't really want to return to Provincetown and its dreary pattern of days. She wanted to stay in New York, with its crowds and frenetic pace. She wanted to eat out and go to Broadway shows, see and be seen.

Wouldn't it be nice to actually be *Ty's girlfriend?* she asked herself. *Instead of just pretending?*

Yes, she thought. It would be nice. She looked toward the bathroom, where she could hear Ty singing to himself in the shower. What would happen, she wondered, if she went and joined him? What if she just slipped into the shower?

She knew Ty was gay, although he still hadn't revealed as much to her. But he was still a man. Could she take things one step further and get Ty away from Reid? She smiled at the thought. What a perfect ending to the story that would be.

Ultimately, though, she knew she couldn't. Straight men might never turn down the offer of a blow job, even if it came from another man, but queers were pickier. They *did* care whose lips were wrapped around their cocks, and even though Devin was sure she was more talented in that department than Reid probably was, she didn't think Ty would give her the chance to prove it. He might *look* all man, she thought, but when it came to sex she suspected it was Reid who did most of the driving. *Pity,* she thought. *It could be fun.*

But really, it didn't matter. She had Ty—and Reid—exactly where she wanted them. Neither, she was confident, knew that she was aware of their relationship, or that she had sold her story—and theirs—to C.J. Raymacher. By the time they did find out, it wouldn't matter.

"All yours," Ty said, coming out of the bathroom with a towel around his waist.

Every woman and fag in America would kill to be me right now, Devin thought as she looked at Ty's well-muscled body.

She went into the bathroom and took her own shower. When she emerged, Ty was dressed, looking every inch the Hollywood star off for a day on the set.

"Time for me to make my exit," he said. "All you have to do when you leave is shut the front door. It locks by itself."

Devin nodded. "Call me," she said, mimicking a girl whose date was leaving.

"Sure thing, sweetheart," said Ty. "Bye."

He left, and Devin reluctantly got herself ready to go as well. When she heard a car honking out front twenty minutes later, she looked out the front window. A nondescript black sedan waited at the curb. There was no sign of the reporters, which disappointed her.

Taking her small overnight bag, Devin left the apartment and went downstairs. She let herself out and carefully closed the door behind her, lingering in case anyone was waiting to ambush her. When no one did, she walked to the car and opened the back door. *He could at least open it for me,* she thought huffily.

As she got into the car, she was surprised to discover that it was already occupied. A man was seated inside.

"I'm sorry," she said, starting to get out. "I thought this was my car to the airport."

"It is," the man said. "You're Devin, correct?"

Devin nodded. "Then this is your car," the man told her. "Get in."

Devin hesitated. She didn't recognize the man, and she'd seen enough bad movies to know what happened to women who got into cars with such people.

"It's either get in or face them," the man said, pointing outside.

Devin looked behind her. Coming down the sidewalk were several reporters, all of them talking at once. They were almost upon her, and the only way out was to get in.

She did, shutting the door just as the first reporter reached the vehicle and began banging on the window. The man beside her motioned to the driver, and they pulled away.

Now that she was inside, Devin looked more closely at her companion. She had to admit, he didn't look too terribly threatening in his khaki pants, light blue shirt, and wire-rimmed glasses. In fact, he looked more like a J. Crew ad.

"Can I ask who you are and how come you're in my car?" she asked.

The man smiled. "The how part I'll keep to myself," he said. "As for the who, I'm surprised you haven't recognized my voice yet. We've spoken enough times."

Devin stared hard at him. They'd talked? She was certain she had never met the man.

"C.J.?" she said uncertainly.

"The same," the man said. "You look surprised."

"What are you doing in New York?" asked Devin. "I thought your office was in LA."

C.J. nodded. "It is," he said. "That's the beauty of the red-eye. I got in just in time to see you off."

"I don't get it," Devin said. "Why?"

"Let's just say I was intrigued," Raymacher told her. "I wanted to see my own little Deep Throat in the flesh."

Devin sat back, unsure of what to say. Raymacher had caught her completely off guard.

"That's not the only reason," C.J. continued. "I also wanted to get a head start on our interview."

"Interview?" said Devin.

C.J. nodded. "My exclusive, remember? I want to get some background information." He pulled a notebook and pen from a leather briefcase at his side. "We have about thirty-five minutes," he said.

Devin was still rattled by the fact that she was sitting in the same car with Raymacher. Up until that point he'd been a vague image in her mind, a voice that came to her across three thousand miles of electrical wiring. Now, sitting beside him, she felt a little trapped. Besides, she hadn't planned on telling her story for some time. Why did Raymacher want to start now?

Then again, what did it matter? He wasn't going to do anything with it until he had the entire story. It wouldn't hurt her to tell him a few choice pieces of information. In fact, it would make him hungry for more, and that was never a bad thing.

"Okay," Devin said, turning toward Raymacher and leaning in. "What do you want to know?"

CHAPTER 48

"The parents of the groom will sit here, and the parents of the bride will be over here."

Reilly watched as Ricky Mialotta flitted around the sanctuary, his hands and mouth in constant motion. Ricky had been Donna's idea. He'd planned the weddings of several of her friends, and he had been the first person brought in when the idea of a marriage had been raised. So far he'd shepherded them through selecting the perfect cake (white chocolate, three tiers) and menu (a choice of duck or halibut), choosing the color of the bridesmaids dresses (light blue) and the flowers (hyacinth and white lilies), and picking music (Bach's Concerto in D Minor for oboe, strings, and continuo for the processional and Steve Tyrell's version of "A Kiss to Build a Dream On" for the first dance). Now he had turned his attention to how the church would be decorated.

"I think sprays of white roses for over the door," he said excitedly. "And maybe some Calla lilies for the altar, although that might be too funereal." He turned to Donna and Reilly. "I don't suppose they'd allow doves?"

Donna turned to Father Michael, who was watching the proceedings. He shook his head gently.

"I don't think so," Donna told Ricky, who gave a tight smile and made a 360-degree turn.

"Then the flowers will have to do," he said, his voice suggesting that without the doves the interior of St. Agnes's might as well resemble a medieval torture chamber.

Donna giggled and leaned over to Reilly. "He is *such* a fag," she said.

Reilly grunted in reply. He knew Donna's remark was made with no malice toward Ricky, but it made him uncomfortable. Ricky, too, made him uncomfortable. He had an unnerving habit of looking at Reilly from time to time as if the two of them shared a secret. "I think he has a little crush on you," Donna had told him after their first meeting with the wedding planner. "And who can blame him?"

Reilly had laughed it off. Now, watching Ricky examine the place where, less than a month from now, he and Donna would be exchanging their wedding vows, he just felt sick. Were he and Ricky really the same deep down? As Ricky ran his finger along the back of a pew and shuddered at the dust that accumulated on his digit, Reilly closed his eyes. *No,* he thought to himself, *we're not the same at all.*

He was going to get married, and that was that. No more thinking about the feelings that had disturbed him more and more as the summer went on. They were just feelings, and they could be ignored. He loved Donna, and he was going to marry her. They would have children. Everyone would be happy. Especially him.

"Candles," Ricky said loudly. "*Lots* of candles. Everywhere. Candles signify romance."

"Are we almost done?" Reilly asked Donna impatiently.

"Relax," his fiancée replied, squeezing his hand. "Before you know it, it will all be over."

Reilly wished it were over already. Then he could get back to the business of his life. He was behind on several jobs, most notably the repairs on the guest house at 37 Oyster Lane. He knew Ben and Ted were expecting him to finish soon, but he just hadn't been able to bring himself to go over there. Not until Josh was gone, which hopefully would be as soon as the warm weather waned and fall chased the summer people away. Then he could go back.

"Have we talked about rice?"

Ricky's question snapped Reilly back to the moment.

"Rice?" he said, confused.

"You can't throw rice," Ricky said. "Something about it swelling up and bursting birds' stomachs or some such nonsense." He made a face registering his disgust at the thought. "Those animal rights people are all over it—Greenpeace or PETA or something. Maybe Robert Redford." He paused, as if remembering the source of his information was crucial. "Anyway," he said momentarily, waving his hands again. "Rice is *out*. We'll use birdseed. Little packets of it wrapped in netting."

"That sounds fine," Donna said. "Is there anything else we need to discuss?"

Ricky swirled around again, taking a last look at the sanctuary. Then he turned his eye on Father Michael. "You'll be wearing black, I suppose?" he asked.

The priest looked taken aback. "Yes," he said.

"Hmm," replied Ricky, as if picturing the father in something more along the lines of a Kenneth Cole suit. He turned back to Donna and Reilly. "What I wouldn't give to do a makeover on the whole fucking Church," he said, rolling his eyes. "For Christ's sake, their leader wears a muumuu."

Father Michael cleared his throat, indicating that he'd heard more than Ricky had intended him to.

"Sorry, Father," said Ricky. "Let's go," he added to Reilly and Donna. "I don't need him sending any more bad press to the man upstairs."

The three of them left St. Agnes's. Out on the street, Ricky stopped at his car.

"Don't worry about a thing," he told them. "I'll have it all taken care of."

"Thank you for everything," Donna told him.

Ricky beamed. "I *love* doing Catholic weddings," he told her. "Not like those fucking Baptists. They always insist on having the reception in the basement, and the mothers want to make the dresses. Ghastly. If I just did Catholics and Episcopalians I'd be a happy man." He glanced back at St. Agnes's. "A trifle goth, perhaps, but very classy. I'll talk to you two next week."

Ricky got into his car, leaving Reilly and Donna standing on the sidewalk. When he was gone, Donna took Reilly's hand and began the walk to where they'd parked.

"Something wrong?" Donna asked.

Reilly shook his head. "No," he said quickly. "Why?"

"You seemed a little distracted back there."

"It's just a lot to think about," Reilly said.

Donna laughed. "Well, it *is* the biggest day of our lives," she said.

"It's certainly the most expensive," remarked Reilly.

"We could just forget about it," suggested Donna.

Reilly stopped and stared at her. "Call it off?" he said, his heart beginning to race unexpectedly.

"Elope," Donna said. "Run off to Vegas or something. Ditch the families."

"Please," Reilly said. "Most of this is for them. They'd never forgive us."

Donna sighed. "You're right," she said as they reached their cars. "Besides, I can't wait to see you in your tux." She kissed him gently. "And then I can't wait to get you out of it."

She kissed him again, harder this time. Her tongue slid between his lips, and he felt her pressing against him.

"Want to go home and get some practice in before the big night?" she whispered.

Reilly looked into her eyes. "I'd love to," he said. "But I have a job to be at in the morning and I still have to draw up some plans for it. Sorry. Rain check?"

Donna kissed him again. "Rain check," she said. "But don't wait too long, or I really will feel like a virgin on my wedding night."

"That might be fun," Reilly teased.

Donna kissed him again, said good night, and got into her car. After she left, Reilly walked to his truck and climbed in. Starting the engine, he began the drive home. He really did have work to do before the morning, and as he drove he thought about the deck he was scheduled to build.

He decided to take the road that ran along the beach and avoid the traffic—both pedestrian and auto—that clogged the streets of the main drag in the evening. Although he enjoyed the energy of the crowds that filled the streets, he was anxious to get to work, to focus his mind on something besides the unsettling thoughts that had been troubling him whenever he allowed his attention to drift.

The sound of the sea calmed him as he drove, the smell of salt and seaweed reviving his flagging spirits. He pushed the wedding and all its accompanying devilments into a corner, to be dealt with later, and simply allowed himself to enjoy riding along in the night, the beams from his headlights cutting through the light fog that had begun to roll in, draping its lazy cobwebs across the dunes and over the road.

He was almost to his turnoff when he saw a car coming toward him, slow, and make its own turn to the right, heading down the narrow road that led to the sea and, Reilly knew, a small parking lot that was used by picnickers and bathers during the day. At night, however, it acquired a less wholesome reputation. What went on there was one of the many things spoken of by Rounders in vague yet clearly disapproving ways. Faggot Beach it was called by some of Reilly's less-refined acquaintances, men who claimed to know (but always declined to reveal how) exactly what went on there under cover of night.

Did the driver of the car know where he was going? Reilly wondered. And what would he find when he got there? He slowed the truck as the turnoff grew closer, telling himself he was just preparing for his own turn toward home and safety. But when he reached the point where the road broke off in several directions, he suddenly found himself making a left and following the path taken by the car before him.

The road went straight on through the dunes, rising up and over a small rise until the highway faded into the truck's rearview mirror and Reilly felt as if he were driving into the sea itself. Then, abruptly, he came to the parking lot. Perched at the edge of the beach, with the sea visible only a hundred yards away, it was almost deserted. Two or three cars, none of them parked too closely to one another, were sitting facing the water, their lights turned off.

Reilly pulled in and drove to the far end. As he passed each car, he saw a shadow within raise its head and look into the car's rearview mirror. Faceless, they were nothing more than shifts in the darkness. Reilly ignored them as he eased his truck into the last spot and turned the engine off.

His heart was beating quickly as he leaned back in his seat and looked out at the beach. He tried not to think about what had caused him to make that turn onto the wrong road, to follow a set of lights to a place he didn't belong. But belong or not, he was there now, and as much as he wanted to start the truck and go back to his own home, he couldn't bring himself to turn the key.

He looked to his left. Four or five spots away, another man sat looking out at the beach. He seemed lost in thought, his eyes staring straight ahead. For a moment Reilly wondered if perhaps he was asleep. Then he saw another shadow rise up into view, a head lifted from the man's lap. Its owner leaned back, and now the first man's head went down, disappearing into the blackness. Reilly felt a tug deep inside him as he watched, and his hand slipped between his legs.

He watched for a minute. Then, unexpectedly, his view was obliterated as another truck pulled in beside him. He looked away as the driver dimmed the lights and the motor sputtered into silence. Reilly looked to his right, as if something there required his full attention. When after a minute he turned his head again, he saw that the truck's driver was watching him. It was a young man, clean-shaven and wearing a white tank top that reflected the light of the moon. He nodded at Reilly.

Reilly swallowed hard and gave a barely perceptible nod back in acknowledgment. In response, the driver of the truck scooted over to the passenger side of the truck, closer to Reilly. He sat, one arm resting on the window ledge. His other hand, like Reilly's, was in his lap. Reilly could see it moving slowly back and forth.

The man lifted his hand to his mouth and spat into it, then resumed his work, this time with more exaggerated motions of his hand. Reilly felt his cock stiffen in his jeans as he watched the man. Growing hard, his dick was pressing uncomfortably against his pants, and reluctantly he unbuttoned his fly to give himself some relief.

The man, seeing him, lifted his body up. His cock was revealed in the window, long and thick as his hand pumped it. Then it was gone again as the man lowered himself back to the seat. He looked at Reilly.

"Let me see it," he said huskily.

Reilly looked down at his cock. Fully hard, it was standing up from his crotch, the head leaving a sticky trail behind where it rubbed against the hair of his stomach. As he stroked himself, more wetness leaked out, slicking his skin. He glanced at the man waiting for him to make a decision. He was watching Reilly expectantly.

Trying not to think, Reilly lifted his ass and shoved his jeans and boxers down. Then arching his back, he raised himself up until his dick was in view.

The man in the truck next to him watched for a moment. Then Reilly saw the door of the truck swing open. The man was framed in the doorway, sitting sideways on the seat facing Reilly. His jeans were pushed to his feet, and he'd pulled the front of the tank top up and over his head so that the material was stretched behind his neck, leaving the front of him bare. His chest was covered in hair that trickled to a thin line at his crotch. His cock stood out from his body as he jerked off.

Reilly put his hand on the handle of his own door, but couldn't bring himself to open it. All he could do was sit and watch as the guy outside his window continued to stroke himself, revealed to anyone who might happen by. The thought both excited and terrified Reilly, and again he felt the urge to start the truck and leave.

Instead, he continued to play with himself, matching his own strokes with that of the man next to him. His eyes remained fixed on the man's cock, watching every move.

"Come on," the man urged. "Show me."

Once more Reilly put his hand on the door's handle, and once again he couldn't bring himself to open it. It was as if he were frozen, incapable of going any further but equally unable to flee. All he could do was watch.

Suddenly, the man came. His head went back as first one burst of white and then another shot from his dick and hit the ground beside Reilly's truck. Reilly looked down at it, gleaming wetly in the moonlight, and felt his own climax break over him. His hand was covered in wet heat as his cock erupted, and he let out a startled moan.

His body shook as he came, his cum sticking to his stomach and to the seat of the truck as he shuddered in a combination of pleasure and growing shame. Looking to his left, he saw the man beside him pulling up his pants and getting into his truck. Then the door shut, the engine came to life, and the truck backed away, its lights sweeping across the rears of the cars still parked in the lot.

Reilly wiped his hand on his shirt and pulled his boxers back up. Already the heat of his excitement was turning to the cold wetness of disappointment. What had he done? His hands shaking, he fumbled for his keys and started the truck. The engine seemed impossibly loud, the headlights when they came on, too bright. Surely, he thought, everyone in the lot would recognize his truck. Never mind that most of the cars carried rental plates, revealing their drivers as summer visitors. No Rounder would dare risk going to such a place. *No Rounder except a pathetic one,* Reilly thought.

He pulled out, rolling the windows up tightly and leaving as quickly as he could. He drove too fast down the road back to the highway, anxious to be away from the lot, away from the terrible enchantment of the place, the rough, wild magic that had drawn him there and made him do something that now haunted him like a nightmare. He pressed harder on the gas, urging the truck toward home, and safety. There, he told himself, he would wash away the effects of his mistake. Then everything would be all right.

Everything will be all right, he repeated to himself. *Everything will be all right.*

CHAPTER 49

"Joe sets his half-empty beer bottle on the bar, turns to Dave, and says, 'If going home alone means I don't have to wake up next to you, it beats the hell out of staying here.' He turns and walks for the door."

Reid made a face. "Not strong enough," he said. "You want his confrontation with Dave to be more forceful. Don't forget, this is the one man he thought he might be able to have a relationship with. He should be a *little* more angry when Dave tells him he wants to see other people."

Josh nodded and made some notes on his script.

"But this is really shaping up," said Reid happily. "We'll get Ty in here this weekend and read through the first act. I think he's going to love it."

Josh sighed. "I hope so," he said.

"What did Nicholson say when you told him you were dropping out of his class to write a screenplay?" Reid asked him.

Josh grinned. "He told me my talents were much better suited to the mass media than to literature, and that he was sure I'd do very well," Josh replied, imitating the patronizing tone in which Nicholson had delivered the news. "The guy may be a brilliant writer, but he's a real asshole."

"Probably manic depressive," remarked Reid. "And has a small dick."

"That would explain why he's been through half the female population of the class already," Josh said.

Reid took a sip of the drink he was holding and looked at the young man seated on the couch across from him. He really liked Josh. He was a good writer, despite the attempt that fuck stain Nicholson had made to convince him otherwise. He was also a genuinely nice guy. Reid had decided that he could trust him.

"There's something I want to talk to you about," he said, making Josh look up expectantly.

"This movie," said Reid, waving his hand vaguely in the air. "I'm not just interested in it because the story is good—which it is."

Josh furrowed his brow, clearly not understanding.

"There's a particular reason why I think Joe would be a good role for Ty," Reid began again. "See, he and I—"

He was cut off by the ringing of the phone. Holding up a finger to Josh to excuse himself, he picked it up.

"Violet?" he said when he heard the voice on the other end, sounding surprised. "Is everything okay?"

"I'm not sure," Violet replied quickly. "I've got C.J. Raymacher on the other line."

"Raymacher?" Reid said dismissively. "You called me because of that piece of shit?"

"He says he has to talk to you right now," Violet said apologetically. "I can't get rid of him."

Reid groaned. "Fine," he said shortly. "Put the little fuck on."

He heard a click, and then Raymacher's unwelcome voice came floating over the line. "Reid," he said, "I hope you're enjoying your vacation."

"I was," snapped Reid. "What do you want? I'm busy."

Raymacher laughed, which irritated Reid even further. "Working on that hot new script for Ty?" the columnist asked.

The question threw Reid off his guard for a moment. "How did you know about that?" he asked. Then he regained his composure and said quickly, "I mean, of course I'd be working on a new project for Ty Rusk. I'd be an idiot not to after the money his last picture made me."

"Right," replied Raymacher. "And it would have nothing to do with the fact that he's sharing your bed, would it?"

"Look, Raymacher," Reid said forcefully, "if you harassed my secretary into putting you through just so you could—"

"Please," said Raymacher, interrupting. "Call me C.J."

"I'll call you a goddamned motherfucking shit smear if I want to," Reid said, trying to keep his voice even. "Now don't bother me again."

"I know about the girl," Raymacher said suddenly.

"What girl?" asked Reid.

"The girl," Raymacher repeated. "The one who's so fond of slipping Mr. Rusk oysters from her plate."

"So what?" said Reid. "Everyone knows about that girl. She's been on the cover of every gossip rag around, including yours."

"So she has," said Raymacher. "But not every rag knows that she's playing the role of a lifetime, do they?"

"I have no idea what you're talking about," Reid snarled.

Raymacher sighed and clucked his tongue. "Why do they *always* say that?" he asked, as if speaking to someone sitting next to him. Then Reid heard some rustling as Raymacher moved something near the phone. "Listen," Raymacher said.

Reid heard some static, and then a woman's voice. "They have *no* idea," she said. "They think I'm pretending to be Ty's girlfriend to help them." There was muffled laughter, and then the recording stopped.

"What did you think of that?" Raymacher asked, coming back on the line.

"Think of what?" Reid responded. "It was just some girl talking." He was trying to sound collected, although his heart had begun to beat more quickly. The voice had indeed sounded far too familiar for his comfort.

"Yes, it's her," Raymacher said, as if reading his mind. "And there's more. A lot more. It's amazing how much a person will say when she trusts you."

"How—" Reid began, his voice faltering.

"It doesn't matter how," said Raymacher. "What happens is what we do now."

"What do you want?" Reid asked, feeling too defeated by the revelation of Devin's betrayal to keep up his act.

"That's better," Raymacher said, clearly pleased with himself. "What I want is a story."

"It sounds to me like you already have one," said Reid.

"That's not the one I want," replied Raymacher. "Although it *is* a good one, I must admit. No, what I want is the Ty Rusk story. An exclusive. Ty Rusk comes out of the closet in a one-on-one with America's favorite celebrity journalist."

"Yeah, you're a regular Barbara Walters," Reid said.

"I just might be, after this story," said Raymacher.

"Don't count on it," said Reid. "Remember what happened when Geraldo finally opened Al Capone's vault."

"Geraldo wasn't discussing the sex life of the most popular new star in Hollywood," shot back Raymacher. "And Geraldo didn't have this tape."

"All that tape of yours proves is that some girl is terribly confused," Reid said, making one last attempt at saving the situation.

"That's something I'd expect to hear in a Joe Esterhaz film," said Raymacher. "We both know what the girl says is true."

"What if it is?" Reid said. "What exactly do you want from me?"

"From you and *Ty*," Raymacher corrected him. "And what I want is a promise, an assurance that when Mr. Rusk is ready to join the ranks of Ellen and Rupert and Sir Ian McKellan, I'll be the one he speaks with."

"And if I say no?" asked Reid.

"Let's hope you don't," Raymacher replied simply. "It's always so ugly when a star has to explain lying to his fans, don't you think? Especially when he's so awfully popular."

"I'll speak to Ty," Reid said, rubbing his forehead as the first stirrings of a massive headache began to course through his temples.

"Please do," Raymacher said. "I'll expect to hear from you shortly. In the meantime, I believe I'll go transcribe the rest of this tape. Just in case I need it. Oh, and one more thing, tell Ty my boyfriend and I love his work," he concluded before the line went dead.

Reid hung up the phone and sat, staring at the floor. When Josh spoke, he jumped, having forgotten all about the young man's presence.

"That didn't sound good," said Josh. "Are you okay?"

Reid shook his head. "No," he said. "It wasn't good. And no, I'm not okay."

"Anything I can do?" Josh asked, sounding concerned.

Reid took a deep breath. "Remember how I said there was a particular reason I want this role for Ty?" he said.

Josh nodded. "That's when the phone rang," he said.

"In scriptwriting terms, that phone call is what we would call a second act plot point," Reid said. "An unexpected turn of events that pushes the action in a new direction." He looked up at Josh. "I might as well start at the beginning."

He did start at the beginning. As the story spun out, Josh's eyes grew larger and larger, until by the time Reid finished relaying the content of Raymacher's recent phone call, his mouth was hanging open in disbelief.

"Get out," he said when Reid was done. "Ty? You and Ty?"

"Yes on both counts," Reid said.

"Get out," Josh repeated.

"So now you know why your story appealed to me so much," Reid continued. "What better role for Ty to use as a coming-out vehicle than the story of a gay man who's your average Joe? It's a chance for people to see that it's not such a big deal."

"He was going to come out?" said Josh.

"Well, that was *my* plan," Reid answered. "I hadn't exactly convinced him of that yet." He paused. "Actually, I hadn't even mentioned it to him yet. But yes, that was the general idea." He sighed. "Now I don't know. This whole thing is my fault. I'm the one who suggested the whole thing with Devin. I still can't believe she would do this."

"And he actually said he and his *boyfriend* like Ty's movies?" Josh said, ignoring the remarks about Devin.

Reid nodded.

"Isn't that a little, I don't know, hypocritical?" Josh said. "I thought the whole outing thing died when *Out* turned into a fashion magazine."

"Ironic, isn't it?" remarked Reid. "But not a shock. People like Raymacher think celebrities belong to the world. And frankly, maybe he's right. I mean, no one gives a shit when they find out Hugh Grant got his dick sucked by a hooker. If anything, it makes them more popular. It's only the gay stars who have to keep quiet, just in case knowing they're queer keeps a few people out of the theaters."

"What are you going to do?" Josh asked him.

"First, I'm going to tell Ty," said Reid. "And then I'm going to kick that little backstabbing bitch's ass. I can't believe she planned this entire thing."

"Why did he tell you?" asked Josh thoughtfully. "Why didn't he just run Devin's story?"

"Because Ty coming out on his own is a bigger draw," Reid answered. "The other way, there's still doubt. People could still believe that Devin or Raymacher made the whole thing up. This is his ticket back into the big time, and he knows it. If he can pull off this interview, every big magazine will welcome him back with open arms."

Josh leaned back on the couch, a strange look on his face.

"What?" asked Reid, noticing the change.

"I was just thinking," Josh said slowly. "Raymacher wants Ty's story because it will be such a big deal, right?"

Reid nodded.

"So what if it wasn't such a big deal?"

It was Reid's turn to look confused. "I don't get you," he said.

Josh leaned forward, his hands clasped together and his fingers tapping on his lips as he thought. After a moment he looked up at Reid and grinned. "I think I have an idea," he said.

CHAPTER 50

"And that, ladies and gentlemen, is why the lady is a tramp."

Emmeline put her mike down and left the stage to wild applause. Her set had gone well, and she was flush with the thrill of the crowd's adoration. But she was also very thirsty, so she headed straight for the bar.

"Water, please, Tamara," she said to the girl working the bar.

Tamara went to get the water, and Emmeline sat down. It was almost two in the morning, but she felt as if she could stay up until dawn broke over the ocean and drove away the night chill. She knew the feeling would pass, given an hour or so and something to eat. Maybe a salad, she thought. Or perhaps, if she asked really nicely, Alison would make her some pork chops. The chef, also a southern girl, rarely got a chance to prepare the food of her childhood in seafood-mad Provincetown, but on a slow night she could sometimes be persuaded to fire up her cast iron and cook for Emmeline as they exchanged stories about their redneck fathers and assorted trailer trash relations.

"Here you go," Tamara said, returning with Emmeline's water. "And there's a phone call for you."

Emmeline took a long drink of the water as she walked toward the kitchen and the phone used by the staff. Who would be calling her? she wondered. Especially at work, and especially in the middle of the night.

"Hello?" she said when she picked up the receiver.

"Emmeline." It was Toby. His voice had a peculiar sound to it, as if he was frightened.

"What is it?" Emmeline asked. "Is it your parents? What did they do?"

"It's not my parents," replied Toby. "It's your mother. I think she's sick."

"Sick?" Emmeline repeated.

"She's breathing really slowly," Toby said. "And I can't get her to wake up."

"Let her sleep," Emmeline said. "I'll be right there. I'm sure she's fine."

"Okay," Toby said, sounding relieved, as if by talking to Emmeline he'd transferred the weight of his worry.

Emmeline hung up. Poor Toby, she thought. He'd never been around elderly people before. Most likely her mother was just in a deep sleep. The doctor had told her to expect that from time to time.

She said good night to Jackie and a few of her well-wishers and left. Ten minutes later, she walked through her own front door. Toby emerged from her mother's room.

"Hi," he said. "I think she's okay. She's breathing more normally."

"I'm sure everything is okay," said Emmeline kindly as she entered her mother's room.

Her first thought was that Lula looked like a child. Her eyes were shut and her mouth was slightly open. Her hands were at her sides, and her body made a small bump beneath the brightly flowered bedspread Emmeline had bought for her a few days earlier. Emmeline sat in the chair Toby had pulled up beside the bed and took one of her mother's hands, squeezing it softly.

"Mother," she whispered. "Mother, it's me."

Lula's eyelids fluttered but didn't open. Emmeline spoke again. "Mother, wake up."

This time Lula's eyes did open, very slowly. She looked up at Emmeline, staring as if she didn't recognize the face hovering above her.

"Where am I?" she asked shakily.

"You're home," said Emmeline, running a hand through her mother's hair and smoothing it.

Lula licked her lips, shut her eyes, and opened them again. "Where's Petey?" she asked hoarsely.

"Petey isn't here," said Emmeline. "But I'm here."

"Where's Mason?" asked Lula. "I want Mason."

Emmeline hesitated. Her mother wasn't recognizing her. Should she just accept the old woman's refusal to acknowledge who she had become and tell her that Mason was sitting there holding her hand? Or was this simply a harmless delusion, a momentary forgetfulness brought on by Lula's stroke and old age, something to be forgiven rather than angered by?

"I'm here," Emmeline repeated, neither contradicting Lula nor succumbing to her desire to have her youngest son back with her.

Lula opened her eyes again and looked at Emmeline. This time some of the confusion was gone. "You're not Mason," she said very slowly, as if suddenly every word hurt her. "You're Emmeline."

"Yes," Emmeline said gently. "I'm Emmeline."

"My daughter," Lula said, blinking.

Emmeline looked at her mother. Her face seemed more worn than it had been even a moment before. Something had taken hold of the muscles, pulling them down so that Lula's mouth twisted half in a smile and half in a grimace of pain. Her eyes, too, had taken on a peculiar look, unfocused and tired.

"Mother?" Emmeline said.

"Daughter," said Lula Tayhill very slowly, like a child sounding out an unfamiliar and difficult word while learning to read. "My daughter."

A shudder passed through Lula's body. Her face spasmed, and her fingers tightened around Emmeline's, clutching them painfully so that Emmeline cried out in surprise. Lula gasped for breath, her mouth opening like that of a fish suddenly removed from its element. A strangled sort of cough emerged from her throat.

"Toby!" Emmeline called out.

Toby ran into the room, saw what was happening, and retreated. Emmeline heard him picking up the phone, then talking excitedly.

"It's Twenty-one Scatterbrook Road," he said. "I think it's a heart attack or something. Yes, she's elderly. What? Okay. Please hurry."

He appeared in the doorway, still clutching the phone. "They're on their way," he said. "Just a few minutes."

Emmeline nodded. She was standing now, leaning over her mother. Lula's eyes had become fixed, unseeing, but her chest continued to rise and fall in the most shallow of breaths. Emmeline continued to hold her hand, not sure what else to do.

"'Lavender blue, dilly dilly,'" she found herself whispering as she rocked gently over her mother. "'Lavender green.'"

The song seemed ridiculous to her, nothing but nonsense, but still she sang. Everything was going to be all right as long as she kept singing, as long as she didn't let go of her mother's hand.

"And if you answer yes," she sang, mixing up the words but not caring. "In a dilly dilly church, on a dilly dilly day." It was all coming out wrong, but it didn't matter. The important thing was to keep singing, to keep soothing her mother with her voice. Then everything would be okay.

It seemed like hours that she stood there, singing to her mother and waiting, yet when she glanced at the clock beside her mother's bed she saw that it had only been a few minutes. Then she heard a knock on the door and voices as Toby said, "In here."

Then she was surrounded by strangers, strangers telling her to move out of the way, that they would take over. They took her by the shoulders and pulled her away gently, but as her mother's fingers slipped from hers she found herself resisting.

"No!" she said sharply. "No."

"Please. We need to be able to work on her."

Emmeline looked at the man who had spoken to her. He seemed young—impossibly young. What could he do for her mother that she couldn't do? She opened her mouth to reply, but found herself being pushed out of the room.

"Here," said Toby, taking her hand and leading her to the couch. "Sit."

Emmeline obeyed, her eyes fixed on the doorway to her mother's room. She could see the paramedics inside, moving around her mother like witches working at conjurations, doing something she couldn't see as they talked to one another in low voices. *Just let her rest,* Emmeline thought. *All she needs is some rest.*

And after her rest, she thought, they would have their talk, the talk Emmeline had been putting off until the right time. The talk that would bring everything out into the open. The talk she had waited nearly thirty years to have. Yes, she thought, then they would have that talk, just the two of them.

Several minutes later one of the paramedics came out, removing a latex glove from his hand as he did. He was, Emmeline was relieved to see, older than the boy who had ordered her out. He, she thought, would know exactly what needed to be done.

"How is she?" asked Emmeline. "Will she need to go to the hospital? She had a stroke a few months ago and—"

She was rambling, but the man wasn't stopping her. Instead he looked at her with a kind of weariness. Why was he waiting for her to finish?

"I can get you her list of medications," Emmeline said, her voice faltering. "And her doctor's name. It's right in—"

The paramedic shook his head gently.

"But they'll need—" Emmeline began, trying to prevent him from saying the words she knew, suddenly, were going to come out of his mouth when he spoke.

"No," she said. "No. She isn't. She's just tired."

This time the man sat in the chair facing Emmeline. "It was another stroke," he said. "This frequently happens in elderly patients."

"There must be something you can do," said Emmeline weakly. "Something at the hospital?"

The man shook his head. "I'm very sorry," he said.

Emmeline expected to start crying. Instead, a sort of calm came over her. She smiled softly at the man. "Thank you," she said.

"We can take her to the hospital," the man told her. "You can have her picked up there."

"Picked up?" said Emmeline.

"By the funeral home," the man explained. "For the service."

"The service," Emmeline said dreamily. "Of course." Yes, there would have to be a service. A funeral. That's what you did when people died.

Died. Dead. That's what her mother was now—dead. Emmeline realized suddenly that so far everyone had avoided saying the word. But that's what had happened, wasn't it? Her mother had died.

The paramedic stood up and went back into the bedroom. Should she follow him? Emmeline wondered. Should she see her mother one last time?

The decision was made for her as the paramedics emerged carrying the body of her mother. They had placed her in a black plastic bag, the kind they often showed bodies being removed from crime scenes in on televison shows. Emmeline watched as they walked with it through the living room and out the front door.

"I'll need you to sign this." The young paramedic was standing in front of her, holding out a clipboard with some papers on it. He indicated a line and handed Emmeline a pen.

"You'll need this to claim the body," the young man said as he tore off the top page and handed it to Emmeline.

Then he was gone, and Emmeline was left holding a piece of paper, a receipt for her mother's body. She might as well have just signed for the delivery of some new furniture, or for the removal of yard waste. But no, the piece of paper she folded neatly in half and laid on the coffee table was a claim check for her mother.

She stood and walked to the bedroom. The floor was littered with small bits of paper and faint with the smell of alcohol. What had they done to her mother, she wondered, to try and bring her back from the dead? Had they poked and prodded her, attempting to convince her spirit to stay for a while longer?

It didn't matter. Ultimately, they had failed. Or her mother had failed. The end result was the same. Emmeline sat on the edge of the bed and ran her hand over the rumpled sheets where her mother's body had lain. They were cool to the touch.

Toby put his arm around her. "Are you okay?" he asked.

Emmeline turned to him. His eyes were kind, filled with worry and fear for her.

"My mother is dead," she said, feeling the tears begin.

PART IV

August

CHAPTER 51

The girl's tits were huge. As she straddled Reilly's lap, grinding her crotch against his, the twin globes of her breasts were thrust into his face. They were bare, and the girl was running her fingertips over the nipples. They were close enough that, if he chose to, he could simply stick out his tongue and lick them.

Thankfully, she still had her thong on, although the tiny strip of shiny gold material did little to cover her. She had, he saw, shaved her pussy completely, so that she resembled a Barbie come to life, her sex a piece of bare molded plastic. He wondered vaguely whether he would find the Matel logo stamped on her backside if he slid the thong off.

The girl flipped her long blond hair and made a face that, he supposed, was meant to inspire lust. Instead, it was just making him feel sorry for her. She was trying so hard.

"Isn't this better than a fucking poker game?"

Peter, or maybe Paul, clapped Reilly on the back.

"Oh, yeah," Reilly said. *"Much* better."

"We really fooled you with that one, huh?"

Reilly nodded as the girl moaned in his ear. "Sure did," he replied.

"So, when's the wedding?" the girl asked him.

"End of the month," Reilly told her.

"Cool," she replied, for no apparent reason. "Do you like my tits?"

Reilly dutifully looked at her breasts, which she was pressing together for his benefit.

"They're real," the girl cooed. "I bet you'd like to fuck them, wouldn't you?"

"I don't think my fiancée would be very keen on that idea," Reilly told her.

Suddenly, the song that had been playing—Billy Idol's "Cradle of Love"—stopped. As if her actions were tied to the song's notes, the girl got off of Reilly's lap and walked away, disappearing behind a curtained doorway. Another song, this time KISS singing "Lick It Up," blared through the room as a new girl, a brunette, entered and almost immediately removed her bra to whoops of appreciation from the men around her.

"Isn't this place hot?"

Reilly turned and looked at his soon-to-be brothers-in-law. All four of them were seated around the table in the middle of the aptly named Kit Kat Box. Each of them had a seven-dollar bottle of Budweiser in his hand and a look of drunken excitement on his face.

"Where did you guys find this place?" Reilly yelled over the deafening music.

"One of the guys Paul works with told him about it," answered Peter, solving the riddle of which twin was which.

Reilly made a mental note to kill Paul's buddy. He'd agreed to an evening of fun with Peter, Paul, Manuel Jr., and Gabe because he'd assumed they wouldn't do anything so stupid. But they had, driving nearly two hours to reach the strip club. The only good thing about it, as far as Reilly was concerned, was that there was no way anyone Donna knew would find out about it and tell her.

"Hey, boys." The brunette had come over to their table, and was smiling at each of them in turn. "Anyone want a private dance?"

The Estoril boys all pointed at Reilly and laughed uproariously.

"He's getting married!" they yelled in chorus.

"Really?" said the brunette. "Then I'll have to give you something special, won't I?"

Before Reilly could answer, she straddled his lap and took up where the blonde had left off. There were the tits again, and the shaved pussy. There was the grinding of the crotch. There were the bargain basement porn film come-ons. Reilly steeled himself for four minutes of feigned arousal.

When it was over, the Estoril brothers tipped the girl handsomely and she left, disappearing into the place behind the curtain where, apparently, an endless supply of girls with enormous breasts and shaved pussies was kept solely for the purpose of entertaining the men who shouted for more.

"Man, I'm surprised you didn't pop off in your pants the way she was dry humping you," Manuel Jr. said to Reilly. "I'd have to change my underwear by now."

"Good thing I don't wear any, then, isn't it?" Reilly said, earning more guffaws from the boys.

"Seriously," Peter said when they all stopped laughing. "It's going to be fucking cool having you for a brother-in-law, man. I mean it."

He put an arm around Reilly and pulled him close.

"Thanks," Reilly said, waiting patiently for Peter to release him.

"Yeah," Gabriel said, nodding. "Welcome to the family." He raised his beer, which was quickly joined in the air by those of his brothers. Reilly lifted his own beer and tapped it once against each of the other bottles.

"To Reilly!" Paul said jovially.

"To Reilly!" the others echoed as they all drank.

Two hours, four more beers, and two additional lap dances later, they were all pretty well shit-faced. Only Gabe, who was driving, had stopped drinking and switched to water.

"I think it's time to get you bad boys home to bed," Gabe said, earning groans of protest from the others.

"Come on," Peter said, sounding like a little boy begging to be allowed to stay up an extra hour. "One more titty dance."

"You've had enough," Gabe said, standing up. "Now get to the car. All of you."

Complaining loudly, the guys all stood up and managed to get themselves to the car without incident. Reilly sat in front with Gabe, while Paul, Peter, and Manuel Jr. climbed into the back. The beer had done its trick, and Reilly was feeling the effects.

"What time is it?" he asked sleepily.

"Half past one," said Gabe, peering at the car's dashboard clock.

"Shit," Manuel Jr. said from the backseat. "We have to take Mom to Mass in five hours."

"Which is just enough time to get home, wash the smell of pussy and smoke off, and get a little sleep," Peter said.

"Man, Reilly's gonna have to steam-clean all the pussy off of his pants," joked Paul.

"How about I just give you my pants to sniff?" Reilly shot back, making the others howl.

They continued to joke with one another on the ride home, but soon a tired silence settled over the car as each man grew too weary to keep up the conversation. Reilly leaned his head against the window and looked out at the passing darkness.

He thought about the women who had tried, albeit purely for financial reasons, to excite him at the club. Some of them had been beautiful, very beautiful. And all of them had done things to him that should have had him aching to get off. Yet he hadn't felt desire for any of them. He liked to think that this was because of his loyalty to Donna, and to their relationship, but the truth went much deeper than that. The fact was, he hadn't been aroused by them because he hadn't been attracted to them. And not just to them, but to the *idea* of them, of being with them.

He closed his eyes. His head hurt. He tried to picture himself making love with any one of the girls who had sat on his lap during the night. But try as he might, their images faded quickly. What replaced them was the memory of the man in the truck beside him in the parking lot, his hand moving up and down his cock, his cum spraying into the air as he came.

He opened his eyes and looked out at the road. In a few weeks he would be married to Donna, he told himself. Donna, whom he loved, whom he made love to. *Yes,* a voice in his head said. *But what do you think about when you make love to her?*

Men. The answer came to him quickly, looming in his thoughts like a monstrous shadow blotting out everything else. Men. He thought about men when he made love to Donna. And more and more lately, the men he thought about all shared one face.

"Here we are."

Reilly looked out the window. Without his even knowing it, they had arrived back in P-Town. Gabe had pulled up in front of Reilly's house.

"Thanks, guys," Reilly said as he opened the door and half fell, half climbed out. "I had a great time."

The brothers all waved and shouted their drunken good-byes as Gabe pulled away, honking the horn three times. Reilly watched them go, then turned to let himself into his house. He was looking forward to sleeping in his own bed.

But as he inserted the key in the lock and started to turn it, he stopped. He didn't want to go inside. He didn't want to get into his own bed, alone, and lay there thinking about his life. He didn't want to close his eyes and see the face that had been haunting his thoughts and dreams.

He turned and walked away from the house. He knew he was too drunk to drive, so he kept walking. He walked down the road and, turning left, kept walking. He walked for perhaps half an hour until he came to Oyster Lane. Then he proceeded to walk up the driveway of number 37 and into the backyard. When he reached the guest house, he pounded heavily on the door.

There was no answer, so he pounded again. This time he heard someone shuffling across the floor.

"Who is it?" Josh's voice came to him through the wood.

"It's me," Reilly said, his tongue heavy in his mouth. "Let me in."

He heard Josh turning the lock, then saw a soft sliver of light as Josh opened the door a crack.

"Reilly?" he said.

"I want to come in," said Reilly.

"Why are you here?" asked Josh, rubbing his eyes. "It's the middle of the night."

"Please," Reilly said. "Let me in."

Josh looked at him for a moment, then opened the door. Relieved, Reilly walked inside. Josh shut the door, then turned around. Reilly saw that he was wearing nothing but a pair of blue plaid boxer shorts. In the moonlight, the dark hair of his body contrasted even more with his pale skin.

"Where have you been?" Josh asked, sniffing the air. "You smell like a brewery."

"I want to stay here," Reilly answered, ignoring the question. "Tonight. I want to stay here. With you."

Josh stared at him. "You're drunk," he said.

Reilly stepped forward and took Josh in his arms. For the second time, he kissed him. Only this time, when he was done he didn't run away.

"Come on," he said, taking Josh by the hand.

He walked into Josh's bedroom. There he kissed Josh again, this time allowing his hands to roam over Josh's bare skin. Touching him, he felt all of the excitement he hadn't felt with the women of the Kit Kat Box.

He felt Josh pulling his shirt from his jeans, tugging at the buttons of his fly. Reilly helped him, sliding his shirt over his head and removing his shoes. Sliding his jeans down, he stood in front of Josh naked, waiting. His thoughts ran together like water, his head spinning in excitement, fear, and wonder.

Josh kissed him. "I'll be right back," he said. Then he turned and walked into the bathroom, shutting the door behind him.

Reilly lay down on the bed. Josh's bed. He could smell him on the sheets, feel the warmth where he'd been sleeping. He breathed deeply. This, he thought, was where he belonged. He closed his eyes and waited for Josh to return to him.

CHAPTER 52

Jackie looked at the back of the box again.

"'Hold the absorbent end of the pregnancy indicator wand in the urine stream,'" she read out loud.

She glanced at the thin plastic stick she was holding in her fingers, one end of which was made of feltlike absorbent material.

"Like hell I will," she said firmly. "I am *not* peeing on my hand."

There had to be another way. Maybe, she thought, she could just pee in a cup and dip the wand in. But a quick search of the cupboards showed that she was out of plastic cups. She briefly eyed one of her coffee mugs before deciding that she didn't want to risk any traces of caffeine or dish detergent that might be lingering inside to affect the outcome of the test. She wanted to be absolutely certain that any results she got were reliable.

Besides, she had to pee really badly. The box said she should use her first urine of the morning for the test, and she'd been saving it up. Now the pressure on her bladder was reaching a critical level. If she didn't do something about it soon, she wouldn't have to worry about peeing on her hand.

"Okay," she said, sighing. "Here goes nothing."

Sitting on the toilet, she aimed the wand between her legs, the tip pointed down as recommended on the box. The accompanying diagram showed the outline of a woman, her urine stream flowing out smoothly and easily as she dipped the wand into it. It was all very natural and beautiful.

The reality was altogether different. At first she tried to let just a little bit out, contracting her muscles in an attempt to pee like the woman on the box. But her body was having none of it, and refused to release even a single drop. Steeling herself for the worst, she relaxed. As soon as she let go, urine sprayed from between her legs in a hot wave of relief.

She held the tip of the pregnancy wand in more or less the center of the stream, feeling uncomfortably like someone attempting to use a straw to sip water from a swirling lawn sprinkler. But at least the wand was getting wet. And why, she thought suddenly, did they have to call it a fucking wand? It wasn't as if she was a fairy godmother or something. The word irritated her unreasonably, her annoyance increased by the fact that not only was the absorbent urine pad sufficiently soaked, but so was her entire hand.

She pulled the wand out from between her legs and laid it unceremoniously on the edge of the sink. When she was finished peeing, she washed her hands thoroughly, steadfastly avoiding looking at the wand. It was supposed to change color if she was pregnant, the tip turning from pale pink to bright blue through some mysterious process she couldn't begin to understand. Something, she knew, having to do with hormones.

She dried her hands on a towel and left the bathroom. It would take twelve to fifteen minutes for the wand to make its prediction, and she didn't want to sit there staring at it. Better to get it over with all at once, she thought. One quick look—a flash of pink or blue—and it would be over. Then she could get on with her life.

She went into the living room. It was early morning. The sun was just coming up over the sea, gilding the beach with gold and slowly making its way along the sand in no particular hurry. It was funny, she thought, how you could tell what time of year it was by how the sun looked. In spring it always seemed crisp and clear, as if it had yet to find its full strength and needed time to grow strong. Summer sun was heavy, full and ripe like the juice of a peach. It covered everything, as if it were attempting to embrace the world. Now, although it was still summer, the light was changing. The hot sun of July had mellowed a bit and become the wiser sun of August. It knew that fall was not too far away, and so it tarried longer in its journey, reluctant to pass away too quickly. It was richer, somehow, and more luxurious. Jackie loved the light in August, and seeing it filling up the morning sky made her smile.

Another Provincetown summer was coming to a close. Yes, there would be visitors after Labor Day. Some people preferred the cooler days of fall, when the ocean turned darker and the wind carried on it the smell of the approaching cold. She would see more of the year-round residents then, many of whom she was convinced went into a sort of reverse hibernation during the summer, holing up in some safe, quiet spot until the summer people were gone.

She, too, looked forward to the coming months, even to winter with its short icy days and long nights of blackness. The Drunken Time, Franny had called it affectionately, and with more than a little accuracy. Winter in Provincetown had a way of bringing out the inner alcoholic in more than a few residents, particularly around February, when the cold had taken its toll and looked as if—despite thousands of years of proof to the contrary—it might choose that particular year to never end. The Drunken Time had been profitable for Franny. It had also, ultimately, been her own undoing.

Winter meant something different to Jackie now that she no longer drank. Now it was a time for reflection and planning, for weaving dreams for the future. She enjoyed the relative solitude. But she would miss the summer, miss the people and laughter and sun. And this winter, she knew, would be different. If she even stayed. That decision had yet to be made.

What the stick on her bathroom sink revealed would have a lot to do with her decision. In what way, she wasn't entirely sure. But she knew it would signal a change in her life one way or another. She calculated in her head. If she was indeed pregnant, she would be giving birth in—she counted on her fingers—early May. Just in time for the new season to begin. *Way to go,* she scolded herself. Could she run her business *and* take care of a baby? She tried to picture it in her mind, but the image faded in and out.

She checked her watch. It had only been five minutes. How, she wondered, could she have so many random thoughts in such a short time? It felt as if she'd been watching the sun come up for hours.

Abigail, she thought unexpectedly. *That would be a nice name.* Old-fashioned, perhaps, but pretty. Abigail Stavers. No, it wasn't particularly—how would her mother have put it?—appropriate. Black, she really meant, but she would never have admitted it. "A child needs a name that fits its heritage," she'd said firmly whenever the topic of what someone was naming a new baby came up.

What would be appropriate for her child? Jackie wondered. With a black mother and a white father, nothing about this baby would be appropriate as far as Wanda Stavers was concerned. She had never approved of mixed marriages. "That's just asking for trouble," she'd said firmly, as if that had been the final word on the subject.

There were times, Jackie thought, when it was convenient to have her entire family dead and buried.

Her mind went back to names. She would *not,* she swore, name her child any of the so-called "African" names. Kiesha. Shenanay. Loquita. Where the hell did people come up with these things? She laughed remembering the name of the clerk at a drugstore she'd stopped at during her last trip to Boston. The girl's name tag had read Benadryl. Unable to resist, Jackie had asked about it. "It's Buh-NAY-dril," the girl had said with some irritation, as Jackie had hurriedly paid for her purchase and left, only to break into uncontrollable laughter in the parking lot.

There should, she thought, be an old black woman appointed to every hospital in the country, her sole duty to review the names black women wanted to give their babies and prevent embarrassment. "Oh, no, you don't," Jackie pictured one saying to a young mother who had just presented baby Tanwisha for inspection. "This child's name is Beatrice."

Beatrice. That was nice. She said it again—Beatrice. *You're assuming it's going to be a girl,* she told herself. *It could just as well be a boy.* A boy. That thought had never really occurred to her. In all of her thinking about the idea of becoming pregnant, she'd always pictured the end result being a little girl. But what if it wasn't? What if, instead of a nice, neat little vagina, her baby came out with a dick?

Then you'll be in deep shit, she thought. *You don't know anything about boy children.*

"He'd just have to be gay," she said aloud. "That's all there is to it."

She couldn't even picture herself with a little boy. Then again, could she really picture herself with a little girl, a little girl who wanted ribbons in her hair and dolls to play with? All of a sudden, the very idea of bringing a child—any child—into the world and being responsible for it seemed like the worst idea anyone could ever possibly have. What had she been thinking?

Maybe I can suck it back out, she thought vaguely. *Before it takes.*

But of course she couldn't. All she could do was wait and see what the stick said. *Wand,* she corrected herself. *The wand.* The wand had all the power now, the power of yes or no. And what if it *was* no? Would she try again? Would she ask Josh to give her another jar of his semen? Would she once again insert the plastic syringe inside herself and deposit a million microscopic sperm into herself and wait to see who won the race against time, the sperm or her unfertilized egg?

It was all so complicated. And why? Millions of stupid women got pregnant every day without even *meaning* to. Why did it have to be such an elaborate ordeal for her? *Why can't I just buy a nice kid at the store?* she asked herself.

Because you're a dyke. The sentence rang through her thoughts like a bell, delivered in Franny's unmistakable ragged voice. *And when you're a dyke in this world, everything is harder. A lot harder.*

"No kidding," Jackie said. She'd learned that particular lesson over and over in her life.

You're better off alone.

"You *would* say that," replied Jackie. Franny had prided herself on not needing anyone. "But I'm not you. I *do* need someone."

That's your weakness.

"Maybe," said Jackie. "Or maybe not needing anyone was yours."

She looked at her watch again. Thirty seconds. Thirty seconds and she would know whether or not she was going to be a mother. She stood up and walked to the bathroom. The wand sat perched on the edge of the sink, waiting for her.

Ten seconds. Nine. Eight. She counted them down on her watch. When the last second ran out, she reached for the wand. The answer to her question lay beneath the cap she'd placed over the absorbent pad. All she had to do was pull the cap off and look.

"Here goes nothing," she said, and pulled. She looked at the tip of the wand for a moment. "Well," she said, "I guess that's that."

CHAPTER 53

"You're sure it doesn't hurt?"

"Not at all," Josh said. "You won't even feel it."

"That's what they say about the first time you get fucked," Toby replied suspiciously.

Josh smiled. He wasn't about to tell Toby that getting his blood taken *would* probably hurt. The poor kid was already nervous enough. He'd even made Josh drive him to Wellfleet so that the chances of his running into someone who might recognize him were smaller. Now the two of them were sitting in the small front room of Positive Outlook, waiting for Toby's name to be called.

"Danny?"

A woman with a clipboard was looking at them, waiting for an answer. Josh gently nudged Toby, who had apparently already forgotten the name he'd given the receptionist when they'd arrived.

"Danny. Right. That's me," Toby said, standing up.

"You can come with me," the woman said.

"Come with me," Toby said to Josh.

Josh shook his head. "I don't like needles," he replied.

"Please," said Toby.

Josh thought about the first time he'd had an HIV test. He'd been a nervous wreck, even though he hadn't really had unsafe sex with anyone and he and Doug had been using condoms at the time. He'd practically fainted with relief when the results had come back negative. He knew Toby must be terrified.

"Okay," he said, standing up. "Let's go."

"I'm sorry," the woman said when Josh attempted to follow her and Toby through the door. "Only partners are allowed in."

"He is," Toby said quickly. "I mean we are. Partners." He grabbed Josh's hand and held it tightly. "Right, honey?"

"Right," said Josh brightly. "Sweetie."

The woman nodded wearily and led them into another room, where a man wearing a white coat was arranging vials of blood in a tray The woman handed him the clipboard and left, closing the door behind her.

"Okay," the man said, looking at the clipboard. "Which one of you is Danny?"

Toby raised his hand. "That would be me," he said.

"Have a seat," the man said, indicating a chair beside him. "I'm Carlos."

"Hi," Toby said. "That's Josh," he added. "He's my partner."

Carlos nodded at Josh. "Is this your first HIV test?" he asked as he read over the paperwork Toby had filled out.

Toby nodded.

"And may I ask why you've decided to get tested?" Carlos inquired.

"I, um, may have been exposed to HIV," said Toby, sounding embarrassed.

"In what way?" Carlos asked.

"Excuse me?" said Toby.

"Transfusion, IV drug use, or sex?" Carlos elaborated, as if presenting the dinner specials of the evening.

"Oh," Toby said. "Unprotected sex."

Carlos glanced at Josh. "With your partner?" he asked.

Toby blushed. "No," he said. "With someone else."

"Oral or anal?" Carlos said.

"Both," answered Toby.

"Passive or active?"

Toby looked at Josh, who mimed fucking by sticking his finger through a hole made by his opposing thumb and forefinger.

"Oh, well, both," Toby told Carlos.

Carlos looked at him for a moment, either in surprise or in subdued disapproval, Josh couldn't tell which.

"You're very young," Carlos said. "We're seeing a lot of guys your age and even younger getting infected. I know it seems as if AIDS has become just another disease you take a couple of pills to deal with, but it isn't."

"I know," Toby said seriously. "This was an accident."

"There are no accidents," Carlos said as he picked up a length of rubber tubing and wrapped it around Toby's upper arm. "There are choices. And it's not just yourself you have to think about," he added, nodding toward Josh. "When you engage in unprotected sex, you put all of your future partners at risk too."

"Hey," Josh said, annoyed by Carlos's lecturing, "he made a mistake. You don't need to scare him even more."

"He should be scared," said Carlos. "We all should."

He ran an alcohol swab over Toby's arm and then pressed the tip of the needle against his skin. As it slipped in, Toby winced and shut his eyes. Josh watched in horrible fascination as blood began to enter the vial attached to the other end.

"I tested positive almost fourteen years ago," Carlos said as he watched the vial fill up. "I've lost thirty-eight friends and two lovers to this disease. Do you know how it feels when I see someone his age come in here testing positive after all the marches, all the funerals, all the education?"

"No," said Josh quietly. "I don't."

"We all thought we were invincible," Carlos continued. "Then we found out we weren't. But somewhere along the line, we've forgotten again."

He removed the first vial from the end of the syringe and inserted a second one. Toby's eyes were still closed.

"I don't mean to sound harsh," Carlos said, his words directed at Toby. "I know how you feel. I really do. I just don't want to bury any more friends."

The second vial filled, Carlos removed it and slid the needle deftly out of Toby's arm. He placed a bandage over the tiny puncture and rubbed it in place.

"How long until I can get the results?" Toby asked.

"A week," answered Carlos. "Just call here and give them this iden- tification number."

"Thanks," Toby said as he stood up.

"Here," said Carlos, opening a drawer and reaching inside. He handed Toby several condoms. "Use them," he said firmly as he opened the door. "And good luck."

Toby nodded and Josh followed him out the door and back to the waiting room. When they were outside and getting into Josh's car, Josh said, "I'm sorry he was kind of an asshole."

"It's okay," said Toby. "I'd be a little ticked off if I was him too."

"Still," said Josh as they got in, "he shouldn't have said those things."

"He was right about one thing," Toby said, buckling his seat belt. "I *am* scared."

Josh turned to him. "You're going to be fine," he said.

Toby didn't respond to the remark. "I don't know why I did it," he said instead. "It was so stupid."

"We all do stupid things once in a while," Josh reassured him. "Especially when it comes to guys."

"Have you?" Toby asked.

"More times than I care to think about," Josh told him. *Like just the other night,* he thought to himself.

"I think I was just trying to prove I *could* do it," Toby went on. "You know, because of my parents coming here and all."

"You don't have to apologize," Josh said. "You're allowed to have sex."

"I know," Toby said. "But it just seemed so, I don't know . . ."

"Sleazy?" Josh suggested. "Dirty? Bad? Wrong?"

Toby nodded. "Yeah," he said.

"But it was also really hot, wasn't it?" said Josh.

Toby looked at him for a moment. "Yeah," he said. "It sort of was. I mean, I know it was dumb and everything, but there was part of me that thought it was really cool too. That's the part I'm scared of."

"You're allowed to find out what you like," said Josh carefully. "And you're allowed to make mistakes. It's not a crime. You just have to be careful."

"Maybe that's the problem," Toby said sadly. "I don't know what I want."

"You and ninety-nine percent of the gay men out there," replied Josh.

"It can't be that bad," said Toby.

Josh laughed. "No," he said. "It's not. But you will find that gay men tend to take longer to figure it out."

"Why?"

Josh sighed. "A friend of mine says that gay men spend their twenties trying to be the guy everyone wants to fuck, their thirties being the guy everybody wants to marry, and the rest of their lives chasing after the guys in their twenties and thirties."

"Is that what you did?" Toby asked him.

"No," said Josh. "I got married as soon as I could so I wouldn't have to." He paused. "And look how well that worked out."

"So what you're saying is it's hopeless," said Toby.

"Not at all," Josh said. "I'm just saying it's harder. Especially at your age."

"Gee, thanks," Toby said.

"I'm not going to lie to you," said Josh. "A lot of gay guys are totally fucked-up. A lot of us screw around for years because we think something better will always come along. But not all of us. If you want to find someone to settle down with, you will. You just might have to look for a while, and you might have to wait for him to grow up. In the meantime, you can have all the nasty sex you want to with couples at the B and B."

Toby shot him a look, then started laughing. "Okay," he said. "I get it."

"There's nothing wrong with having sex," Josh said. "As long as you're doing it because you want to and not because you're trying to prove something. *And* as long as you play safe."

"Okay, Carlos," Toby teased. "I'll be a good boy. No more free willy."

"Besides," said Josh, "if anything happened to you, Emmeline would kill you. How is she doing, by the way?"

"Okay, I guess," Toby said. "She hasn't said a whole lot since it happened. She's been on the phone most of the time, trying to track down her brother and find out if her mother had a will."

"Where did they bury her mother?"

"They didn't," Toby answered. "She was cremated."

"Poor Emmeline," said Josh. "It must be hard."

Toby nodded. "They didn't get along all that well," he said. "But still—she was her mother and all." He looked out the window and grew quiet.

"You okay?" asked Josh after they'd driven a few miles in silence.

Toby nodded. "Just thinking," he said.

"About your mom?"

Toby nodded again but didn't say anything.

"You know what I said earlier," Josh said. "About maybe having to wait for the guy you're looking for to grow up?"

Toby looked at him and nodded.

"Well, sometimes that applies to families too," Josh said.

CHAPTER 54

"Coming up on *Dateline*, an interview with one of the hottest young stars in Hollywood—Ty Rusk. Speculation has been swirling around his relationship with a mystery woman. Now, in an exclusive, he talks for the first time about fame, being a sex symbol, and falling in love. Could marriage be in the not-so-distant future? Find out after the break."

"Jane Pauley?" Josh looked at Reid, who shrugged. "He grew up with her on the *Today Show*," he said. "Besides, she's more respected than Barbara Walters and better looking than Larry King."

"I thought we were going to wait awhile to announce our engagement," said Devin, who was seated next to Josh on the couch in Reid's living room.

"We decided to step things up a little," Reid told her. "This way, we get a jump on all the tabloids who have been sniffing around."

Devin shifted in her seat, looking slightly uncomfortable.

"Here we go," said Reid as the commercial for Pepsi faded away and Jane Pauley's smiling face blossomed across the screen.

"He had a major hit with the number-one smash *Hat Trick*," Jane said. "According to *People* magazine, he's the object of every woman's fantasies. But has someone finally captured Ty Rusk's heart? Let's find out."

The camera pulled back to show Ty seated across from Jane. He was wearing a black suit and a pale blue shirt. One leg was crossed over the other, and the fingers of his left hand toyed absentmindedly with the lace of one shoe.

"I have to say, this is something of a surprise," Jane began. "You've been very reluctant so far to discuss your new relationship."

Ty nodded. "Well, Jane," he answered, "I thought it was time to set the record straight. There have been a lot of rumors flying around about what's going on."

Jane smiled sweetly. "So, what is going on? First of all, what's this young woman's name?"

A photograph of Devin and Ty walking through Central Park flashed on the screen. They were holding hands and laughing.

"We had to walk through there three times before a photographer finally showed up," Devin told Reid and Josh.

"Her name is Devin," said Ty as the photograph faded away and the shot of Jane and Ty returned.

"She's very pretty," remarked Jane.

"Yes," Ty agreed. "She is."

"So who is she?" asked Jane. "Everybody wants to know."

Ty laughed. "I'm sure they do," he said.

"Tell us this," Jane continued. "Are you in love?"

Ty hesitated a moment before answering. "Yes," he said. "I'm in love."

Jane beamed. "Does that mean there are wedding plans in the works?"

Ty shook his head. "Not until this country changes its laws," he replied.

A shadow of confusion passed over Jane's face. "I'm afraid I don't understand," she said. "Why can't you and Devin marry?"

Ty leaned forward. "Oh, Devin and I could marry," he said. "But the person I'm in love with and I can't."

Again Jane looked perplexed. Before she could formulate her next question, Ty went on. "I'm in love with another man."

"What?" Devin said, staring first at the television and then at Reid. "What did he just say?"

"Listen," Reid said, a smile beginning to creep across his face.

"I'm not in love with Devin," Ty was saying to a shocked Jane Pauley. "I'm in love with a man. Reid Truman."

"Shit," Reid exclaimed as Josh clapped and crowed with delight. "I didn't know he was going to say who I was."

"You're gay?" Jane was looking at Ty, clearly unsure of where to take the interview next.

"Yes," Ty said. "I'm gay. And I *am* very much in love. Just not with Devin."

Somewhere offscreen, someone or something caught Jane's attention. She stared blankly for a second over Ty's shoulder, then nodded.

"We're going to take a quick break," she said. "When we come back, we'll talk more with Ty Rusk."

As a commercial rolled, Devin stared in shock at Reid, who hadn't stopped grinning.

"I don't understand," she said weakly.

"Let me explain then," Reid replied. "We decided to beat you and Raymacher at your own game."

Devin's face collapsed into an expression of disbelief.

"Yes," Reid continued. "We know about your deal with him."

"How?" Devin asked.

"He tried to double-cross you," Reid explained. "The same way you tried to double-cross us. Only now both of you lose."

A sudden beeping came from inside Devin's purse, which sat at her feet.

"That's probably Raymacher now," Reid said.

Devin stared at her purse, not moving.

"Go on," Reid said. "Answer it."

Reluctantly, Devin reached into her handbag and removed her phone. Flipping it open, she said, "Hello?"

"No," she said defensively. "I didn't. You're the one who—"

"Give me that," Reid said, reaching over and taking the phone from her hand.

"C.J.!" he said brightly. "Enjoying the show?"

"I don't know what the fuck you think you're doing," the columnist shrieked. "But whatever it is, you are *totally* fucked."

Reid laughed. "Why's that, C.J.? What are you going to do?"

"I still have the story about how you hired the girl to be Ty's beard," Raymacher said. "That should go over really well with his adoring public."

"We'll see," Reid answered. "He's about to tell Jane all about it when they come back from the commercial."

There was dead silence from Raymacher for a long time. Then he said, "This is the end of his career, you know."

"I wouldn't be so sure about that," replied Reid.

"Women aren't going to fantasize about a faggot," Raymacher told him. "The studios will drop him."

"That's your problem, C.J.," Reid said. "You have so little faith in the moviegoing public. It's sad, really. I feel sorry for you."

"Fuck you," shouted Raymacher as Reid laughed.

"Sorry," Reid said. "I've already got Ty for that. Good-bye, C.J., and enjoy the rest of the show."

He hung up and handed the phone back to Devin, who took it and stared at it helplessly.

"Don't ever trust a gossip queen," Reid told her. "They'll turn on you every time. Oh, and by the way—you're fired."

Devin stood up. Without a word, she walked out of the house.

"Not a very dramatic exit after everything she did," remarked Josh. "I thought she'd come up with something spectacular."

"Only in the movies," Reid said. "They're back."

They returned their attention to the television, where Jane Pauley—looking her old self—was ready to resume her chat with Ty.

"Why did you decide to reveal your homosexuality?" she asked.

"You make it sound like I have a fatal disease," Ty said, earning a tight smile from Jane. "I was tired of pretending to be someone I'm not. I make believe for a living; I don't want to do it in my private life."

"Aren't you worried that this revelation might end your career?" Jane said, sounding like a worried mother.

"I like to think my fans are better people than that," Ty said. "I'm sure there will be some who can't get past their prejudices, but I think the people who expect my career to be over will be surprised."

"Let's hope so," said Jane encouragingly. "What are your plans for the future?"

"I'm finishing up a film here in New York," Ty said. "And then I don't know. There's a script I'm interested in by this great new writer. I want to see where that goes."

"We have to take another break," Jane announced. "But stay with us for more with now openly gay actor Ty Rusk."

"I can't believe how calm he looks," Josh said. "I'd be a nervous wreck."

"Oh, he is," Reid answered. "Trust me."

Again the air was filled with the sound of a ringing phone, only this time it was Reid's. He picked it up.

"Hey," he said. "How's it going?"

"I feel bad for Jane," Ty said. "I really threw her for a loop with this."

"It was the only way," Reid assured him. "It had to be a total surprise."

"I told her we'd take her to dinner at Le Cirque to make up for it," Ty said, laughing.

"Any word yet from Pamela and Jeremy?"

"Six messages on my cell," Ty said. "I haven't listened to any of them yet."

"I think we can guess the gist of them," said Reid.

"It doesn't matter," Ty told him. "I'm firing them anyway. Oh, I have to go. We're about to go back on the air."

"Good luck," Reid told him. "I love you."

"Love you too," Ty said.

"Everything okay?" Josh asked Reid.

Reid nodded. He watched as the program resumed, but turned the volume down. "We already know this part," he said as Ty began to explain Devin's part in recent events.

"What do you think will really happen to him now?" Josh inquired.

Reid sighed. "Honestly? I don't know."

"Would studios really drop him?"

"I wouldn't be shocked if they did," said Reid. "For an industry run by queens, we're surprisingly quick to turn on our own. He'll still get work in independents, and in anything I produce myself, but other than that, I can't say."

"And he's willing to give it all up?" Josh said incredulously.

"What's to give up?" asked Reid. "The lying? The pretending? The constant fear that someone is going to expose you?" He looked at Josh. "The film industry is all about illusion," he said. "Unfortunately, the people involved in that illusion start to mistake it for real life. The money. The fame. The image. They all make it seem real. The problem is, too many people start to mistake who they're pretending to be for who they really are. They have to pay more and more to protect that image, and ultimately what are they left with?"

"Being the subject of the next *E! True Hollywood Story*?" suggested Josh.

"Exactly," Reid said. "Ty deserves more than that. And if I can help him get it, I will."

Reid turned the volume on the television back up. Jane was wrapping up her interview with Ty.

"I hope you'll come back and talk to us about what happens next for you," she said.

"I'd love to," said Ty.

The camera zoomed in on Jane's face. "Join us tomorrow, when we'll have a report on the scandal facing Texas Republican gubernatorial candidate Gary Trittiver. A fourteen-year-old baby-sitter claims she and Trittiver had a yearlong affair. Is this another Monica Lewinsky in the making? Find out tomorrow. Until then, I'm Jane Pauley for *Dateline.*"

Reid turned the television off. "And they think queers are the ones with problems," he said. "God bless America."

CHAPTER 55

Emmeline looked at the plastic bag that held all that remained of her mother. It sat on her kitchen table. It had been delivered half an hour earlier, and Emmeline had immediately removed it from the box it had been mailed in. Unable to hold it in her hands, she had set it on the table next to the salt and pepper shakers shaped like lobsters standing on their tails and bowing. The lobsters had been her gift at a holiday party the Christmas before, picked from a pile when it was Emmeline's turn to draw. Each of them stood on a small stone that said Provincetown on it in loopy script. They were the sort of thing tourists would buy on a whim, ridiculous not only in the absurdity of the lobsters' poses, but in that while P-Town was memorable for many things, its lobsters were not among them. Probably, Emmeline thought, there were dozens of such lobsters sitting on gift store shelves along the eastern coast. Only the rocks on which they stood would be different, reading Bangor, Camden, and Rockport.

She reached out and lifted the bag. She'd been surprised at the weight of the box when she'd taken it from the driver. She'd expected something less substantial, but her mother's ashes weighed probably close to three or four pounds. There was, Emmeline thought, more to the old woman than she'd realized.

The question now was, what was she going to do with the ashes? Petey didn't want anything to do with them. He'd made that clear to her when, after repeated tries, Emmeline had finally reached him on the phone. He'd reacted to the news of their mother's death with no emotion, simply saying, "I'll check with the lawyer to see who gets what" before hanging up. That had been almost two weeks earlier, and she'd heard nothing from him. Not that she wanted to. He could keep the house and everything in it for all she cared. Her mother didn't have much to leave behind, and she wasn't going to fight with her brother over what little there was.

She left the bag of ashes on the table, picked up a large cardboard box she'd brought home with her from the restaurant, and went into what had been her mother's room. With the old woman gone, it could become *her* room again. But she'd yet to clear out her mother's things. Everything remained largely as it had the day of her mother's death. She'd cleaned up a little, changing the bedclothes and removing the hallmarks of illness—the bottles of pills, the wheelchair, the bedpan her mother had refused to actually use. All of these had gone into the trash.

But there were still her mother's personal effects to deal with. Her clothes, what little she'd brought with her, were in the closet and the bureau. Some small items—a hairbrush, her wedding ring, a half-empty bottle of perfume—sat on the dresser top. Everything else remained in her house back in Louisiana, where it would stay until Petey either sold it or left it for the trash men. All Emmeline had to do was put the few things Lula had brought with her into the box. Then her mother would truly be gone.

Emmeline sat on the bed that her mother had died in. She wasn't sure she would ever sleep in it again. For now she would remain in the bedroom upstairs, next to Toby's. She liked knowing that he was in the next room, that she wasn't all alone in the house. She'd retained more than a little of the superstition bred into children who grew up in the ghost-haunted South, and she half expected to wake up one night very soon and find the shadow of her mother standing beside her bed, demanding to know why she hadn't done enough, hadn't saved her from death.

She *had* done enough. She knew that. Everyone had reassured her that it had been Lula Tayhill's time to go. Nothing Emmeline could have done would have prevented it. Still, she sometimes found herself wondering if perhaps she had in some way hastened her mother's departure from the world, if not at the actual hour of her death, then at some point long before.

She'd promised herself that she wouldn't think about things left unsaid. It wouldn't do either of them any good now. Her mother was gone, and she was left with what memories she had. Good or bad, they were hers to hold on to.

She looked at the bedside table. She might as well start there, she thought. On it was a magazine and a small tape player, given to her mother by Toby so that she could listen to music when she felt too tired to do anything else. Emmeline picked it up and started to put it in the box. Then she hesitated. What, she wondered, had her mother chosen to listen to?

She placed the earphones in her ears and hit the play button. She was shocked to hear her own voice filling her head. It was her singing "The Man I Love." But when had she ever recorded herself singing that? She couldn't remember doing so.

She fast-forwarded through the tape and hit play again. This time she was talking. "I learned *that* one when I was a little girl," she said. An audience laughed. Then Emmeline broke into "Sweeping Cobwebs Off the Moon."

She turned the tape off and popped it out of the player. There was no label, nothing to tell her what it was or where it had come from.

"I made it."

Emmeline looked up and saw Toby standing in the doorway.

"I taped you singing at Jackie's," Toby said. "A few weeks ago. Your mother told me she'd never heard you sing. I couldn't get her down there, so I figured this was the next best thing. I'm sorry I didn't tell you. I wasn't sure you'd want me to do it."

Emmeline shook her head. "No," she said. "I'm not mad." She hesitated, then asked, "Did she like it?"

Toby nodded. "She listened to it all the time when you weren't here," he said, smiling at the memory. "She said you reminded her of Judy Garland."

Emmeline gave a little laugh. "I'm sure I did," she said. She looked at Toby. "Thank you," she said.

"I thought she should hear you," Toby replied. "That's all. Do you want some help in here?"

"That would be nice," Emmeline said. "Why don't you start with the closet?"

As Toby opened the closet and began removing Lula's clothes, Emmeline inserted the tape back into the player and carefully wrapped the headphones around it. The sadness she'd been feeling had lifted somewhat. Maybe she hadn't been able to talk to her mother, but thanks to Toby, she'd at least been able to share some of who she'd become. If that was as close as the two of them ever got to understanding each other, it would have to be enough.

"The clothes can all go right in the garbage," she said, looking at the pile Toby was making on the end of the bed. "I don't think *anyone* would want them."

"How about this?" Toby asked. "It was underneath her sweaters." Emmeline looked at what he was holding. It was a shoe box.

"What's in it?" she asked.

Toby opened the lid and peered inside. "Holy shit," he said.

Emmeline, wondering what her mother could have put in the shoe box that would elicit such a reaction from Toby, reached out for it. "Let me see," she said. "And please don't tell me that it's naked pictures of my father. My cousin Laura-Ann found a stack of those when her daddy died, and it wasn't pretty."

"It's not naked pictures," Toby said as he handed her the box.

Emmeline looked inside. The box was filled with money, stacks of bills wrapped in rubber bands. On top of them was a piece of paper, folded in thirds. Ignoring the money for a moment, Emmeline removed the paper and opened it. It was a letter, written in a spidery but firm hand.

"'Dear Mason/Emmeline,'" she read out loud. "'Your mother asked me to pack this for her. Petey don't know about it, and you aren't to tell him. This is for you. Let that son of a bitch have the house. It's ready to fall into the ground anyway. If you're reading this, I'm guessing your mother is dead, which grieves me. She was a good friend. But you still have a lot of life left to live, and that's what this is for. Your mother never could say it very well, but she loved you. I heard it in her voice when she talked about you. Sometimes people just can't say what they should while they're alive. Take care of yourself, and come visit one of these days. We have a lot to talk about. Your friend, Binny Labordeaux.'"

Emmeline set the letter down and looked at the shoe box again. She picked up one of the bundles of bills and thumbed through it. They were all twenties.

"How much is there?" asked Toby.

Emmeline removed the rubber band from the stack of bills and counted. There were fifty in the stack. "Fifty times twenty," she said. "What is that?"

"A thousand," answered Toby after doing the sum in his head.

Emmeline emptied the box onto the bed and began counting. "There are fifty bundles," she said when she was done.

Toby thought for a few seconds. "That's fifty thousand," he said, his mouth falling open. "Fifty thousand dollars."

Emmeline stared at the pile of bills. Fifty thousand dollars? Where had her mother gotten such a huge sum of money? Why hadn't she used it on herself, or to repair the house when it needed it? She couldn't believe it.

"Mama," she said aloud, "I don't know why, and I don't know how, but thank you."

"What are you going to do with it?" Toby asked.

Emmeline looked at him, a smile spreading across her face. "I'm going to live my life," she said. "Thanks to my mama, I'm going to live my life."

CHAPTER 56

Nothing happened.

Reilly stared into his coffee. The cream he'd just poured in was swirling around in gentle eddies, turning the coffee a milky brown. *Carly Simon was wrong,* he thought as he stirred. *It doesn't look like clouds at all. It looks like mud.* He sighed. Nothing happened.

You can't even turn gay right, he admonished himself.

He'd tried. He'd gone to Josh's house. He'd kissed him again. He'd taken off his clothes and gotten into Josh's bed.

And then he'd fallen asleep.

The next thing he knew, it was morning. He'd awakened to the sound of someone moving around in the other room. It had taken him a moment to realize that the person making the noise wasn't Donna and that he was in a strange bed. Then, all at once, it had all come back to him. For a brief, wonderful moment, he believed that he'd actually spent the night with Josh. But when he couldn't remember anything after getting into bed, he started to worry.

He didn't want to think about the rest: the way Josh had looked at him when he emerged from the bedroom, the pounding in his head as the beer took its revenge, and especially not the revelation that Josh had returned from the bathroom to discover him dead asleep and had covered him with a blanket before going to spend the rest of *his* night on the couch. Reilly had listened to it all with a growing sense of embarrassment, and although Josh had been as kind as could be expected under the circumstances, Reilly had gotten the distinct impression that Josh wouldn't be terribly disappointed when he took his leave.

He'd done so as soon as possible, mumbling an apology and walking out into the too-bright morning. Squinting and cursing himself for having drunk so much the night before, he'd walked home quickly, praying that no one would see him plodding along the road unshaven, tired, and decidedly wrinkled. Thankfully, fortune had been with him, and he'd arrived home with only his own disapproval to shoulder.

That was more than enough. In the four days since the incident, he had beaten himself up constantly. He was a bad person. Worse, he was a liar. But whom was he lying to: Donna, Josh, or himself? That was the question he was having a hard time answering. He'd gone to Josh's house for a reason, he knew that. But had it been to prove something, to disprove something, or something else entirely?

He'd *wanted* to go there. He admitted that. He'd wanted to go to Josh. But for what? Simply to indulge in the fantasies he'd been having, to see if they were simply passing curiosity? If he wanted to do that, he could just return to the parking lot, or roam the dunes at night. He could do it and remain faceless, unknown, safe. Instead, he'd gone to Josh, someone who wasn't at all faceless or safe, someone who knew him.

And if all he wanted was to feel another man's hand on his dick, or to take him in his mouth, why couldn't he just get it over with? He wasn't afraid of the sex, at least not much. It was something deeper than that he feared, the passion behind the act itself. It was the desire he was terrified of, the *need*. The sex could be over and done with quickly, but the need wouldn't go away. He understood that now, although he had fought the truth of it for a long time.

"Hey, buddy. Enjoying your last days as a single man?"

Reilly looked up from his coffee. Parks Danner had taken the stool next to him at the counter. His dog, an old mutt named Scudder who looked as if someone had cobbled him together from scraps of retriever, shepherd, and bear, settled with a tired sigh at his feet, defying all public health laws with an air of decided indifference. Parks and Scudder were regular fixtures at the coffee shop, and Maggie, the waitress, knew what both wanted without asking.

"Coffee for you," she said as she placed a mug in front of Parks. "And scrambled eggs for you," she added, putting a bowl beside the dog.

"Thanks, Mags," said Parks as Scudder lifted his snout and partook of his breakfast. "You're the best."

Maggie sniffed. "If only you tipped as well as your dog does," she joked.

Parks turned his attention once more to Reilly. "So, when's the big day?"

"Week from Saturday," answered Reilly. Although he wasn't in the mood for questions, he was glad to see Parks. In his early sixties, Parks was one of the town's more eccentric characters. A postman for thirty-two years, he'd given it up to run the town library. Now he spent his days cataloging books, organizing the children's hour, and chasing horny teenagers out from among the stacks when their makeout sessions ran past what he considered a decent time. He'd become something of a legend a few years previous when, confronted by a woman who demanded that certain books be removed from the library's shelves due to their "questionable moral character," Parks had chased her out of the building brandishing a copy of *Ulysses* and yelling, "It ain't *words* you need to be afraid of!"

"Week from Saturday," Parks repeated, as if filing the information away for later use.

"You're invited, you know," Reilly told him. He had addressed and stamped Parks's invitation himself.

Parks nodded. "Just checking," he replied. "Not so good with dates anymore."

Reilly smiled to himself. He knew this was all part of Parks's old man act. The truth was, he was probably sharper than most of the people a third his age.

"You bringing a date, Parks?" asked Reilly. "Invite's for two, you know."

Parks turned a watery blue eye to Maggie, who was refilling Reilly's cup. "Hear that, Mags?" he said. "You busy a week from Saturday?"

"Sorry," Maggie said. "I got my grandkids coming in. Besides, last time you took me dancing I almost broke a leg, remember?"

Parks laughed. "Guess I'll be coming solo," he told Reilly. "Unless you don't mind Scudder coming. He could use a bath anyway."

"I don't think Donna would be too happy about that," Reilly answered. "Sorry, Scud," he added as the dog looked up at him and wagged his tail sadly.

"Couple of old bachelors, aren't we, boy?" Parks said to his dog.

Reilly sipped his coffee. Something about Parks's statement made him think. Had Parks ever been married? He'd known the man his whole life, but couldn't recall ever seeing or hearing about a Mrs. Danner.

"Were you ever married, Parks?" he asked.

Parks shook his head. "Nope," he said simply.

Why not? Reilly wondered. How could someone go his entire life being alone? It didn't seem natural to him. People were supposed to pair up, find someone to love and get old with. But Parks had no one except his dog.

Then another question crossed his mind: Was Parks maybe queer? Was that why he'd never married? He tried to picture Parks with an other man. He couldn't really see it, but you never knew.

"I was engaged once," Parks said, not looking at Reilly as he spoke. "Regina was her name. Most beautiful girl you ever saw."

Parks's voice had changed as he spoke, softening and taking on a gentleness that was unexpected. Reilly waited for him to continue.

"She died," Parks said simply. "Before we could get married."

He stopped, leaving Reilly wondering how Regina had died but not wanting to ask. Parks seemed to consider the story over at that point, and went back to drinking his coffee. Reilly, unsure of what to say, poured some sugar into his cup, even though the coffee was too sweet already.

"I'm sorry," he said finally.

Parks nodded his acceptance of the condolences. "For a long time I thought maybe it would happen again," he said. "Falling in love, I mean." He paused, taking another sip of coffee. "I guess sometimes you really do only get one chance. Important thing is to take it while it's there."

Scudder, finished with his eggs, sat up and whined softly. Parks set his cup down. "There's my alarm clock," he said as he fished a dollar out of his pocket and laid it on the counter. "Time to go open up."

He put his hand on Reilly's shoulder. "Don't feel sorry for me," he said unexpectedly. "I don't. Just be thankful for what you've got."

He and Scudder left Reilly sitting alone at the counter, contemplating his now-empty coffee cup and thinking about what the old man had said. He knew Parks had been telling him to be thankful for Donna and their relationship. But Reilly was thinking about something else. He was thinking about chances that were gone, opportunities that for whatever reason slipped away when someone hesitated, afraid of taking them. Parks had lost the love of his life to sickness, accident, or something else out of his control. But what about if it *had* been within his control? What if he had been given the opportunity to change the situation?

He would have taken it, Reilly told himself.

"What else can I get you?"

Reilly looked up at Maggie. She was clearing Parks's cup, neatly pocketing the dollar he'd left for her as she swept away his spoon and napkin.

"I'm good," Reilly told her. "Thanks."

"Sad, isn't it," Maggie said as she picked up his cup. "To have something that close and then lose it."

The waitress left to take the dirty dishes to the kitchen. Reilly watched her go. Standing up, he reached into the pocket of his jeans and pulled out some bills.

Thanks for the tip, he thought as he laid the money on the counter.

CHAPTER 57

"That's a big yes for Rebecca Wilmont and a resounding no for Randi Colburn."

Marly looked at the list in front of her, which contained the name of every instructor who had taught at the Arts House during the summer session. She was engaged in the annual end-of-summer ritual she'd come to call the Weeding. Classes would run through Labor Day, but on a reduced scale, so she was free to start wading through the piles of paperwork that came with finishing up another successful season. Many of the instructors were already finished as well. Some had chosen to remain in their rent-free accommodations for a few weeks of rest. Others had already left or were leaving shortly.

In the meantime, Marly was going through the list, putting stars beside some names and crossing others off. The scratch-outs would be added to the secret list she kept (but always denied keeping) of artists to be avoided at all costs. She shared this roster with a select few of her counterparts, those responsible for inviting visiting lecturers to artsy enclaves such as the Iowa Writers Workshop, Jacob's Pillow, and the Omega Institute. It was a favor they did for one another, designed to help preserve one another's sanity in a world known for its distinct lack of mental stability.

This year's crop of guests was almost equally divided between yeses and nos. Currently, Marly was holding her pen above the name of Brody Nicholson. She adored the man's books, but she'd seldom seen such unenthusiastic reviews for an instructor. Six people had dropped out of his classes, two demanding refunds in exchange for not suing the Arts House for contributing to emotional cruelty. Reluctantly, she put a red line through him, increasing the nos' score by one and putting them in the lead.

"Knock, knock."

Marly looked up from her desk. Garth was standing in the doorway.

"You busy?" he asked.

"Just ruining a few careers," answered Marly. "Nothing urgent."

Garth gave her a confused look.

"I'm reading student evaluations," she explained.

"Anyone say anything interesting?"

Marly sifted through the pile of forms on her desk. "Let's see," she said, selecting one. "One of Perry Lawrence's poetry students said that his teaching was, and I quote, 'as engaging as watching the last presidential election results.'"

"Is that good or bad?" asked Garth.

"The sad thing is, I can't tell," replied Marly. "Oh, and here's another of my favorites. 'Taney Fuller is an amazing songwriter. Too bad he's not much of a person.' I think that one definitely qualifies as bad."

Garth winced. "Harsh," he said. "I hate to think what they wrote about me."

"All raves," Marly informed him. "They can't wait to have you back next year."

"And how do *you* feel about that idea?" he said.

"I'd love to have you back," Marly said. "Unfortunately, I have to select new people next year, so if you do come back, it will have to be as my personal guest."

Garth laughed. "Somehow I don't think your husband would enjoy having me around the house all summer," he said.

Marly smiled. "Probably not," she answered. "So, why are you still standing in my doorway instead of coming in?"

"Ah," said Garth. "Because I have something for you." He retreated to the hall and returned with two large, flat packages wrapped in brown paper.

"What are those?" Marly asked, intrigued.

"Going-away presents," Garth said, leaning the packages against her desk. "Open them."

Marly stood and came around to the front of her desk. She ran her hand over the first of the packages.

"Just open it," said Garth, sighing.

Marly pulled at the tape that sealed the package shut, then folded the paper back. Underneath was a large framed photograph, about three feet square. Marly looked at it and gave a little laugh.

"It's one of the photos Nellie took of me," she said, looking at the image of herself lifting a nutcracker into the air and beaming up at it. "I look—"

"Happy," said Garth, cutting her off. "Beautiful and radiant and happy."

Marly looked at the photograph again. She did look happy, she saw, like a little girl having one of her dreams come true.

"Open the other one," Garth instructed.

Marly placed the photograph to one side and tackled the second package. Free of its paper and tape, it, too, revealed a photograph. It had been taken by Garth. It caught her in the process of working on the portrait of him. The painting loomed in front of her, only a rough sketch covering the canvas. Marly was staring at it with intense concentration. Her brush was poised in the air, and there were smears of ink on her hands.

"Look at your eyes," Garth said quietly.

Marly nodded. She *was* looking at her eyes. She recognized the emotion in them. It was joy. Joy in creation. Joy in doing something she loved and had missed terribly.

"That's how I'll remember you," Garth said.

"You sound like you're leaving," said Marly.

Garth nodded. "I am," he told her. "I fly out later tonight. I got a call to go on the road with the White Stripes."

"The who?"

"Some new band," Garth said. "Supposedly they're bringing rock and roll back to life."

"What happened to taking it easy?" Marly asked him, sounding more than a little like an anxious mother. "What about the MS?"

"It will still be there," said Garth, grinning. "Besides, it's only for two weeks. Then I can go shopping for a rocking chair and a pipe."

Marly nodded absentmindedly. A sadness had come over her, the feeling that something very important was leaving her before she was ready. "I haven't finished it," she said suddenly. "The portrait. I wanted to have it done before you left."

Garth put his hands on her shoulders. "I'll come back for it," he said. "Or you can bring it to me in New York when it's done."

Marly felt tears forming in her eyes. "Okay," she said, staring at his shoes.

"Hey," said Garth softly. "Look at me."

Marly looked up.

"It's not like I'm breaking up with you," said Garth with mock seriousness.

Marly laughed, causing tears to run down her face. She gave Garth a hug, wrapping her arms around him and holding tightly for a long time. When she released him she sighed and wiped her eyes.

"I needed this," she said. "You. I needed you, and this summer, and this." She indicated the photos. "All of it."

"Even if we didn't actually have an affair?" asked Garth. "Because you know, it's still not too late. I have a couple of hours before my flight leaves."

"Sorry," said Marly. "I'm a married woman."

"Don't say I didn't offer," Garth said. He looked at his watch. "I should go," he said.

Marly stepped forward and gave him another hug. "Be safe," she said. "And call me when you're done playing rock star."

"I have fillings that are older than these kids," said Garth, giving her a final squeeze before letting go. "I'll be lucky if I can stay awake for the entire show."

"I think you'll manage," remarked Marly.

Garth looked at her in silence for a moment, then raised his hand. "Bye, Mrs. Prentis," he said.

"Bye, Mr. Ambrose," answered Marly.

Garth turned and left her office. For a moment she almost ran after him for a final hug, a final word. But she made herself stay where she was. Garth would be back, she knew.

She looked at the photos he'd given her. There was a spot on the wall across from her desk, a blank expanse that had been waiting for just the right thing to hang there. She went to the supply cabinet and located a hammer and some picture hangers. There were, she thought as she returned to her office, a great many benefits to working for an arts organization.

Half an hour and several misplaced nails later, the two photographs were hanging side by side. Marly stepped back and looked at them. She'd always been slightly irritated by people who hung photographs or, worse, paintings of themselves in their own spaces. But she was pleased by the photos of herself. They captured parts of her she wanted to see more of, the parts that took risks, that weren't afraid to look foolish, to fail.

It had taken almost having an affair with Garth to remind her that these parts of herself still existed. She'd needed that shock, that feeling of standing on the very edge of possibility, to bring her back to life. It hadn't been about sex at all; it had simply been about waking herself up. *Although the sex probably would have been amazing,* she thought idly as she returned to her desk and resumed looking over the evaluations.

"Hey there."

She looked up, half expecting to see that Garth had come back. Instead, she was surprised to see her husband and daughter framed in the doorway.

"You're back," she said. Drew had been in Europe for three weeks on business. He wasn't due back for another two days, and his presence in her office was unexpected and, given that her mind was crowded with thoughts of Garth at the moment, slightly unsettling.

"How long can you stay in Paris?" said Drew. "It's filled with French people."

Marly laughed. She and Drew had spent their honeymoon in Paris, and he'd first used the line then to describe the city to friends and family upon their return. It had since become an in-joke, a way to describe any particularly unpleasant social gathering, place of business, or travel destination.

"I'm sorry to hear it," Marly replied.

"Don't be," Drew said. "It means Chloe and I can take you to dinner and a movie. Sound good?"

Marly looked at her husband and daughter. She hadn't seen much of either during the past few months. Drew's hair was longer, she noticed, and he'd put on a little weight. It looked good on him, she thought. Chloe, impatient as ever to be doing something other than waiting for her parents to get going, was chewing her gum loudly. They would have to have a little chat about that later.

Behind them hung the photos of herself. They floated above Chloe's head and just over Drew's shoulder, reminding her of a painting she'd seen once at the Metropolitan Museum of Art in New York. Visiting on a rainy afternoon, she'd turned a corner in the third-floor gallery and stopped short. Covering most of one entire wall was a painting depicting Joan of Arc. Behind her hovered three visions, angels come to seek her help and inspire her to bravery.

What had struck Marly most about the painting was how Joan was depicted reaching forward, despite the angels being behind her. It was as if their very presence was enough to fill her with inspiration. Because of them, Joan was able to reach for something unseen, something she knew awaited her if she was brave enough to trust, to risk failure by setting foot on the path even though she had no idea what lay in store for her.

Drew and Chloe were hardly Marly's ideas of angels. They were often demanding, sometimes oblivious, and generally maddening. But maybe that was what she needed. Maybe they were the voices telling her to reach for the next thing, whatever it was, to stretch her hands out toward the unknown while keeping her feet firmly planted in something real—home, family, the day-to-day ups and downs that sometimes seemed overwhelming.

And Garth? There were, she reminded herself, *three* angels in the painting. He'd helped her to see that there was still a great deal of passion inside her, and also that she didn't need to go too far to find an outlet for it.

She gathered up the evaluation forms and put them into a drawer, along with her hit list. "Yes," she said, standing up and going to join her daughter and her husband. "Dinner and a movie sounds *very* good."

CHAPTER 58

"Oh, shit," Josh said as he peered out the window. "Here we go again."

Reilly was walking up the driveway, and he was heading for the front door. Josh quickly pulled the curtain back into place and stepped away from the glass. *Maybe if I hide,* he thought vaguely, trying to figure out a way to avoid talking to Reilly. *Or just don't answer the door.*

The whole Reilly thing was just way too weird for him. Weird and frustrating. He almost preferred it when Reilly was ignoring him.

"Josh?" Reilly's voice startled him, as did the firm rapping on the door. "Are you there?"

Josh held his breath, as if letting the air in his lungs escape would be so audible that it would betray his presence.

"Josh?" Reilly called out, again knocking on the door. "I need to talk to you."

If I were home, *don't you think I would already have heard you pounding?* Josh thought irritably. *You sound like the big bad wolf trying to knock the three pigs' house down.*

Reilly knocked a third time. Josh exhaled with a groan. *Here we go again,* he thought as he went to the door and opened it.

Reilly, his hand raised to pound on the door again, paused in mid-knock. He looked at Josh with a surprised expression, as if he'd finally resigned himself to the fact that Josh was in fact not at home.

"Hey," he said.

Josh nodded silently. He wasn't going to make this easy for Reilly. Not after everything that had already happened. *Or not happened,* he thought as he waited for Reilly to explain what he was doing there.

"Can I come in?" Reilly asked.

Josh hesitated. Part of him wanted to send Reilly away. But Reilly looked so hopeful that he couldn't do it.

"As long as you don't fall asleep in my bed again," he said.

Reilly followed him inside, where they stood in the living room. Reilly put his hands in his pockets and looked at the floor as Josh waited for him to say what he had to say. For several minutes they waited in silence, until finally Reilly spoke.

"I'm supposed to be marrying Donna," he began, then stopped, as if unsure of how to proceed.

"But you wondered what it would be like with a guy," Josh said. "I get it. It's okay. You're not the first straight guy to want to try it once."

Reilly shook his head. "It's not like that," he said.

"Really?" Josh asked. "Then how is it? Because so far you've kissed me and run away and fallen asleep in my bed without actually doing anything. I'm sorry, but I really don't have time to be your experiment. Go. Get married. Be happy."

"That's just it," Reilly said. "I'm not happy. I thought I was. I thought this was what I wanted. But then you . . ." He stopped, the sentence unfinished.

"You what?" Josh said. "Please don't say you fell in love with me and everything changed, because that's just bullshit."

"No," Reilly replied shortly. "I'm not in love with you."

Josh looked at him, slightly wounded. Despite his speech, he'd half expected Reilly to pour out some misguided declaration of love. Wasn't that what confused straight guys were *supposed* to do in these situations? Weren't they supposed to get all dramatic and tragic?

"I'm not in love with you," Reilly repeated, as if trying to hammer the point home. "I haven't known you long enough to be in love with you."

Josh looked away. "I'm sorry," he said. "I didn't mean that. I shouldn't have—"

"But I want to get to know you," Reilly interrupted.

Josh stopped speaking.

"I don't know how to do this," Reilly said, running a hand through his hair. "Fuck!"

"What are you saying exactly?" Josh asked carefully.

Reilly took a deep breath. "I'm gay," he said. "I've always been gay, I guess. I just thought marrying Donna was what I was supposed to do. Everybody wants me to."

"But now you don't want to?" Josh asked.

Reilly shook his head. "No," he said. "I don't."

Josh sat on the arm of the couch. "I'm glad I'm not you," he said before he could stop himself.

"What the hell do I do?" Reilly asked. "How do I tell Donna I can't marry her because I'm a fag?"

"First of all, I wouldn't use the word *fag,*" Josh said. "It's bad PR."

"My family is going to freak," Reilly continued, ignoring him. "Her family is going to freak. *Everybody* is going to freak." He was pacing back and forth worriedly. He stopped suddenly and looked at Josh. "I can't do this," he said. "I can't do it."

"Oh," Josh said, "so you're just going to marry her and think about guys every time you fuck her and be miserable?"

Reilly nodded. "How bad can it be?" he said.

Josh laughed despite himself. Reilly watched him for a moment, looking wounded, then burst out laughing himself.

"I sound like an idiot," he said when he regained his composure.

Josh nodded. "You won't get any argument out of me about that," he said. "But I sounded pretty much the same way when I was thinking about coming out to my family, so don't feel bad."

Reilly laughed again. "Coming out," he said. "I can't even believe I'm thinking those words."

"Not that it's any of my business," Josh said, "but have you ever actually *been* with a guy?"

"Not since . . ." Reilly began. "No," he said. "Not really."

Josh contemplated this information. "You mean I would have been your first time?"

Reilly nodded as Josh grinned. *I would have been his first time,* he thought happily. Then he realized that Reilly was looking at him, and he tried to sound serious.

"Never mind what your family or Donna's family want," he said. "What do *you* want?"

"I want to find out who I am," Reilly said. "What kind of life I could make with someone I love. Someone I *really* love," he emphasized. "Not someone I'm with to make other people happy."

"Then it sounds like you're going to have to make some tough decisions," Josh told him. "And soon."

"I know," Reilly said. "I just don't know how to start."

"Well—" Josh started to say. He was cut off by another knock on the door.

Who else is coming over to come out to me? he wondered as he went to answer the door.

"Hi," Doug said when Josh stepped outside. "Remember me?"

"What are you doing here?" Josh asked.

"I brought you some stuff," Doug said, holding up a cardboard box.

"Thanks," Josh said cooly.

"Can I bring it inside?" Doug asked, nodding toward the door.

Josh hesitated. He didn't want Doug coming in. But he also didn't want him to think it was because he had a trick inside. He wasn't going to give Doug any ammunition he could use against him in post-breakup conversations with mutual friends.

"Okay," he said finally. "But just for a minute."

He went into the cottage, followed closely by Doug. When Doug saw Reilly, he stopped.

"Oh. I didn't know you had *company.*" He emphasized the word, imbuing it with all kinds of meanings that Josh understood immediately.

"Reilly is a friend," he said. "Reilly, this is Doug."

"Doug," Reilly repeated, as if the name were familiar but he'd forgotten why. "Oh," he said. "Doug."

"I see my reputation precedes me," Doug said, giving a little laugh. "So, have you two been fucking long?"

Josh looked at him, stunned. "What did you say?" he said.

"You two," Doug repeated, nodding first at Reilly and then at Josh. "Have you been fucking long? I mean, did you wait until after you broke up with me, or was he just the reason you ended our relationship?"

"*I* ended the relationship?" Josh said. "If I recall, you were the one who cheated on me."

"Oh, come on," Doug replied. "It was one time. I told you that. Nobody else thinks it was a big deal."

"Nobody else was with you for eight years," Josh shot back. "And we both know it wasn't just one time."

"Grow up, Josh," Doug said. "There is no happily ever after in real life. You're not going to find a perfect knight in shining armor."

"I didn't ask you to be a knight," Josh said quietly. "I just asked you to be a man."

"I tried to give you a second chance," Doug said. "But I guess you think you've found something better." He gave Reilly a withering look.

"I'll put the rest of your stuff in storage," Doug said, setting the box he was carrying on the floor. "You can arrange to pick it up."

He turned to Reilly. "I'm sure the two of you will be *very* happy," he said smugly as he prepared to leave.

"Just one thing before you go," said Reilly quietly.

Doug turned around. "What's that?" he asked.

Reilly's fist flew through the air and landed squarely on Doug's jaw. Josh watched as his ex-lover staggered backward, his hand clutching his face, and then fell to the floor. He lay there, groaning, as Reilly looked at Josh.

"Sorry," Reilly said.

Josh looked at Doug, who was trying to stand up. His lip was cut, and blood spotted his face.

"Don't be," Josh told Reilly.

Doug had gotten to his feet. He looked at Reilly and started to speak.

"Just go," Josh told him.

Doug looked as if he might still say something. Then, without another word, he turned and left, slamming the door behind him.

"I hope I didn't just make more trouble for you," Reilly said.

Josh shook his head. "What's he going to do?" he said. "Keep all my Armistead Maupin signed first editions for himself?"

"Who?" Reilly asked.

"It's a gay thing," Josh told him. "You wouldn't understand."

"You'll have to teach me," Reilly remarked.

Josh looked at him for a long moment. "I'd be happy to," he said.

CHAPTER 59

"To us."

"To us."

Reid and Ty clicked glasses. Reid took a drink of his wine and set the glass down.

"Well, honey, how was your day at work?" he said, channeling June Cleaver.

Ty laughed. "Well, my boss is a jerk and that new secretary tried to feel me up in the copy room again," he replied.

"The hussy," Reid said.

"It does sort of feel like we're married now, doesn't it?" Ty said as he cut a piece from the steak Reid had removed from the grill just minutes earlier.

"Coming out on national television will do that, I guess," replied Reid.

"Now I know how Ellen and Anne must have felt," Ty said, chewing.

"I think only the space aliens who control her brain know how Anne felt," said Reid. "As for Ellen, I don't think she had any idea what was going to hit her when she did it."

"And we do?" asked Ty.

Reid shrugged. "More or less," he said. "Why, are the people on the set giving you a hard time?"

"Not at all," answered Ty. "You know, apart from the 'Which one of you is the wife?' questions."

Reid stopped eating and looked at him, horrified.

"Just kidding," said Ty. "Everyone has been really supportive. It's the press that's making me nuts."

"Which reminds me," Reid said. "Violet called today. The *Advocate* wants us on their cover in two weeks. I told them I'd have to talk to you first."

Ty made a face. "Do we have to?" he asked.

"They are the largest gay news magazine in the country," Reid said. "It says so right on the cover."

Ty laughed. "I know," he said. "But if they feature us, doesn't that mean they'll have to cut an article about Melissa?"

"Be nice," Reid admonished him. "It's not every day the hottest actor in America comes out."

"That's because we're all afraid *The Advocate* will interview us and ask us a bunch of idiotic questions," replied Ty. He sat up and affected a serious tone. "So, Ty," he said, "are there any other gay actors whose names you can share with us? Will you be doing a full-frontal nude scene in your next film? Do you know Cher?"

"You're going to hell," said Reid, laughing. "A lot of people read them."

"Maybe so," said Ty. "They're still colossal ass-kissers."

"You have to talk to the gay rags," Reid said. "If you don't, you'll look homophobic."

"Thank you, Larry Kramer," said Ty.

Reid gave him a look. "I'm serious," he said. "This is a great opportunity to show that you're still confident about your place in Hollywood."

"But I'm *not,*" Ty said. "How many offers have come in since I came out?"

"It's been a *week,*" said Reid firmly. "And you've gotten tons of press. All of it pretty positive, I might add."

Ty nodded. "I know," he said. "But who knows what the suits are saying about me?"

"I'm one of the suits, remember?" Reid told him. He watched Ty, who continued to eat in silence. "Hey, are you sorry you did this?"

Ty looked up. "No," he said. "I'm not sorry. I'm just a little, you know, worried."

"It's going to be fine," Reid reassured him. "And we're in this together, remember?"

Ty smiled. "How could I forget?" he said sweetly.

Reid rolled his eyes. "Fuck you," he said playfully. "Use that face when you're interviewed and you'll be replaced in no time."

"Ooh," Ty said. "Just what I've always wanted to be, the *Advocate*'s celebrity of the moment."

"Well, Cher won't be around forever," Reid said thoughtfully.

"Speaking of girls of the moment," Ty said. "Any sign of Devin?"

Reid shook his head. "Not a peep," he said. "I think we've probably seen the last of her."

"Don't count on it," said Ty. "That one has *plans*. She'll probably turn up on an episode of celebrity *Survivor*. She and John Wayne Bobbitt will be the last two and she'll win by flashing her beaver at the jury right before they vote."

"I didn't need that image in my head while I'm trying to eat," Reid said as he stabbed at his meat. "Anyway, I feel a little sorry for her. She's sort of pathetic, really."

"Like O.J. is pathetic," Ty remarked. "The girl is poison."

"And ninety-nine percent of the people in Hollywood aren't?" said Reid.

"She and Raymacher are a perfect match," Ty continued. "Too bad he's queer. Then again, she could always use a strap-on."

"You're charming tonight," Reid said. "Very charming."

"Charming enough to get you into bed?" Ty asked.

"If I have any more wine you will be," Reid answered.

Ty picked up the bottle and refilled Reid's half-empty glass. "Drink up," he said.

They ate for a few minutes in silence, enjoying the last of the sun before it returned to the sea. The heat of the afternoon was dissolving into the cool of evening, and the house had taken on an almost dream-like quality, as if it existed apart from everything else in the world, protected in its golden bubble. Reid wished he could fix time and stay there, not forever but long enough to enjoy time alone with his lover.

"Have you thought about what we're going to do when we get back to LA?" he asked Ty cautiously. It was a subject that had been on his mind for a while, but he hadn't raised it with Ty until now.

"Can't we just stay here?" Ty replied, sounding irritated.

"Not if we're going to keep working in the film industry," replied Reid.

"Then let's not," Ty said. "Let's get out."

"And do what?" asked Reid.

"I don't know," Ty said. "Run a B and B. We could do that." He looked at Reid hopefully.

Reid began laughing. "Nice try," he said. "You almost had me."

Ty grinned. "Just seeing if I still have it," he said. "But you thought about it for a minute, didn't you?"

Reid shrugged. "It would be fun for about a day," he said. "Then we'd want to pack our bags and get on the first flight to LAX."

"You're right," Ty admitted. "As much as I hate the place sometimes, and the people in it, it's still home."

"Which brings us back to my original question," said Reid. "What are we going to do when we get back?"

"I assume you mean about living arrangements," said Ty, spearing a green bean and biting it in half. "Shacking up."

"It had crossed my mind," Reid answered.

"First we have to get a few things cleared up," Ty said seriously.

Reid looked at him quizzically. "Like what?"

"No commitment ceremony," said Ty. "I think they're dumb."

"Okay," Reid said. "What else?"

"Our anniversary will be the day we first said 'I love you,' not the day we first fucked."

"Very romantic," Reid said. "Agreed. But I'm not sure I remember the exact date."

"Sunday, May twenty-fifth," Ty said instantly, earning a surprised look from Reid.

"I wrote it down," explained Ty.

"May twenty-fifth it is then," said Reid. "Is there more?"

"We're getting a dog," said Ty, ticking the items off on his fingers. "A big one, not one of those little yappy things Joan Rivers has. You have to watch baseball games with me, if one of us goes on location we call every night before bed, we do Thanksgiving at home, don't ever call me 'pumpkin,' and don't interrupt me while *Buffy the Vampire Slayer* is on."

"Okay," Reid replied. "And *you* don't drink milk from the carton."

"Done," Ty said. "Man, you make a lousy agent. You agreed to every one of my demands."

"It's because you're so adorable," Reid said. "Pumpkin."

"That's grounds for divorce," Ty informed him sternly. "Say it again and I'll have my lawyer all over your happy ass."

"I love it when you talk like rough trade," Reid said.

Ty gave him the finger. "And there's more where that came from," he said afterward.

"Young people," said Reid, shaking his head. "No respect for their elders."

"Careful," Ty said. "If you keep it up, I'll have to call you 'Daddy' when we do our Barbara Walters interview."

"Do it and I'll tell Jon Stewart how you jack off when you watch him," Reid retorted.

"Bitch," Ty snapped.

Their repartee was interrupted by a knock on the door.

"Please don't tell me it's Devin," Ty said.

"Relax," Reid told him. "It's Josh. He's bringing me the script. He finished it today."

Reid went to the door and let Josh in, giving him a big hug.

"How's the most famous gay couple in America?" Josh asked as he patted Ty on the shoulder and sat down at the table.

"Siegfried and Roy?" Ty said. "They looked okay when we saw them at the market."

"He's on a roll," Reid said to Josh. "Ignore him. How's the script?"

"Finished," Josh announced, dropping a bundle on the table and pushing it toward Reid.

"This might just be your next big hit," Reid told Ty as he picked up the script and flipped through the pages.

"It's still rough," said Josh hesitantly. "It will need a lot of work."

"Then you'll have to come visit us in LA to work on it," Reid said.

"Yeah," Ty agreed. "What *are* your plans, anyway? Heading back to Boston when the summer's over?"

Josh groaned. "I don't know," he said. "Things have gotten a little complicated."

"Sounds interesting," said Ty. "Tell us everything."

"I don't even know where to start," replied Josh. "It's a long story."

Reid picked up the bottle of wine and poured Josh a glass of it. "Start at the beginning," he said, handing it to him. "We have all night."

CHAPTER 60

"Negative."

"Congratulations!" Josh high-fived Toby, as if he'd just scored the winning run at the World Series. "Now just promise me you won't do anything like that again."

"Three-ways with guys I don't know?" Toby said.

"Three-ways with guys you don't know without using *rubbers*," Josh clarified.

"Don't worry," Toby replied. "That was a onetime thing. In fact, I've decided not to have sex at all for a while."

Josh regarded him suspiciously. "Are you sure you're gay?" he asked.

Toby laughed. "Oh, yeah," he said. "There's no question about that. I'm just not in any hurry is all. Besides, I can do it myself and do it better and faster." He lifted his hand and waggled his fingers.

"Man's best friend," Josh said, nodding.

They were sitting at a coffee shop on Commercial Street, catching up and watching the world go by. It was a gorgeous afternoon, and the street seemed even more crowded than usual, as if everyone was trying to squeeze in as much time as possible before the summer ran out.

"Look at them all," Toby said. "This place is a like a zoo of gay people."

"Just don't tease the bears," Josh remarked.

"I never imagined a place like this existed," said Toby. "I thought all the gay people lived in New York and San Francisco."

"They do," Josh told him. "They just come here to get away from New York and San Francisco."

"You know what I mean," Toby said. "I've met guys from all over the place working for Ben and Ted. This morning we had a couple check in from Knoxville. That's in *Tennessee,*" he added, as if perhaps Josh didn't know.

"There are gay people in Tennessee?" Josh said, pretending to be shocked. "Does the FBI know about this?"

"I'm serious," Toby protested. "When you live in a small town, like I did, you don't think there are any gay people around besides you. Being here makes me feel like I'm part of this big family or something."

"Yeah," Josh said, nodding. "A big *dysfunctional* family."

"You're bitter," Toby said. "It's not pretty."

Josh laughed. "I forget what it's like when you first discover that there are other gay people out there," he said. "But I know what you mean. I remember going to my first Gay Pride parade and feeling like I was in heaven."

"I can't wait for my first Pride parade," said Toby excitedly.

"You're *in* it," Josh said. "If it gets any more festive around here we'll have to build a float."

"I'll practice my wave," said Toby. "Should I go for the Queen Mother or the Miss America?" He waved stiffly, then with more flair.

"What *are* your plans?" Josh asked. "Are you just going to hang around here?"

"Ted and Ben said I could keep working for them," said Toby. "And Emmeline wants me to apply to some colleges."

"She's an amazing lady," Josh said.

Toby nodded. "She's been really good to me. I don't know what would have happened to me if I hadn't met her."

Josh hesitated before asking his next question. "Any word from your parents?"

Toby shook his head. "No," he said simply.

Josh didn't respond. He wanted to tell Toby that things would work out with his family. He knew that's what he was supposed to say. But maybe it wasn't true. Maybe sometimes parents didn't come around. He hoped Toby's would, but he wasn't going to make promises he couldn't come through on.

"My family is here," Toby said, looking out at the people walking by. "Emmeline. Ben. Ted. You." He looked at Josh. "That's all I need."

Josh smiled, not saying anything. He knew what Toby meant. He also knew that somewhere inside himself, Toby wanted his other family back. But that would take time, if it happened at all. In the meantime, he had a lot to learn about who he was and how he fit into the gay world.

"Long time no see."

Josh looked up to see Ryan standing in front of him.

"Hey," he said. "Where have you been?"

"Oh, I met this guy," Ryan replied. "You know."

"'Summer loving,'" said Josh. "'Had me a blast.'"

"'Summer loving, happened too fast,'" Ryan said, grinning.

"I take it the romance is over?" asked Josh.

Ryan sighed. "It's what I get for falling for a guy from Lubbock."

"Roped yourself a longhorn, eh?" Josh teased. "So, when are you heading back to the big city?"

"End of the week," said Ryan. "You?"

"I'm not sure," Josh told him.

"If you need a place to crash for a while, *mi casa es su casa.*"

"I'll let you know," Josh said. "Thanks."

"Well, here come the boys," Ryan said, looking over his shoulder. "I should go." He looked meaningfully at Toby.

"Later," Josh said.

Ryan departed, joining up with Al, Bart, Phil, Eric, and Aaron in the street. As they walked away, Bart, Phil, and Al waved at Josh and Toby, while Eric and Aaron looked steadfastly in the other direction.

"Do you think he really believes nothing happened?" Toby asked, his eyes on Eric.

"He knows," said Josh. "He just doesn't want to believe it."

Toby shook his head. "I don't get that," he said. "What's the point?"

Josh thought about his own recent brush with infidelity. There had been a moment, however brief, when he'd truly wanted to believe that Doug would never cheat on him again. The prospect of ending their relationship had terrified him. He wanted to maintain the security he'd enjoyed for eight years, the comfort he felt in coming home to the same man every night. He didn't want to be back out there, looking, alone, waiting. Maybe, he'd thought at the time, having the illusion of that security would be enough.

"He's scared," he said. "That's all."

Toby looked at him. "He's still an asshole."

"Yes," Josh said. "He is. And there are a lot of them out there."

"For some reason I thought gay people would be more supportive of one another," Toby said. "Boy, was I wrong."

"Being gay doesn't make us more morally right," Josh said. "It just means we have better taste."

"Some of us anyway," said Toby, nodding toward a man walking down the street wearing shorts that were way too small for his expansive stomach.

"Just pretend he's straight," Josh said. "It makes it easier to take."

Toby looked at his watch.

"Do you have an appointment?" Josh asked him. "That's the fourth time you've checked the time."

"I have to drive Emmeline somewhere," Toby answered.

"I heard she wasn't going to be performing for a couple of weeks," said Josh. "Is she okay?"

"She's fine," answered Toby. "She just needs a little break. You know, after her mother died and all. She's going to go away for a couple of days."

"That's the first time I've heard of anyone *leaving* P-Town for a vacation," said Josh. "But I guess this summer hasn't exactly been a holiday for her."

"Not really," Toby agreed. "First I came along, then her mother, then *my* parents. It's been rough. She needs some time off."

"Well, hopefully she'll come back a new woman," Josh said as he took out his wallet and removed some bills.

Toby nodded, smiling to himself as he stood up.

"Give her my best," Josh said. "And call me later this week. We'll see a movie or something."

Toby gave Josh a hug. "Thanks for the coffee," he said. "And everything else. I really appreciate it."

"Any time," said Josh.

"I hope you don't go," said Toby. "Back to Boston. I hope you stay."

Josh smiled. "Well, the jury is still out on that one. I'll let you know."

Toby put his sunglasses on and waved good-bye. Josh watched him join the stream of people moving along the street. Soon he was swallowed up in the sea of bodies, difficult to distinguish in the ever-moving mass of bodies in shorts and tank tops. Josh caught one final glimpse of his blond head before he turned a corner and disappeared completely.

Picking up the notebook he now carried with him almost every-where, Josh began walking in the opposite direction. He was going to the beach to write, or at least to think about writing. Now that he'd given up on his novel and discovered the joys of writing scripts, he found himself coming up with one idea after another. Most of them, he had to admit, were bad. But at least he was having them.

He was walking along, daydreaming, when he ran into someone rushing out of a store.

"Sorry," he said automatically before realizing that the body he'd just bumped into was Jackie's.

"Oh," Jackie said, picking up the bag she'd dropped. "Hi."

"I'm sorry I haven't been in in a while," Josh said. "I was working on the script with Reid, and then things with Reilly got all weird again."

"It's okay," Jackie told him. "I've been sort of crazy too."

Josh looked pointedly at her stomach. "So," he said, "when will we know?"

"Actually," Jackie replied, "we already do."

Josh suddenly felt dizzy. "We do?" he asked.

Jackie nodded. "I was going to tell you right away, but I did the test three more times just to make sure."

Josh stared at her, waiting for her to continue. Jackie stared back, not saying anything. Josh tried to repeat the question, but his mouth wouldn't form the words.

"Are you?" he finally blurted out at the same moment that Jackie said, "I am."

"That means you're . . ." Josh said, the words trailing off as he looked at her stomach again.

"Going to have a baby," said Jackie. "Yeah, I guess so. I did the fourth test this morning, and it was positive, just like all the other ones."

"I . . ." Josh said. "We . . ." He kept looking from Jackie's face to her belly.

"You can't see anything yet," said Jackie, noticing the direction of his gaze.

"Oh," Josh said slowly. "Wow."

"Are you okay?" Jackie inquired.

Josh nodded. "Sure," he replied. "I'm fine. I'm good. I'm going . . . to . . . be . . . a . . . dad."

He looked at Jackie again. There was a baby growing inside her. His baby. He was going to be a father. *Technically, you already are,* he told himself.

"You look like you need to sit down," said Jackie.

"Good idea," Josh said as the dizziness returned. He felt Jackie take his arm, and he took two steps before blackness overtook him and he felt himself falling.

CHAPTER 61

"There's a casserole in the refrigerator," Emmeline said. "All you have to do is put it in the oven."

Toby nodded. "Yes, Mom," he said. "And I promise to wash behind my ears when I take my bath."

"You watch it, young man," Emmeline said sharply. "Keep it up and there'll be no porn for you for a week." When Toby blushed she added, "Don't think I don't know what you hide in your sock drawer."

They were in a hospital room. Emmeline, wearing a pink silk bathrobe over the awful scratchy paper gown they'd made her put on, was sitting up in bed. An IV tube led to her left wrist, and she was tapping nervously on the tape that held it in place.

"Don't pull on that," Toby told her. "Godzilla will come in and yell again."

Godzilla, otherwise known as Sheila, was the nurse assigned to Emmeline's ward. A thin, washed-out woman, she resembled the star of scores of Japanese monster films not in appearance but in her steely resolve to stamp out anything she found not to her liking. This included, but was not limited to, floral arrangements she considered too pollen-heavy, small children who did anything other than sit quietly on the hard plastic chairs provided for visitors, television shows featuring laugh tracks, and humor of any sort. Already she'd glared disapprovingly at Toby when he'd promised to bring Emmeline a candy bar from the snack bar and rebuked Emmeline for not removing her nail polish before arriving, as directed.

"I just pray she's not the one who shaves me," Emmeline said. "I might not be able to control myself."

Toby shuddered. "Don't even joke about that," he said. "That woman makes *me* wish I didn't have a dick."

"Well, if everything goes as planned, five hours from now I won't have one," said Emmeline.

"Are you scared?" asked Toby.

Emmeline thought for a moment. "No," she said finally. "I spent a lot of years being scared, and I think I got it out of my system. Now I'm just ready for it to be over."

"You know what you have—down there," Toby said cautiously, "doesn't matter to me."

Emmeline took his hand. "Thank you, sweetie," she said. "I love you for saying that. But it does matter to me. And it's going to be fine."

Toby nodded. "I know," he said. "I just wanted to tell you that. I mean, for Christ's sake, I didn't even *know* when I met you."

Emmeline smiled, remembering how innocent Toby had been that first night in her kitchen. "You were like a stray puppy," she told him.

"I had no idea what was going to happen to me," said Toby.

"Nobody does, honey," said Emmeline. "Nobody does."

"Okay, it's time for someone to get prepped."

An orderly had come into the room. The young man stood at the foot of Emmeline's bed, holding a towel, a plastic bowl filled with water, and a razor. He was very handsome.

"Bingo," Emmeline whispered to Toby, who laughed.

"I'll wait outside," Toby said, walking toward the door. As he left, he turned and gave Emmeline a big wink.

"All right," said the orderly when Toby had shut the door. "This won't take long."

Emmeline undid the belt of her robe. The orderly lifted up the edge of her paper gown and folded it back, revealing her lower body.

"Whoa," he said when he saw what awaited him. He looked at Emmeline, who smiled daintily. "I didn't know," he said. "No one told—"

"It's okay," said Emmeline. "I can do it myself if you like."

The orderly shook his head. "No," he said, clearly trying to calm his nerves. He took the razor in one hand and with the other reached for Emmeline's penis.

"Be gentle," Emmeline said, enjoying seeing the young man flinch.

Five minutes later, the job finished, the orderly left and Toby returned.

"What did you do to him?" he asked Emmeline. "He looked like he'd seen a ghost."

"Ah," Emmeline said. "I'm going to miss having a dick. It can be so much *fun* sometimes."

Before Toby could reply to the comment, Sheila strode into the room, looking at her clipboard.

"Dr. Tulevitch will be in to see you in a few minutes," she said. "Have you had a bowel movement?"

"Yes," Emmeline answered.

"Good," Sheila said as she checked something off on the clipboard. "I won't need to give you an enema then."

Emmeline and Toby exchanged a glance of horror, as if the thought of Sheila coming anywhere near their rectums with a pointed object was the most horrifying ordeal they could imagine.

"You've been shaved," Sheila continued, blissfully unaware of the effect of her remark. "And you have your IV. Good. Now all I need you to do is sign these releases."

She held out the clipboard to Emmeline, who took the pen attached to it and scribbled her name at the bottom of the three pages Sheila turned over for her.

"What are those for?" Toby asked.

Sheila regarded him cooly, as if questioning his right to speak.

"They're in case they leave a glove or some forceps in me," said Emmeline as she signed the final page. "I can't sue anyone."

"A bit simplistic," Sheila remarked as she took the clipboard back. "But yes, essentially."

"Why would anything happen?" Toby asked worriedly.

"Relax," said Emmeline. "Nothing will happen." She hesitated. "But if it *does,* I want you to know that everything goes to you."

"Everything what?" asked Toby, confused.

"In my will," Emmeline explained. "It all goes to you. You're officially my next of kin now."

Toby took her hand. She could see tears forming in his eyes.

"You weren't listening," she said. "I said nothing is going to happen."

Toby nodded, his lip quivering. Emmeline felt her own eyes growing moist as she looked into his face.

"Good morning!"

Dr. Tulevitch breezed into the room, his long white coat flapping behind him.

"Good morning," Emmeline said, wiping her eyes as Toby did the same.

Dr. Tulevitch looked at Emmeline's chart, giving them a moment to compose themselves.

"Everything looks great," he said. "How are you feeling?"

"Like the luckiest woman on earth," answered Emmeline.

"Do you have any questions?"

Emmeline shook her head. "We've been talking about this for almost three years," she said. "I think I've asked every question there is."

"Twice," Dr. Tulevitch said, smiling. "In that case, I'll see you in the operating room in about twenty minutes."

He left. Emmeline shut her eyes and took a deep breath. When she opened them she looked at Toby. "You don't have to wait," she said. "I'll be fine. You can come back tomorrow."

"I'm waiting," Toby said firmly. "And don't argue."

Emmeline nodded. She was glad he was staying. She'd done things for herself for most of her life. It was nice to know she had someone to help her now.

"Time to go." Sheila entered the room accompanied by two orderlies pushing a gurney. Sheila transferred the IV bag to the gurney's pole while the orderlies helped Emmeline slide over. Toby came and leaned down, giving her a kiss.

"I love you," he said.

"I love you, too," replied Emmeline. "See you in five hours."

She waved as the orderlies wheeled her out. Closing her eyes again, she tried to relax as they pushed her down the hall and into an elevator. The orderlies chatted with one another about nothing important—the vending machine on the third floor that ate quarters, the new schedule, how badly the Red Sox were doing again. Emmeline listened to it all, the litany of everyday life. It was beautiful in its simplicity, even in its meaninglessness. The two men couldn't care less about her or why she was there. Yet they were taking her to the one thing she'd wanted for as long as she could remember, and for that she was thankful.

The elevator stopped and once again the gurney was propelled forward. They came to another set of doors, this one leading into the operating room. As they exited the cool white tunnel of the hallway,

Emmeline found herself surrounded by a constellation of lights and sounds, the machinery of medicine. She was lifted onto another table, and a sheet was placed over her, as if she were being tucked into bed.

All around her people moved, speaking in low voices as they tended to machines, arranged instruments on trays, and checked monitors, dials, and gauges. For a moment Emmeline felt embarrassed, as if she should apologize to everyone for going through so much trouble on her account. "Thank you for coming," she wanted to say. "But you really shouldn't have."

A face suddenly appeared directly over her.

"I'm Dr. Yu," the face said. "And I'll be your anaesthesiologist today."

"I'll take everything you've got," Emmeline told him.

"I'm going to inject this into your IV," the doctor told her, holding up a syringe filled with pale brown fluid. "I want you to count backward from ten."

Dr. Yu did something out of her sight. A few moments later, Emmeline felt something entering the vein in her wrist. It felt thick, and it stung slightly.

"Ten," she said silently as her eyes grew unbearably heavy. "Nine." Her countdown was interrupted by an image of her mother. Lula was holding a baby in her arms and smiling down on it.

"Welcome to the world, baby girl," she heard her mother whisper as the warm embrace of sleep overtook her.

CHAPTER 62

"Can this wait until after we meet with Ricky?" Donna said as she walked briskly up the street toward St. Agnes's. "We're late."

"I really think we should talk now," said Reilly. "This is important."

"More important than the wedding?" Donna said as she led him up the stairs and into the church, where Ricky was waiting for them to discuss some last-minute details.

"There they are!" Ricky called out, as if he'd been just about to leave after waiting for hours.

"Sorry we're late," Donna apologized. "Mrs. Crisfer's perm wouldn't set and it was a nightmare."

"I understand," Ricky said sympathetically, laying a hand on her arm. "It's hard to be an artist."

"Donna—" Reilly said.

"Wait until you see what I found for the altar," said Ricky, interrupting. "It's to die for."

Donna went with the wedding planner to look at his latest discovery. Reilly followed along after them. He'd been trying to talk to Donna all day, but things had kept interfering.

"I think this will be *perfect,*" Ricky said as he pulled what looked like a tablecloth out of a bag.

"It's gorgeous," said Donna, fingering the material. "Reilly, look at this."

"I see it," Reilly said tiredly. "It's a cloth."

"Oh, and look at these candlesticks," Ricky said, going back into the bag. "Have you ever seen anything like them?"

As Donna inspected the candlesticks, Reilly tried to think of a way to gracefully pull her away from Ricky. He felt as if every minute that went by was pulling him closer and closer to disaster, and he desperately wanted to stop things before it was too late.

"Father Michael," Donna said brightly.

Reilly looked up to see the priest coming in from the side door that led to the church offices. The cleric eyed Ricky warily as he greeted Donna.

"And how are you?" he asked, turning to Reilly.

"I'm gay," Reilly said.

Father Michael looked at him blankly, the smile still on his face. "I beg your pardon?" he said.

"I'm gay," Reilly said again. "Gay. That's how I am."

"Reilly, what did you say?" Donna was staring at him, a candlestick in her hand. Ricky was watching, a look of disbelief on his face.

"He said he was *gay,*" said Ricky helpfully.

"I know what he said," snapped Donna. She turned back to Reilly. "Are you out of your mind? Father, I'm sorry about this. He didn't mean that."

"Yes, I did," Reilly said defiantly. "I'm gay."

Father Michael, Donna, and Ricky stood there silently, looking at him as if they were waiting for him to tell them that it was all a big joke. Finally, Father Michael cleared his throat.

"I think the two of you should be alone for a moment." He looked meaningfully at Ricky, who was still staring, wide-eyed, at Reilly.

"What?" Ricky said. "I didn't make him gay."

Father Michael took Ricky by the hand and pulled him toward the door. When the two of them were gone, Donna put one hand to her temple, as if she'd suddenly realized that she had a pounding headache.

"I'm sorry," Reilly began. "I didn't mean to tell you like this."

Donna nodded wordlessly, not looking at him.

"Say something," said Reilly.

"You're not gay," Donna said quietly. "You can't be gay." Finally she looked at him. "You've made love to me." She said it as if stating a scientific fact, undeniable proof that she was right.

"I know," Reilly said. "But I am."

Donna gave a strange little laugh. "No," she said. "You're not."

Reilly walked toward her. "Donna—" he said, reaching for her hand.

"Don't touch me," Donna said, raising the hand with the candlestick in it. "Not until you tell me you're lying. I don't know why you're lying, but you are. Now tell me."

Reilly shook his head. "I'm not lying," he said. "I'm done lying, to myself, to you, to everyone."

"You made love to me," Donna said again, her voice plaintive.

"This isn't about making love," said Reilly. "It's about *being* in love. I'm not . . ." He hesitated, taking a breath before finishing his statement. "I'm not in love with you."

He'd stood in front of Donna many times, looking into her eyes. But as he did so now, he looked into a face that was unfamiliar to him. Instead of happiness, he saw uncomprehending sorrow. He wanted to reach out and pull her close, to tell her that everything would be fine. But it wouldn't be. Not now.

"I'm sorry," he said helplessly. "I wish there was something I could do or say, but there isn't. I'm just sorry."

He waited for her to respond, to do *something*. Even having her scream at him would be preferable to the silence that engulfed them. But she didn't speak. She simply stood there, the candlestick for their wedding altar in her hand, and looked at him with eyes reflecting hurt and confusion.

"I should go," Reilly said finally.

Donna nodded.

"We can talk tomorrow," Reilly said.

Again Donna nodded, but still she wouldn't meet his gaze or speak.

Reilly started to tell her again that he was sorry, but stopped himself. He'd said enough. There would be time for talking later, he knew. Now both he and Donna needed to be alone.

He turned and walked quickly out of the church, not looking back. He half expected to hear Donna call his name, or to feel the weight of the candlestick against the back of his head. But nothing stopped him as he pushed open the doors of St. Agnes's and exited into the summer heat.

He tried not to think about what was going to happen next. Donna would tell her family, of course. The story would spread quickly, likely within hours, and he would find himself with a great deal of explaining to do to everyone. Perhaps, he thought, it would be a good idea to go talk to his parents, before they heard about it from someone else. The cancellation of the wedding was going to be tough enough on them; the reason behind it would be even more difficult to understand.

No, he decided, he wasn't going to do any more explaining tonight. He was going to have a lot of time to explain. *Like the rest of your life,* he told himself. There would be conversations, and tears, and most likely a *lot* of yelling.

But that could all wait. Tonight he wanted to be by himself. And so he walked. He walked through town, past the shops and restaurants and bars he'd seen thousands of times. But now they looked different to him, pulsing with energy and life. The laughter that floated out of open doorways and windows lifted his spirits. The rainbow flags fluttering in the evening breeze became banners celebrating his arrival.

He walked through it all, not stopping, and continued on until he reached the beach. Although the light was fading, there were people walking along the shore. Several bonfires had been lit, and he saw clusters of people sitting around them. Two dogs chased each other, barking at the waves.

He stepped out of his sneakers and pulled off first one sock and then the other. His T-shirt came next, slipped over his head and deposited carelessly on the sand. His jeans and boxers joined it a moment later, and he stood naked looking at the ocean.

He ran, not caring if anyone saw him or not. The warm sand turned cooler where the waves had touched it, and then he was in the water. The coolness of it was a shock, as it always was, but he plunged forward into the waves. When it became too difficult to run, he dove, his head slipping beneath the water.

The rush of the water over his bare skin took his breath away. It slid around his torso and between his legs, caressing him with cool fingers. He spread his arms and let the ocean turn and lift him, bringing him back to the surface.

He broke through the watery ceiling and into the air, shaking his head and letting out a whoop of joy. A wave lifted him up and he floated on his back, buoyed by the sea. His heart beat fiercely, working against the cold and making him feel more awake than he had in a long time.

Looking toward the shore, he saw the lights of Provincetown reflected in the ocean's surface. Tiny dots of white flickered like stars around him, the sea their cosmos and he some kind of winged creature flying through on his way to who knew where.

"Who cares where?" he called out happily.

"Are you all right?" a voice asked. On the shore, he saw someone looking his direction.

"I'm okay!" he called back. "I'm okay," he said again, this time to himself.

The sea was carrying him back to shore. Each wave moved him another few feet closer to the beach. When he reached it he would find his clothes and put them on. Then he would go home, to bed and sleep. In the morning he would face Donna and his family.

But until then he was going to float, cradled in the sea of stars.

EPILOGUE
Labor Day

"Are you two almost finished?"

Josh peered over the box he was carrying. Ben was standing beside the newly acquired picnic table, arranging dishes.

"Almost done," Josh told him.

"I don't see what else could *possibly* be in that truck," Ben said. "You've brought out enough stuff to furnish the Four Seasons."

"It's books and CDs, mostly," said Josh, setting his box down and wiping the sweat from his forehead.

"I'll vouch for that," Reilly said, emerging from the cottage and coming to stand beside Josh. "I don't think my back is ever going to be the same."

Josh gave him a kiss and ran his hand over Reilly's back. "Don't worry," he said. "There's a massage in it for you later. But right now go get another box."

"Yes, sir," Reilly said, saluting.

"How are things going with his family?" Ben asked Josh quietly as Reilly went to the truck.

"His mother has stopped crying for the most part," Josh answered. "His father doesn't really talk about it."

"Poor guy," Ben said. "And the girl?"

"She's in the Caymans with some friends," said Josh. "They were supposed to go there for their honeymoon, so she's there getting some sun and fruit drink therapy."

"I'm just glad he has you," said Ben, taking the plastic wrap off a bowl of potato salad. "And I'm particularly glad you've decided to stay with us."

Josh laughed. "For someone who was supposed to be here for a weekend, I've turned into the guest who wouldn't leave."

"I just hope all of that stuff fits into the cottage," remarked Ben, looking at Reilly as he carried another two boxes past them.

"It's really not much," said Josh. "I let Doug keep just about everything. I figured it was better to start over and make new memories instead of surrounding myself with old ones."

"What are you two yakking about? And why isn't that grill going?"

"Hey there," Josh said as Jackie came over and hugged him. "How's the mother of my baby?"

"Hungry," answered Jackie as she handed Ben a dish. "That's sweet potato pie," she told him. "When do we eat?"

"As soon as one of these big butch boys gets that charcoal lit," Ben told her. "I'll go see if I can get my husband out here."

"I see you're moving in," said Jackie.

Josh nodded. "Looks like I'm a Rounder now."

"That's what this place does," Jackie said. "It sucks you in. Next thing you know, twenty years will have gone by."

"Is that a bad thing?" asked Josh.

Jackie shook her head. "No," she said. "It's not a bad thing at all. At least not if you have something to stay here for."

"I think I do," Josh said as a very tired Reilly came out and collapsed onto one of the picnic table's two benches.

"It's all in," he said. "Every box." He nodded at Jackie. "Hey. How's the little one?"

"About the size of a peach, I think," Jackie said, placing her hand on her stomach.

"So if my boyfriend has a baby with a woman he's not married to, that makes me the what?" Reilly asked.

Jackie looked at Josh.

"A fairy godfather," said a voice behind them.

They all turned to see Emmeline and Toby coming up the driveway. Emmeline was dressed in a white dress patterned with strawberries, a straw hat perched on her head. She was carrying a large bowl, also patterned with strawberries, which she set on the table beside Jackie's pie.

"Three-bean salad," she said. "A favorite with white trash everywhere. It's my mother's recipe."

"You look great," Josh told her.

"Yes, I do," replied Emmeline. "And I feel even better."

"I keep telling her she needs to rest, but she doesn't listen to me," Toby said sternly.

"I have all winter to rest," said Emmeline. "But while there's still some sunshine in the sky, I'm going to enjoy it."

"There's our houseboy," Ted said, appearing from the kitchen with a tray of chicken, hamburgers, and steaks, Brewer trotting along at his side. "Toby, can you help Ben in there? He's having a breakdown over the deviled eggs."

Toby dutifully went off to assist Ben, while Ted approached the grill.

"All right, men," he called out, "let's fire this baby up."

Josh and Reilly started to get up, but Jackie put up her hand to stop them.

"This is a job for a dyke," she said firmly. "You all just sit there and be pretty."

She took the matches from Ted and went to work on the charcoal. Ted stepped back, watching her work.

"That's my woman," Josh said. "I'm so proud."

"This must be the place."

"And there's my boss," Josh said, waving at Reid and Ty as they entered the yard.

"We weren't sure what to bring," Reid said, putting a paper bag on the table. "So we just emptied out the refrigerator."

Ty set an identical bag beside the first one. Josh peered inside.

"Caviar?" he said, pulling out a small jar. "Goat milk gouda?"

"This is the last weekend I have the house," said Reid apologetically. "I didn't want it to go to waste."

"Going back to LA?" asked Josh, inspecting a tin of smoked oysters.

"Tomorrow," Reid answered. He sighed. "I'm going to miss this place."

"It'll always be here," Emmeline told him. "It's not going anywhere."

"And we'll be back," Ty said confidently. "We're thinking of buying a place."

"After the movie you wrote us hits big," Reid teased Josh.

"That's great," Josh said dramatically. "Now I have to worry about supporting a kid *and* you guys."

"The hors d'oeuvres are served," announced Ted, stepping from the house with a platter loaded down with vegetables, dips, and the infamous deviled eggs. Toby trailed behind him, pitchers in both hands.

"We have margaritas for the drinkers among us and iced tea for everyone else," Ted explained as the latest additions were added to the bounty already covering the picnic table. "And as soon as I get the corn, we're all set. How is the meat coming?" he asked Jackie.

"Keep your apron on, Mary," Jackie said, blowing on the coals. "It's almost there."

"That poor child," Ben said, shaking his head. He looked at Josh. "Thank heavens it will have at least *one* good influence."

"I heard that, queen," Jackie called out. "Keep it up and you'll be getting tables near the kitchen for the rest of your life."

Ben pretended to be offended. "And after all of the marvelous tips I've left there," he said.

"Okay," Jackie said, ignoring him. "We're good to go. Who wants what?"

For the next few minutes, orders were placed and meat was thrown onto the grill, filling the air with smoke and mouthwatering smells. As each person's order came off the grill, she or he returned to the table and began eating. Before long, both sides of the picnic table were filled.

"This is just like the Waltons," remarked Josh as he looked around at the faces of his friends.

"Thanks, Josh Boy," said Reid.

"I'm serious," replied Josh. "I feel like you're all my family now."

"We'll remember that when we need to borrow money," Toby told him.

"Josh is right," said Ted. "I mean look at us. We're the perfect traditional American family."

Everyone laughed.

"Well, we're traditional for P-Town," Ted amended.

"All I know is that this is a *lot* more fun than any Labor Day picnic I ever had with my family," said Reilly as he cut a piece from his steak. "My father always made us play horsehoes."

"Three-legged races," Josh said.

"Softball," said Jackie.

"No wonder you're a dyke," Ty told her.

"And what excuse do *you* have?" demanded Jackie.

"I was exposed to *Valley of the Dolls* at an impressionable age," Ty said. "I blame it all on Patty Duke."

"I believe there's a twelve-step program for that," Emmeline drawled.

The afternoon wore on, filled with conversation, food, and laughter. As the sun began to drift down from its vantage point high above them, the yard filled with the golden haze of twilight. Slowly, as if reluctant to bring the day to a close, they all stood and began to gather up the plates and cups, the empty bowls and crumpled napkins.

"I'll help you wash the dishes," Toby told Ben as he made his way toward the house.

"I'd offer to dry," Reid said, "but we should get going. Our plane leaves at an ungodly hour."

After they'd said their good-byes to everyone else, Josh walked Ty and Reid to the street.

"Thanks for everything," he said as he hugged them each good-bye.

"We'll call you in a couple of days," Reid said. "And don't get too comfortable. It will be time for rewrites soon."

"I'll be good," Josh told him. "Promise."

The two men walked to their car, and Josh returned to the backyard. Reilly was sitting by himself at the picnic table.

"What did you do with everybody?" asked Josh.

"They're all inside," answered Reilly. "Probably fighting over the right way to do dishes."

Josh laughed and took a seat beside him. "Did you have a good time?"

Reilly nodded. "I had a great time," he said.

"Good," said Josh. "I have a feeling there will be a lot more holidays like this." He leaned against Reilly, feeling the solidness of him. "I don't think this could get any better," he said.

"I think it could," Reilly replied.

Josh pulled away and looked at him. "How?" he asked.

Reilly reached into his shirt pocket and pulled something out. "These," he said, holding his hand out.

"Sparklers," said Josh, laughing.

"I've been saving them since the Fourth," said Reilly.

He took some matches out of his pocket and struck one. Touching it to Josh's sparkler, he held it there as the stick burst into a frenzy of golden sparks. He then lit his own, which turned out to be red.

Josh moved his sparkler through the air, writing his name, just as he had so many times when he was a kid. Reilly did the same, his sparkler looping in the air. Gold and red sparks tumbled through the air, glinting in the fading light. When the sparklers finally died out, Reilly looked at Josh.

"So, Tinkerbell, did you get your wish this time?"

Josh looked at him for a moment, then leaned in and kissed him. "Yes," he said when they parted. "I did."

In the critically acclaimed bestseller LAST SUMMER, Michael Thomas Ford brought to life the trials and triumphs of a cast of characters spending one remarkable summer in Provincetown. Now, in LOOKING FOR IT, he introduces a diverse group of men in a small, upstate New York town struggling with dreams and desires, coping through friendship, and searching for the things they want—or the things they think they do.

Mike Monaghan is the bartender at the Engine Room, a meeting place for the small but thriving community of gay men in Cold Falls, New York. As Mike pours beer, wipes glasses, and hears everything, he's also witness to the men who come here looking for what they need—sex, direction, friendship, spiritual fulfillment, and love. People like:

Stephen Darby—As an accountant, he knows many secrets. But Stephen has his own secret, one he's never been able to share with anyone close to him. Being the perfect son costs him dearly, and now it may take from him the one man he longs for.

Pete Thayer—Playing it straight, Pete takes out his frustrations on transmissions and engines during the day, then spends his nights trying to quench his needs through anonymous sex. But once the thrill of the forbidden begins to fade, what will he be left with?

John and Russell—The golden couple in town has the ideal relationship everyone wants. But behind the scenes, their storybook marriage is on the verge of facing some explosive trials that will shake both men completely.

Father Thomas Dunn—More and more the gentle priest is feeling a need to express the secret desires that conflict with his devotion to the church, sending his faith into a tailspin and making him question what he really wants from life.

Simon Bird—He's a fixture in town, an old queen everyone finds amusing and entertaining. Still mourning the loss of his longtime lover, Simon yearns to find love and a place in a culture that worships youth and beauty.

As Mike hands these men their drinks, he marvels at their determination, strength, and foolishness. But most of all, he begins to question his own dissatisfaction, pondering what's missing from his own life, and what risks he may have to take to find fulfillment.

LOOKING FOR IT is an extraordinarily human tale of community, friendship, and the search for happiness. With unflinching honesty, keen insight, and his trademark humor, Michael Thomas Ford weaves together the unforgettable stories of these seven men, chronicling their dreams, hurts, heartbreaks, joys, and hopes, while taking readers on an emotional journey to find what it is we're all looking for.

Please turn the page for an exciting sneak peek of
LOOKING FOR IT
coming next month in hardcover!

CHAPTER 1

"Another fireman. That makes five." John Ellison took a sip of his vodka tonic and regarded the man in the yellow slicker and red plastic helmet with an air of weary disdain. "You'd think they'd at least try not to look like overgrown kindergartners."

Mike Monaghan, preoccupied with trying to remember the order the nun waiting at the other end of the bar had just given him, nodded absentmindedly as he poured gin over the ice in a glass, neatly popped the caps from two Rolling Rocks, and searched beneath the counter for the bottle of vermouth. *Damn it, Paulie,* he thought, silently cursing the barback whose duty it was to set up before the evening rush. *Why can't you ever put things back where they belong?*

"I know this is the Engine Room, and I'm sure they think they're being very clever, but can't they show a little more imagination?" said John.

"Actually, engine rooms are on ships and submarines, not in fire stations," Mike remarked as he grabbed a pile of napkins to hand to the nun along with his drinks. "Technically, they should be dressed as sailors."

"That makes it even worse," said John, draining his glass. "Not only are they unoriginal, they're ignorant."

"Well, it was very original of *you* to come as Mr. Rogers," Mike told him, eyeing the blue cardigan John had buttoned almost all the way up. "I know I definitely want to be your neighbor."

"Fuck you," John shot back. "For your information, this is what all self-respecting high school science teachers wear."

"The stuff of teenage boys' wet dreams," joked Mike as he took John's empty glass and refilled it.

"What have I missed?"

A man took the seat next to John at the bar. Leaning over, he kissed John quickly on the mouth.

"Nothing," said John. "Just the annual Halloween Faggot Parade and Masquerade Ball."

"Russell, I don't know how you live with this bitter queen," Mike said. Anticipating the request he knew was coming, he poured a rum and Coke and slid it to the man who had just joined them.

Russell took the drink, lifted it to his lips in salute, and took a deep swig before replying. "I'm just with him for the sex," he said, earning a laugh from Mike and a roll of the eyes from John.

"How was the sale?" asked John, changing the subject.

Russell groaned. "Three hundred overweight women all insisting they were size fours," he said wearily. "I barely made it out alive."

"Oh, the perils of retail," said John.

"I didn't even have time to come up with a costume," said Russell.

"Thank God," John told him, sounding relieved. "There are enough cowboys, Batmen, and lumberjacks here to recreate an episode of *Let's Make a Deal.*"

"Actually, I think those lumberjacks are lesbians," Mike teased. "And since you're asking, I'll take what's behind door number two."

Russell laughed. "You don't have to be so uptight," he said to his lover. "Halloween is supposed to be fun."

John snorted. "Excuse me if I'm a little tired of this nonsense. All day long I had to teach chemistry to children dressed as gangbangers and hookers," he said. "Not that *every* day isn't like that."

"You should have gone as Grand Master J," suggested Mike. "Pimp Daddy of the science lab. You could show them how to make their own street drugs. That would get them interested in chemistry."

"I don't see you in a costume," John retorted. "If you think this is so much fun, how come you're not dressed in some inane getup?"

"I *am* in costume," Mike said. "Can't you tell? I'm a straight guy."

Russell laughed as John shook his head. Mike, noticing a ghost waving a ten-dollar bill at him, excused himself to attend to the customer.

"Can we go now?" John asked Russell.

"Go?" Russell said. "They're just about to start the drag show."

"That's exactly why I want to go," said John. "I've got a splitting headache, and being here isn't helping."

Russell looked down into his drink. "Yeah," he said quietly. "We can go. Let me say good night to Mike."

John stood up. "I'll be outside," he told his partner.

As John pushed his way through the crowd toward the door, Russell finished his drink and set the empty glass on the bar. He caught Mike's eye and waved.

"You're leaving?" asked Mike, coming over and automatically sweeping the empty glass into the plastic tub beneath the counter.

Russell sighed. "Her majesty has a headache."

"So send him home by himself," suggested Mike.

Russell shook his head. "It's okay," he said. "I'm pretty beat anyway. I'll see you later."

Mike nodded and watched as Russell left. Russell and John had been coming into the bar regularly for the six years Mike had worked there, and still he hadn't figured out what kept them together. One of these days, he thought, he'd unravel the mystery. But tonight wasn't the night. Tonight he had too much else to do.

He turned his attention to the customers lined up three deep at the bar. Within moments he was busy mixing drinks, his hands finding the bottles, ice, and wedges of lime as his mind ticked off the orders: three martinis for Wonder Woman, a shot of Jack Daniels and a Cosmo for the scarecrow, and a Budweiser for the devil with the wicked smile. Then he was on to a new set of faces and the next round.

"What's an old queen have to do to get a sidecar around here?"

"Simon!" Mike said, leaning across the bar to kiss the cheek of the man addressing him. He eyed the old-fashioned black dress and powdered wig Simon was wearing. "What are you supposed to be?" he asked as he began putting together the sidecar.

"What did I just say?" asked Simon primly. "I'm an old queen."

Seeing Mike's confusion, Simon shook his head. "You children have no sense of history," he said. "Victoria. I'm Queen Victoria."

Mike nodded. "Oh," he said. "I get it."

Simon took his sidecar and handed Mike a five. "Don't feel badly about not knowing," he said. "Someone else complimented me on my Zsa Zsa Gabor costume. There are, I'm afraid, disadvantages to being the oldest one in a room."

Behind Simon a drag queen sporting a pink-sequined dress, enormous breasts, and a beehive hairdo that added a good two feet to her height stepped onto the small stage that had been erected for the evening. Taking up a microphone, she flashed a red-lipped smile, batted her false eyelashes, and addressed the crowd.

"Happy Halloween!" she shouted. "Welcome to the Engine Room. So, what will it be tonight, tricks or treats?"

"Tricks!" shouted the crowd.

The crowd around the bar thinned as people turned to watch the show. Simon pulled out a stool and sat down. "She got that from Walter, you know," he said to Mike.

Mike knew. He'd heard Simon's stories about Walter many times. Everyone in the bar had, particularly in the year since Walter had died.

"He was so lovely," Simon said, speaking to no one in particular. "So beautiful."

Mike looked at Simon's face. Caked with makeup, it reminded him of a crumbling painting. How old was Simon, he wondered? Surely he must be over seventy. And Walter had been even older. Mike, picturing Walter, tried to imagine the wrinkled little man with the white mustache who'd worn corduroy trousers and neatly pressed plaid shirts dressed in drag.

"I remember the first time I saw him," Simon said. "It was at a party given by my friend Harold Carver. We didn't have a bar to go to back then, but Harold was wealthy and had a big house in Saratoga. Every weekend we went there. Escaped, really. From our lives. One weekend someone brought Walter along as a guest. Friday night he made his entrance to dinner dressed in a beaded gown, and I fell in love with him."

Simon looked at Mike and smiled, the pancake makeup on his cheeks cracking and flaking off. "I know it all sounds terribly fey," he said. "But he wasn't playing at being a woman. It was just his way of having fun." Simon sighed deeply. "It all seems so much easier now, doesn't it? We have our bars, and parades, and we're on television for everyone to see. People talk about how terrible it was back then, how we had to hide who we were. But they forget that it was also magical. We had our own secret world. Maybe we were afraid sometimes, but we weren't unhappy."

Simon looked down into his glass. "We weren't unhappy," he repeated. "Not then."

"Would you like another one?" Mike asked him, nodding at the empty drink. "It's on the house."

Simon shook his head. "Thank you, but no. One makes me maudlin. Two will make me positively morose. I think I should probably take myself home before I become a spectacle."

"You're going to miss the costume contest," Mike told him.

"That is a misfortune I will have to live with," Simon said, standing up. "I pray that I am up to it."

He waved away the change Mike had placed on the bar. Mike pocketed it as Simon turned and melted into the crowd. With only a few customers waiting, Mike enjoyed the relative quiet. The drag show was in full force, but he was able to block it out. It was a trick he'd developed during years of bartending in places whose clientele favored the cover of blaring music over the ability to communicate with those around them. He simply tuned the noise out, losing himself in his work or his thoughts.

He observed the action from within this sphere of artificial silence, surrounded by the chaos that was Halloween at the Engine Room but at the same time removed from it. As he straightened the bottles and restocked the napkins, he watched the faces of the patrons. Many of them he recognized, but others were strangers to him. This was to be expected. The Engine Room was one of only three gay bars in a two-hour radius. The towns of upstate New York had many charms, but the availability of entertainment for the queer community was not one of them.

Oddly, this was one of the things that appealed to Mike about life in Cold Falls. He'd lived in larger cities, Albany and Syracuse for several years and a brief three-month stint in Buffalo one summer, but he preferred the quieter atmosphere of the smaller towns. Not that Cold Falls was merely a flyspeck on the map of New York State. An hour north of Utica, it shared with that city a history and economy based in brewing. Founded a hundred years earlier, Cold Falls Ale continued to be the bar's best seller, beating out Coors and Budweiser by almost three to one. An image of the falls that gave the town its name graced the label, and the brewery's motto—"Give me a cold one"—was regularly shouted out by customers, each of whom Mike rewarded with a friendly laugh suggesting that it was the first time he'd heard such cleverness.

He didn't mind. He liked his customers. Like the town itself, they had quickly become familiar to him, until he knew their faces and names in the same way that he knew the most recognizable of Cold Falls's landmarks: the brewery, the falls, the statue of the town's lone celebrity (Cuthbert Applewhite, a dairy farmer who had distinguished himself in 1892 by preventing an assassination attempt against presidential candidate and former fellow upstate New Yorker Grover Cleveland during a campaign stop, and who after Cleveland had secured his second, improbable, term in office, had been awarded a medal of distinction that he wore for the rest of his life, even when mucking out the barn).

In addition to their names, Mike knew their stories as well. He fell easily into the time-honored role most bartenders held along with their ability to mix drinks, that of father confessor and unpaid therapist. The tips he received were just as often tokens of appreciation for the advice he dispensed as they were for the strength of his cocktails, even if all he'd done was nod sympathetically during a patron's rambling, boozy dissection of a recent breakup.

Stories. It was all about stories. Everyone had one, and almost everyone wanted to tell it. All he did was listen to them, and for that his customers were thankful. He was like a book they were writing, recording the events of their lives in his head. Maybe, he thought occasionally, one day he would write them all down. But who, he asked himself, would want to read it? To whom would the individual stories of heartbreak and joy be of any interest besides those who told them? It was, Mike thought as he washed and dried a wineglass, one of the less appealing characteristics of human beings, the ability to be completely uninterested in the lives of those around them while desperately longing for someone to pay them attention.

A burst of cheering made him look up. On the stage, the beehived drag queen was putting a crown on the head of a muscular man half-heartedly dressed as a pirate, the primary clues to his identity being the patch on one eye and the stuffed parrot somehow affixed to his shoulder. Apart from these props he was nearly nude, which Mike assumed was the reason for his popularity.

"How about showing us your Jolly Roger?" the drag queen teased, shamelessly pawing the pirate's chest as the crowd roared.

"Can I get a cold one?"

Mike looked away from the action to see a skeleton standing at the bar. He wore a black turtleneck and pants painted with crude representations of bones. His hair was slicked back and his face, too, was painted black and white to resemble a skull. His eyes were misshapen white spots above a ghostly mouth, and the overall effect was unsettling.

"Great costume," Mike remarked as he pulled a beer from the ice-filled chest and handed it to the man.

"Thanks," came the short reply. "How much?"

"Two bucks," answered Mike.

Three dollar bills were slapped on the bar. Then the skeleton man turned away, scanning the crowd.

Mike took the money, putting two of the bills into the register and adding the third to the rest of his tips. The man, he guessed, wasn't one of the regulars, otherwise he wouldn't have had to ask the price of a beer, which hadn't changed in well over a year. Probably he was one of the visitors who came in only on nights like this, when they could hide behind the anonymity of a costume. Maybe there was a wife at home, perhaps a kid or two. Mike saw a lot of guys like that. They came to the Engine Room from other small cities, driving an hour or more to ensure invisibility while they spent a night living other lives.

Usually he saw them only once, but sometimes they showed up at regular intervals. Apart from their nervousness and unfamiliarity, they were easy to spot. Often they forgot to remove their wedding rings. He glanced at the left hand of the skeleton man. It was bare. Still, that meant nothing. Not all of them were married, of course. Some were simply afraid of who they were.

The man moved away, out of Mike's sight. Looking for something, Mike thought. He was looking for something. They all were. That's why they came there.

CHAPTER 2

What was it with faggots that they liked to dress up like women? Pete Thayer stared at the drag queen standing on the stage. He was rambling on and on, grinning at everyone and throwing his hands all over the place. Pete couldn't stand to look at his face, painted up like a clown's. Someone needed to take the queen out back and show him how a real man acted.

That was the problem with fags; they wanted to be women. Not all of them, but most of them. That's why so many of them were wearing dresses or girly costumes. Even the ones dressed as men were trying too hard to look masculine, hiding their sissiness behind military uniforms and football player getups. But Pete knew that once the clothes came off, the masculinity would fall with them to the floor of the bedroom, discarded like so much make-believe.

He took a swig of his beer and leaned against the wall. His eyes scanned the bar, looking for anything to relieve his boredom. The possibilities were few and far between. There was a cowboy by the pool table who wasn't too bad, and at the back of the room a guy dressed as a baby wearing nothing but a diaper. The costume was a turnoff, but the guy at least had a hairy chest and didn't seem too swishy.

Pete decided to give the baby a shot and started walking toward him. Halfway there he found his way blocked by a guy in a devil outfit. The devil looked him up and down and smiled.

"Nice costume," he said.

Pete nodded. He wasn't in the mood to talk.

"That paint sort of glows," the devil continued. "Is it fluorescent?"

"Yeah," said Pete curtly. Fluorescent? Who the hell cared? It was paint. He'd grabbed the can from the back room at the shop. The costume was a last-minute thing, pulled together in about ten minutes.

"You should have won a prize," the devil said, grinning broadly. "It's really cool."

Behind the devil Pete saw the baby getting ready to leave with someone dressed as Dorothy from *The Wizard of Oz*. He quickly looked for the cowboy, but he, too, was gone.

"Can I buy you a drink?" the devil asked him.

Pete looked at the guy. He was shirtless, like the baby, although his chest was smooth. But at least it was well muscled. His skin was painted red. On his head was perched a set of horns, and he had a goatee. He was wearing red boxer briefs and black work boots. He would do.

"I have a better idea," Pete said. "Why don't you and I take a little trip to hell."

The devil looked at him, confused.

"Let's get out of here," Pete explained.

The devil nodded. "Oh," he said. "I get it. Funny. Well, I'm sort of here with some friends. I should—"

"Okay," Pete interrupted. "No problem."

He turned to go, but the devil grabbed his arm. "I guess I could leave a little early," he said.

"Then let's go," Pete told him.

He walked toward the door, knowing the devil would be right behind him. They always were, predictable as Monday morning. As the door of the Engine Room closed behind him, the devil was there beside him.

"I'm Mark," the devil said.

"Dan," Pete told him. "Where's your car?"

"Over here."

Pete followed Mark to his car, waiting for Mark to unlock it and then getting in. When they were inside, Mark leaned over and tried to kiss him. Pete put his hand on the back of Mark's head and pushed it down to his crotch instead.

Mark's fingers fumbled with Pete's zipper, pulling it down and reaching inside. Unrestrained by underwear, Pete's dick slid out easily. A moment later Mark's mouth was sliding up and down it hungrily and

Pete was growing hard. He leaned back, shut his eyes, and lost himself in the warmth of the mouth that serviced him.

When he felt himself begin to come, he said nothing. His load exploded into Mark's mouth and he felt Mark gag for a moment before swallowing hard. When he was done, Pete pulled his softening cock from Mark's mouth and zipped up. He opened the car door and got out, leaving Mark looking up at him with a puzzled expression.

Pete shut the door quickly, blotting out the sight of Mark's face with its smeared red makeup and the horns hanging askew. He walked briskly away from the car toward the one he'd driven to the bar. It wasn't his; it belonged to a customer from the shop. He would never drive his own car to a fag bar. It was too recognizable.

He got into the borrowed car and left the parking lot. He was home within fifteen minutes, where he parked the car in the garage and shut the door. Once safely inside the house, he went to the bathroom, where he turned the shower on, stripped off his painted clothes, and stuffed them into the small garbage can beneath the sink.

The water was too hot, but he left it that way. It would help wash away the dirt. Maybe, he thought vaguely as he soaped himself, it would also kill anything the queer's mouth had left on his dick. He scrubbed his skin hard with a washcloth, wiping away the oily drugstore makeup he'd bought to create his skeleton face. He watched it run down his body and into the drain, a milky stream that ran clear after several minutes. Still he scrubbed, making sure he was rid of any lingering taint. You could never be too careful.

Turning the water off, he stepped from the shower and dropped the washcloth into the trash on top of the clothes. Grabbing a towel from the hook behind the door, he dried himself and walked into his bedroom. He flopped onto the bed and reached for the remote on the bedside table.

The TV came on with a click. Another push of a button set the tape inside the VCR whirring, and a moment later the image of a big-breasted blonde getting fucked from behind filled the screen. Pete stared at the TV, idly playing with himself while the girl's partner, an unattractive but hugely endowed man, thrust in and out of her pussy. The girl's tits jiggled and her lipsticked mouth was open in an expression of ecstasy as squeaky little "ohs" and "yeahs" filled the air.

After a few minutes the camera moved in, moving behind and

above the couple to focus on the pink folds between the girl's legs. The man pulled his cock out and rubbed the swollen head against the girl's asshole. Pressing it against the pinkish-brown pucker, he slid inside her, the length of him disappearing between her cheeks.

Pete lay back and spread his legs. His cock angled across his belly, untouched, as he wet a finger and slid it beneath his balls and began to rub his asshole. His eyes were fixed on the dick that was pounding the girl's butt. It moved in and out with increasing force, stretching her wide. The skin was slick and shiny with lube. He wondered what it felt like for the girl to have such a thing inside her.

He'd fucked a girl like that once. Like the girl in the film, she'd had blond hair and store-bought tits. He'd met her at a party. Fourth of July, maybe. He couldn't remember. What he did remember was how he'd been fucking her from behind and suddenly wondered what it would feel like to stick his piece in her ass. Without asking, he'd done it. She was so drunk she hadn't even really noticed, groaning a little at first and then going right back to mumbling some foul-mouthed crap she apparently thought was sexy.

He'd blocked out her voice, concentrating on how tight her ass felt around him. He'd come quickly, before he was ready, and it had made him angry. He'd left the girl on her hands and knees, pulling on his jeans and leaving before she could ask him where he was going.

What would it feel like to have something as big as a cock in your ass? He slid his finger inside himself, poking gently. Just a finger hurt a little. He couldn't imagine what a dick must feel like. Especially one as big as the one on his TV screen. Christ, it had to be a good ten inches long. His own was eight. He knew because he'd measured it once just for the hell of it. Eight inches. Man, those faggots loved his big cock. They always said so when they sucked him off.

He'd never fucked a guy. Some of them had wanted him to, but he wouldn't do it. Who knew what kind of shit you could get from that. Not that the idea didn't have some appeal. The girl—what was her name, Amy? Kelly?—had been virgin tight. Probably a guy wouldn't be, though, especially some queer who'd been plowed by everything he could get in there.

He slid more of his finger inside himself. His ass tightened around him and he felt his balls give a jump. He moved in and out a little, fucking his own ass. In the film the guy was pulling almost all the way out and slamming back in. The head of his dick would appear for a moment, the girl's asshole almost closing. Then he would push back into her, his balls slapping against her as he nailed her.

Pete added a second finger to the first, gritting his teeth as he stretched himself open. How did those fags stand it? He was about to pull his hand away when suddenly his ass relaxed, as if something had stopped resisting and opened up. The pain ebbed and his fingers were simply surrounded by heat. He could almost feel the blood pounding in his ass.

He started to fuck himself with his hand, matching the motions of the guy in the movie. With his free hand he gripped his cock tightly. He imagined fucking the girl. His fist was her ass, tight around his dick. She was moaning as he pumped her. He was giving it to her hard, the way he liked it.

Behind him was a guy. Maybe the man in the film, maybe someone else. A cock was pressing against his asshole, pushing its way inside. As he fucked the girl, he too was getting fucked. He closed his eyes and imagined it, the three of them rocking together on the bed, his dick and the other guy's moving in tandem, sliding in and out like the pistons of an engine. It was like they were both fucking the girl, the other man's dick connected to Pete's inside.

He heard loud moans and opened his eyes. On the screen the man had pulled his dick out of the girl's ass and was spraying a thick load over her back. Pete pumped himself harder and came too. His ass tightened around his fingers and he erupted with a shout. Cum splattered across his chest in thick drops, leaving behind a pearly trail caught in the dark hair of his stomach.

He pulled his hand away from his ass and reached for a T-shirt on the floor. He used it to wipe the stickiness from his skin, then tossed it back on the floor. The TV was shut off and he was left in the darkness of the room, looking up at the ceiling.

He reached for the pack of Marlboros on the bedside table. Pulling one free, he flicked his lighter to life and lit it. The smoke felt good as he drew it into his lungs, a cloudy darkness that surrounded his thoughts. The end of the cigarette glowed redly in the dark like a star.

He exhaled, blowing the smoke into the air. He lifted his fingers to his nose and inhaled the scent of himself. It clung to his skin, thick and ripe, like the smell of leaves in the fall. Is that what he smelled like inside? He had expected it to be different, dirtier. But it wasn't; it was rich and dark, like the smoke that fell over him like invisible rain.

He licked a fingertip, expecting to taste something sour. Again he was surprised. The taste that met his tongue was nothing like that. Instead it had a sweetness to it. He sucked on his finger, drawing it inside. Minutes ago it had been inside his ass, filling him. Now he was tasting himself. He was both repulsed and thrilled by the act. He thought about the times when girls had sucked him after he'd pulled his cock from their pussies. Watching them lick their own juices from his skin, he'd wanted to fuck them all over again.

He was no girl, though, he told himself. He didn't get fucked. His fantasy had been about something else. What, he wasn't sure and didn't want to think too much about. It was just something that had popped into his head, that was all. He'd just wondered what it might feel like. Nothing more. And now he knew.

He removed his finger and took a long drag on his cigarette, blotting out the taste in his mouth with the bitter kiss of tobacco. In a few minutes he would get up and wash his hands. He would use lots of hot water and soap, just like his mother had made him do when he was littler. "You can't be too careful," she'd always said as she watched him to make sure he didn't just run his hands under the tap to fool her.

"You can't be too careful." He repeated the phrase out loud. It was the guiding principle of his mother's life, and like a good boy, he followed it himself. Well, mostly. He suspected his mother wouldn't approve of certain aspects of his life. But still, he was careful.

He'd almost totally forgotten about his encounter with Mark earlier in the evening, but now the guy's face came to him. He recalled the red skin, the two little horns.

"You got a blowjob from the devil," he told himself. He laughed. The idea was so ridiculous he couldn't help but find it funny. After all, he was a nice Catholic boy. He'd done altar service, gone through CCD, all that crap. Sometimes he still went to Mass, at least on holidays or when his mother demanded he accompany her. What would Father Fitzpatrick think about his former altar boy getting a knob job from Satan? Maybe he was a cocksucker himself, although Pete doubted it. Despite the recent rash of abuse revelations, he could honestly say that Father Fitzpatrick had never once done anything like that to him or, as far as he knew, any of his friends.

Maybe he would stop by the church tomorrow, he thought. It was, after all, All Saints' Day. He could light a candle for his grandmother. It had been a while since he'd done that. His mother would like it if he did.

He stubbed out his cigarette in the ashtray and got up. Going into the bathroom, he turned on the water in the sink and began to scrub.